RUN

— *A Novel* —

JANET BAKER

Malapert Press

Chicago, IL Copyright © 2015 by Janet Baker

All rights reserved, including the right to reproduce this book or portions therein in any form whatsoever.

This book may not be reproduced in whole or in part, or in any form or by any means, electronic or mechanical, including photocopying, recording, or by any information storage and retrieval system now known or hereafter invented, without explicit written permission from the publisher.

This book is a work of fiction. Any references to historical events or real people are used fictitiously. Other names, characters, places, and events are products of the author's imagination, and any resemblance to actual events or places or persons, living or dead, is entirely coincidental.

Library of Congress Control Number: 2015901509
Run, by Janet Baker
ISBN: 978-0-9863621-0-1
ISBN: 978-0-9863621-1-8
ISBN: 978-0-9863621-2-5

Malapert Press
Chicago, IL
https://malapertpress.wordpress.com/
Printed in the United States of America

This book of science fiction is most respectfully dedicated to Archbishop Marcel Lefebvre (1905-1991). It is not to be supposed from this that the Archbishop was an avid reader of science fiction. He was a successful missionary to Africa from France, as busy with a thousand practical details as any sincere man in those circumstances must be, and had as well his prayer life; he had also the epic battle with the liberals of Vatican II, and later the care of his priestly family in the order he founded to resist the effects of the disaster, the Society of Saint Pius X. He was unjustly excommunicated for his resistance, although finally, posthumously, that has been withdrawn. Those were very difficult times. Science fiction in the evenings? Probably not.

But still, Archbishop Marcel Lefebvre made this book, this plot, these characters, possible by making their fight plausible, the greatest necessity for fiction. He understood the calamity when the Council abandoned the Catholic religious state, both in practice (there were still five left at the time of the Council) and theoretically. How he struggled! In the end, by keeping the idea alive, he has won! (We have won.) Archbishop Lefebvre fought the injustice of secularism for Christ's sake, because Christ *should* be our King, having died for us on the cross, and not for political reasons, although he was acutely aware of the purely natural social chaos caused by secularism.

Capitalism, compared with the blessed Catholic state which it replaced after it bribed English brigands to do the ripping off of the monasteries and English land, is also horribly, disgracefully cruel to the poor. The economy of wage slaves which replaced the medieval economy of small owners was--and is--brutal, and so is the reaction to it, socialism, communism. Only the old way shows any hope, and astonishingly, it will work *best* on the High Frontier where we are going.

Sinner and ignoramus that I am, unworthy to do so, still I dedicate this work to Archbishop Lefebvre, and pray that he helps us from heaven, for we poor are in a world of trouble now.

The Civic

    The whole public amphitheater was still dark. It wasn't time yet for the Civic. Two figures stood close to the wall on the lowest circle, where it was darkest. One was a child. They wore loose jackets with hoods pulled low over their faces, like many others. People streamed past them on the broad ascending walkway; not many yet.
    The amphitheater was a series of stacked circles, three in all, connected by risers, each bigger than a football field. The structure was supported by three columns rising from the gleaming center of spokes that ran out to the ends of the sphere that was Earth's first space colony. One spoke was lit, a green glow in the darkness, with a red and white streak—a train—running down it. The other five spokes were dark, because the villages they connected to were still empty. In fact, they were still unbuilt. Much to be done here on *Halliburton's*.
    Marley held tightly to Laney's hand. She held her cell phone in her other hand. They kept their heads down, avoiding eye contact with any others. They were waiting for their own people before they went up to the largest circle for the telecast. When Marley raised her head for a moment to scan the faces moving past her, the white light caught her young face, highlighting her prominent cheekbones and straight dark brows. She glanced around quickly and then lowered her face again, but it was too late. One of the freaks had taken interest.
    She raised the cell phone to her ear, but he didn't buy it—or didn't care. Young and white, he had a dirty neck and shaved head. His eyes shifted evasively, as if he were listening to an invisible wire. He spoke to her, but gazed crazily over her shoulder.
    "How you doin', sister. Are you going up to the Civic? Me, too." His eyes rolled around to her as he wound up. "In the name of peace, in the name of the living God, I will tell you the truth." He was trying to sound educated. It wasn't working. "I didn't find the truth in no book. I don't need a book to tell me the truth. The Spirit speaks to us; he is speaking to you and to me."

He thumped his chest dramatically, hard. Marley imagined how hard he could strike her or Laney. It could happen, even out here in the open.

She raised her face and looked him dead in the eye.

"The Spirit is telling you to leave us alone," she said quietly but firmly, as she slipped her phone into her pocket and grasped the mace there instead. Then she lowered her gaze, and her face again disappeared into the darkness of her hood.

His eyes blinked rapidly and his jaw clenched, but he did not respond to Marley's remark. Averting his eyes, he went on with his rant. "Saint Paul is my uncle, and Jesus is my father. My uncle told me, where you and I are, there is our church. You and I! Just the two of us!" He loved those words. "Just the two of us."

He moved closer, and Marley pushed Laney sideways so she was between them and began to edge backward into the throng, nudging Laney behind her.

As three or four men in mining coveralls swept past them in a group, Marley snatched Laney's arm and darted around them. She and Laney moved quickly up the walkway to the second level. Again, they waited against the wall, scanning the crowd for either the crazy man or their own people. Slowly, their breathing eased.

It was lighter here, but they still had not turned on the main lights for the civic. Those would illuminate the interior of the sphere for miles.

Marley bent down and peered into Laney's face. "Are you okay?" She searched his serious little face. "Listen, he couldn't hurt us. I had my mace in my pocket, all ready to go. He was nothing!" She grinned at him to try to make him smile. "The Spirit doesn't speak to us personally," she added. "That's crazy talk."

Anyone could see Laney was Marley's little brother. The same straight dark brows; same thick, wheat-colored hair; same cheekbones that spoke of some ancient people from long ago and far away. *Really* far away, now—on another planet. But Laney was only five, and whereas his sister's face was fierce, his was frightened, though he was trying to hide it. His mouth smiled, but his eyes didn't.

"I know," Laney said. "I was ready, too."

He didn't say for what he was ready, what he was ready to do, Marley noted. She would talk about it with him later, at home. Laney *had* to know exactly what to do. Anything could happen.

A gaggle of pierced Goths scurried by, walking quickly, almost flying in the reduced gravity and on the moving walkway besides. Their metals clinked enticingly and they wore it thick as armor. Purloined platinum dripped from every orifice a human could pierce. Marley knew from her contacts that their black-market sales were good. Well, she would like to condemn their theft, but their contracts, while paying them well for their processing skills, did not allow them to build up any kind of ownership in the Company. They would never be more than they were now: middle-management, sub-techie slaves with three weeks' vacation and worthless market-based retirement plans. When it came time to use those retirement accounts—oopsie !—gone, seized to prop up the bank failures or forestall site closures. Then, quiet euthanasia, most likely. Any illness that landed them in the clinic would be their last. And their bodies, down to the Combs.

One of the Goths noticed Marley and Laney, and her face lit up with recognition—although "lit up" amounted to a little half-mouth twitch, the default deadpan among their kind. It was Stephanie, who worked where Marley worked, on the loading dock. This week, Marley knew, she was sleeping with the guy walking beside her on her right. What was his name? Last week, it was the guy now on her left. Stephanie loved them all, at least for a minute, the worse for her. Marley got a full dose of Stephanie's angst for every new guy.

Stephanie glanced back at Marley again and fluttered her eyelashes in goodbye. Cats did that, Marley thought. Except Stephanie made it look sad. Funny to think of cats. Laney probably would not remember cats at all pretty soon. They had flying pigs in the farm pods, and cows and sheep for wool and milk and meat (so far the vegans hadn't gotten their way). But the colony had no cats yet—which they could use in the Combs. Who knew what they would catch there? She glanced at Laney. He heard things in the Combs.

"Marley!" a voice called out, a few decibels above a whisper.

Here they were, her people. *Deo gracias!*

Marley and Laney stepped away from the wall and onto the walkway, melting into the crowd from Honesty Village. With them were her mom and dad, Amy with little Anka by the hand, and Tomás, her fiancé. Wonderful! Marley fell in beside him, with Laney between them, still holding her hand. Tomás took his other hand. Anka leaned forward and peeked at Laney. Where was Ferdi? Marley thought with a spike of anxiety. Oh, there he was, just behind them, tall and broad and comforting. They walked along quietly, their eyes lowered, as close to invisible as they could manage. That was the best policy.

They swept along with the growing crowd, up to the huge top circle of the amphitheater. It seemed to float in the interior sky of the sphere. It hung like the colony's own private moon far above the misty surface below, where the bay docks and much of the colony's office spaces were. The top sphere was lit to imitate the phases of the moon—the moon as seen from Earth, of course. The seats on the third level retracted and made the disk flat and white, for dancing or what passed for it.

A giant screen tethered to the amphitheater was running ads until the Civic would begin. The heads alone were five feet tall, at least. The ads didn't focus on their heads, but on their gyrating, thrusting torsos, and Marley's family did not glance up at them. They did not have television. They did not like television. They had thought it would be easier to avoid it, here, on *Halliburton's*. Not like Earth. And it was still true, to a degree, but only because the screens weren't installed everywhere, yet, here on the colony. Not like Earth. The screens were everywhere on Earth: *You Will Buy. You Will Believe.*

Tonight, the Civic was supposed to be a special transmission from the president about Earth. It could not be good. None of the news from Earth ever was. To gather them for a special Civic meant it could be seriously bad. Even this crowd, inclined to be boisterous, some to be just plain dangerous, since so many of them were prisoners released to work on the colony, had family on Earth. Everyone looked pretty thoughtful, for a change.

Marley's family found their section among the tiers of shining aluminum bleachers arranged around the amphitheater's outer ring. The colony's elite were arriving, too, in their noisy private pods, and they hovered around the edges. There were the rest from Honesty village, about five hundred people. Next to them was Harmony village, and the contrast was great, and illegal.

Harmony Village was Muslim; Honesty Village was Catholic; Diversity village was Hindu. The Protestants were no longer numerous enough to have their own village, though. Nor was there a village for people of African heritage. Not enough black people to have one, even if it would have been tolerated. Hadn't Marley just heard that, back home, there were fewer than a hundred thousand black people left in all the Americas! The several blacks on the colony happened to be Catholic and lived in Honesty.

The colony was not supposed to be segregated like that. It was forbidden, officially. Regardless of the laws and the hype, though, things functioned the same way on the *Halliburton* as they did on Earth. That meant access to money and com links and language skills could usually result in bending the rules. Such was the case with enforcing "diversity" in housing, rules got bent. Because artificial diversity in housing just didn't work.

People preferred—to put it mildly—to live and raise their children among their own kind, usually a cultural, not a racial distinction, although they often overlapped. They would be pushed so far in this, but then, no further. They wanted their own, when they came home. In that, they were resolute, and it was an embarrassment to Earth, as they were often lectured. But the government tolerated it because they had to, at least for the time being, and of course there was always the possibility they'd be able to leverage the division later, for their own ends. It had been done in the past.

So, for the present, the colony administration tolerated it, and no one could deny that it made for better organization. Similar values and experiences made for fewer details to explain, and even if it didn't matter, anymore, if any piece of work took too long or cost too much on Earth (which was the price of "diversity" there), life cut closer to the bone on the colony. There, getting it right the first time mattered. Eating depended on it. Breathing depended on it. And bathing and sleeping.

So things got arranged, by a phone call and a visit, and in the end there was a Muslim village, a Catholic village, a Hindu village, and a Buddhist village. Of course, there were also any number of secular villages whose values were mixed, your basic paganism, and life was much more chaotic there, but, some argued, more "interesting," more "diverse." Poor, small-denomination Protestants with their thousand sects usually lived among the seculars, always bitterly complaining about the abandoned deist values of the Founding Fathers and so forth. The colony even had a fair share of tiny cults, like Chinese Wang Gong. It was just like Earth, only smaller—crazy, unsure, unstable, unbearable. Made slightly more bearable by the villages. Just like on Earth. (They had really thought it would be different! Chumps!)

The colony's aldermen apparently were tolerating the religious villages, for now, at least, as well as the black market and the purloined platinum and all the rest, because the colony was about to come online, fully online. Self-sustaining. It meant a lot to Earth. There would be time later to bring the *Halliburton* into compliance with the law in the little matter of neighborhoods. Meanwhile, it was like the old Wild West, hey? Rules were bent, and that came with an upside. The walls between the rule-makers and the ruled were more penetrable on *Halliburton's*, although Admin had its own village in process, and the rumors flew about the amenities there.

The religious villages would have argued that their way was kinder and more efficient, if anyone would stoop to ask them, if anyone would bother to listen. It wasn't about kindness and efficiency, though; not for ordinary people. It was about surviving, intact, with the beliefs your parents had handed on to you. That wasn't possible anymore on Earth, and that's why so many religious people had applied for colonial assignment. Life on Earth had become quite difficult for those who wished to live as if God existed.

So Marley's Catholic family had responded to the opportunity to relocate to the space colony. It had seemed to them, at the time, that with the great distance between Earth and

Halliburton's, they could leave behind at least some of the problems of Earth. And that was true. There *was* less conflict here between the religious villages. But there was perhaps more between the religious villages and the secular villages, whose lifestyles were ugly and expensive and noisy.

Problem-wise, though, the Catholics on the colony had one in particular not shared by the other religions. They had to have a priest, and they didn't have one. They had to have a validly consecrated, and that meant theologically educated, priest to give them the sacraments and offer mass. So far, no priest (of the precious few remaining on Earth, let alone a traditional priest like Tomás's brother!) had been granted permission to immigrate to the colony. Marley, among others, was trying to arrange it.

Marley was an expert at getting things arranged, whether it was managing a clandestine shipment of medicinal herbs or arranging a housing swap between her village and another to get a Catholic into Honesty. But so far she had not been able to get them a priest. The matter was particularly urgent to her, because she and Tomás were waiting for a priest to marry them.

"Chumps," is what her workmates thought of them, for waiting. Because today, who got married? Apparently it was important only to Catholics, and now, since all the changes of the last century, not important even to all Catholics, not even to the Vatican, judging from the absence of pastoral attention they had gotten so far on *Halliburton's*. That is, zip. No priest. Apparently, civil marriage was all the Church required now.

Marley had tried every avenue she knew. Only this morning she had tried another possibility, but so far had received no response. Apparently, the Church was satisfied with the current solution: to send consecrated hosts via a monthly "Eucharistic minister" courier and to recommend sincere acts of contrition, in the absence of a priest to hear their confessions. About marriage, nothing at all was said, nor about anointing the dying. Apparently, the Church now thought Catholics could survive without a priest, mass, marriage, or the sacraments.

Marley's cell phone tingled in her hand. She disappeared into the privacy of her hood for a moment, chatted briefly, and then looked into the eyes of her parents and shook her head: not yet.

Suddenly, the screen abandoned the dancers and began a dazzling display of light that culminated in the opening shot: the President of the World surrounded by . . . who?

"What?" Tomás muttered.

Marley glanced up at the screen. Assembled with the president were religious leaders, it seemed. There was a Sikh guru, you could tell by the turban, and, wow, the Holy Father, and on either side of him were Muslim imams, and beside them several saffron-robed Buddhists. There were also some women in suits and clerical collars: protestants.

The audience in the amphitheater hardly noticed the assemblage of people on the screen, however, nor did they pause to interpret what the presence of religious leaders at the side of the President of Earth might mean. They were all intently watching something else on the screen.

Blue sky.

On Earth, the sky above and behind the platform on which the president and religious leaders stood was azure. The blue sky of home. Marley's mom had tears in her eyes. Suddenly, Marley was aware of it, their longing: Earth! Home! Home sick! They were well and truly homesick.

Marley glanced around at what they now called home—a place where the dirt was thin beneath you, no, not *beneath*, on the inside surface of an enormous sphere. A sphere separated from the emptiness of space by nothing more than a membrane. A sphere so big it had its own sky inside, where little engineered white clouds floated. But it was not blue sky, just kind of a silvery mist. It was not Earth sky.

You couldn't see through Earth sky. You could *almost* not see through the mist and clouds to glimpse through windows the second sphere that ringed the center sphere where they were gathered. That outer ring held the living sections, with many future villages. There was a big wall of windows in the top of the center sphere, too, above them, like a row of large skylights, and outside those windows was the *real* sky. It was black. It was huge. Galaxy after galaxy glowed in the immense distance, pulsing like lightning storms on a summer night. Not in Kansas anymore.

Framed outside in the blackness, to one side of the observation windows, hung the biggest mining mobi-pod of the whole fleet. On the side of this formidable pod, in nostalgic green and gold, was the logo: Halliburton. The pod had moved very close to the window, as if the pilot and crew, too, were watching the huge screen inside, like a drive-in movie of old times.

But it fit, didn't it? To be together in the picture? The President of the World and the biggest machine of the biggest company in the world, the company that owned most of the world and *everything* off-world, as of now.

Oh yeah. Halliburton. The American success story.

They lived on *Halliburton's Colony*. Halliburton—the company that wished to own the universe. The obscene song sung about it floated unwelcome through Marley's head.

The president began to speak. The *Halliburton's* darkened and obediently quieted. All eyes focused on the screen, even if the eyes of many continued to watch the blue sky rather than the arresting face of the President of the World.

It was a big-boned, masculine face, with features thrown together from an assortment of the world's races, the nose from here, the brow from there, the forehead pure Sudan, the chin jutted like a Swede, and with a bluish five o'clock shadow (really?). Surrounding the face, a woman's blond hair. It was real—the hair, so they said.

The president was registered as a woman. There had been some question, putting it mildly, about *that*, but her gender registration documents were circulated widely on the nets for all to see. And it worked for her. Her voice was deep, but then again, not too deep. Everyone admired her oratorical ability.

She began to speak, resolutely, looking off into the middle distance. They dutifully admired the proffered profile. "My fellow citizens of Earth, I bring you greetings, wherever you are. I send special greetings to our brothers and sisters on *Halliburton's Colony*. All reports indicate that through your hard work, more and more services and goods are coming online. We hear you've got wheat, and as everybody knows, that means pizza."

The president paused for the requisite laugh. Media reports of severe dietary restrictions on *Halliburton's* mentioned nothing about the vigorous black-market food trade. The government was making aggressive propaganda use of the colony as a measure of the success of its partnership with Halliburton for the "economic good" of Earth, a policy that had cost Earth's taxpayers dearly. The best propaganda was pity. And, of course, there *were* real shortages. Just not like what was portrayed.

"I will arrange to visit as soon as you get a rose garden," the president added, milking the moment.

The laughter rippled upward again.

"Because I cannot be bought for pizza."

Now, the laughter had a hysterical edge. What could she be bought for, then? Ha ha ha! Hilarious.

"But I'm not here to talk about cuisine." The president, who delivered all her speeches in a quasi-Southern accent, drew out the word *cuisine*. The crazy guy Marley had encountered earlier had used the same drawl. It was the enunciation of a con man.

"I'm here to talk about faith," the leader of Earth proclaimed.

Marley's people exchanged surprised glances.

"I'm here to talk about faith because we know two things about faith. We know it has a bright side, and we know it has a dark side." The president smoothly changed cameras, and her eyes sought the prompters. She smiled for the lens. It was her specialty. She used it whatever the content of her remarks, and it made her seem, well, a little off, among other things.

"It is very easy to talk about the dark side, because you all know, and I know, and we will never forget, all that we have *suffered* because of religion." She paused again, casting her eyes down with an expression of mournful sadness, to allow everyone to remember the fiery explosions, the rains of slashing metal bits, and body parts, and blood, all done in the name of religion. A false one, of course. But—although the "experts" would have vigorously protested the use of the wrong programming language or even an inauthentic salsa on the tacos—they conveniently refused, Marley thought, to acknowledge differences among religions. Because the law said they were all equal.

"The people of every land have suffered, and we do not want their dead to be forgotten." Again, the president paused so her audience could remember the horrors, the rapes, the mutilations.

How bitterly Marley and her family had heard their kind referred to in that way. None of that had anything to do with Christ or their faith; it lay with the madness of the sects. Catholics had always believed in respect for life. Their followers were always the ones left cleaning up the mess, healing the wounds, burying the dead. And suffering the blame. They could feel the eyes of the others upon them, even now as the President of the World spoke of it, eyes filled with hatred.

The president's voice raised a notch in intensity. "Innocent people have *died* because of religion. Racial *divisions* have *deepened* because of religion. Women, especially, have *suffered* because of the cruel teachings present in the cultures of many of the world's religions. It is painful to mention the way *rape* is used as a tool of war."

She paused and struck a tragic pose, allowing everyone to appreciate with what authority she spoke for the women of the world, particularly, of course, black women. Marley remembered an African woman telling her mother, long ago on Earth as they waited in an eye clinic, how the US government-aid program had once, in her homeland, offered her sterilization in trade for food for her kids. How it hurt. But the president was all for *those* programs. That was *health* care.

"And religion is used the same, as a tool of war," the president added solemnly.

"But let us not forget the bright side of faith," she said with a lighter tone, a half-smile, letting a little sunshine in. "Let us not forget the many good things that religion brings to our planet. The many things that respect for a god gives to humankind. How it can also bring us together, forgiving hurts and insults, letting go of the past."

Her voice deepened, serious again. "Yes, religion can be used to hurt people, but it can also, in the hands of wise government, be used to help people."

The president took a deep breath. "One situation in particular needs the help of religion. As you know, the very prudent policy of population control pursued by our Founding World Fathers suffered a setback. We sought a balance, in which the population would remain steady and neither grow nor decline. That has not come to pass."

Indeed, it had not. The president's audience reflected on what, instead, had come to pass, in country after country. Both men and women, having been taught from childhood to avoid unwanted conception, had gone to great lengths to prevent it altogether and en masse. Parenthood was difficult. Houses had gotten so small. Raising a kid had gotten so expensive. Marriage was so stressful. Who needed it? Even sex itself, real sex, was difficult—at least more difficult than a video and a hand-job, to put it bluntly. Not worth the effort. So, before long, the world population had fallen to the 2.2 children per family that the UN called "balanced." Then it had fallen again, and again, and again, and the population of Earth had finally, after the older generations died off, halved and now was halving again. In forty years, the experts predicted, there would not be enough people of working age to keep the infrastructure running—the electricity, sewage plants, water purification plants. Governments had already given up the demolition of abandoned buildings and homes. Whole cities were wastelands roamed by packs of starving dogs.

And nothing seemed to have worked to get people interested in love and procreation again. Most countries were still glue-stuck in the old, sterile, low-fertility model. Take, for example, the mining asteroid adjacent to the colony, where it was forbidden to have children. It had something to do with the big Asian population; they had clung to China's old one-child concept, and it had mutated, metastasizing into a repulsion for children, for the very idea of children. On the mining asteroid, that was official policy: children were not only unwanted, they were illegal. The colony had the same policy—though it was unofficial. There, the threat of worse work schedules and diminished career advancement was quite enough to dissuade most couples from having even one child.

The president resumed her speech, and for a second, the sadness in her eyes seemed genuine. "But there is one place where the people were able to increase their population, over time. You may already have heard this on the media: the government of the Republic of Georgia, in the Caucasus, where the Orthodox version of Christianity is widely practiced, was able to motivate their citizens to take up the burden of procreation once again. Georgia is the only nation on Earth that has been able to accomplish that for a sustained period."

Everyone knew the extreme efforts and enormous expenditures other nations had thrown at the problem, only to have their birth rates bump up a smidgen for a year or two, but never longer. Then the birth rates fell even below previous levels—after all that mommy money they could so ill afford!

"Demographers have determined the country's success is due to their religion. Apparently, it works to encourage fertility where money does not. That is why I have gathered us here today—to forge something entirely new on Earth, but long overdue."

The president slowly and deliberately looked around the platform, and the camera followed her gaze, as if all those representatives from Earth's religions were speaking with the president. The camera lingered on the Holy Father as the president continued.

"We have learned from little Georgia. The world's religious leaders have joined me today to announce the beginning of a new world faith, a faith that will unify us in love and respect. And boost our birth rate. No longer will religion be used to divide us," she said, her tone warming noticeably with that last statement, the repetition of her favorite words. "That is because we will be joined in *one* faith, an evolved religion stemming from the best of the beliefs of the world's faiths."

Again, the president glanced expectantly at her companions on the platform. Some of them took her cue and turned to those around them with smiles, but others looked confused and uncomfortable. Still, they responded politely, especially the Holy Father. He seemed eager to stand with his companions on the platform; it was said he had already forged his epitaph: Lived for Brotherhood.

"We are not speaking empty words, here, my dear friends," the president went on. "Henceforth, ministers of One World One Faith will host public, transmitted services for all. There will be no need for private services around the world to divide us. There will be no rogue ministers to confuse us, to lead us to violence, to destroy our civilization." She appeared triumphant now. "This is the new Freedom of Worship Act, the crown jewel of my presidency and the highest achievement of mankind's great history of achievement. I know I can count on you to support our efforts to achieve, once and for all, lasting world peace and security for everyone in everything."

There was a second of silence. Then, the unseen listeners at the location on Earth where the president spoke erupted into wild applause. *Halliburton's Colony* followed, somewhat delayed, with some applauders more delayed than others. Marley's people were too stunned even to pretend to applaud. Their eyes were glued to the screen, on which they could see the face of the Holy Father. He appeared to be serene. Could he be drugged?

When the applause faded, the president continued. "There must be a period of transition, we realize that. Our new ministers will have to be thoroughly trained in the official liturgy." The president's voice suddenly hardened. "Of course, from this time forward, all private, selfish pursuit of religion is forbidden. There will be a time of patience and forgiveness, after which there will be penalties. Security measures have been put in place, and they will be utilized. Make no mistake: this is change, this is the future. The power of religion to divide and hurt us is gone forever. Its power to unite and motivate us will remain, at the service of democracy and freedom. For *nothing* is as important as freedom."

She wound up for the big finish: "One World, One Faith! Let's make that happen, for the good of all mankind! God is with us now! Freedom now! Freedom now! *Freedom now!*"

The cameras cut to celebrations around the world, one after another. People cheering in Paris. (Paris! How sweet the one glimpse!) In Malta, a group of young people weeping, for joy of course. An incredibly diverse group of people applauding under Big Ben. Some Australians standing by a beach in what looked like, yes, it was, Melbourne. Tiananmen Square filled with cheering Chinese. Sober men in Mongolia cracking a smile. It must have taken some arranging and producing, that lightning-fast set of images from around the world.

The crowd from Honesty Village was suddenly acutely aware that they were the only ones not cheering in their section, but their confusion was so great that they ignored this breach in security. What they had heard was unthinkable! Couldn't everyone see? It was like saying, from now on, they were all married to each other! It was like saying that all gods were the same. How could anyone not realize that meant there was no God at all?

It didn't seem like freedom, it seemed like prison! Peace? It seemed like death! And yet, everyone was cheering.

No, not quite all. Besides the Catholics from Honesty Village, the Muslims also looked worried and serious. So did the Hindus. There were others, as well, in small groups. The longer the cheering went on, the more exposed they all were. Some managed a little smile or a small wave with the others. It was pathetic.

Marley was trying to process the implications. Whatever could it mean? For one, surely no priest was ever coming now! Maybe they'd have some kind of transmission, at best. How could they ever celebrate mass? How could they ever receive communion again, via *transmission*? It wasn't possible! If there was anything Catholicism *wasn't,* it was *virtual.* How would they be Catholic, then? What was the Holy Father meaning, being there, seeming to agree to all that? Maybe there would be no mass, no communion, no confession, no holy matrimony ever again!

The screen faded to black. People rose to leave.

Her parents looked stunned. Her dad seemed mad, too. Tomás caught her eye, and they exchanged a worried look. He leaned close to her; she could smell the good scent of him, and it both thrilled and saddened her. How would she be married now?

Tomás knew her concern, and whispered, "Don't worry, Marl. Patience. Let's give God a chance to help us work it out." He smiled, his blue eyes twinkling, and it reached into her heart.

Energy filled her again, and hope. In spite of all that it happened and how crazy it had been for Marley's family to immigrate to the colony, she had met Tomás there, and that made it all worthwhile. She smiled back at him.

Then they concentrated on getting their little flock through the crowd and getting home, where they could manage to talk about things and pray. Marley and the others proceeded as usual, with Anka and Laney in the middle, where no one could bother them.

Out of the corner of her eye, as they turned, Marley saw a private pod begin to descend and caught a glimpse of Graham Fletcher's cold face at the back of the amphitheater. Fletcher was the superintendent of *Halliburton's*. He seemed to notice her. Bad luck! Quickly, she dropped her head but not before catching sight of the expression on Fletcher's face. It chilled her to the bone. He liked her.

Marley's group fell in beside some Muslims from Harmony Village. Adn was among them; she and Marley worked together on the dock. Everyone on the job steered clear of Adn because she was Muslim and wore *hijab*, but Marley liked her, anyway; she couldn't help liking her. Adn was so cheerful, a good worker, and kind to everybody. Besides, the others gave Marley a hard time, too—for her clothes, her rejecting the colony fashion of skintight jumpsuits for women, and for a million other little things, like sex jokes not laughed at and crude invitations not accepted. Marley and Adn gave each other a little wave. It was so discrete only their mothers saw them. Adn's mother frowned.

The second circle had been transformed into a dance floor for the after-Civic celebration. It was packed. You could see the crowd from the moving walkways. Many of the partiers wore masks or animal headgear. Most of the girls weren't wearing much of anything. The music was turned up loud, and the dancers wore or held laser lights, which flashed all around the interior of the *Halliburton's*, some striking the dark skeletons of empty habitats stretching into the horizon, some striking the inhabited villages.

Marley's group was almost through the moving walkway on the second level when a young man wearing the horns of a bull, a shirt with red syringes printed all over it, and a belt that flashed with many colors stumbled onto the walkway and almost fell before righting himself and peering into Marley's face. "Hey baby," he slurred, "Why don't you come and have a little dance and a little toke with me?"

But before he could finish the sentence, Tomás had reached around Marley and grabbed him by the collar. Shielded by the crowd on the walkway, Tomas then gave him an illegal shake and thump and tossed him back onto the dance floor. It was never legal to use any form of violence on *Halliburton's*, even in self-defense. Of course, the bad guys used it easily enough. They had less to lose, and prosecutions were rare. Not enough manpower.

Some of the man's friends saw him land on the floor and rushed over to him. One of the men pointed in their direction as he said something excitedly to his friends, who turned and glared at Marley and her family as they continued to descend the walkway.

"Freaking Catholics!" yelled another of the men. "Guess the president gave it to you tonight! Now, you're illegal!" He made an obscene gesture. "Ha ha ha ha!" he brayed, his laughter echoing far out into the sphere.

But then Marley's group descended out of his vision and to the lowest rung, where they continued on to the train that took them to their village. It was late when they reached home, and Tomás was going to head to his place, but Marley's dad stopped him. They all sat down on the faintly curved aluminum "sofa," and Marley's dad broke out the whiskey. Each of them, except Laney, of course, sipped an aluminum thimble-full.

After they sat thoughtfully for a moment, Marley's dad held out his jigger and said, "Fill 'er up again, Mary. I guess this night will be worth remembering someday—as the day we turned into rabbits." They all knew he was speaking metaphorically. He dare not speak the actual words out loud, under the assumption that everything was bugged. The new restriction would be unbearable, but everyone knew a way around it: the Combs. Now, they would need the Combs more than ever.

What Marley's dad meant was that they would have to go underground, like rabbits. She had expected him to say something like that, because they would not give in. They would not give up their faith. The Church would be underground. If they ever got a priest, he would be underground. It was not the first time Catholicism had been forbidden. It wasn't the first time on *Halliburton's*, either, despite the colony having been advertised as more free than Earth. As it turned out, that "freedom" meant you had to conform even more openly to secularism. It made for a lot of burrows. The Combs.

Actually, they had been expecting this new law, along with the Church's apparent complicity, for a long time. Every passing day had given more evidence of the Church's confused response to government pressure. Marley's family had been part of the movement to reverse that, to recapture tradition in the Church. They had achieved some discussion of the issues in Rome, and in the process had gotten for themselves shadowy, quiet parishes of tradition. Their traditional parish in Florida was the hardest thing on Earth to leave. They had done so only with the intention of fixing the situation as rapidly as possible. When they had left Earth, the Church seemed to have gained some momentum toward tradition, toward Restoration, but it had faded again. Or rather, as Marley put it to herself, the Church seemed to have found a way to mouth solemn bits of traditional doctrine just before it sneaked in liberal practices, and many people were fooled.

That they'd been expecting this turn of events didn't make the new law any easier to take, though. And there seemed to be no solution. They had tried to run to the colony. But the colony was just like Earth.

Well, except for a bigger black market. A lot of that back-alley commerce happened in the Combs, which could not be electronically snooped because it was so heavily shielded. Down under the habitats, between the living surface and the inner surface of the outer hull, was the area that had been built first, by robots, before people ever came to the colony. It was a big, empty space designed to be used for storing nonessentials and anything that would shield from radiation. Everything that could be stuffed between the habitat level and the hull was put there— at first, space rubble the debris sweepers hauled in. Then, after the people came, the colony's sewage, dried into bricks once the water and organic compounds were extracted. Later, the dead were "buried" there. All necessary. Because of the radiation, of course. The colony interior had to be shielded from the radiation of the sun. It could cause all kinds of savage effects on organic matter.

So the dead found their final resting place there. The dead shielded the living. And the living found a place to hide.

They called it the Combs, short for catacombs, according to the Catholics. Everybody else said it was named for a guy back in the day—Mike Combs or something like that—who'd first come up with the idea of a near-Earth orbit space colony. Initially, the government was going to name the whole colony after him, but Halliburton said no. So then they started to call the shielded space the Combs. But the catacombs explanation worked, too—for Christians, life was more and more like life in old Rome. Only the bots that buried the dead and compacted the trash were allowed there. It was illegal for any of the colony's residents or visitors to go into the Combs.

Everyone said it was haunted. Everyone expected the radiation to work some kind of mischief on whatever organic DNA it could find. Some believed they just saw ordinary spirits, good ones and bad ones. Whether haunted or tainted or both, the Combs was heavily shielded from the habitat level on the one side and from the hull on the other, with both electronic and visual shielding. It was also shielded horizontally both by the materials packed into it and by actual wall-shields. In the end, the authorities believed they might have overdone things. They could not get human workers to go into the area, and despite the hype over the "intelligent" bots, the fact was, they were stupid, next to useless for unaided surveillance.

Everybody who went into the Combs did so on the sly, working around the cameras. The Combs hid many secrets. Marley's family had a private entrance to the Combs. Others did, too. No one knew all of the mazes of the Combs. It was kind of like the colony's own lost continent.

"Fill 'er up," Marley's dad said again, faintly. It was, of course, a joke. He was speaking of a teaspoon. Whiskey was dearer than gold on the *Halliburton's*. But they sat on their aluminum couches in their aluminum habitat on humanity's first space colony, sipping their teaspoon of whiskey and mourning the newest development in secularism: an official, co-opted state religion. And the Holy Father had sat right there with the others, seemingly going along with it. They felt--scalded. That's what betrayal felt like. Their skin felt burned. Their hearts felt hot.

From this day forward, practicing Catholics—those who would not deny Christ as the Way and the only Way to the Creator Father, as He had said numerous times—would be officially illegal. There could be no Christ the Savior God in the new religion--maybe just Jesus, the good man, a prophet perhaps. Not God.

How would they live now?

Tomás stood up to leave. He had to rise early the next morning to make a run to the asteroid.

"Will you be back by supper tomorrow?" Marley asked. He ate with her family often.

"I hope so," he said. "Things are so bad on the asteroid, though, it's hard to say what will happen. Always chaos and delays!"

Tomás had to fill up the pod with the processed mineral ore, aluminum, lead, and silver as well as with minerals to be used in the colony's farming or oxygen synthesis. Then, once back to the colony, he had to offload all the materials to the manufacturing sectors, on the docks where Marley worked.

Marley walked Tomás to the entrance. He looked troubled.

"Do you remember Maki? The Catholic Asian girl?" he asked her. She nodded. "I hope she's on duty tomorrow; I want to talk with her. Maybe there's some way I can help. It's *really* bad for the women there."

"Wait," Marley said, and kissed him on his chin. She dashed to the storage cube by the door and pulled out a small rosary. Pressing it into Tomás's hand, she said, "Give this to her. Tell her I'll pray for her, and ask her to pray for me."

Tomás gently drew her closer to him and kissed her on the forehead. She lifted her mouth to his, and they kissed tenderly.

"Do you think we'll have to forget about a priest now?" he asked.

Marley thought for a moment. She glanced around, and then put her arms around his neck and discretely repositioned herself so that her face was shielded from the cameras.

"Look," she said, leaning back to look up at his face. "Things didn't seem any better back in the day. Catholicism has been illegal in the past, too! Remember Henry the Eighth? They had no priests then, or only a couple priests they had to hide! But they didn't give up. And we won't either."

He smiled at her determination. But sadness filled his eyes.

"Have faith!" she said, grinning hopefully at him. "So we won't get any help from the Vatican now; nothing new about that. Let me try again, see what I can do. There *has* to be a way." Marley looked thoughtful, the expression Tomás loved best. "Maybe there's a black market for priests."

"Okay," is all he said, but his voice was relaxed again. She could always affect him that way. He squeezed her hand goodbye and walked down the quiet habitat street to his single guys' dormitory—a home that colony administration knew nothing about. It had been set up—in violation of mandatory mixed-sex dormitory rules—by Catholics in this Catholic neighborhood, who had rules of their own.

The path Tomás walked along consisted of pebbles instead of vegetation, because pebbles were cheap on the asteroid. It was a very Japanese landscape. The amphitheater now glowed above him, lit like the quarter moon. The real moon, actually in its quarter phase as viewed from Earth, but in its dark phase as viewed from the colony, showed ghost-like through the observation window. In a couple of hours, the window would frame the black Bernina Harrison asteroid where Tomás was headed in the morning.

The Bernina Harrison

Tomás got ready for docking. He thought of the old joke, that piloting a mining pod involved long days of boredom interrupted by seconds of sheer terror as you approached the docks or a new rock. But Tomás was really good at it. Just a matter of staying alert—and avoiding collisions with badly programmed bots, like the one heading straight for him! Tomás scooted quickly left and then right as the bot zipped past and another approached. Thank you, Mother Mary!

A smiling image suddenly appeared on his screen, the boss of the docks. A Hindu and a nice guy, Ramdoss Krishnamurthy was the traffic controller on the 931 Bernina Harrison Asteroid, *Halliburton's* first asteroid mining project.

Tomás grinned. "Hey hey," he chuckled into his headset. "Hey hey! What's going on, buddy?"

"It was all good, but now here you come," Krishnamurthy . "Ready for docking? What did you bring me?"

"Brought you a big fistful of hurt," Tomás laughed. What he'd actually brought him, tucked under his shirt, was a whole half pound of cranberry red, 100 percent wool yarn from the Shetland Islands, for which Krishnamurthy had traded Tomás an ounce of pure-grade platinum. The precious metal wasn't stolen or anything shady; Krishnamurthy had a legal right to the platinum as part of his labor agreement with Halliburton, negotiated on Earth, in which colonists could buy the ore they mined cheap, but they had not worked out much else, like where colonists could sell it. They weren't supposed to sell it on Earth, thereby protecting the market. Native ingenuity was taking care of that, though. He hadn't sold it at all. He traded it.

Tomás didn't like the casual trafficking. You had to sneak, and Tomás was not a good sneak, although, he had to admit he sometimes kind of enjoyed the game of fooling the technology to bring in something from Earth, like wool, that colony administrators had decided was not a necessity—a decision they made without any input from colonists, of course. But these were strange times. States and companies joined forces.

They were making all the decisions. And they wanted the colony to become profitable—quickly. Pushing up prices was part of the game. What's more, in their dogged pursuit of fat and fast profits, they were not above exacting harsh punishment on colonists caught selling or trading *Halliburton's* booty at less than its inflated value.

Tomás unstrapped himself and stepped out into the Regina Coeli's first big bay, where the doors had already been opened and a tiny woman, an asteroid worker, was struggling with a stubborn lever. She wasn't familiar to Tomás. He stepped over and helped her, and then exited the pod. His crew was already beginning the ore transfer.

Ten minutes later, Tomás was sitting across from Krishnamurthy in the little office beside the loading dock. It was little more than a couple of freestanding wall panels surrounding some stacked cubes to sit on and to serve as a desk. David Booth's geeky official photograph leered at them from its aluminum frame hung crooked on the wall. Booth, an engineer and programmer of legendary talent, was administrator of the mining asteroid, Bernina Harrison. It was rumored he liked boys, and the average age on the mining asteroid was twenty years younger than on Earth. The Bernina Harrison was certainly taking advantage of Asia's new export, the dwindling reserves of its young labor force—though for different reasons than Booth's. Krishnamurthy followed Tomás's glance, and reached over and turned the photo down.

"How's the wife?" Tomás asked.

"She's great," Krishnamurthy said. "Thanks!"

The question had not been rhetorical. Krishnamurthy and his wife were expecting a child. Hardly anyone knew—Tomás, a very few others. There was a lot of well-concealed excitement about it. No one had been sure whether human beings could actually conceive under the almost-weightless conditions on the asteroid, not to mention it was against the contract. The couple, like all asteroid workers, had signed a contract agreeing to practice birth control and to abort any fetus.

The contract had not been tested yet. The Krishnamurthy's were hoping against hope that they could somehow conceal the pregnancy and that common sense would rule when it was discovered. Labor was the single most precious commodity in space. Surely, faced with executing a future worker, the asteroid owners' greed would win out over their default Earth-bound prejudice against new human life. Of course, common sense had not yet prevailed on Earth. Surely here, the expectant parents reasoned, where the shortage of workers was most acute, surely here common sense would kick in. Right? So they hoped.

It was possible Administration already knew of the pregnancy but was divided. That had happened In China, until it was too late to reverse the one-child policy. For so many years, Earth had pursued a relentless policy of zero-population growth, and although the situation had changed drastically as the economic consequences of no-growth rolled out, it now was now proving difficult for people to switch gears mentally. Women, in particular, having spent the last several generations obtaining educational levels in excess of their male counterparts, were not easily being persuaded to become mothers. Most associated the idea of motherhood with slavery, biological slavery, as they had been carefully taught.

Nor had the deformed economy, running on speculation, coupled with the labor shortages that appeared like cancers and blighted any new economic growth, made it easy for the state to lose women workers to motherhood. Women were more necessary than ever to the workforce and also to take care of their parents, especially in Asia, which had no national retirement insurance. The colony, too, needed workers desperately, even more desperately than on Earth. There were habitats to be built, and crops to be grown, and orders to be processed, and new asteroids to be brought in, and tomato paste and refined wheat to be developed so they could have pizza. Even the children on the colony, mainly belonging to the religious groups who had sought refuge there, had after-school jobs as soon as their little heads could clear a counter. Two hats? Try three!

They needed workers on Earth, too. But on Earth, where the thinning and aging population was spread out over an entire planet so that, the rural populations having been hollowed out of their young, the cities still seemed cheerfully populous, the impact of the demographics was easier to ignore. Besides, all the media, following the script, continued to attribute the decline in Earth's economy to a multitude of factors, none of them the depressed birth rate. That message was muted, blocked. Every article speaking of the birth dearth always ended with the comment that fewer humans just had to be good, given Global Change, and no one had the nerve to argue. Besides, Planned Population was a big donor to the President of the World's political war chest. In return, the government helped Planned Population with their elegant solution for poverty--killing the impoverished.

Female mining colonists on the asteroid were all on birth control, too. Any pregnancy was to be terminated. That was the law. Many women had ceased to menstruate, anyway.

It was such a mess. Current profits relied on women working. Future profits relied on women reproducing. Nobody—except "religious extremists"—had even thought of any guidelines or rules for any purpose other than protecting and growing profits. The present laws protected only current profits. If they made new laws, suddenly reversed the ban on births, those guidelines and rules would be only to protect future profits. Those were the only two choices compatible with profits. Forced abortion or forced reproduction. Current conditions called for abortion--so governments thought. In order to escape Earth, men and women alike had signed the no-child agreement.

Krishnamurthy was thus extremely worried. All he could do was count on Administration thinking about *future* profits, and so far the jury was out on how they would respond to an actual pregnancy on the colony or the asteroid. Rules were broken in space, though. Although Krishnamurthy's face was drawn, he made every effort to appear cheerful. Tomás deeply respected the man's self-discipline.

Krishnamurthy took out a couple of ceramic tumblers, and fished a bottle out of his desk. He poured a little of the precious liquid into each glass, and handed one to Tomás.

"To week twelve," Krishnamurthy said, raising his glass in a toast. "This fine liquor is supposed to be sherry. But maybe that was the color of the bathtub."

Tomás grinned. He tossed back the sherry, with his eyes closed. When Krishnamurthy offered him another, he waved his hand.

"I'm driving," Tomás said. "So how are things going here in paradise?"

"If I owned it, I guess I'd say great," Krishnamurthy answered with a grin. "We're getting a big ice shipment from Luna this afternoon, and I'm shorthanded."

Luna ice was big, bulky, and unpredictable at low gravity. During the last delivery, a chunk of the rock had drifted from its mooring and crushed a girl against the wall of the bay.

"But here's something." Krishnamurthy leaned forward and lowered his voice, his face intense. "I think a scout found something very interesting: an asteroid, not on the grid. A big one. It was this crazy accident they saw it. It was Laiq Amanpour and that crew." He paused to let Tomás recognize the implication.

Laiq Amanpour was a Muslim and presumably reliable in his opposition to the secular administration of the Bernina Harrison. This finding would therefore not necessarily have been reported. In fact, the odds were it hadn't.

"It's in the Oort Cloud," Krishnamurthy whispered. Again, he paused to let Tomás consider the implications.

The Oort Cloud was a big place, putting it mildly, huge, the last outpost of Earth's sun, a band of asteroids and comets on the far outskirts of the solar system. Its heavenly bodies were full of absolutely everything—ices of all kinds, methane, ethane, carbon and cyanide and nitrogen, and everything heavy and rare in Earth's hard-to-get-to center, where, back in the hot-liquid stage of Earth's formation, gravity had sunk all the heavy elements to the center. On an asteroid, all those goodies were right there on the surface. Aluminum! Platinum! Gold! Like scooping ice cream.

There were millions and millions of asteroids in the Oort Cloud. So many that they screwed up communications, acting as a natural shield against transmissions. You could get well lost in the Oort Cloud. Rumor had it that Oort was shielded from solar radiation, too. Rumors also circulated about ghost ships. Such details were of interest to those who—well, had things to conceal.

An enormous wild space in a universe of sinners and saints who needed to hide.

"Wow! The Oort Cloud!" Tomás said, his voice low. "I don't suppose you got the coordinates?"

Krishnamurthy grinned wanly and shook his head. He didn't, and likely wouldn't, get the coordinates, he admitted to Tomás. Laiq Amanpour was no fool.

Anyway, Krishnamurthy went on to explain, he wasn't absolutely certain of what Laiq had found, let alone where. It wasn't as if Laiq had actually said anything. It was just that Laiq and his team had been headed for the sector adjacent to the Oort Cloud, according to their flight plan. It was the longest and least desirable run of the regular routes, usually boring. When Krishnamurthy had checked them in, Laiq had been excited, really excited, and muttered something about getting off-course, way off-course. And when Krishnamurthy had joked, "What did you do, find a rainbow and a pot of gold?" Laiq had turned to him wide-eyed and open-mouthed, as if to say, How did you know? So Krishnamurthy had a strong suspicion—that was all it was, really—that Laiq had found something in the Oort Cloud, and he could see, glancing down at the log between them on the desk, that nothing had been recorded about it. Nothing. Laiq shut up then and calmed down, too. He shrugged, laughed, and turned his back so Krishnamurthy could not see his face.

Tomás pondered this information and then observed Krishnamurthy's sober face. "But congratulations! Week twelve. Wow!"

"Yeah, isn't it great? But Dhwani hasn't been to a doctor. Naturally."

Tomás looked worried himself. He had known this moment would come. Krishnamurthy was really nothing more to Tomás than a seemingly nice guy who worked for the Man, the same as Tomás. He wasn't a Catholic; he wasn't one of Tomás's people. But he was in as much trouble as a person could be in, and it was possible that Tomás could help—mainly because Marley had made it a point to know where to get darn near anything.

But in helping Krishnamurthy and his wife, Tomás would make himself liable. He could possibly expose his family, and

Marley. They could be sent back to Earth, at the very least. Presently, although he missed Earth and especially missed his brother, who was stuck there by his disability, Earth was an even worse place to be than the colony, especially for Catholics.

To hell with all that! Tomás had a heart. "Krish, look, I can't promise, but it's possible I could put you in touch with someone who can help. I don't know if she's, you know, available. But I can ask. I will ask."

Krishnamurthy put the tumbler on the table. His hand trembled a little. He knew what Tomás had undertaken with his offer, putting himself and his whole family and friends on the line for the life of a stranger, a baby still in the womb, and outside their circle. He didn't trust himself to speak, but he nodded and held Tomas's gaze for a moment.

They changed the subject. "I'd sure like to talk to Laiq," Tomás said wistfully. "I don't guess you could convince him to give me those coordinates!"

Before Krishnamurthy could joke back, the door flew open and a young woman burst in. Something wet and oily was spattered across her chest.

"Krishnamurthy! Come!"

The alarm began its demonic shrieking. Krishnamurthy ran toward the dock.

After tucking the wool into Krishnamurthy's desk, Tomás followed him into the nightmare world of the mining asteroid, with alarms screeching, lights flashing, and thin, frightened women scurrying toward their emergency stations.

A Florida Parish Priest

This was the worst attack yet! It was so hot! No air, and the humidity vibrated like a steel drum. But he couldn't think about that. He could think of only two things; his next breath and the woman's voice.

He couldn't look at the dark wood of the confessional. If he looked at it, it rushed toward him. He had to hold on to the next breath: a sip of air.

"The next thing, I gossiped." The woman's voice. Disembodied, distorted, it became a devil's falsetto.

His heart was thudding in his chest. Something was coming for him! Don't think about that, hold on to the woman's voice. Concentrate!

"How many times?" He could get out only so many words on the exhale. Three was about right, before the panic would catch his throat. Would there be air when he needed to inhale? He gasped the next sip.

"Once. This week."

Think about something good, something with air. Air! Cool, dry, silky over the lips. Oh God, help me! I can't! Can't get air!

"Did it hurt?" Sip. "Anyone?" Sip.

The woman paused and thought. "I suppose it made someone mad."

No. No, don't go there. Not therapy. Sin.

"Anything else?" Sip. Poison air, like melted wax. Nauseous; gonna hurl. Help.

"The Seventh Commandment."

"Yes?" He was drowning. Christ drowned. Couldn't get air. The way they stretched His arms. There was no air, just her perfume, hair spray, awful. Panic was right there, where he could touch it. Something was coming. All he had to do was scream— but then, no air. What would happen next? It couldn't be worse than this. Help!

"The one against stealing, Father." She sounded exasperated to have to tell him, or that's what she thought. It hurt his pride!

"Yes?" Could she hear him panting?

"Oh. Well, I bought some of them pirate DVDs for the kids."

Restitution, oh Lord. How could he explain in three words? "Any good?"

"What? Good? How do you mean?"

"Good. Catholic."

"They're *cartoons*, Father."

"But good?"

"Yeah, well, a couple, I guess."

"Bad ones . . . in trash. Five dollars . . . good ones . . . poor basket. And."

"Yes, Father?"

"Read to them. Books." Sip. "And work on the gossiping." He barely got it out. "Penance: decade rosary. Say the Act."

"Oh, my God, I am heartily sorry . . ." the woman began the Act of Contrition.

Tim held onto her voice in the dark confessional and, trying not to think about air, said the ancient words of absolution as clearly as he could. He still said them in Latin.

When she was finished, he said, "Go in peace. Pray for me. How many waiting? Please?"

A moment later, she whispered on the other side, "No one left, Father."

"Thank you," he murmured, but she was gone.

Five more minutes. Just five more minutes in case somebody showed up late.

Finally, Tim opened the heavy wooden door. He took off the purple stole. He started to hang it over the door knob, but the satin was soaked with sweat, so he draped it over his shoulder. It could use an airing, and so could he. He groped his way out of the confessional.

He knelt to say goodnight to Christ present in the tabernacle. What a relief, to kneel in the open air of the old church. They had designed it for Florida, and the hot air found its way up and out through the stairway, up to the steeple and out, drawing relatively cooler air in through the windows at ground level. It was still hot, but the attack faded instantly in the wonderful sensation of flowing air.

Tim looked at the tabernacle. As he thought of the confessions he had heard that evening, he prayed for them, the straggly men and women who had knelt beside him, one by one, in that hot box: Help them to be strong against their sins, Lord. Then, he amended it: Help *us*.

He was too tired to pray in words. Well, that was also something to offer to God, for the world. He was so hungry he was trembling, and he smelled rank, and he had to pee. He offered all that to God, too. He offered it for his penitents tonight, like a chess move, for that's what Saint Teresa of Avila said about prayer, it was "like playing chess with God," she had written. He often wondered what she must have meant, since she hadn't explained further. If God were a kind God (although that jury was still out, what with the Bible brimming with brimstone and all, the evidence pointed toward mercy), God's next move (since Tim, on his part, had consciously and formally accepted all of his discomfort and offered them with a willing heart) would be to grant that prayer, and give the requested help for those who had come and told their sins and hoped for divine assistance in the endless struggle. Sort of like chess. Or maybe poker. (Saint Teresa didn't say that!) Father had a sudden feeling that all that he offered was so small compared to the struggles of his penitents, even the least of them, and he cringed in shame at offering God such feeble suffering, compared to the roughneck old world as he heard of it in the confessional. It was a sad feeling. So he offered that, too, with a wry smile. What was he, God's own personal *Comedy Central*?

His penitents! What a struggle, to be really sorry for their sins. All we humans ever wanted was to make excuses. Yet, the only necessary thing was to be truly sorry. Of course, it was also the hardest thing. Deceptively simple. What did the mass say, when the priest put the incense in the censor? "Help me put a wall at the door of my mouth, to not make excuses in sin."

But, ah yes, they made excuses! Like dime-store lawyers, they were inclined to argue their cases. They stole because they were poor or thought they were poor.

They lied because the truth hurt, and they dodged it like a blow.

They gossiped because no one listened to them otherwise.

They dressed immodestly because otherwise no one looked at them, really looked at them.

They committed adultery because they were so lonely in the hell that marriage can be, if it goes bad. And it went bad so often. Because they insisted on contraception, without knowing it's the death of love. Because they lusted in their hearts. Because they cheated. And then made excuses. All of it hands around the throat of their love.

Besides, too many men didn't want to grow up. They secretly hated being the breadwinner, and they covered it up with sweet talk about "equality." So women ended up doing both jobs, and the marriage died. Or the wives! Couldn't do a nice thing for a husband if the world depended on it. Fifty-fifty, all the way, like a business!

So they argued their cases.

They always had a point. Monogamy is so delicate and so difficult. Men could really act like pigs. But women have a trick or two themselves. He'd learned a lot in the confessional. For one thing, he'd learned to appreciate celibacy!

Humans! They cheated on their taxes; they littered; they killed other human beings in public; they kicked their dogs in private. They found it really hard to stop. He could understand it. He knew them. He was one of them. "Our sins are all we have." He'd heard a song like that once. Seems like the truth, sometimes.

Yet, God said, "Stop." But really quietly. Because He knew.

God knew He overwhelmed men. He could *make* men stop sinning, but He didn't want to. That wouldn't be love. God tried to make up for it by invisibility, and He said "Stop" in a tiny voice, like the wind or the whisper of leaves, so faint anyone could pretend not to hear. Truly, He wanted the real love of free men and women!

The tired people at confession tonight hadn't ignored Him. What a miracle! It moved Tim to prayer. He locked his heart on the Presence in the tabernacle and begged. Help us. He wished his heart said that to God with every beat. Help us, or the world will end. Because that was pretty much the way it was around here on Earth now: end game. Extinction.

He walked back to the rectory. The sky was rich with stars to the east, and in the west towering rain clouds still gilded from the sunset pulsed with energy, full of heat lightning. The smell of his housekeeper's jasmine billowed all around him, but he was okay now, he could even appreciate it. His claustrophobia seemed a very mild penance compared to the problems and sacrifices of some of his parishioners—even though it had kept him at home in Florida all his life while his twin brother was already in outer space.

If you had to be *somewhere* on Earth, though, this was the place. Oh, sure, the cities were dangerous now; in spite of the mandatory news blackout, there were plenty of ways to find out things had gone to hell pretty fast around certain parts of the globe, including Miami and Tampa. But people in rural Florida had armed themselves long ago, and Catholics and Protestants saw their way clear to a kind of awkward cooperation around the Ten Commandments, more or less. Catholics had to stand silent about divorce and promote social justice, maybe over-promote it, to compensate for the economics they'd inherited. Protestantism had begun with a king's lust and greed, and protestantism still held to the lust and to the vicious economy the rebellion had produced . But they kept the peace between them, one way or another. Central Florida still had food and power, too.

The Church bureaucracy, from incompetence, left him alone to say the old mass and to do things the old ways. He thanked God for it often. He would be happy right here, except for one thing: he missed his brother, Tomás, on the new space colony, up there with the stars. Tomás was the only family Tim had left, since their parents had died. It was a constant ache, a hole in his heart; he offered it up, automatically. He missed his brother. Missed him. Missed him. Missed him. Offered it up.

He opened the screen door and entered the back porch quickly, and closed the door quickly again to keep the mosquitoes out. The rectory kitchen was as old as the church and just as thoughtfully designed for the heat. It was a separate wing from the house, with its own porch, so the cooking heat and odor dissipated. A cast-iron wood-burning stove complete with a smoke oven in the flue dominated one side of the room. An enormous window opened the sink area to a view of the sweet, slow creek below, where otters sometimes played and water lilies bloomed.

There now at the sink, his housekeeper Dovie stood firmly planted on her house slippers, washing dishes. She turned when she heard him enter. "I'll get your supper, Father. You'll be wanting to wash your hands."

When he came back from the bathroom, she was standing by his chair holding his dinner plate. She would give him, as usual, a thorough examination before she put the plate on the table. If he failed any part of it, she would absentmindedly return the plate to the counter and set out to rectify whatever was amiss. He hoped he'd pass. He was starving.

"You've had another attack, from the looks of you," she finally said.

"It wasn't so bad. I got through it. But my stole could use some sunshine, okay, Dovie? I left it out. Thank you." He seated himself and held his breath to see whether she was going to put down the plate.

She weighed his words syllable by syllable. Satisfied, she placed his dinner carefully before him, and then returned to the counter for the hot rolls, salt and pepper, and his juice. Fried chicken from their own little flock, mashed potatoes, collard greens from the rectory garden, and the juice squeezed fresh from oranges growing by the doorstep—another benefit of living in Florida, if you still lived on Earth. It was possible it would go on forever, if the crisis did not result in any kind of nuclear war or invasion, and people outside the world's cities just might survive.

He wondered what Tomás had for supper tonight. Many things were coming online on the colony; maybe they had fried chicken and collard greens by now. Anyway, that's what the news said, if you could believe it. He'd have to ask Tomás the next time he emailed, if it wouldn't be too much like gloating over his own dinner and making things tougher. Different folks from around here had someone on the colony—a relative who'd been evacuated or volunteered, a friend, an old co-worker. And everyone felt sorry for the people on the colony—to be living with only the thinnest layer of air and a micrometer membrane between you and a very dark, very large solar system, and besides that, war at home, and no fresh food and possible terrorist destruction. Just hung out there like a big target at a shooting range. From what Tomás had told him about black-market activity, clearly security was imperfect. Things, and even living people concealing themselves by various devices, had gotten through. Once they got there, no one on the colony wanted to turn them away. Labor was hard to get!

Dovie interrupted his thoughts. "Well, Father, we've had a crank phone call." She had a slip of paper in her hands.

"How is that, Dovie?"

She handed him the slip of paper, and he peered at it while he took a bite of mashed potatoes.

"It's long-distance," he observed. And not even normal long distance; there were too many numbers.

"Well, listen to this, Father: It's worse than long-distance. He said it's Rome!"

Father Timothy and Dovie locked eyes for a moment. Rome! She might as well have said the moon.

"But it has to be fake, Father," Dovie said. "Look at the name. Isn't that the Vatican Secretary of State?"

"It is, Dovie," Father Timothy said. "It is, indeed."

He finished his supper, though, before he punched the numbers into the rectory phone. The call went through, not even through a switchboard, but straight to the renowned Cardinal and Vatican Secretary of State, who answered it personally and even sleepily, as if it were his private line. Only then did Tim realize how late it was in Rome.

"This is Father Timoteo Monaghan. From Saint Anne's? In Melbourne, Florida?" he ran on, as His Eminence said nothing. "You called here and left a message? The message said it was urgent. I realize it's very late there. Or maybe there was some kind of practical joke; if so, please excuse me. Do you speak English? I'm sorry," he finally wound up as the voice said nothing.

There was a heavy sigh on the other end of the line. "No, it is not a joke, Father Monaghan," the voice said in perfect English. "I've been waiting for your call. You are the brother of Tomás Monaghan, yes? The astronaut? The space pilot?"

"Tomás? He's alright, isn't he? He's on the colony. Has something happened?"

"No, nothing has happened to Tomás Monaghan; at least we have heard nothing like that," the heavily accented voice continued. "No, it is simply that Catholics on the colony must have a pastor, and we are thinking we have been tardy in recognizing that need. But no more. You, Timoteo Monaghan, are about to be a bishop."

His Eminence paused to let his words sink in. Then, he continued. "You must come to Rome tomorrow. You must be consecrated, and—"

"Bishop of what?" Timothy said, realizing how dumb he sounded. But he was stalling for time, trying to think of what to say.

"—And then you will join Tomás." The cardinal finished his thought before answering Tim. "You will be bishop of . . . of everything that is not Earth. You will be Bishop of the Universe. I suppose that is how we shall have to put it." He chuckled dryly. "Or bishop of at least as far as our galaxy."

The cardinal sighed. "We have been slow to understand." He sounded regretful and sad. "I think we are beginning to see the whole picture, now, though," he said, a little more cheerfully. "So you are to be the first and perhaps the only, for now, bishop in space. But someday you will consecrate other priests and other bishops."

Tim held his breath as the cardinal paused for a moment. Lowering his voice, he continued, "There are many things we will discuss when you arrive. Let me just say, there have been some developments. I cannot discuss it presently. But please let me say that the situation is--developing, and urgent."

It had, of course, occurred to Tim earlier, when Tomás left Earth, that this was coming for the Church. The Church would have to act, for Tomás was Catholic and there were other Catholics among the evacuated, and that meant eventually there had to be priests. He had thought they'd come and go from Earth, of course. Visiting. Rotate in and out or something. Not that different from mission assignments to remote locations on Earth. For those who could fly, of course. Never for him, personally. But it had to happen. Even with all the changes in the Church, priests were still a necessity for Catholics. But he was not the one, in spite of how well it must line up to others, with his brother already being on the colony and everything.

He started to frame his objection, scrambling for a delicate way to put his problem, when the cardinal continued briskly, "And so you must come to Rome, and then you will be evacuated. We will talk about that at more length later."

"But I can't!" Timothy blurted. "I can't!"

"Of course," His Eminence said. "Of course, you must have time to think. This is very sudden for you. It is true that you will give up many things, and even the saints had time to consider that." His voice grew gentler. "But we don't have time, Father Timoteo. That's the problem. That's why I'm calling you, not the Papal Nuncio. That's why there's no fine letter on linen, in Latin. Nothing is normal. Our civilization is dying, Father Monaghan. And our Church, our Holy Mother Church, is wounded. There is a new development." The fine, confident, richly masculine European voice faltered for a moment, and then regained strength. "But the Church is not dead, much as they wish it. Listen: the shuttle leaves in five days. There must be a bishop on it, traveling incognito."

He stopped then and waited for the young priest's inevitable question about that last part, the incognito part. But that question didn't come.

"No, I mean I can't come to Rome." Father hesitated for only a fraction of a second before he lied. "I can't fly. I—I have an ear infection. I'm taking antibiotics. The doctor was very clear." He bit the inside of his cheek and felt terrible. Lying! And for what? He had to tell them!

He was only putting off the inevitable. What did he think, that there'd be some kind of miracle down the road? He was not, no way, ever going to get on a shuttle and fly to the space colony. It would never, ever happen. Not even for Tomás. Certainly not to be a bishop! Why had he lied in the first place and led the cardinal to believe anything otherwise?

His Eminence hesitated only a moment and seemed relieved. "All right, then, Father Monaghan. No problem. Can you arrange local accommodations for, let's see, myself and three other cardinals? We'll bring everything we need. And call your bishop and let him know I'll be in touch. He must attend. If you cannot come to Rome tomorrow, Rome shall come to you." Before Tim could say anything, the connection terminated.

The Pilots' Lounge on the Bernina Harrison

After his shift, Laiq Amanpour headed for the 24/7 pilots' lounge maintained on the asteroid. Actually, he was off early, some malfunction in the bays, traffic shut down. So he had to kill a couple hours before his ride back to *Halliburton's*, and the lounge was as good a place as any. At least, he hoped it really would be just a couple of hours and not a whole night's delay, as had happened before. This official lounge was better than the local dive, because the liquor had to be concealed here, even if the pilots weren't flying—professional appearance and everything. Not a big difference to some people, even an annoyance, but it meant Laiq could relax there without compromising his faith.

He removed some objects from his pocket and laid them on the anonymous aluminum table: A book, on real paper—*The Ornament of the World*, about Medieval Spain and the peace enjoyed there for a few centuries. A notebook, also paper. A pocket reader, with his pilot's schedule loaded. If he'd had a pistol in his pocket with the rest of his gear, he'd have laid that down, too, among the other tools. Why had he thought of a gun? He'd never had a gun; maybe it was because he usually felt like a wanted man in this lounge. Muslim pilots were a rarity for a reason—they were hated. And to have to spend time there today, of all days. He already felt like a dead man when he walked in.

Dead man walking, just like the song, after what happened today. He was a dead man! And from good luck! Laiq had experienced the asteroid jockey's dream/nightmare: he'd found the perfect asteroid—the perfect composition, the perfect location, the perfect size for profit or living, the perfect everything. An over-achiever of an asteroid! It had been an accident. A stuck gyrator had thrown them way off flight path, into the Oort Cloud. That was where he found it.

And he'd not turned it in.

He'd told no one.

But--his flight path had been digitized and recorded by the box. Bots analyzed every bit of data coming in from the pods. They physically synced it, no wireless to be hacked that way, so it took time to update. But eventually, someone could know—no, *would* know. Then they'd kill him. First, of course, they'd torture him to get him to confirm the coordinates—not because he hadn't turned it in; that didn't matter. What mattered is that it was the perfect asteroid, and he knew where it was. They'd kill him no matter what. He was a dead man.

Naturally, he'd wiped the mainframe drive. But not before he'd written the coordinates on paper, in the notebook in front of him on the table. He couldn't get to the box itself, of course. Only the bots had access.

Laiq could blow up the pod. But he didn't know how. Some Muslim, right?

His only other option was to fill his mining pod with seed stock and DNA, take his family and as many others as he could, and make a run for it, black box and all. He had to move fast, now, before the bots synched the box, while he was still the only person with those coordinates.

They could get well lost in the Oort Cloud. The mining pod was equipped for oxygen generation from water, and water was widely available on this rich asteroid! The asteroid's profile was outstanding for terraforming. They had solar and nuclear in the pod for the short term, and the pod was big enough for the long haul, if necessary.

But they weren't ready for that. They weren't nearly ready. To try such a thing too soon, ill-prepared, was the wrong step! But he had no choice. Things were happening too fast. At any minute, someone or some data sorter would start to analyze the digits and spit out one word: bingo! Or two words: gold mine!

Laiq would have buried his face in his hands, but he would not give the other pilots in the lounge the satisfaction. He knew they were watching him. They were always watching him.

He noticed, then, that one of them was, in fact, looking at him, though it seemed with curiosity more than animosity. Still, he deftly covered his notebook.

He had not expected the first blow to come from that direction, from another pilot! How could that be?

Then, he remembered. When he'd first arrived back and was checking in, perhaps he had not been discreet with Krishnamurthy. What had he said? Nothing! But Krishnamurthy had made that joke. That had to be it.

The most difficult equation to calculate is the character of a man who has your life in his hands, Laiq thought, to work out the probability of him sacrificing your life to better his own. How tall, inside, is he? How hard, how tough is he? How smart, how cunning? How easily bought or bribed or bullied was the man? Krishnamurthy had a wife, and Laiq had heard, perhaps a secret child. It might make him more vulnerable. Or less. Laiq hated these thoughts! Allah did not favor the man who went about judging and weighing other people.

When Laiq looked up from this tedious equation, Tomás Monaghan, the pilot who had been watching him before, was now standing by the table.

"Okay if I join you?" Tomás asked.

Laiq hesitated, but then nodded toward the chair next to him. Everything he had heard about Tomás Monaghan was good—good pilot, good guy, not a hothead, knew some people. Catholic, from that Catholic village, Honesty. Laiq had heard these things mainly from people who worked under Tomás, his crew, not from other pilots, since other pilots rarely spoke to him at all, about anything. Oh, and, of course Adn had heard all about Tomás from her workmate, that girl, Marley, who was engaged to him. There was a problem about them getting married, Laiq suddenly remembered: They had no priest or something. He could not see how this conversation could be good, but Tomás was respected by those Laiq respected.

So, more graciously, he gestured for Tomás to sit down and smiled, although without much enthusiasm.

"I'm Tomás Monaghan," Tomás began. "You're Laiq Amanpour. I've been waiting to meet you. My fiancé, Marley, works with Adn, on the docks."

Tomás took a breath and considered the man across the table from him. He was good-looking, maybe a little younger than Tomás. He was wearing one of those Muslim skullcaps; his was white. Tomás wondered if it was because he wasn't married yet; maybe married guys wore the black ones. The guy looked worried.

"Well, I hope you have heard good things," Laiq said. "As a matter of fact, I've heard about you, too. Our fiancés do talk." He glanced at Tomás's face and then quickly looked away.

"There's a lot of things we shouldn't talk about these days, or I mean, things that are dangerous to talk about," Tomás said. Might as well get right to the point.

"I agree," Laiq said.

Three pilots walked in together, joking around. A foul word for women flew by, and then another, worse. They found a seat noisily. Laiq and Tomás turned slightly away in distaste, causing them to make eye contact with one another, which they held for a moment.

Tomás plunged ahead. "I was with Krishnamurthy this afternoon, before the accident."

"Oh? What did you two talk about?" Laiq answered.

"We didn't talk about a rainbow and a pot of gold," Tomás said. He glanced at Laiq and was almost happy to see that nothing registered, not a flicker of an eyelash or the twitch of a finger. Hard to read; good. Or Krishnamurthy was full of it, and the guy didn't find anything. "Krishnamurthy can't afford to say much, in his situation."

"'In his situation.' Right," Laiq said.

"Me, on the other hand, I'm very interested in rainbows." Tomás paused to see whether Laiq would take the hint. But Laiq sat quietly, his arms folded in front of him on the table. "I don't want a pot of gold, though. I want a village."

"You want a village. You already have a village," Laiq said, though he figured Tomás wasn't referring to that one.

"Yeah. But our well is poisoned. That—uh—that new law. We're Catholic. That doesn't work for us."

It didn't work for Muslims, either! Laiq thought, but hesitated to respond.

"Us, either," he finally said. "But I don't know another solution. I mean, his argument, the president's, it makes sense. We're in a mixed-up mess. We can hardly talk to each other anymore. It's like we're drowning. Know what I mean?"

Tomás nodded but remained silent.

"Maybe they've got it right this time: Pick one god and stick to it," Laiq continued. "Maybe that's the *only* solution to this mess." But, as he said this, his voice trailed off and his head hung.

"To my mind, that is *no* solution," Tomás replied. "One god, one state-designated religion, is not a solution. It's oppression."

Laiq gazed into the distance, a light flickering in his eyes, for a moment. Then, he turned his attention back to Tomás. "We used to have a different solution—I mean, it wasn't something we had; it was a condition we enjoyed. For a time. It's gone now," he said. "My dad called it the 'dear distance.'"

"The 'dear distance'?"

"We were far enough apart. Just far enough, time-wise, to worship, and raise our children, and bury our dead the way we wanted, under Allah's sky, but we could also trade, too, when we wanted," Laiq explained as Tomás listened intently. "My dad thought the prophet taught this, but I've never found a reference to it anywhere. But I certainly understand it."

"The dear distance. Just far enough apart, huh?"

"Yes," Laiq said. "But we lost it."

"What if we got it back?"

They looked at each other. They were each thinking the same thing.

It was like an ache in Laiq's chest! To be distant from the new law, to be distant from *Halliburton's*. To be free of them and their suicidal tendencies, free of their ugly and stupid interpretation of human sexuality, and work, and government, free of their obtuse denial of the supernatural and their boring pride. They built such lovely rooms, and then all they ever talked about in them was … shit. You see, it rubbed off. He was even talking like them now.

Laiq longed to be gone from them, like Moses from the Egyptians.

To be free, in the desert, to worship the One True Blindingly Beautiful God.

To be among his own.

To be distant from unbelievers. Like this one, here, for example, with his annoying trinity of gods. Although, otherwise, Laiq liked him.

To be gone. Like those Israelites from Egypt! Boom! In the morning light—gone! Just gone.

Impossible, to be gone. At least, Laiq thought so.

Tomás, considering the possibilities, thought otherwise. Of the two men, he was the more optimistic. His faith believed in miracles, for starters. Perhaps Tomás and his people were also more prepared. They had been living in a social underground for at least two generations, ever since that Council, that cursed Council, which had resulted in the rapid fall of the Catholic Church and the breakdown of everything. They'd had to live on the fringes of the world. Real Catholics were a hated minority. Europe picked on Catholics relentlessly in the hope the Muslims who'd immigrated there would take the hint to shut up. Then it spread to the US.

Conversely, Laiq had been among the majority in his realm on Earth, in Egypt among the protesting throngs who had wanted to bring Islam into the modern world. He had never been in a minority until his transfer to the colony.

Well, Laiq thought, to be 'dearly distant' was impossible now. At least for Tomás and his people, since there was only one vacant asteroid. Because Laiq, alone had the coordinates and was not about to share them, least of all with Catholics. Of all the world's religious groups, Catholics surely qualified as the ones Muslims would most like to be distant from. Those corrupt Catholics! Anyway the kind Laiq had known. It was unlikely Muslims and that kind of Catholics could share an asteroid—unless they subscribed to religious "freedom," which Laiq got the feeling somehow these particular Catholics might not go for! They didn't seem lukewarm!

It was an unsolvable puzzle, Laiq was convinced. You were alone. Or you were back stuck with 'religious freedom,' and that always seemed to break down, to eat away at society like acid, gobbling up its values, consuming its young. If all religions were equal, they were equally worthless!

Laiq sighed. He wondered if his dad had known how dear the 'dear distance' had been. "You don't know what you've got/ 'until you lose it." Fine old song. Very Koranic.

No, there could be no dear distance far enough apart now, after all that had happened. They each needed their own asteroid.

Tomás interrupted Laiq's thoughts and replied to the earlier question: could we get those peaceful times back, reverse the flow of history, reset to a cleaner time before liberalism? "It is possible. For your people and mine," Tomás said, as if he had read those thoughts. "And you hold the key. Or rather, the coordinates."

Again, Laiq refused to engage in that conversation, refused to even entertain that possibility. (How, how could they live in peace? It wasn't like they hadn't been discussing it for generations now!)

"They will kill you," Tomás said, acquiescing to Laiq's silent rejection of his invitation to discuss the matter.

"Not if I can help it."

"Do you have plans?" Tomás asked.

"Not exactly."

"The box?"

"Not yet, as far as I know." Laiq looked at Tomás. "They'll probably question you. They'll know you talked with me. They'll question everybody who talked to me." He glanced around. "I'm sure we're on camera."

"Actually, I don't think we are. A friend of a friend said they took care of the pilots' lounge. Professional pride." Tomás knew people. "But I do take your point."

They again fell into silence.

That Laiq was sitting there, in the lounge, doing nothing, underscored the grim truth of his statement that he did not have a plan.

Finally, he asked Tomás, "So. What would you do?"

Tomás didn't hesitate. It was all he'd been thinking about since Krishnamurthy had shared the information with him. "I'd run. I'd get so far out of Dodge, all they'd see is my vapor trail. If I had a pod. And a place to go."

He paused to let that sink in before continuing. "You do have a pod—well, the key to a pod. And I think you have a place to go. Even if you didn't, you could live in a pod for a long time, until you found a place." He looked narrowly at Laiq. "But you *do* have a place to go. Right?"

Laiq hesitated a long moment. He truly believed that "dear distance" was impossible. Or a very long shot, at best. But he desperately needed help to figure it out, the analysis only another pilot could understand and contribute to. To hell with it! He was a dead man, anyway. He plunged ahead.

"Yes. The data showed it. Then, I did a fly around." He couldn't help but sound a little excited.

Tomás leaned forward.

"You—we—could terraform it," Laiq went on. "It's got everything: stable orbit. Heavy metals. Little tilt to the axis. Seasons. It's loaded with frozen CO_2. It's already at forty percent of Earth's pressure. We'd just need to warm it a little, using the mirrors. We'd have atmosphere."

He was referring to the mirror technology used to stream solar to the colony. Every pod had its own set of solar mirrors as well. With sufficient mirrors, they could heat the asteroid enough to release carbon and oxygen, and that was all it would take to generate human-friendly air.

"We could blow out an underground bunker, at first, and seal it in," Laiq added. "That could sustain a generation."

"It's completely shielded?" Tomás asked.

"Yes."

"How do you know?"

"I scanned it. Three times. Got nothing. It's a ghost! You cannot see this asteroid with instruments." Laiq grinned. "Location, location, location!"

"Nitrogen?" Tomás asked.

"Oh yeah. Rich."

"Wow."

"Indeed."

Just then, the television blared an ad featuring the word *freedom* sung in ascending ecstatic notes to a jiggling, dancing bank name animated in the foreground.

Another group entered the lounge. A woman was with them. Her male companions took a table, but she strolled around the room. She had a funny way of walking and a strange look on her face, too, bold and hungry. Or *was* she a woman? She paused at another table of men, and then approached the table where Laiq and Tomás sat together. She came very close to them, stood with her pelvis thrust forward provocatively while her face melted with sexual interest. Then, as if she had accomplished something, she turned and joined her set at the table. One of the men reached over and fondled the woman roughly. But *was* it a woman?

Tomás felt his stomach turn, and grimaced. Laiq noted his reaction, which matched his own.

As the two men quietly resumed their conversation, they continued to watch the new group, warily. Anything could happen with a bunch like that.

"So you'd run?" Laiq asked. "And leave all this?"

"In a heartbeat." The tone of Tomás' voice expressed disgust and weariness.

"So would I—if I could."

"What would you do when you got there?" Tomás said rather absently, looking at Laiq while simultaneously observing the rowdy group's reflection in the window behind him.

He watched as another of the men let out an angry exclamation and punched the woman smartly on the side of her head. His buddies laughed. The woman—or was it a man?—looked confused, the confident mask crumbling. Tomás shivered. She sure was ugly! Ugh!

"Live!" Laiq answered Tomás's question. "Harvest the sun, mine the planet, grow food, get married, have kids. And vote for president." Ah, the lesson of the Arab spring, not yet fully realized. "All that good stuff. You know, just live. Without all this. And according to the Koran," he added.

"You don't like the state's new Ramadan? We're all gonna share it, and then you'll celebrate the state's new Christmas. Isn't that how the new one-god religion will work?"

Laiq shrugged. "You know, actually, it sounds okay. I'm tired of *this*." He gestured between them. He hoped Tomás understood him.

Tomás knew what he meant. The relentless discord and distrust between all the different faiths.

"And I'm sure tired of *that*." Laiq gestured behind him, toward the group now engaged in some squabble that involved much cursing.

Tomás knew what Laiq meant by that, too: maybe the state's new uni-religion would help. Maybe the president was right about diversity of religion causing problems. Maybe one god and one faith would bring peace, at last.

But Laiq knew his people were hotly discussing it at that very moment, as only Muslims can discuss an issue. And he knew he would end up siding with those who argued that you don't just make up a religion. That would be admitting the religion is false in the first place. It has to come from God. It isn't ours to make up. Otherwise, there is no God. There's just a god app, news we can use to soothe ourselves to sleep. Anytime it pinches, we turn it off. Anytime we need it again, we turn it on. Just an app. We'll all just pretend.

One would think such duplicity would be impossible. But, no, some could live with it. Life was not so long that some could not go along with that. But Laiq couldn't. Wouldn't. Of course, there were many among his people who would. They liked the colors and the music. It made them feel good. It would make them feel even better to be in one thing, with all others. Those Muslims had never leapt to their feet in defense of the truth, and they had no interest in doing so now.

It came clearly to him then: a made-up religion has no power to save us.

"If I had the chance, I would live according to my own religion, the religion of the Prophet, the true religion. I think I would have to be sick to convince myself otherwise," Laiq told Tomás. "And yet I see the problem. Because we just can't go on like this."

Laiq gestured again behind him. Then, he nodded at the television in front of them, where, in what he guessed was a newly released movie, a woman gyrated on a pole.

Her rear-end was made up, or maybe it was some kind of prosthetic, to look like enormous breasts, and she wore a prosthetic of a derriere on her head, so that she was a creature entirely sexual—top and bottom, left and right, front and back—

with no brain at all. It was so horrible, and he could not look away because it was on every wall. He felt so hopeless.

"We can't go on like this. We are killing ourselves with this poison." He glanced at Tomás. "You could start to hate sex, you know?"

They both laughed and ruefully shook their heads, each deliberately avoiding any thought of, respectfully, Adn or Marley. Not their fiancés, not here. Adn and Marley had brains and souls.

"I would do the same—if I had an asteroid," Tomás offered. "If I had an asteroid, well, I think maybe we could go back to the old ways."

He looked up shrewdly at Laiq. "I have to tell you, I'm not so sure about your democracy. It doesn't solve all evils."

"I thought it was *your* democracy," Laiq answered.

"Well, it's nobody's democracy. You know, the fact is, it really doesn't even work. Think about it: why do you think—in our country and other countries in the West; I don't know about your countries, but in our country—one party wins by a half percent for four years, and for the next four years the other party spends all its time cutting them off and not cooperating, and nothing gets done. Then, we have an election and the other party wins by a half percent, and the preceding four years is repeated except in reverse, and nothing gets done. Or nothing important, it's always easy to give in to some things." He gestured at the television.

Everyone knew how the new president had made a very big deal on television about "freedom of speech," which boiled down to a whole lot more cursing and sex but not more truth.

"And everything has gone to hell in the meanwhile," Tomás went on. "There's only one trend for wages, and that's down. And only one trend for profits, at least for the big guys, and that's up. They have found out just how cheap they can buy us, and they do. Every election. So that's how democracy works."

"You have another way to do it?"

"Yeah! Actually, I thought I learned it from you." Tomás grinned.

"From me?" Laiq asked.

"Well, part of it. See, I think we Catholics need to go back to a religious state—like the Muslims. You guys have been trying to get religious states, right?"

"Yes," Laiq said. And so they had, in several homelands in the Middle East, even now.

"Well, to some of us, at the time, it seemed to make a lot of sense. Catholics can do that, too. In fact, we once had religious states. We lost them, somehow." Tomás looked perplexed. "I think we thought secularism was going to work, you know, to end all the struggle. We had been fighting among ourselves about what to do, how to live, since, what, like, 1517. Could we co-exist with the rebels? Or did we have to go back, and could we go back, to the old way? There was much bloodshed. I guess we got tired." He shrugged. "But not everybody gave up."

Tomás thought of Marley's family, of his brother on Earth, of others in Honesty Village—of Ferdi, Kioshi, Laney, little Anka, hundreds of others. Catholics bred and buttered! And without a priest. They had not gotten "tired" of the Faith of Ages. Even without a priest. They wished only to live it, in peace. They wished only to live serenely in this life and pass happily into the next to live with God. That would be a fine life! Worth every ache and pain of it.

"But how can you have a religious state now?" Laiq gestured at the depravity around him. Things had not gone that far, not yet, in Muslim countries. There, things were still decent, more or less. Oh, *this* was on the rise, sure. But he had confidence in his Muslim brothers to keep it under control where they were a majority. He could not see how the man sitting with him could ever achieve such a thing here. Bernina was ruined.

"Well, see, that's what I mean. Before, it was the craziest dream."

"'Before?'"

"Before you found the perfect asteroid."

They sat there in the pilots' lounge on the Bernina Harrison, looking at each other, the television blaring. Laiq went back to contemplating the problem: he had an asteroid. What was he going to do about it? He had to act fast. Soon, the authorities would come to kill him.

And then they did.

Laiq spotted their reflections in the television screen seconds before they entered the lounge. He had just enough time to sweep his things into his bag and grasp Tomás's hand in a quick farewell before he ran for it, knocking over the table and a chair. In the confusion, Tomás slipped away, too. Later, the authorities would discover the looping camera malfunction in the pilots' lounge. The Bernina Harrison went into lockdown, but Laiq had already disappeared into the warren, where, because he was a good pilot and a good man, he still had a few friends, in spite of his religion.

The Bar at Cape Canaveral

Albert Taylor got in by mistake. He knew the deal. Al had gotten in more than a few places in his life by being six two and 250 pounds; being black had helped sometimes, too. Mary always laughed when he said that. She always thought he had it all wrong; it had nothing to do with Al's size or color. She always thought he had a particularly lucky guardian angel. Yet and still, she admitted, being very tall and very black might have changed things a tiny bit. Yet and still! That was another thing Mary always said—"yet and still"—which, to tell the truth, Al had never completely understood. Something like "yes and then not," he supposed.

"Yet and still," he signed to Mary under the table, a little clumsy, out of practice, "to get a seat in this bar, this night, with this crowd, you have to be somebody special." That's why Al was pretty darn sure he'd gotten in by mistake. "Yet and still, pretty Mary." Mary had been dead for, let's see, three years now. He still talked to her--signed to her.

Al sipped his ginger ale as he scanned the crowd. Everybody there had more than a few things in common: they had a report letter or an e-mail from EVAC and they had the ID to back it up—good to go. They were either NASA or medical or special support. They were young, healthy, educated, and had no addictions, not counting their massive egos. Except him! Oh how he felt it!

There were other exceptions, too, although none he could spot right off the bat, there in the bar. The exceptions fell into two categories. For one, released prisoners, who had been brought to the EVAC facility in cuffs, and then, on the other side of the security barrier, suddenly uncuffed. The wonders of modern medical therapy! A sure miracle, by God! Naw, forget God, a miracle brought to you by the world government. Their evacuation to the colony took a load off the prisons and a load off the tax rolls, leaving nobody to complain but the colonists suddenly living next door to felons. Of course, they were all nonviolent offenders, supposedly.

The second exception was the religious evacs. If you could convince the Man that life on Earth had "become unbearable" due to your religious convictions, you had a chance for an e-mail from EVAC. They'd been a little surprised at the result. Didn't expect that many people! God was supposed to be dead, and now here He comes again, in the most unlikely place, outer space. Well, not so outer. Near Earth Orbit. Yet and still.

How many people would rather live next door to a white-collar criminal than a religious nut? Plenty.

Al was neither a released criminal nor a religious nut. He was an aging engineer with no ties anywhere. Maybe that's why they'd picked him.

It sure made for a crazy mix. But it was just like almost every nation on Earth now, the most unlikely people put shoulder to shoulder by the massive immigration of the latter part of the last century, when the population began to collapse. At first they'd thought the declining population was a good thing. It had put labor into short supply, which caused the great shifts in population and the breakup of the traditional centers of religion. That, in turn, had . . . well, it had made a world government possible—necessary. That, too, was supposed to be a good thing.

Yet and still. Al Taylor had thought he'd never live to see the day when he'd miss the city's south side. The sound of jazz from the corner bars, the smell of ribs, and the sweet sight of black women sitting on back porches waiting for kids to come home. It all smelled like stir-fry now, or salsa, one or the other. Not that he had anything against that. He was just sayin.' He just missed it. Where had the black people gone, anyway?

His eye fell on a young man standing close to him. Let's see, what category did the kid fall into, religious nut or convict? He looked like one of the nerds, not like a gangbanger on early release. He was clutching a large, black satchel. A nerdy con? The kid glanced at him, caught his eye, and Al could see how young he was and that he was scared half to death. Damn.

"Here, stash your stuff," Al called to him on impulse when the guy sitting next to him suddenly went to squeeze in next to a petite blond in a booth.

When the young man maneuvered onto the bench, Al took the bag from the his grip and slid it under the bench next to his own bag.

"Albert Taylor, NASA," he said, extending his hand, unable to resist the little thrill of pride he still felt every time he identified himself. He hadn't added his profession: civil engineer. Specialty, sanitation—the shit detail.

"Timoteo Monaghan," the young man said as he took Al's hand.

It seemed to Tim like it had been a long time since he hadn't added the word *Father* in front of his name, although it hadn't been all that long since his ordination. It felt awful to be without it! And it felt awful to be without his cassock. On his way there, he had come around a corner and, suddenly, for no reason whatsoever, gotten the distinct feeling he was wearing no clothes at all. Of course, he had on this costume; that's what it amounted to. But for a moment, he'd felt as if he were stark naked. The feeling had stayed with him, even though he could look down and see the khaki pants and the unbuttoned button-down shirt. His disguise.

Great! Tim's heart speeded up just thinking about it. A fine situation! He directed that last complaint to God and mentally tipped a hat to Saint Teresa of Avila, who had said more or less the same thing when she'd fallen off a horse in the middle of a river while burning up with fever. As she picked herself up, she said to God, "Well, if this is how you treat your friends, it's easy to see why you have so few of them!" It is not reported what God replied.

Distracted, thus, by self-pity, Tim made the first mistake of his career in the underground: he'd given up his real name. And he didn't even realize it yet.

"Tim, good to meet you." Al sized up the kid's grip. Not bad. "Timoteo Monaghan, you say? McTaco, huh?"

The young man grinned. "Something like that. Mom and Dad."

"So you got your papers?" Al asked. "You on the shuttle?"

Tim looked thoughtful and vaguely patted the breast pocket of his black jacket. "Yeah," he said, "I got my papers." He paused and glanced at Al. This was the first person he'd talked to in his new persona, given him by the Vatican along with an explanation that bordered on the fantastic.

Sitting across from the Vatican cardinals before his consecration, Tim had been unable to disbelieve them—"they" being the solid, serious, well-educated men of the Church and of the world that they were. Now, so far away and alone, he felt a greater sense of the unreality. He had the papers establishing his false identity, and he had been rehearsed in the responses that would be necessary to get him across the checkpoint. But he had never been good at lying. Growing up, Tomás had always done the fast talking. Tim would always blow the story. Now, that was over. Now, Tim *really* had to live for Christ. He had to *lie* for Christ.

Of course, Tim would never get to the checkpoint, anyway. He wouldn't be able to even stand in the doorway leading to the shuttle, not with all those people. He had already checked it out. Never in his life had he entered a space that small and that packed with other air-breathers.

What was he doing here, then? Why hadn't he told the cardinals about his problem? Why was he here? What the *hell* did he think he was doing? Was he actually going to look for some kind of miracle at Cape Canaveral?

Tim looked at Al Taylor. The man's face was kind. He hadn't much hair on top and wore a small mustache on an otherwise smooth-shaven face. He was a big guy, even sitting down. He was black. His eyes were mild behind an impressive set of spectacles. He *looked* like an engineer. He also looked like a very nice person.

Tim swallowed and offered that he was a human-relations specialist, class one, on his way to facilitate negotiations on the colony, a temporary assignment. His voice trailed off. Lying felt so shameful. Tim glanced at Al to see whether he'd believed him. Only then did he realize his mistake: he'd given the man his real name instead of the alias! Dumb!

His false name was Roland Connelly. Roland was the same age as Tim. He had gone to his same schools. But in the disguise he was a junior HR specialist. But he had already blown it, and now he would have to get away from this guy, and that was a shame because he liked him.

Of course, Tim was a newbie "felon," and the preparation had been somewhat abbreviated. The cardinals had explained to Tim that the papers he would be carrying were false and had been purchased at no small price. On the colony itself, Tim would disappear into the habitats of Catholics, and his seat on the return trip would be filled by someone who needed to get out of the colony, using Tim's papers. Tim had been surprised at the casual way in which the cardinals had mentioned this. Since when had they become skilled lawbreakers? (He'd failed entirely to consider their related work experience in the political machinations of the Vatican.)

Meanwhile, they were all *de facto* underground now. The Church would appear to cooperate, the cardinals said, at least for the moment—as, indeed, the Church was bound to do by its own rules, in normal circumstances. The Church wasn't in the business of fomenting rebellion, liberation theology notwithstanding. The Church had worked with some strange national arrangements over the centuries since Christ. This world government was a legitimate secular government. It had been elected by the people, even if the system was basically corrupt. To disobey one's government was a big step, and under normal circumstances, it was forbidden. "All are called to obedience." "Render to Caesar," as long as you can. ... "On pain of sin." Mortal sin!

Despite that, the Vatican was protecting itself. Setting up underground. Protecting its teachings. Something was *that* wrong.

Of course, it was not the first time the Church had gone underground. This time, under the Terrorism Act, the penalty for being caught was undoubtedly death; certainly, it would be the penalty on the fragile and generally freaked-out colony. So Tomás would wear a disguise. The Vatican had contacts on the colony, the cardinal had repeatedly said, and a plan was in progress. The contacts had not yet had the opportunity to speak in a shielded conversation with Tomás, but, the cardinal assured Tim, his brother was well and living in communion with the faith.

"Father Timoteo, do you have any reason to believe that your brother would object to the plan? Would he submit to your endangering his security, as would be the case if you accept this assignment? More to the point, Father Timoteo, will you do it?" With that, the cardinal speaking had leaned forward with his hands on his knees, waiting for Tim's assent. (If material eyes could have seen, five guardian angels leaned forward at the same time. They were quite beautiful; the cardinal, not so much.)

Tim had looked at the cardinal with, literally, his mouth open. The cardinal had looked morosely back at him, his own lips set in a firm line.

Wait, wait! This is supposed to be an explanation? Tim had thought with alarm. But then he'd remembered having heard something about it on the news, something to the tune of "the world churches have agreed to greater understanding" or something like that. No big deal; they were always saying wild things on the news. But that all churches had been officially *dissolved*? That was the *literal* meaning of the new Freedom of Worship law? Tim hadn't realized that, prior to his meeting with the cardinals! On the news, it had sounded much less extreme.

"How could they do that?" Tim had finally managed to say.

The cardinal had simply shrugged and looked incredibly sad. He'd taken the whole new development as a personal defeat because it so clearly had stemmed from policies adopted by the Church of his youth, with his enthusiastic support. And he was too old, just too old, to find out the bitter truth—that his life had been spent on the wrong side. There had been that magical time—actually, the majority of the years of his life—when he'd thought mankind to be on a path directly to God, without the need of all the negativity taught in tradition. So many rules! It had seemed throughout his life that penance and hell and original sin, those ugly concepts, could be forgotten, and that the Time of Rejoicing had come.

Oh well. The Church had taken some wrong turns before, and like an enormous ship, it had slowly but surely come around. It had been, what, almost seventy years now, since the council? Not a long time in the Church. Not too late.

Then the cardinal had answered Tim's question as best he could. "They—the President—demand that the Church meet with the World Council of Churches to form this One World Church 'required by our times.' Actually, they already have the structure. They have consecrated six bishops in China and prepared a catechism that these new bishops have signed off on—without the consent of the Holy See. Of course, they asked for this consent *after* the fact. But they don't care what we think."

The cardinal had said nothing of the raging debate the developments had set off in the Vatican over the last two weeks. It had been fiercely argued on one side that this "one-world religion" was both a necessity and a heaven-sent opportunity to do what the Church had been trying to do for more than a half century since Vatican II. The other side had argued with equal passion that the new state religion was just the modern world's newest and next-best form of apostasy, supported by Vatican II's ambiguous wordings. The false doctrine, the Council itself, needed to be repudiated once and for all, they argued; it was exactly what those break-away groups had been yammering about all these years since the Council.

Rome needed time to think and to pray. It needed time to consult theologians on both sides. Meanwhile, it seemed prudent to have a bishop … somewhere else, anywhere else, and hidden. A bishop with all the very considerable powers of a bishop tucked safely away—in outer space. That seemed far enough.

And so here was this—what would you call him, actually? The cardinal looked Tim up and down, from the top of Tim's brush cut to the tips of his scruffy black loafers. Such inappropriate shoes to wear, and with a cassock, of all things! The cardinal smoothed the luminous nap of the fine, black, tropic-weight, wool gabardine suit he wore, glanced at his understated alligator Tanino Crisci shoes, and shook his head. What a—wait, how did they call it in English?—what a *loser*! That's how the cardinal would refer to this Timoteo Monaghan, this first Bishop of the Universe, when he told this story over brandy, home in Rome on his patio.

Still, the cardinal would not have wished this on his worst enemy. The boy was being asked to live in the most distant exile ever known, and possibly to die there, an outlaw. Well, he had to stop this line of thinking! What had the Holy Father said last week, after the Angelus blessing? "The great sin of our age is an excess of pity."

Now is the time of the cross, the cardinal had thought, and I will not be sad! He controlled his trembling lips. He was still that much of a Catholic, and a man.

At that moment, while the cardinal had been lost in thought, Tim had not actually been thinking about the death he could suffer for being caught or how he would live "on the run" in outer space. He had been thinking only of being on the space shuttle.

Everything he'd heard about the crowded conditions had weighed heavily on him as he'd met with the cardinals. The thought of being inches from the wall or from the next seat, not just side to side, but also up and down. Front and back. Above and below. Like sardines. Like being in a coffin. Tomás had joked about it, but Tomás had never had a problem with small spaces.

Me on a shuttle? Tim had been thinking. Not gonna happen. Never in a million years. Not going to get on that shuttle.

But that wasn't what he'd said to the cardinal. What had come out was, "Your Eminence, did you know, do you know, that I celebrate only the old mass?"

The cardinal had looked at Tim's bishop, who was sitting in what was usually Dovie's chair in the living room of the rectory, where she would sit evenings watching the news with Tim before retiring.

The clerics had already discussed Dovie and agreed she would keep the house there, in Florida, where his replacement would live as long as the political situation allowed it. They had discussed and agreed, too, that Tim's salary would be deposited into the church account from Vatican resources, through the diocese. Dovie would be okay.

However, at the same time, the cardinals, to a man, each had thought there was a distinct possibility that Tim's replacement (not the simulacrum the New World Church might put in his place) would be unable to openly occupy a rectory, any rectory, on Earth. They'd found it to be astounding that, in the year 2030, in the United States of America, a remote location like this particular parish could prove useful in the very near future for *hiding* Catholics. For hiding *priests*. If they had to go underground on Earth—which, incredibly, looked more and more likely with each passing hour. Just like in China. It had spread so quickly.

And now this priest, Father Timoteo, was about to go to the remotest location of all.

What had he said? Oh yes, the mass. The cardinal had looked at Tim's bishop. "So this is true, you let him deny the new mass?"

The bishop had nodded with downcast eyes, ashamed, as if Tim's celebration of the traditional mass was a weakness of his own.

His shame hadn't surprised Tim, because he knew the conditions in the Church, in general. Instead, it had made him grateful for the sacrifices his bishop had undoubtedly suffered in order to indulge Tim in what his own superiors must have seen as some kind of aberration. Tim had left it at that, he had never said to his bishop or to anyone else that he found the new mass to be about the ugliest and most dishonest thing he had ever had the misfortune to be involved in. Let them think he simply liked incense! Let them think whatever they liked, as long as they didn't mess with him, especially now, at long last, when faced with this new crisis, they seemed finally to have turned their attention to the real problems caused by the profound changes in the hectic, heady days of the last century when the Church crashed.

The Cardinal had swallowed and glanced down at his manicured hands. "That would be acceptable," was all he'd said. He had not added any qualifications whatsoever. He had not said, notably, any nonsense about the mass depending on the "wishes of the laity" on the colony. Nor, apparently, would they try to force him to celebrate the *Novus ordo*.

So Tim would in charge—as true leadership required. But it needed to be crystal clear. Everything the Council was not.

"This is what I need," Tim had said, looking at each of the men in turn. "I need for the traditional mass to be the ordinary form used on the colony—not the extraordinary form."

This reversed the rule on Earth, since the Council. It seemed a small detail. Of course, it was not. It had been struggled over for the last half century. Bishops had been excommunicated over it.

Tim had held his breath. Did they realize what he was asking? The cardinals had blinked but said nothing, so he went on.

"Another thing I need is no interference in my decisions on the colony. No collegiality, and no committees." Then, he'd laughed, a trifle giddily. "I guess it's going to be like that anyway, isn't it? I might never see any of you again, isn't that right? But I just want to be sure and for it to be known that I'll be the boss there, in my diocese, on the colony, which I understand is pretty large." Even bigger than the American Southwest, back in the day, he thought, and looked inquiringly at his superiors.

The cardinals had glanced at each other: another bullet point on the Holy Father's agenda back home! Is that why they'd selected this particular young priest, then? Collegiality was the other big change from the council. Liberals had tried to compromise the authority of the pope, parcel it out to national bodies, and substitute democracy for authority. It wasn't Christ's management model. Not at all. They had done it by hiding behind their innocent national personas instead of openly and honestly declaring their liberal philosophy. It was always "the German church says" or "the African church says." Nothing was argued by philosophical persuasion, as in the old days. Never what *Christ* had said, either. Christ had so specifically and, apparently, very deliberately named Peter as *the man in charge*. Christ had emphasized His intention by making a play on his name that pushed the singularity of his power: Peter the Rock. Peter was the *man*. That was Christ's clear management style, and the Council had been equally clear in changing it. But, it had been argued to the Council's stacked jury, it was a "necessary modernization."

Collegiality had caused the most shocking conformity to error from then on. The national bishops' conferences had become liberal enclaves that turned the council's hidden agenda into policy—and woe betide anyone who opposed them. Every man at those conferences had known, privately, how it worked, but none would ever admit it publically. Each man had his secrets, how he had muddled the authority when it had been granted—and after all their childish cries for "Freedom! Freedom!" at the Council! Christ had been right. And they had almost destroyed the Church to learn that lesson.

"One last thing," Tim had said, after the cardinals did not respond to his request, which he'd taken as their assent. "I want you to know that, should anything happen to me that would cause you to have to write the record of our conversation here, I'm *not* doing this for your 'religious liberty.' I want that clear. I'm doing this for Christ—only for Christ! For the teachings of the Holy Catholic Church. I'm not doing this for the equality of Buddha's teachings, or Krishna, or Mohammed! I think we've had just about enough of that group church thing, don't you? Given where it's brought us, right?"

Tim had waited until their understanding was evident in their faces. That smirk of shame! Now, they saw where the bs had led.

"So all I'm trying to say is don't use me as a poster child for anything but *our* faith. Okay? Am I clear? No fake ecumenism," Tim had continued. "And regarding the secular state, this is war. The secular state has attacked us. Do you agree? Does the Holy Father agree? We're done with them? Our deals are off?"

He'd been referring to the council's abandonment of the traditional Catholic religious state. That had still been a blessed reality for five countries, at that time, and a dream for the rest, the Catholic state had been an alternative, call it a threat, which had kept the poor in the secular nations hopeful and the predators careful. The Council had changed all that, had substituted the endorsement of the secular state for the old preference for the Catholic state, had enthusiastically declared their support for a secular state where all religions would be "treated equally." What a joke that had turned out to be. They had become equal, all right, equally irrelevant. Just as all previous traditional, non-liberal popes had predicted, had explicitly warned, had *shouted* in warning. Pleaded. Begged. Only for the likes of Congar and Rahner and Ratzinger at that cursed council to dismiss the warnings and plunge headlong into the abyss. Apostasy!

Tim knew all about it. He was well aware of the arguments that had simmered at his family table over the years as they discussed exactly this point with other Catholics. Now, he had the chance to say it to the Church's face: enough with the phony ecumenism! Enough with phony religious liberty! It was like he had been wanting to say that forever! It felt good. He hadn't said it to the pope himself, but he'd said it to these cardinals who'd sit down with the Holy Father very shortly to report to him their agreement to certain terms their new bishop had negotiated. Tradition would finally be heard in Rome!

The cardinals had simply nodded at Tim's assertions and demands. Tim had heard no argument from these important men, although his words must have pained them. There certainly had been argument enough all those years since the Council. All that had just ended—wow, just like Tim's dad had said it would!—with the Freedom of Worship Act. That law abolished all private worship and established the new state religion. It was Syncretism, if you wanted the theological term. Incredible, the exact opposite of where they had begun, and yet it was the logical conclusion to "freedom of religion," its antithesis, its punishment for the social chaos caused by the dangerous new teaching of religious liberty. Radical liberty, not just freedom of conscience as of old but freedom of *action*, to do as you willed, not just in secular states but even in Catholic states. Liberal bishops had seized control of the Council and substituted this intoxicated impossibility for the traditional Catholic guarantee of interior freedom. It had to end like this, of course. Just like his father had predicted. The heart of it had been exposed now: religious liberty was *impossible!* In theory, it had looked so cool, in practice, not so much.

Tolerance, the old teaching prior to the Council, wasn't impossible, of course, with a strong religion at the center. But absolute freedom? No. Because religions *aren't* equal.

Too few people knew the difference, though. Such a small difference, but so critical! For one thing, the potential craziness of purely private "religions" had not been anticipated back in the liberal heyday. They had forgotten about original sin. Apparently, some people's religion is to eat other people. Some people's religion is to kill their own offspring. Some people's religion is to blow up bystanders. Who knew? (Everyone.)

But you needed it. China had seen it early. Without it, kids begin to reject family ties and stop sending money back home to Mom and Pop, and then the state has to fund some kind of retirement plan. But no new generation is contributing to the fund. There *is* no new generation! People begin to "marry" for a week. Their unstable lives led to lowered production. Control fertility? Ha! Women don't *want* to reproduce. "It's too much work!" "I can't express myself!" So no babies are born. And contracts honored? Forget about it! You couldn't even trust organized crime anymore! And the suicide rate! The suicide rate! Young people in the prime of their working lives flinging themselves out of factory windows!

A vision, maybe a YouTube flashback, flashed by Tim's distracted eyes: the Chinese dragon, smoke still escaping from his jaws, standing upright on his back legs and scratching his confused golden-scaled head with a sharp front claw: *this was not supposed to happen. This was not in Mao's little red manual of Chinese Marxism!* But they adapted. One day they were still preaching old-style communism—"Religion is the opiate! Free yourselves!"—and the next morning, the party leadership showed up at church. Imagine the Politburo meeting! The Chinese leader exclaiming bitterly, "It's as if the bastards need God!"

China had showed them how it's done. Get a real bishop whose line of consecration goes all the way back to Christ, and then force him at the point of a gun to consecrate other bishops under the state's control. Sometimes you don't even need the gun.

The World Government had simply taken the next logical step.

The new law demanded that all the remnant churches come together and drink the Kool-Aid, that they all would emerge as the One Faith, a brand new World Faith controlled by a brand new World Government. It was a risk, but they must have thought the people were ready. Their own most liberal supporters would be their biggest obstacle now, but experience had shown that liberals were always the easiest to frighten.

The popes, at the beginning of the age of the modern state, had called out the heads-up regarding secularism. Tim had grown up on those encyclicals, when rabid secularism was first sprouting its milk fangs. The cardinals sitting in the rectory living room of a remote church in rural Florida cracker country with the crickets going to town outside in the gathering dusk must at one point have read them all, too: Leo XIII, Pius XI, Pius XII. The liberal bishops who had gathered in Rome in those first fateful months had argued against those popes, but in the end, they had changed the teaching. They had changed the traditional theology to include all churches and all gods in the "work of salvation," using the argument that "society had evolved" to some stage at which this redefinition of brotherhood was both possible and necessary. Anyone could be an 'anonymous Christian.' Anyone at all, as long as you *felt* it. Vatican II had taught world politicians the way forward, building on China's formula. How to destroy a civilization.

Tim wondered what had happened to the old "times are different now, we don't need those old rules" argument. The traditional teaching was still standing strong, was even back in the catechism: Christ is the Way. No other. It had just proven to be too hard to find and discard all those bibles around the world! Not that revisionist Rome hadn't tried. But in the end, the contrary Conciliar teaching had just evaporated. No more ecumenism. No "dialogue." The diocesan newsletters and papal directives no longer mentioned how Islam and Buddhism led to heaven, although the inflammatory doctrine had worked its way deep into practice and even into canon law. They would have to untangle decades of perverse social engineering. Thank God they had the Holy Spirit to help them!

Those had been Tim's thoughts as he'd met with the cardinals.

Those esteemed men of the cloth had been following similar trains of thought, prompted by Tim's stipulations. May God have mercy on us! the Vatican Secretary of State had concluded as he shivered in the heavy Florida air, made cool and damp by the rain they'd had that afternoon. He'd been turning things over in a manner remarkably parallel to Tim's, except in Italian. His contemplation had one addition: this young man who had just declared his loyalty to Jesus Christ would be sitting or standing somewhere—the cardinal had been unable to picture it and had it somewhat confused with 'upside down,' but anyway—

this young man would be sitting or standing or hovering somewhere very, very far away from Earth, saying to an unimaginable group of humanity or—oh, heavens!—to aliens: "As Christ promised us long ago, on Earth, in a little spot they call the Holy Land ..."

Just the thought of it had made the cardinal want to cry, though he hadn't known whether the surge of emotion was from joy or sadness. Mankind was taking Christ out into the universe. No, following Christ, of course. So, then, the cardinal had decided, it had to be joy that was making his eyes smart. *Deo gratias*. But he was kind of cried out. He was not a good traveler. Plane travel wore him out. The dry air.

So, then, that's how it had come to pass, there in that Florida rectory, that Tim had failed altogether to say what he *ought* to have said to those men. What he probably should have said, instead of those theological points he had so tediously negotiated, was that, never in a thousand years—no, a thousand *light* years—would he be able to actually set foot in a space shuttle. That's how caught up in the passion of the moment Tim had been, in case anyone a hundred years down the road wondered how that little oversight could have happened. But whoo-ee! He'd made some major deals for whoever *would* eventually be the Bishop of the Universe! One thing was certain: it would not be him!

"Something wrong?" Al's voice brought Tim back to the present. The boy had been a million miles away. A million *light* years.

"No, no. Just thinking about when I was getting ready to come here. I was, uh, a last-minute addition. Lot to arrange," Tim said. "How about you? Are you temporary or what?"

"Yeah," Al said. "Open contract. I got guaranteed re-up, though." Al reflected on it. That was a good contract. The best. Good options. Work was hard to come by on Earth.

Indeed, it was "stimulating the economy" that had caused the World Government to fund the colony project in the first place. They had argued that once mankind was out in space and actually beginning to mine asteroids and to harvest solar energy, the investment would pay off for Halliburton, and then the government would get paid back. The World Government had put together a good technological plan—hell, it was a *great* plan, Al had to admit it in spite of himself—but they'd overlooked, as they had all along, that the problem was economics, not technology. They'd disregarded the impertinent fact that, thanks to the crisis, they were going to have more raw materials than they knew what to do with. Markets were depressed on Earth already; the economy was apparently in perpetual contraction. They just didn't *need* any asteroids. No one was buying!

"All dressed up with no place to go," Mary used to say. But she hadn't meant what Al meant now, about the colony. The colony was a dream from another time, when there was hope. Too late for it now. The world had been seized with the ill notion that there were too many humans. That was the problem, they all learned to bleat it like sheep, too many children, and the obvious solution was to stop having children and to contract and contract until—until what? But nobody finished that sentence. And so they had discouraged having children and encouraged instead sex for fun, health, better sleep, and the cure for baldness. Eventually it had wrecked everything, not just the markets. It had wrecked it all. They had finally succeeded in making love boring.

"Are you temporary?" Al asked the kid.

Before Tim could answer, the bartender gave them ten seconds of his precious attention, and they both ordered a Coke. Might be a while before I get another, Al was thinking, might as well splurge. He meant splurge on the sugar, and he was thinking of Mary because she never let him drink those sugary drinks.

"Yes, I'm pretty temporary," Tim said after they ordered. But then he quickly added, "They're not sure how long my assignment will last. I might come back right away, if a lot has already been done. Or later. They're not sure." Tim was trying to plan ahead for his new identity, in case Al might notice him on the colony months or years from now. Who knew how much they could observe each other's comings and goings there?

He was NASA! For all Tim knew, this guy might be the *head* of the colony or at least somebody very important. And he'd already told him his real name!

"So what kind of work will you be doing on the colony? Are you somebody important?" Tim asked with a fake grin. If he'd really blown it, as he feared, the grin was for Saint Michael the Archangel, who might have to help him get out of the jam he'd put himself in.

But Al shook his head. "I'm just an engineer."

And not an especially good one, either, Al thought. Lost my edge when Mary died. So why am I here? She'd been his reason for doing every hard thing he'd ever done, including getting up each morning and facing the NASA pressure cooker, and he had nothing to put in her place. Without Mary, why do any of it?

Al inadvertently pictured the small envelope tucked into his left pocket. The envelope with the special pills he'd been carrying with him ever since the funeral. His back-up, or back-out. When he just couldn't stand the emptiness another minute. But he was still afraid. Now, he was letting himself be evacuated, when he knew he didn't have what it took to be a hero. To even be a man.

He knew he was being melodramatic, but that was the whole thing in a nutshell: he'd lost all his perspective. It was terrifying. It was exhausting. He shook his head, casting away his thoughts. They just led nowhere.

"I'm a sanitation engineer," Al added.

All of his introductions always ended the same way: "How do you do. I'm in charge of the shit around here." But he'd never minded it at all—before Mary … left.

"Oh. That's good," the kid said. "I can see how that would be a permanent assignment."

A joke, then! Al's eyes crinkled for a second, and then his face went serious again. What was *is* it about this kid? Al thought. He's so—different. And pale as a sheet!

Tim glanced up at Al and tried to smile. Then Al could see in his eyes that, besides being a nice enough guy not to mind at all that Al was nobody important, just a grunt engineer of the smelly, untouchable class, the kid was simply scared. *Really* scared. And sick to death of it. He was worse off than Al himself!

"Is something wrong, Tim?" Al said quietly, the way Mary would have.

"No!" Tim said. "Well, yeah. See, I took this job because they offered it. But it was a mistake. I'm the wrong guy for the job."

"Funny, I was just thinking the same thing about myself," Al said, and laughed. "So why are you the wrong guy for the job?"

"I can't fly."

"You can't fly? What do you mean, you can't fly? You didn't tell them?"

"I really want the job," Tim said.

"You can't fly? You've *never* flown? You've never flown at high altitudes before?" Al asked.

That wouldn't surprise him. They were breaking all the rules with this evacuation, and it would settle an argument NASA had been having for years, whether space riders had to be trained astronauts. Now, they were evacuating these yo-yos, just willy-nilly. Because they had to. They needed the labor! It was a recipe for disaster!

"No," Tim said. "I can't fly at any altitude. That's why they made a mistake. I have claustrophobia."

"You sure? You're not kidding?"

"Nope. Had it for years. Had it all my life. But it's funny, I can drive. Some claustrophobics can't. I'm okay, it seems, if I can just look outside. Being by a door helps, too. But, you know, never in a plane. No. I just couldn't breathe."

The doctors had suggested various reasons for his claustrophobia. Tim had never mentioned to them that he already knew the reason. It was simple: he'd been the littlest twin, stuck in a corner, folded in half, and he had almost not made the journey alive, because Tomás was bigger and took up all the room. Not that he remembered it. But somehow he knew it.

"So why did they offer you the job?" Al asked. "If you'll excuse me for asking right out."

"I didn't tell them." Tim glanced up at Al. "They were so—rushed. And they were so sure. And it really is perfect, Tomás being my twin brother and everything." Al wouldn't understand that part, but Tim went on. "Okay, I don't know why I didn't tell them. I just packed my stuff and came to Canaveral. Maybe I'm hoping for a miracle."

Tim shot Al a desperate look and then, to Al's surprise, buried his face in his hands.

Miracle, huh? Al thought. Well, don't look at me! This dog is barking at the wrong door. Al Taylor was not about miracles. Engineers were not about miracles.

"Let me tell you a joke," Al said.

Tim didn't answer, so Al plunged in. "There was this doctor, this priest, and this engineer playing golf, right?"

Tim groaned behind his hands.

"No, no, you'll see," Al said. "So they were playing golf, and they were behind this group that was going really, really slow. So they ask a groundskeeper, 'What's going on?' And he tells them they're behind a group of blind firefighters. See, these firefighters had lost their vision saving people in a big fire right there at the country club, so the golf course lets them play for free, anytime they want. This is what the groundskeeper tells them.

"So the doctor says, 'Hey, that's really nice of the club. Maybe I can help, too. I think I'll ask this ophthalmological surgeon I know if he thinks anything can be done for them. They call him a miracle worker.' And the priest thinks for a minute, and he says, 'I'll help, too. I'll pray for them. I'll ask God for a miracle.' And the engineer thinks for a second, and then he says, 'Well, why can't they just play at night?'"

This still delighted Al, and he laughed heartily at his own joke. "Get it? Play at night! Engineers! No, we're not much for miracles!"

Tim tried to fake a smile. "Right. Right, that's a good joke."

Al felt a small moment of panic, the embarrassed kind that comes when you've told a joke that's all wrong for the situation and told it badly, to boot. Why had he told that joke, again?

Oh, yeah, here's why. "See, Tim, the engineer didn't think about some medical breakthrough or some religious miracle. He just thought of how to *fix* the situation."

"Oh," said Tim. "Oh. I get it. Ha ha. Well, how would you fix it? My situation." His tone was light, but his face was serious.

"Well," said Al, leaning back, all business now, thinking as he glanced around the bar, and watched the bartender work.

That guy really is excellent, holding up under *this* crush, Al thought. Then, suddenly, it came to him, just like that!

"I guess I could get you 'hella drunk,' like the old folks used to say, and just *put* you on the shuttle—*if* you can get through the door, *if* they let you. I'm pretty sure they can sedate you once we're up. I'm pretty sure. But that could take a while, however long it would take to set it up," Al said. "What are you going to do when you first wake up? Die?"

"I might," Tim said. "I've never had an attack before that I couldn't get out. I don't know what would happen. It's pretty fierce. It *feels* like I could die."

But Tim wasn't thinking of that. He was thinking of something else: maybe Al was wrong. Maybe God had led him right here, after all those doctors, to this person, to this engineer who could just 'fix' him. That *would* be a miracle.

Tim believed in miracles. It came with the collar. Besides, he had more faith in God than in his own efforts to control his anxiety, since, in the end, he truly could not.

"Well, you want to try it?" Al leaned back in his chair like a poker player with a good hand—or a poker player trying to bluff a good hand.

"Getting drunk?" Tim looked at Al hesitantly, and then dropped his eyes. "I've never been drunk. But that's not it. There are many things I've never done. But, see, I don't *want* to, either. Getting drunk, I mean, drunk enough to get on that shuttle, to go through that door. Really, really drunk. No. If that happened, well, I might do things I don't want to do. I might—commit sins."

Well, this was getting awfully personal with a man Tim didn't even know! He didn't know if this guy could possibly understand what it meant when you believed that sin was serious. Because people usually didn't. Still, Tim went on. "So I don't want to. When you get drunk, they say, you give up your faculties."

"Well, that's probably why people like it so much," Al said. "But okay. Sure. Easy problem. Simple fix: I won't let you do anything sinful."

Al paused to study Tim for a moment. "What is it with you, anyway? Women? Guys?" He was tempted to add the laundry list of perversions but stopped there. The kid just didn't seem the type. "Cussing? What?"

"No. I mean, I don't know. I—I don't want to know," Tim stammered.

"Don't worry. I can get you on the shuttle with everything intact. And I'll stay with you. I won't let anything—uh—indiscrete happen."

Exactly how he would get a presumably unconscious man through the checkpoint Al didn't know. It was going to be a challenge, but nothing he couldn't handle. Okay, maybe that was a bluff. Up to now, though, being NFL-linesman big had never hurt.

"I'm straight myself, by the way," Al added.

Tim bit his lower lip and stared at the table. What a mess! Ever since their mom and dad had passed away, Tomás was all he had. He missed him so badly, and now this chance to be with him again, to be on an incredible adventure with him that was part of his vocation, too, his chance to serve the Church and God—it was so perfect. Except for that one little thing. Suffocating. He'd wake up—up there—in the tightest space he'd ever been in his whole life, outside the womb, anyway. His stomach rolled over, just thinking about it.

Therapy hadn't worked; it was a joke. Hypnosis, a bust. He'd tried deep breathing during an attack, but his body just wouldn't cooperate. Once the panic started, it was over, he had to get out. The best he could do was hold on for a minute with those little sips of air.

They'd tried pills, too. But he had to be almost unconscious, apparently, because the one time he'd tried pills, for a field trip, he'd bolted from the SeaWorld aquarium and thrown up in full view of the parish's Sacred Heart Society, whose members had seemed to regard him with a shadow of suspicion ever after.

Some doctors thought that if a person with claustrophobia could suffer through one attack, voluntarily, no running, no hiding, it would be over. But that last extra five minutes in the confessional waiting for a straggler was all he could ever manage, and that was only because he knew he could get out, he would get out. There'd be no getting out of the shuttle.

No getting out! The very idea made him dizzy with dread. It must be what Gethsemane was like for Jesus.

That last thought made the decision for him, though, because it was the same decision he made every morning when he put on his collar. This time was no different than every other day. Only this time he'd follow Him into space, which was a funny word for it, because he was pretty sure he was going to feel like there was no space at all, which might be the last feeling he'd ever feel, because his heart would explode.

"Okay." Tim looked up at Al Taylor, who was gazing down at him with amusement. "Okay. Let's do it."

"You sure, now?" Al said. "What'll you do when you wake up?"

"I don't know. I guess, at the worst, could you just knock me out?" He glanced at Al's fists. Ouch!

"Let's deal with that when we get there. But listen: I will if I have to," Al said. "Give me your papers so I can get us both on board, first."

The papers!

Al noticed Tim's stricken face, but misinterpreted. "How's your stomach? You got a weak stomach?"

Tim was silent. Now, he was risking something more. Claustrophobia was one thing. Breaking the law was another. He couldn't put another person in danger. He had no choice now but to tell the truth. He'd already told him his real name, anyway, and it wasn't the name on the papers Al was now asking for.

What if Al turned him in! The airwaves were full of reward offers for turning in terrorists. You could keep their property—not that Tim had any, but this stranger wouldn't know that.

Al waited, watching the turmoil on Tim's face. 'Wait for it,' Mary would say, signing the words. Mary taught the deaf, and Mary was deaf. She thought teachers hardly ever waited long enough for a child to answer a question. She'd once told him she tried to ask some questions every year that the child might not answer until they were all grown up. She believed in waiting. So Al waited. He sensed there was something the kid wasn't saying. Al took a swig of his Coke and kept waiting.

Tim sighed. He took the papers out of his pocket and dove in. "Listen. There's another—issue." He paused, took a deep breath, then continued. "I am who I said I am." He paused again, and looked at Al, who just kept listening. "I mean, who I said I was. I mean, I gave you my real name. That was a stupid mistake on my part, to tell you. It just came out. And it's true, for sure, I'm claustrophobic. But I'm not an HR temporary worker like I said." Tim took a deep, ragged breath. Here goes. "I'm a priest."

Again, he paused and looked at Al, to see how it registered. Well—not horror, at least!

Dropping his voice and his head, Tim rushed headlong into what was very possibly quicksand. "I'm traveling incognito. I don't know exactly why I'm traveling under, you know, false pretenses. With forged papers. But my—boss—said to. There's some government thing going on with the Church. I don't keep up much with it, but the bishop in charge of me asked me to. And--they made me a bishop."

He looked up at Al. It was Tim's turn to wait.

Al hadn't taken his eyes off Tim's face, but he was no longer seeing him. His mind was working a mile a minute. A priest? No, wait, a bishop? Incognito?

"Yeah!" Tim blurted, reading his expression. "Really! Believe me, I'm as surprised as you are!"

"But why wouldn't they just apply for a religious evacuation or something?"

"I don't know. They seem to think something really bad is going to happen behind this One World Church thing. Because, of course, you know, Catholics can't do that. We'll have to resist."

Tim paused and looked at Al to see if this would make him angry, as it did some people. Al's expression didn't change.

"You understand, don't you?" Tim asked. "We just can't. We believe in something. You know, it's like love. You just can't. You know what I mean?"

Al did. To him, the shoe was on the other foot. What would a kid like this know about love? And a priest, besides? But apparently he did. Because that's just how it was.

"Yeah, I know. I get it," Al said aloud.

Love. It was a very hard concept to explain, as Al had found whenever some well-meaning somebody would suggest he marry again, that he had to "get over" Mary and "move on." What a hoot. Idiots!

Tim, believing Al actually did get it, continued. "So I think it's like I've been sent to the outskirts of town, if you know what I mean. My superiors expect some kind of suppression of the churches that won't cooperate. I think they're hiding me on the colony, kind of like a spare bishop. Bishops have, uh, special powers. Legal stuff. But important powers. They can ordain priests, keep the Church alive. How I'll live hidden on a space colony, I don't know, but they said they had contacts and a plan. I guess they figure the colony is kind of like the wild, wild West or something. Is that true?"

Al just blinked.

Tim continued. "My brother is there, my twin brother. He's a pilot. I could get him in trouble, I think. I have no clue. I wasn't even paying enough attention while the cardinals were explaining it. I was thinking of my other problem." He sighed and shook his head. "All I know is that someone is meeting the shuttle."

Al considered the young man beside him as if he were interviewing him. For a long time he had handled job interviewing for the Chief. In Al's humble estimation, the department had an overrated opinion of his people instincts. He looked at the applicants' qualifications, but in the end, he just trusted how he felt.

So how did he feel about this kid? Would he be someone he would like, if he had to work with him? Yes. Something in the way he held his head and set his shoulders made Al think that, in a tight spot, the kid would not fold.

Al tried to sum it up. "Okay. You're claustrophobic. And you're a bishop. The Catholic Church has decided that, given the new developments, they need an underground wing, and you are it. You have fake papers, and you think, in this day and age, you will be able to pass a security checkpoint with those fake papers. When you get to the colony, you're going to disappear. So, if I help you with the claustrophobia part, I have to buy into the illegal priest part. I wouldn't just be getting somebody drunk and walking through the gate with him. I'd also be helping to smuggle a potential terrorist onto a space shuttle, because I'd need to carry your fake ID through the checkpoint, the plan being you'll be too drunk to do it yourself. Is that about it?"

"Well, I'm *not* a terrorist. And I already got through the first check to get in here. They did everything, and it hit all the data bases, right? So it worked. And couldn't we work out a cover story, like, where you wouldn't have known? Not the whole story? Like you were just helping a guy you thought was claustrophobic?" Tim reasoned. "But I do see your point. I suppose they'd shoot first and ask questions later, the way things have been going. But they said, my boss said, the papers would work. They said they had the best contacts for that kind of thing. And the papers already did work once to get me in here."

Both Al and Tim sat quietly and recalled vague memories of rumors and exaggerated stories in sensationalist magazines about Mafia contacts with the Vatican, and secret meetings with money launderers, and who knows what else? The Catholic Church was as international as it gets, and older than all existing state organizations. They probably *could* get a plausible ID. It had been several hundred years since they had needed to, but that is a short time in history—and, come to think, in space time, too.

Finally, Tim shook his head, as if to clear it. "It's too much. It's too dangerous for you. I have to do this on my own. Look. I don't know how to ask this, but is there any chance you could just forget about this conversation? If you just don't turn me in, I'll be okay." Tim reached for his bag.

But Al shook his head. "Hold on. The thing is I don't want you waking up on any space shuttle I'm on and freaking everybody out with a claustrophobia attack," he said, realizing this only the moment before. "It's contagious. So, if you're going to try to board anyway, I'd like some say-so in the deal."

And that was the truth, but it wasn't the whole truth. The whole truth was it riled him. This One World, One Church thing riled Al Taylor. "All religions are interchangeable" was as stupid as saying all women are interchangeable. They should just leave people alone.

Besides, who was he to say anything about false identities? Him, with his little stash?

Al took off his glasses and put them on the table. "This looks like a job for Superman," he said, only half-jokingly. He struck a corny little pose. "Notice the resemblance? What do you think?"

That's what he'd always said to Mary when things got tough, and she'd always laughed and believed him. "My Superman," she would sign, the little chest thump, the letter S quickly sketched with her beautiful quick fingers. She was the cutest woman ever, making her little Superman sign and smiling. It touched something so deep inside him that you'd need a seismograph to register it. If the state thought any other woman could take Mary's place just because she had all the parts, they were wrong.

"So ... ready to do this?" Al grinned.

Tim laughed weakly. "Oh yeah, sure!" Then, he stopped laughing. "You mean it?"

Al put his glasses back on and nodded. "Yeah." He let that register, all it meant, for a moment. In for a penny, in for a pound, yo! Then, he went on. "Okay. First, give me your papers. And *do* you have a weak stomach?"

"Yeah, I do," Tim said, remembering SeaWorld. He slid the papers over to Al.

Al read the documents, absorbing the information, and put them away with his own. Then, he considered the problem at hand: weak stomach. That ruled out tequila. Vodka? Yeah. They had about two hours before passengers would start boarding the shuttle. He had to time it right.

Al caught the barman's eye and nodded. If the kid had soda first, it'd be easier on his stomach. No more Coke though; no more caffeine. "Can you bring me, uh, two ginger ales? And a coupla' vodka martinis, Grey Goose, straight up. And keep 'em coming. My friend here is on a mission."

"Aren't we all," the bartender sighed.

"Put it on this," Al said, handing him his card.

"I gotta charge you the up tax."

Al grimaced.

"It's more liquor, man, without the ice," the bartender added. Then, he grinned. "And whadda *you* care? It's on the company tab, anyway, right?"

Everybody in the room had a card, having been given one at the preflight check. Nobody knew exactly how it would work, but everybody in the bar was now on the government-Halliburton payroll, and everything they bought came from the company store. Al's own paycheck was still signed by NASA, though. Separate budget. But, nevertheless, part of the government's underwriting of Halliburton. Said it was an investment for the people. "Fascism," some whispered.

As investments went in this day and age, it was an incredibly good one. The State foresaw no drastic social welfare problems because everyone had a paycheck, and they expected no unemployment on the colony, not in the near future, at least. Everybody worked. How could they not? They had a whole miniature world to set up. Their problem was different: labor. Not enough.

Presuming the technology worked and the physical existence of the colony was achieved, there were other risks. The possibility for revolt, for example; it was huge. The distance between Earth and the space colony, as with the original American colonies centuries before, made political independence just about inevitable. The investment in the colony made those old sub-prime loans look mighty safe, indeed. Independent economies weren't inevitable, though. Halliburton wasn't worried. They'd bought whole countries before, and named their price, too. They'd long ago learned how *that* was done, although Islamic states had proved remarkably stubborn, until the Arab Spring had finally set them on the road to liberalism and eventual secularism. They were catching up fast.

The colony's first job, along with subsistence, was to provide solar energy to Earth via microwaves. Until that was accomplished, everybody got paid just enough to maintain a minimum standard of living. The recruiters had promised big raises, though. The second job had been to set up mining the first asteroid they'd lassoed, braked, and towed into the colony's orbit. The potential for profit was enormous. The government backing ensured the potential for risk was minimal. Win/win.

Mulling over the situation, Al grinned sardonically. Yeah, win/win, right? Not exactly. Who would speak for the working people, you know, *them*, the ones grinding out the profits and taking all the risks? In spite of the labor shortage, all their champions had been eliminated: the old Soviet had fallen—what, sixty or seventy years ago already—even though it had been only a front anyway, all talk. The labor unions had co-opted. And now it looked like the Church was gone. Working people were fragmented, despite having instantaneous communication anywhere across the globe, and wages had reached new lows competing with China, where it was rumored they were harvesting their elderly for protein.

Here was the payback, though: they were within months of having their hands on all the platinum they could carry away, right from the surface of the 931 Bernina Harrison asteroid. With its implications for engine design, platinum would change the energy picture completely. Between that and solar energy, wasn't the future rosy!

But no, even that was tainted. The opposing gears of the system were beginning to freeze up. Demand was down. The push for profits that had driven down wages had ground also against the fall in consumption due to that very feature. With the birth rate drying up, too, there was no natural growth in demand. There were no new hungry mouths to force a concession from profits. The existing population had eaten all the cheap food it could, had all the housing its skills deserved, didn't want to put on anything but sweats, and simply could not consume another dumb-downed college course on which no job depended. And they simply refused to reproduce. They just wanted to watch porn on TV. The world had conveniently stationed a television about every ten feet. Entropy. Therein lay the irony: they had all the platinum and sun power they'd ever wanted right within their reach—and didn't need it now. Didn't want it. Couldn't sell it. Mankind had dried up.

Al had the curious feeling that the activity he was observing there, in what should have been a hopeful moment for his species and his race, was simply the reflex motion of an animal already dead. The "free market" (which wasn't and probably never had been *free*) had slit its own greedy throat. He shook his head to drive away the sad images. So what was he doing here, again? Could somebody tell him? Oh, yeah: running.

He sure was in a mood for questioning the basics tonight. Whether a cocktail straight up should cost more or less than one over ice. Who should own the company store. What women wanted—might as well add that in, too.

More than a few things about the set up on the colony, aside from the economics, worried Al. The structure itself was so fragile, literally, the skin just a thin, flexible membrane. But he understood how all that worked, the mechanical parts, the electronic parts. It was the human part that he struggled with. They would have to build a civilization there, in that huge emptiness. He didn't know why they wanted to anymore. He didn't know anybody else who cared as much as he did, and that was a reflex with him, too, Mary had cared about everything that affected people, and she'd taught him how. Without her, though, he didn't care. That was her job, to help him want to live. Mary gave him something to live for. Then, she up and went! Fine thing!

It occurred to Al that he had been thinking of himself as simply human, not as black or as an American or even as a man, a male of the genus Homo. Maybe it *would* be like that, finally, in space. All of us united as a species, out there, waiting with awe and dread for other species to turn up and come knocking. What did this mean for him personally? Maybe nothing. Maybe a lot. He'd been black for a long time. It meant good things and bad. It meant things he could say and things he could *never* put into words, things deep inside him. He thought again of the pills hidden in his pocket and of Mary, and it pulled him out of the drowning sensation. But not all the way out. He never came all the way out, now.

Or maybe they wouldn't be united as a species. Maybe they'd develop other identities that would take the place of species and nation and race. Lot of maybes. Al had no "maybe" about one thing and one thing only: they'd always have plumbing issues. And he would always be a sanitation engineer.

The bartender put the ginger ales and vodka martinis in front of them, and then handed the debit card to Al. It was silver, NASA's favorite color. Al put it away, along with his gloomy thoughts. Or so he hoped. Maybe this kid and his problem would distract him from his dark musings.

"Drink this first. Keep you from puking. Hopefully," Al said as he slid a ginger ale across the table. "Let me ask you something, Tim ..." Al rubbed his forehead. How to put it?

"Ask away."

"Are you actually going to do some kind of missionary thing? In space? Or what? 'Cause I just can't see it. First of all, I can see how any human being could offer, well, what human beings have to offer, given the mess we've got ourselves in. I mean, let's face it, we're *fleeing* Earth. We're not reaching out. We're running! From ourselves!"

Al was referring to a recruitment ad that had run internationally when governments were selling the colony deal to taxpayers around the globe. The ad featured a colony immigrant and an alien, and referred to their encounter as "reaching out." The alien's low-cut top revealed three breasts. "Join the new space race now!" You'll reach out, all right! That was the message.

"The other thing is Jesus Christ was a guy, right? A human; I mean, created in the image of man." And lily white, Al thought, meanly. Sorry, Mary! "What could He have to do with whatever forms of life we find out there? Including ourselves."

The priest was watching bubbles rise in the ginger ale and enjoying breathing. "Well, back at you," he said. "Why are *you* going, Al? Aren't you taking human culture out there, too? Idiotic as you say it is?" He finished the ginger ale, and Al pushed the first martini in front of him.

Al thought again of the pills (What, they were his obsession now?) in his inside pocket, where he hoped security wasn't interested in checking. He had another option to the human culture thing, and he wasn't sharing.

"I asked you first," Al said.

"Okay. Fair enough." Tim picked up the martini glass and drank deeply as he considered his answer.

"Go easy on that," Al said with a chuckle. "Seriously. So it'll go into your bloodstream nice and slow. We got time."

"Who gets saved? That's the real question." Tim glanced at Al, trying to judge if he cared about the issue of an afterlife at all. But Al was poker-faced and, besides, was making eye contact with the bartender to keep those grey geese marching, as Tim took another big sip.

"The Church teaches the same as always: you have to believe in God—just one!—to be saved, and you have to be sorry for your sins," Tim added, and killed the first drink.

Al pushed the second martini over to Tim and thrust his chin forward: drink up. Tim did.

"You don't need the Church to tell you that. Saint Thomas taught that God gives every person the grace to believe in God and the grace to be sorry for your sins. But it's easier to do those necessary things if you have the Church to help, you need the sacraments the Church has for strength, you need the mass. Now, I'm figuring Saint Thomas included alien life in there, or would have if he'd known there were any." The priest took another drink. Vodka didn't taste bad at all. It tasted like winter, or at least the way Tim, a lifelong Florida resident, imagined that winter would taste—bitter, cold, sharp—this libation made from hard, red berries sheathed in rime.

"Are you sorry for your sins, Al?" The liquor was already making him dreamy. He'd never ask such a question of a stranger, otherwise.

Al didn't hesitate for a second. "Yeah," he said. And let it stay there.

"Me too," Tim said. "Because it hurts Him." Tim took a manly drink and made it seem liturgical. "That matters to me. I can't explain it. I just love Him. And, personally, I don't care if God *does* give every single creature in the universe, no matter how many arms or heads it has, the grace to believe in God and to be sorry for whatever sins the creature has knowingly committed so he can go to heaven with or without specifically knowing the Catholic Church or knowing Christ. That's okay with me. But if I meet them I'm going to tell them about Jesus."

Father threw back another mouthful of the silvery liquid and grinned. It made him look about twelve, Al noticed with amusement.

"Because He makes everything better," Tim added. "He's the man. The best, surest way to heaven."

"Jay-sus," Al murmured and shook his head. But Mary'd always said the same thing the priest did! Of course people could get to heaven without the Church--it was just so much harder!

"I don't care," Tim said. "Go ahead, joke. But Jesus changed the world! Take what he taught about the poor. To love them. That was revolutionary! Do you know how much most people still, to this very day, care about the poor? They don't care at all! They still have "untouchables" in India, you know that?"

Tim had sprung to his feet in indignation, and the whole packed room was suddenly looking at him. He sat down sheepishly.

Al whistled. Alcohol did strange things to people! Al hoped this stage was brief. Even though the priest was a light-weight, the last thing Al needed was a fighting-drunk Irishman. Mexican-Irish, even worse!

The barman slapped down two more. Tim picked up his third Grey Goose and took a sip. "But not Christ," he said with satisfaction. "Here's what Christ said: 'Whatever you do for the least of my brethren, you do for me.' Whatever you do for the *least* of them, you do for me! For *me*! Now, *that* is a real revolutionary! And you know what? The Church has actually walked that talk ever since. Saint Paul baptized slaves and sent them back to their Christian masters to be treated as sons. No other Church has a record like that."

Al had to slow things down or this kid would get sick before he passed out, and then they'd have to start all over. He distracted Tim with a question. "How long you been a priest, Father?"

"Not very long," Tim replied thoughtfully, his mind elsewhere. "And now I'm a bishop! I'm the bishop of the rest of the universe." He put down the glass and buried his face in his hands again.

Oh no! First combative, now weepy, Al thought. Well, but it *was* a tall order. I'd be scared, too.

But Tim recovered. With a shaky breath like a man taking up a cross or a sword, he said, "If, out there, they don't know God, or know that there's another life after death, or if there's any slavery or stealing or lying out there, or if anybody's beating up on women or working people to death, I'm bringing Christ—

and His Church!" He thumped the table with his fist. "That means laws, or it used to. Before the Council."

Tim took a sip of the soda. "Baptism by water. By desire. By blood. All kinds. The whole shillelagh. I'm gonna bring it. Without the gospel, human beings are just too—dangerous. And lonely. Probably aliens are, too."

"We're pretty dangerous *with* it, Tim," said Al dubiously.

But, in his heart, Al knew how it was. The kid was right. Mary called them "the others," the sign an exaggerated swing of the thumb toward an imaginary gentile. Gentiles were always killers behind their happy salesmen's smiles. Not Christians, for whatever else you wanted to hate on them for. There was something civilizing in that cross, which was strange, on account of how savage the act it symbolized actually was. Christianity didn't seem so different from any other way to live not by *that* much, anyway. It was like an eighth of an inch. Just the tiniest little bit more, mostly from saying *yes* instead of *no* to suffering. That's what Mary had taught him. Or tried to. He'd never listened. But now he knew. 'Cause, make no mistake, suffering is part of the deal. And it's got plenty to do with *not* killing. (Not even yourself. So, sorry, Mary! He patted his chest. Yep, still there. His hidden pills.)

Not that Al had given Christianity and everything much thought in the past. Al had only one image to go with the word *suffering*: Mary's face. And it came to his mind unbidden. Isn't that what the Buddhists said? Heaven was just an eighth of an inch over. An eighth of an inch from madness. An eighth of an inch of metal skin separating you from space vacuum. Things broke down exceedingly small, right, 'bra?

Tim finished the drink. Al ordered up. Time for some serious drinking, Father Timoteo Monaghan. Or whoever you are.

The level of frantic merriment in the packed bar seemed to have gone up another notch. These people were saying goodbye to the world. The world was going to let them say it in style, which Al figured would work in their favor when he got this little man to the checkpoint.

Two or so hours later when the crowd began to drift toward the launch site, Father Tim Monaghan was completely soused. Seemed just about right. Al could count on him to sleep for several hours, at least through the launch, if all went according to standard procedure.

Al's heart constricted briefly as he took one last look around. Goodbye! Goodbye! But he didn't have time to dwell on the fact. The way things were going, there probably wouldn't be an Earth to come back to. The old blues song floated across his sadness: "You don't know what you've got until you lose it / You gave me all your love, but I abused it." Or maybe it went the other way round. *I gave you all my love, Earth, but you abused it.* Maybe it went both ways.

Anyway, goodbye.

Al checked Tim's papers and then his own. He gathered both their duffels, and then got his arm around the priest and hauled him to his feet. They joined the raucous, staggering crowd leaving the bar. In the broad outside hallway, lines were already forming. They went fast enough, the biological identification having been completed outside the main gates. Papers, photo ID, interview, scanner wall to walk by. Still, Al had to wonder if they'd let an unconscious, scrawny, white guy (with a phony ID) being hauled by a big black guy (with contraband pills in his inside right pocket) get through. The kid cooperated, though. He was walking on his own, more or less, and singing some Latin tune that sounded surprisingly like a waltz.

Suddenly, Tim raised his head and looked straight into Al's eyes, just inches from his own. "Stay away from the bad angels," he said. "Stay 'way from those little devils."

Al thought suddenly and guiltily of the pills. Christ! Ditch 'em! But how?

Yet, the idea of not having that option, that power, was even scarier. Terrifying.

He guessed it was because Mary was gone now. Why, when she was with him, had he never understood how much she meant to him? That gentle touch and sweet smile that she so generously gave him in good times and bad, always there for him when he needed it most. Why hadn't he smiled first sometimes, been the one to reach out to her once in a while? Why couldn't he feel sorry that he'd let her do all the heavy lifting? Why couldn't he feel *anything* now? Why was he carrying little white pills that would make it all go away forever? Why was he planning his death instead of being dead already? And why was he toting this absolutely useless kid who thought he was some kind of bishop? And his feet hurt.

He peered over the irregular lines to see how far they had yet to go.

Tim lurched toward Al and repeated his warning. "Stay away from the bad angels!"

"Who are the bad angels?" Al asked.

"You have to listen," Tim said.

"What? Are they singing or something?" Al asked absently. He was watching the youngest guard at the checkpoint, their line's guard. Too hot on the job, he thought bitterly. Damn!

"No. Not singing. *Talking*. Him." Tim pointed upward with his index finger. "*God* is talking to you. You-have-to-listen," he carefully articulated, as if giving Al a formula. "God always tells us all the bad angels. But we just aren't *listen*-ing. Listen." He cupped his hand behind his ear.

Al deliberately dropped a duffle. As he retrieved it, he managed to slip sideways into a throng that was leading to a different checkpoint guard—an older blond woman. Al hoped he could manage her a little more easily than the guard for which they'd been queued up.

They finally reached the scan-wall. The blond held out her hand. Papers.

"Here's mine," Al said. "I've got my friend's here, too. He's, uh, had a couple too many. Guess he's not real experienced." Al grinned his best grin and looked her dead-on but only for a second. "Tell me when you want his." Then, he shut up to see if she'd buy it.

She hesitated. "How do you know this guy?" she finally asked Al. "Did he ask you to take him across? Did he give you anything to hold?"

"No, no, no. Nothing of that. I just picked up his duffle on my own. He had a few too many is all. We just happened to be sitting next to each other in one of the bars, The Launch Pad. You know it? He's HR! His papers will say. I'm an engineer. You see on my papers there."

Wow, human resources and sanitation. A double-speaker and a drainage expert. Couldn't the Vatican think-tank have gone for something a little more glamorous than HR guy?

This could work either way for them, Al knew. He hazarded a peek at the guard's face. Geez! The iron maiden! He'd hate to play poker with her! She glanced down at his papers. That's good. Now, she'd either ask for Tim's, or pull them over for a full search, or reject either or both of them on security grounds, or reject only the priest for not being able to respond to questions.

"And his papers?" she asked, holding out her hand.

Phew! Al fished them out.

Iron Maiden scanned the papers. "Sir? Sir?" she addressed the priest. "Sir? Mr. Connelly?"

Al shook Tim a little. Tim stirred and raised his head. He looked straight at the guard—and smiled.

"Is she one of the good angels?" Tim asked. "Are you one of the good angels?"

She ignored the question. "Are you Rolland Connelly, sir?" she asked.

"No, I am not," Tim smiled beatifically. "Rolland Connelly doesn't drink. And I do. Are we going to the shuttle? I'm ready." He studied her calmly for a moment. "You're a good angel," he added and gave her one last dazzling smile. Then, he laid his head on Al's shoulder again and closed his eyes.

Al looked at the guard and tightened one side of his mouth into a lop-sided grin. *Be that angel*, he said in his heart.

She hesitated a moment longer and then jerked her head sideways. "Walk the wall," she said.

As Al walked the length of the wall dragging Tim with him, the guard strolled down it with them, checking the X-ray. Al tried not to think about the pills in his pocket. There was a lot to see in a short time. She might miss them. She might decide to miss them. Pills were not plastiques. They were a different sin. Maybe she had her own stash. Maybe she could care less for a bunch of a-holes that Earth would never see again. *Go ahead, kill yourselves, like I care,* she might be thinking. Al held his breath.

She hesitated, and Al's heart began to pound.

"This would be the moment to step in and give a little push," Al said to God. "If you're listening and haven't made up your mind yet, ha ha, which is highly doubtful. I mean, why would you care about a couple of losers, anyway? But God, please help me, please help us."

Then, the guard simply handed him the papers and turned back to the next evacuee.

That wasn't God, Al snorted to himself. Nah. That was just a woman picking her battles. All in a day's work, all in a day's work. He started shuffling them toward the shuttle doors far ahead, although he was well aware of his disgusting lack of gratitude. He covered it with a promise of sorts: here comes my turn to work, he said silently to his great Whomever. That is, when the kid perked up.

Al could not see the outside of the transit tube in which they were walking, nor could he see any part of the shuttle, except for the big bay doors at the front on the line they were in. But he knew the vessel was huge, half a city block with the staging, and that it had many doors, as passenger loading was done from the outside into compartments. Although, theoretically, one could pass through from compartment to compartment, the shuttle was designed so that pressure loss in one compartment could be sealed off from the rest. They had all the safety features available. Comfort features, not so much. No frills. Only sixty cubic feet per passenger, less than the old shuttle days, and it had been famously cramped even then.

NASA had learned that human beings adapted quickly to weightless conditions, opportunistically using all the space around them, where previously they could have used only the floor or the tray. You could put your glasses up by your ear, and if you did it gently enough, so they'd have no momentum, they would still be suspended there by your ear when you awakened from your nap. You could put your coffee (in its closed container, of course) by your hand, and it would still be there. And your tablet reader on the other side. You could use all sixty cubic feet. So that's all you got.

But that was another thing different on the colony itself. The colony was surprisingly generous in size. Room to grow and then some. Big spheres. An atmosphere, complete with clouds and rain. Even a horizon. Of course the colony had gravity, except in the center where the loading was done, and the famous recreation arenas for flying sans aircraft. And someday they'd have material to build other smaller colonies in orbits around them.

On the shuttle, though, you were as weightless as the day before you were born. And it could be a pain.

Passengers were stacked like cordwood into seats the size and shape of normal airline seats turned on their backs. They were slightly more padded than airline seats, for the few but powerful minutes of the trip when they were accelerating out of gravity. The shuttle's seats could not be completely straightened out like a bed, but they could be stretched out like a recliner. Passengers could stow their gear in a compartment under the seat above them, except for those on the top row, of course.

Al had tried out a seat once, when visiting the launch site on a job. It was like those ergonomic chairs that are good for your back, where your knees are raised a tilted 180 degrees. Except in these chairs, on the launch, you were looking at the underside of another seat just inches from your face instead of the nice high ceiling of, say, your living room. Al knew he was going to be uncomfortable himself. What about the priest? What would he do? Would he scream? Vomit or something else gross? And what if the priest's panic caused Al to panic? Because, let's face it, sixty square feet of space was roughly the size of a coffin. And if you copped to that, you were cooked. Everybody's claustrophobic when the conditions are ripe. It was all about control. That's what Al had always thought, anyway.

Once, he'd had to do some work inside the double hull of a navy sea vessel. It was on his first job, way back in the day, just out of school, before he'd specialized. He was checking the ship's sanitation pipes that ran inside the tight space between the double hull. Some of the guys couldn't take it, where it seemed the air wouldn't circulate away from your face. The brass had assured the guys that it was all checked out: there *was* circulation, it *was* safe. Like brass gave a rat's patootie. It always took somebody getting hurt and suing before anything was really checked out. It did not make for confidence.

But Al had been okay crawling in and setting up for the work, okay and fine until a welder started to hot-weld ten feet or so away from him, and Al suddenly felt like all the air had been sucked right out of the confined space. But even *then* Al had kept control. After one horrible second, he was able to latch on. But that second had taught him all he needed to know about terror.

Later, when he and his buddies talked about it at the local joint, after that third beer, he didn't tell the whole story. He never said that, as the last resort, he'd remembered his mother's face and held on to it, and that that's how he'd talked himself out of panic and made himself find the air in the mean, nasty soup around his face. Like cobwebs. He just couldn't take it one more second. Oh yeah. He knew what the priest felt. He just wasn't that naked. He could in the end always put something between himself and fear. Up to now.

Now he'd remember his wife's face, Mary's face, not his mother's. If it came to that. Man, he hoped it wouldn't! Why, exactly, had he volunteered to help this dweeb, would somebody tell him?

Well, because what difference would it make if the guy started screaming two rows down instead of right next to him? It would still get to Al, big time, either way. It was like throwing up; one person starts it, and you could have a room full of up-chuckers! Panic, air panic, space panic—they all spread the same way. At least this way he'd be seated close to Tim and could do something sensible to fix it. Knock him out. And not take too long to do it, either.

Well, we weren't weightless yet, Al thought with regret as he shifted his hold around the priest. He had to admire the man's attempts to carry his own weight, though, after the martini assault Al had subjected him to.

They shuffled forward with the rest, and soon they came to the beginning of the escalator mechanism and the entrance to the bay doors. Al was almost glad to have the troublesome arrangement of priest and luggage, which gave him no time or opportunity to glance back at the ugly green-walled transit tube and very possibly his last glimpse of Earth. Home. The bones of his people. His Mary. All he knew. Goodbye. *Adios*. He thought it as reverently as he could, for an engineer, and then turned his attention to getting himself and the priest up the access stairs with all their gear intact. So much for goodbyes.

They ended up in about the middle of the vessel and the middle of the compartment. Al would certainly have preferred to have been in the first bank of seats, but nothing was going to make it any easier, even if he could have bartered some kind of switch. There was, at least, an aisle seat, and that seemed roomiest. He got the priest strapped into it, stowed the gear, and took a little more time with his own adjustments. Finally, like all the rest, he hunkered down in his nest and waited for what came next. Liftoff.

Al had read about liftoff, and he had heard astronauts talk about it. There would be an initial sensation of vibration as the engines ignited, which would quickly grow to unbearable in the moments before actual liftoff. Then, the noise would begin—first, the pop as the hold-down bolts were blown, followed by the roar of burning propellant, and finally, the howl and hull smacks of the violated atmosphere as the ship accelerated and ultimately punched through the sound barrier. The cabin would buck, but, Al hoped, hold together—like a kid in a cardboard box bumping down a steep hill until coming to a stop at the bottom, or in this case, at the top, where the atmosphere thinned and the silence began.

Most people slept through all that, aided by the gelatinous little cocktails the attendants were administering to passengers even now, mere minutes before liftoff. But Al thought he'd have to tough it out awake, in case his companion awoke. Neither one of them ought to drink the Kool-Aid, right?

On second thought, the priest had shown he was tougher than he looked, metabolism-wise. So Al decided not to worry about the combination of drugs and booze. When the attendant reached their row, Al took both containers, and when she moved on, he gently and very slowly poured the liquid of one cup into Tim's mouth, waiting until he swallowed each mouthful, before tossing back his own cup of elixir. It was pink and tasted like—good heavens!—Mexican *horchata*. Nice touch! Goodbye, Earth. Goodbye, *horchata*, until we've got a sweet little Guadalajara in space, anyway.

Al drifted off remembering the trip south of the border that he and Mary had enjoyed just before her diagnosis. They'd been making a big show of a tight border at the time, but nothing had stopped the flow of Mexican labor to the greedy markets of the north. (They would not get across the border of space, though—right?)

The Shuttle *Swiftsail*

Al didn't wake for twenty-four hours, which he gleaned from the cabin countdown clock when he finally opened his eyes. Six and a half to go, he noted. He didn't feel it yet, harnessed, but they were weightless. Al could tell from the black ball-point pen floating near the wall. He quickly checked the priest. Tim still slept and appeared none the worse for wear. His color was good, his breathing even and relaxed. So far, so good.

Suddenly, Al was aware of movement below him. Someone was climbing the access ladder, hand over hand, weightless but not soundless. Seemed like two people. They came nearer, and Al glanced at the priest, who was stirring and muttering—sounded like Latin—in his sleep.

A flashlight suddenly flickered across them, and a woman's voice said, "Are you awake?" She played the light first over sleeping Tim, and then over Al. "I'm sorry to disturb you, sir."

Al could make out her NASA shuttle crew uniform and glimpse a uniformed man standing on the ladder below her.

"We are looking for a Catholic minister. Are you, or—" she consulted a list on her handheld device. "Or your seatmate here, or anyone on this flight, to your knowledge, a Catholic minister?"

"Why would you want to know that?" Al asked. Tim's fantastic predictions in the bar suddenly looked a lot more plausible.

"I don't have time to discuss it right now. We have to find a Catholic priest or deacon or whatever. Are you? Is he?" She flicked the light over Tim again. "Do you know anybody on this flight who is?"

Al considered it. "Well, I'm not," he finally answered. "Is this some kind of emergency?" He could have just blown them off, but he had a feeling Father Tim Monaghan wouldn't want him to.

"What about your seatmate?" The man had floated into view just behind the woman.

"I don't know. Maybe. People generally like to keep their business to themselves, know what I mean? He might be. He might have said something like that. You'd have to ask him."

The woman sighed and shook her head in exasperation. Clients! "Could you wake him, please?"

Al raised his eyebrows and whispered. "Well, there's a little problem with my seatmate. He might wake up screaming." Al didn't miss the effect that the word *screaming* had on the woman! Could she *be* any paler?

"He's drunk, see. Or he was drunk, for the launch. Then he took your knock-out drink. So he's out, and believe me, you want him to stay asleep. Like, he might be a full-fledged claustrophobic or something. That's how it sounded to me."

NASA's nightmare. Al watched it register on her face. Her errand had just turned uglier.

"Unless you have something to knock him back out with, after you wake him up," Al added.

The man floated up behind the stewardess and whispered into her ear. Although Al couldn't make out what he'd said, he did hear his voice. Distinctive. Very firm, authoritative. and—what was that accent? Southern. Uh-oh. Probably upper management. More bad. He had taken the hint to speak softly, though. Smart, at least.

The woman went on as if she hadn't heard the man, which told Al all he needed to know about labor relations in outer space. "If you think there's a chance your seatmate is a priest or whatever, we have to wake him. We have an emergency situation requiring a priest. So, actually, we can't knock him out again, anyway. Who are you? Family? Friend? Co-worker? Or what?"

Or what? An *accomplice*! But that wasn't important! An emergency situation requiring a priest, Al thought with alarm. What on Earth could it be? Or rather, what in space? Ha ha! Hysterical! Whoa. Get a grip!

"What kind of emergency requires a drunk priest?" Al deliberately directed his question to the man over the woman's shoulder.

The man hesitated only a fraction of a second. "There's been a . . . problem . . . on the International Space Station. And one man is badly hurt. He's a Catholic, and he's asked for the Last Rites, they said. It was all over the nets. And they knew the shuttle was going by. And so they, the brass, upstairs, asked if we could check. And you know, you understand, with the religious riots and everything, with the new law, they don't want to screw this up. This is an opportunity. You know what that means to brass, right?" He shot Al a look. Al did. "They said find a Catholic minister. So, is he?"

Al tried to reason it through: maybe the kid and his wacked-out church were just paranoid. There's not going to be any kind of persecution. Even if there is, Al was pretty sure Tim would still want to help. And these crew members might be more inclined to give him something to deal with the claustrophobia, just to allow him to assist them. So Al went with it.

"He might be. Seemed like he could be," Al said. "What kind of problem on the station?"

"Never mind now. It's functioning, just the air locks are not, and inside there's some minor debris," the man answered. "Help us get him downstairs. Unhook his harness, alright?"

"Where are we taking him?"

"Conference space, downstairs, as I said," the man replied.

Oh, that's good, Al thought. A whole room ought to be easier than this seat, panic-wise.

"Uh, does it have observation units? Windows?" Al asked. "And a door? A doorway?"

The man thought and nodded. "Yeah. Why?"

"You'll see," Al said and began to unhook Father Tim's harness. Tim stirred once or twice as Al floated him free and lightly steered him over to the railing. "It's okay, it's okay, we're good," Al whispered to Tim, as he guided the priest's weightless body down the access ladder and followed the man and woman to the section's exit and down a short hallway.

Every piece of wall space had some gadget, or screen, or storage cabinet door embedded in it. There was a "floor" for walking, under gravity on Earth; in space it was more like a metal pathway surrounded by gear lashed to walls, which were outfitted with lockers of every size and shape. Every wall had handholds, and very moderate force provided sufficient propulsion.

Al continued to follow the two attendants. It was awkward at first, pulling himself along with one hand and towing Tim with the other, but he got the hang of it. He hadn't had time to appreciate the fun of weightlessness yet, but he could already tell it sure beat hell out of walking on his bad knee.

They entered a small room—an area, actually, with only two walls defining it and a sliding door between them, and an outside hull wall with an observation window. There was another area beyond, on the fourth side, with folding doors, probably to more storage, and another window. There was seating and a table in the "floor" area. The windows were about double the size of a Boeing 747 passenger window, and the view outside one was filled half with Earth and half with space. It was magnificent! But Al did not stop to appreciate it. He was assessing the room for what it could throw at a claustrophobic.

There was a door. There was air. There was "outside." Except, here, *outside* didn't mean more air; it meant *no* air. Al hoped Tim would not think of that. He hoped it would be enough for Tim to be able to see beyond the crammed hard surfaces inside, just like on Earth.

Al deposited Father Tim in the seat nearest the open door and belted him in. Tim breathed slowly and regularly. After glancing around the room for any sign of a camera, Al swiveled Tim's seat around toward the door, with the window at his back. Tim stirred but slept on.

"Is the air circulation in this room up to the maximum?" Al asked the supervisor. "Can you jack it up any?"

"Yeah, sure." The man rotated effortlessly and threw a switch on an array by the door. "That's the max—hundred cubic feet per minute."

The woman pulled herself into a seat but didn't bother with the belt. Both had obviously been weightless before.

Al inhaled deeply and frowned.

"What's the matter?" The man looked at him anxiously.

Al couldn't notice much difference in the air after the guy turned it up. There was air, all right. But it wasn't moving much. "Like I said before, he's claustrophobic," he said. Al had almost said Tim's name but caught himself. They hadn't asked. He shouldn't tell. Tim slept on in the easy comfort of weightlessness. "He's *big-time* claustrophobic. So you better tell me what's so important that we should wake him up. I mean, what's he got to actually do at the space station?" Al glanced between the jump-suited man and the female attendant.

The woman had put a hand over her eyes, and the man had shed the affected über-composure of a senior officer. Now he looked distraught, and one tuft of hair shot off unflatteringly. He was staring at his subordinate with slack-jawed confusion. Whatever was happening was their professional worst-case scenario.

"What the heck is going on?" Al said more quietly but urgently.

The man took a deep breath and held out his hand. "Sorry. Name's Hank. Officially, Henry Collums. NASA flight crew." He gestured at the ID clipped to his pocket. "This is Miss Renfro." He spoke softly--with a Louisiana drawl! That was the accent.

"Julie," the woman smiled shakily.

"Al Baylor," Al said, blurring and slurring the last name. No sense giving it away, if they hadn't already ID'd him. "NASA engineer. And, uh, presently guardian angel of this guy. I helped get him on board. He had gotten himself really drunk, and I kind of carried him on."

Your turn now. Al waited.

"Okay, the thing is, like I said, we've had a distress call. There's been an accident at the ISS. And a crew member, he's Catholic, is hurt pretty bad. The word has been out all over the net that we are in the air with a boatload of religious refugees. He's asked for a priest. The call said for the Last Rites, that the priest would know what that meant."

Al noted that they hadn't said the crew member's name yet. Nor did they have the name of a specific priest. Okay, good.

"So you want him to transfer over to the ISS? In a *suit*?" Al asked. He did some calculations; they must be almost to the station by now. "With what, like an hour's orientation?" Man, NASA must be in complete chaos of some kind! All the years of training they gave astronauts, and now they were actually thinking of letting completely untrained civvies just run around all over space! And this *particular* civvie! Al sat there slack-jawed.

"Yep, afraid so," the man continued. "The accident damaged the docking station and the big back-up lock, too. The minister has to go in through a utility airlock. He has to put on an EMU. He has to space walk."

The two men looked at each other. An EMU—a spacesuit—was no joke. Men had crashed out of astronaut training because of the EMU. Just getting into it and then going under water in the huge training pool was too much for some, even though they'd never had any previous signs of problems. It was really hard to move in the suit, and the feeling of helplessness evidently increased the panic. It weighed three hundred pounds—on Earth, of course. That wouldn't be a problem now. But pressurized, it was as hard as a radial tire! And you had to get into it stark naked!

Then there was the helmet. The terrible helmet into which you could not suffer one of mankind's most common physical responses to stimuli, from bad sushi to a panic attack. You absolutely could not throw up. It could kill you, drown you, suffocate you. There was no place for the vomit to go inside the helmet except into your lungs.

The air lock the priest would have to enter through wasn't much bigger than a foot locker, as Al recalled. Another nightmare for a claustrophobe.

Al thought. "Couldn't he just do the praying thing over the radio? Did they think of that?" he asked the guy.

"Well, yes, actually, I did think of that. But, apparently, the ritual has to be face-to-face. Some kind of oils involved, I think they said. For *anointing*." He shook his head. Religion! "And the confession thing—that can't be virtual either."

Father Tim stirred and muttered something in Latin. Time was getting short; he'd wake soon by himself.

Al plunged in. "Okay, Henry—uh, I mean, Hank. What do you know about claustrophobia? Did they talk about it in training? Is it in the manual?" One thing engineers knew—good engineers—was when they didn't know anything about a problem, the best strategy was to see if anybody else knew anything, especially those closer to the problem. Failing that, they read the manual.

Al realized, a little too late, that he'd left Julie out of the question when she threw him a look like a long left hook, and spoke up.

Her voice was shaky, but she clearly *had* read the manual. "We talked about it in training! We didn't talk about it much, because, well, they didn't want to have to scrub the whole plan because they hadn't screened the flight manifest for claustrophobes. Really, we just swept it under the rug. But this is what they said." She didn't look at her associate and superior while she was speaking, and Al figured he'd not been in on this training, which was probably on the check-list for attendants.

"They said you have to do this part ahead of time, ahead of the event that could cause the claustrophobia. First, you—I mean the helper—has to rehearse all the steps that will happen— describe how everything will look, and not only that, but how the person will probably feel.

"You have to, second, talk about what you'll do, the steps, to reduce your attack: breathe calmly, visualize, and one more thing, it was like acupuncture, they said, but without needles, let me explain. You just touch some pressure points. There's two here," she pointed to two spots just above her breasts, one on each side, while Al tried not to notice benefited from the lack of gravity, "and five here." She touched her face.

Julie Renfro, you're a pretty girl, Al thought.

"You tap them in a rhythm, seven times each," Julie continued. "Then, you do some points on the hand. In between, you roll your eyes and sing 'Happy Birthday.'"

She paused for effect. She wasn't kidding. "Tell you the truth, I think it works because it distracts the person. I mean, *if* it works. But what do I know!" She shrugged and dismissed the brass.

"Yeah, right?" Al offered. "Okay, but that could help, I can see that, for just waking him up here in the room. But it won't work in a space suit! You can't touch your face at all. In fact, I heard that's another real problem with the helmet." You couldn't scratch your nose. You couldn't get something out of your eye. You realized it and panicked.

"Well, they didn't think we'd be suiting up a claustrophobic guy and sending him outside!" Julie said.

She looked at her supervisor with exasperation; obviously, *she* would be responsible when Father Tim freaked out. The brass had "covered the topic" and their own asses. But in the end, it always came down to the guy or gal on the ground, who, as likely as not, turned out to be the woman in the air. She sighed. She had the worst luck! In love, too!

Julie continued. "Well, anyway. The eye part of it, I was thinking when they talked about it, how you could do that in a helmet, without your hands. Because, see, my brother's a dive instructor, and some guys wash out of SCUBA training because of their helmet, you know, and I'd been thinking for a long time about how you maybe could still use the pressure points even in a helmet. This one part of the sequence, you could use your eyes instead of your fingers to touch those spots, the acupuncture points, and you can move your mouth to touch the other ones. You can actually touch those same spots. Here, watch." Julie closed her eyes and began to move her eyeballs. She was rolling them in a circle. "See? It touches those same spots—from the inside. And you just move your mouth around, too." She demonstrated.

Well, at least she made a dumb idea look cute, Al thought.

She glanced at Al and saw the look on his face. "I'm just saying. Do it, you'll see! It touches those same points!"

Al leaned back and exhaled. This must beat all in NASA gullibility!

Unfortunately, since knocking the priest out with whatever drugs they carried on board for panic attacks wouldn't work in this particular application, and since Al himself had no better ideas, he had to go with it. That is, if Tim chose to do it. After all, he had a choice, didn't he? Really, the fact was, he *couldn't* do it. Al had a feeling that Rome or the Vatican—Tim's boss, whoever that was—wouldn't give permission if Father asked them. Why would they risk their one and only Bishop of the Universe?

Meanwhile, Tim slept on.

"So what's our time line? *If* he is a priest," Al said. "When do we get to the station? Who's gonna train him in the steps? Where's the schematics of the station?" Al paused briefly, thought hard. "And I gotta go with him."

He watched fresh dismay on Hank's and Julie's faces. They weren't authorized; they'd have to ask management, and so on and so forth.

"Just say it's a religious thing. That he has to have an assistant." Al waited for that to sink in. "Anyway, it might not matter. He might not get the helmet on."

"We've got about an hour and a half. I can get the schematics and I can call the brass, but I'm telling you, they aren't gonna like it," Hank said. "And I don't think we've even got a suit that would work for you." He eyed Al and shook his head.

Then, he went on. "We've got to go over the schematics and get it down to steps, because I suppose we have to rehearse him, like Julie said. It's not that bad. He'll go out our lock, that's all automatic, and we'll throw up the gridway first. We'll have to talk to him about how to grab onto it to move. But you know, it's pretty simple, just hand over hand—unless you freeze up. I mean, they say the view from outside is pretty . . . challenging. Especially if you're afraid of heights. Is he afraid of heights, too?"

Al shrugged.

"He'll have to open a lock on the other side, that's all," Hank continued. "He'll have to key in a sequence to get into the lock, and they'll be waiting for him on the other side, I guess. He can take off the suit inside, at least—as far as I know, anyway, right now. And only the one guy was hurt bad. So it shouldn't take too long once he's on the station."

"How long is the gridway?" Al asked.

While Hank keyed his hand-held to find that in the schematics, Tim woke up.

Julie noticed first. She gently pushed herself out of her chair and floated sideways until she was at the side of the dazed-looking priest. She smiled a pretty, professional smile. "Sir?" she crooned.

He looked at her. She wanted him to keep looking at her. She pushed a little tendril of blond curl back over her ear and kept smiling.

"Sir, welcome to Flight 101! Just sit back and relax. We're here to make sure you're comfortable. I'll bet you're thirsty." She gestured emphatically behind her back to her co-worker.

Hank looked blank for a moment, but then glided over to the wall and fetched a drinking cup from a locker. Tim turned his head to follow Hank, so Julie moved just enough to block Tim's view and caught the priest's eye again. *Just keep looking at me for a minute*, she thought as she smiled at him brightly.

"My name is Julie Renfro. I'm from Chicago. Have you ever been there?" When Tim only blinked, she went on, undaunted. "I've been a flight attendant for eight years, and I'm happy to help with anything you might need or want."

Hank slipped Julie the cup and she waved it gently in front of Tim. "First, you'll want to sip this real slow."

Tim looked away from her face to the cup as if he'd never seen a girl or a cup in his life but was willing to like both of them. Julie gestured with the cup the way she might offer a treat to a very good dog, and waited for Tim to reach out for it.

But he didn't. Tim's head hurt. Why was that? Then, he remembered the last shot of Grey Goose, and his stomach turned over and he quickly drew in a shaky breath. Julie was on it. She put the cup in his hand and helped his hand to his mouth, and he sipped a sweet little pull of cool water through the self-sealing mechanism. Strange cup, he thought. What kind of franchise is this, anyway? Ahhh, he thought after a couple more sips. Better.

Tim closed his eyes for a second. No chance on going back to sleep, is there? His head hurt, but otherwise he felt comfortable. Nice chairs they have here. Very nice. What kind of chairs are they, anyway? Really comfortable. He opened his eyes enough to peep down at his. Navy blue. Nice fabric.

Then he noticed he wasn't sitting, exactly. He was close to the chair, but he wasn't actually sitting on it. He was floating. He let go of the cup. It floated, too. Julie reached out and took it, and he realized her feet weren't touching the floor at all. Suddenly, Tim was completely awake, wide-eyed and heart thumping.

Al leaned forward. This could be where it goes bad. "Hey, there! Remember me?"

Tim looked at him and finally nodded. "Al ..." The memory of Al and the bar and their conversation flooded him. "We made it?" he asked.

Al smiled, exhaled, and nodded, waiting for Tim to suddenly panic. Okay, what's the drill? Rehearse. Breathe slowly... what else, what else? He couldn't think of a single thing to rehearse, but so far, Tim's breathing and everything else seemed pretty good for a guy with claustrophobia and a world class hangover to boot. They'd been lucky! The room was as good as it gets, shuttle-wise. A window—okay, with a strange view, but. And a door. The air seemed okay to him, too.

"So how'd you like getting drunk?" Al grinned. Might as well just chat, then.

Tim grinned weakly back, wincing when that slight movement set off what felt like pin balls the size of grapefruits in his skull.

"You were a perfect gentleman and all that. Nothing to worry about there," Al assured the young priest. "And see—it worked. We're here, and everything is fine."

"*Deo gracias*," Tim finally got out. He wasn't talking to Al or the other two people in the room, either. *We're here. I'm in outer space. I'm on my way to Tomás. I'm on the space shuttle, just like we said. Thank you, heavenly Father*. He took a breath. No problem; there actually was air. Maybe as long as I don't think about it! Okay, fine!

Cautiously, Tim glanced around. Hank and Julie and Al were gathered around him, pretending to sit. He could see a hallway through an opening. On the other side, he saw another window. Outside the window ... Oh, dear Lord! Outside the window was half an Earth, all tilted! Oh shit! (So much for sainthood!) Tim's stomach lurched, and he quickly looked away. It was way better to look at the room and the people. This was opposite the way it usually worked! Usually, outside was better for him. His heart slowed a little. Okay. Okay. Okay.

"How you doing, buddy?" Al asked.

"I'm not sure. I'll tell you in a minute." He shook his head. "Well, I have a headache. My stomach isn't too good. This is a very comfortable chair I'm not sitting on." He gave a little chuckle and took another sip of water. "This water is excellent, too. Floating's not too bad." His back felt—good, as though weightlessness was just what it had been waiting for.

Al sighed with relief. No screaming, yet. "You just keep drinking it, buddy. We're gonna switch to coffee in a minute, because you're hung over and coffee'll help." He glanced at Julie. "Tell me you can get him some toast and some coffee," he pleaded. "And maybe Alka Seltzer?"

She nodded, and took off. Literally.

Tim's eyes got wider, watching her fly down the hall.

"It's gonna be fine," Al said. "It's gonna get better. See? It's just fine."

"Thanks, Al. Thanks. You did great. This is—fantastic! How far are we?" Tim asked, carefully keeping his eyes away from the window, carefully not watching his breathing.

"From the *Halliburton*? We're about three quarters of the way there," Al said, evading several issues at once.

"So how much longer?" Tim persisted.

"Well, about six hours. Give or take." Al glanced at Hank, silently urging him to back him up on this dubious statement. There wasn't any give or take with space flight; they knew to the second. But Hank was watching Julie, returning now with her hands full. And Al figured the priest wouldn't know that, and there was no sense in making him nervous about time and oxygen supply on top of everything else.

"Listen, let's get this into you, and you'll feel better," Al said, nodding to the parcels Julie had placed in his hands.

She had brought them all coffee and bagel-bites (no floating crumbs), and for a minute they were just a group of professionals stopping at Starbucks for a little something-something before hitting the El, if you discounted the fact that downtown was way, *way* downtown, on that blue and white globe below them, the view of which they were all ignoring. Beyond the room, crew attendants moved back and forth through the hall, towing similar refreshments for other waking passengers in the seating alcoves. It was rather normal! Tim found that he could eat, as long as he kept his field of vision really blurry and as long as that little breeze kept up.

Finally, Tim said, "That was good. Thank you." His headache was just a little ache now and then, and he did feel better. "Listen, Al, where's my bag?"

The others glanced at each other sideways and looked away. Something was wrong.

"Did the bags not make it?" he asked Al. That would be bad, but maybe not a disaster. Presumably his essentials, his mass kit, the unconsecrated hosts, and the oils, could be replaced on another flight.

"No. I got it all. But there's something else." Al took a deep breath.

Subconsciously, Tim imitated him and breathed deeply, too. Noticing that, Al took in another breath. Tim did, too. It worked again!

"Okay, what?" Tim said a little impatiently. "Damaged? Confiscated? What?"

"No. Your bag is intact; everything's there. But—" Al looked at Hank and Julie as if it were their fault, the news he was about to deliver. "—the reason we're down here in the conference room is, uh, Julie and Hank were coming through the passenger section looking—ah, for a Catholic who could administer the last rites. Like a priest—or whatever."

Al paused. He was trying to signal Tim, by communicating that Julie and Hank didn't seem to know that only priests could give last rites, that Tim might be able to conceal his priesthood, at least for the moment. He was hoping to give Tim a chance to try to pull the thing off in some fashion without revealing his identity—either identity, priest or HR nerd!—so that they could both still slip away when they got to the station and the priest could, presumably, be concealed—how, Al couldn't fathom. *Don't introduce us, buddy!* he tried to say with his eyes and body language.

Of course, Al couldn't see how they could fail to get around to exchanging names, eventually, since he was betting the shaky World Government already saw the media possibilities. "The new World Religion at Work in Space." Pure bleeping gold. Any minute now cameras would begin to roll. Had he done the right thing, outing Tim? This could end up so bad!

Al winced, but pushed on. "See, there's been an accident on the International Space Station. A guy is hurt bad and he's a Catholic, and they know the shuttle is going by with some religious immigrants, probably, and the thing is, they, he, somebody there, wants, uh, a Catholic person to come and give the injured man those last rites, they said."

"Oh! Well." Tim's face registered concern. The things they'd never mentioned in seminary! He inventoried. He had everything needed.

"Yes, I have everything, uh, a Catholic would need to do that. Is it possible for the shuttle to stop like that and get off schedule?" Tim turned and asked Hank, just like a rational person, in complete sentences even, instead of like the serious phobic he was. "Is the injured man being treated medically on the station? Is he conscious?" The man could still be anointed if he were unconscious, but there was the matter of confession.

Hank answered. "About how long are we talking about this rite thing taking? We've got some schedule leeway, but not a whole lot." Then he added, "I don't know anything about his condition at the moment, except that he's alive."

"A few minutes," Tim said, thinking about the priests in days past in the battlefields of the world, bringing God to the dying. Had to be quick then, too! "Ten, fifteen minutes."

"But that's not all," Al continued with details Hank had omitted, and Tim turned back to him. "The regular air locks were damaged, so you have to go in through an emergency lock."

Tim looked blank.

"You have to put on a space suit to do that."

Tim still looked blank.

"You have to put on a spacesuit and a helmet, and you have to pull yourself through a, um, scaffolding, like a wire enclosure." He didn't say *cage*. "You have to go outside, in a space suit and a helmet, and pull yourself along the scaffolding. Then, you have to use a code to open a door on the hull of the station, and go inside the air lock. The space inside is tiny." Al paused. "And the space outside is—huge. It's huge."

Tim understood then. He forced himself to glance at the window. Dear heavenly Father! Out *there*? He looked quickly away.

Hank continued. "The scaffolding is safe. You can't let go and drift away or anything."

Not a pleasant turn, Al thought, and hurried to undo the possible alarm. "Hey, you don't have to do this, Tim. This is optional. Right? Above and beyond. You can talk to the guy on the radio. Nobody even expects you to do this. It's just, they've never had a—you know, a trained Catholic—available before, in the neighborhood, as it were. So they were just asking. Since the government is so religious now."

Hank had been reading his handheld. "It's negative on you going with him, Al. No suit for you. Only standard sizes on this run. I've requested they fix that for the future."

"So you'd have to go alone, without me, I mean," Al said to Tim. "Way outside the call of duty."

"I'm pretty sure no place is outside the call of duty." Tim said. For a priest, his eyes said to Al.

Al squinted his response back at Tim: how about for a claustrophobic priest incognito?

Tim lifted his eyebrows back at him: what's gotta be's, gotta be.

Then Al rolled his eyes, and everybody got that.

"Well, okay, then," Hank said. "I'll go get the suit ready."

He turned and floated away down the shadowy corridor outside the little conference room. The space seemed much larger without him. Julie looked meditative, and Al imagined she was thinking out what had to happen next. They had to rehearse each step.

"If you're sure you want to," Al said to Tim. "I think you can do this." Al hoped Tim wouldn't know he was lying. Did priests have some kind of extrasensory perception in that area?

Julie settled back in the chair. Forgetting it was fixed, she tried to scoot it forward and flashed a rueful little smile. She gently propelled herself forward and into a seated position, sans chair, very close to Tim, facing him on his right side.

"Do you think you could eat anything else?" she asked him. There was time still for it to settle in his stomach before he put on the helmet, and the energy might help. "We have, I happen to know for a fact, a very nice Chicago hot dog in the crew galley. It does come in a package, but it's really not too bad." She was trying to get him to smile. She didn't really think he'd want a hot dog, but it was comforting to her at least, the word *Chicago*. What could ever go wrong in the world where there was a Chicago? Plenty, apparently.

Tim sat with his face carefully shielded from the observation window and breathed in shallow, quiet gasps. He looked pretty miserable.

What Julie had to teach him about going to the scaffolding and opening the outer door would be difficult for any ordinary civilian. It was a crazy idea to suggest, but not impossible. She just had to help him each visualize each step of the way and to overcome his claustrophobia. He did not appear to be a particularly receptive student. Not nerdy enough.

But little Julie Renfro had always been a girl who followed orders faithfully, and who could be counted on to overlook only one thing: being overlooked. She sighed. It made her think of the last guy who'd overlooked her. And that made her think of something else.

She glanced at Al. "Could you give us a minute?" she asked.

"I beg your pardon?"

"May I have a moment alone with your friend? There's another room right on the other side there," she gestured.

Al looked dubious, but hey, Tim was awake now and could protect himself, temptation-wise, so maybe it was okay. Al had to trust her a little, so okay then. He enjoyed free floating around the corner.

Julie gazed at the crown of Tim's bowed head. He had fine, silky, light-brown hair that floated gently with his breathing and revealed a rather bad haircut. Her own locks were controlled under a cap with an insignia, but someday she wouldn't mind a photo of her hair in freefall—a golden halo all around her in a beautiful dress. And she could see the dress too. Dresses would be tricky but wonderful in freefall.

"Sir? I'm going to ask you a personal question. Is that okay?"

Tim raised his head and looked at her. He had a stunned and dazed expression, but she had a corner of his attention. He nodded cautiously.

"Are you a priest?"

She could tell the question bothered him, and she'd been following the news. "Hey, listen, I don't know what's going on, but anybody can tell that things are—weird. But I noticed you didn't say anything, and the other guy didn't say anything, and I know last rites and confession and everything *have* to be—or, at least, *used* to have to be—administered by a priest. I'm only asking for myself: are you a priest?"

After a moment, Tim answered haltingly, "I'm not sure... I don't know what's going on either.... It was suggested that I... that it would be safer if I... didn't say...."

"I want to go to confession."

Tim's face relaxed. "Yes. I am a priest."

His purple stole was inside his jacket, in the inner pocket. Dovie had brought it, freshly clean, to him as he'd packed. Her face had been stony as a statue's.

"You'll want to put this where you can get at it, I suppose?" she'd said, her lip quivering. But she would not give in to sorrow. It was right for him to go, right for the faith, so it was all right with Dovie. Where he might put on this stole next, out there in whatever they called a "near-Earth orbit," was out of her pay grade to imagine. Her job was to make sure the stole was clean, and she had done it. No pity. She'd heard a sermon once saying that if the Romans hadn't done it, Mary would've nailed Jesus to the cross herself, because she knew He had to save mankind. That saying always made Dovie picture Our Lady as being a little bit like that old movie character, Sarah Conner, only better.

But Tim had seen Dovie's trembling lip. It hurt him and made him stronger at the same time.

Tim had completely forgotten where he was, thinking about Dovie. The woman floating at his side filled his whole frame of vision and blocked the view, and that was fine. He slipped the stole out of his jacket, made the sign of the cross, kissed the stole as required by the ancient rubric, and put it around his neck. He had to hold it together at the bottom to keep it from floating upward, and the gold fringe at the bottom danced all around with his breathing. It would seem that fringe will be a problem in some parts of my diocese, he thought in passing, and came very close to giggling, but only for a moment before he turned to the matter at hand.

Five minutes later, Julie floated around the corner, gave Al a curiously happy smile, and invited him back into the conference room. "I'm going to start the training now," she said.

What the hey? Al thought. First, the guard at the gate and now her. This guy sure has a way with the womenfolk! He found that reassuring, in point of fact, and floated around the corner behind Julie thinking rather cheerfully, *Let's get 'er done*, an ignorant white-trash phrase his Mary had hated, which he never therefore said out loud.

Hank had returned with his arms full of diagrams. Al and Julie arranged themselves on either side of Tim, and Hank took the role of presenter. Being able to hang the printout of a spacesuit right in the air was rather convenient. Hank composed himself, pushing away all the expressions and gestures of irony and perplexity he was feeling about the nature of this particular presentation, just one of many in his career and yet so different and, in his opinion, so crazy of NASA to attempt.

But he was a professional and he'd carry on. And every molecule of his body communicated that very attitude. Hank was *expressive*. And then some.

"This is a spacesuit," he began. "You're going to put this on. It's bulky because it shields you from radiation, but it's weightless. Right here is your tether; see where it's attached on the side there? So there's no chance of you floating away, even if you *could* get outside the grid."

Hank glanced at Julie, who was following his instructions carefully. He took a quick breath and continued. "The joints are designed to flex as easily as possible. You see the hooks at the belt line? That's where you'll carry any gear you need for this job."

He looked at Tim. "How much gear you got? Will this work?"

Tim envisioned the small black bag with the material necessities for the last rite—the oils, the cloths, the crucifix—and envisioned the bag floating and its handle hooked to this belt the man was pointing to. He had the sudden image of the bag bungeed around the rear rack of a bicycle that Tim was peddling madly through space like the witch in *The Wizard of Oz*. Really? And where was *this* at seminary?

"Sir? . . . Sir?" Hank said, reeling Tim back. "Will that work?"

Tim nodded slightly, and Hank continued.

"This other thing is the helmet. You put it on last. Look." He pointed at the wrap-around. "It's got fantastic peripheral vision. And see those lamps on the side? Switch is right here." He indicated a slide-switch on the belt section. "You have radio contact in the helmet, too. You don't have to push or activate anything; it'll be open. Someone will be on the radio with you the whole time."

Hank glanced at Julie. "Anything you want to add?"

She just looked thoughtful for a moment, and then shook her head slightly.

"Sir, you have any questions?"

The young priest carefully turned his head from the schematic to Hank's face. As long as he did everything very slowly, he could keep the level of panic just below the boil. It was as if his eyeballs were moving through molasses. He tried to think of a question, but the only one that came to mind, and it came to mind often, was, *Are you serious?*

Finally, Tim said, "So I'm going to put on a spacesuit and a helmet? Because somebody's hurt? On the space station?"

Hello? Is there intelligent life in outer space? Hank thought sarcastically. Still, he was glad to see some sign of awareness, any kind of animation, in this priest, or whatever he was.

"Yeah, that's about it," Hank said. "You get into the suit naked. There's some plumbing issues, but it's easy, no worries. Heh heh. The suits are comfortable inside, nice and padded, nothing to irritate or itch, because, you know—" Because if something itched, you couldn't scratch. Oops! He was sorry he'd brought *that* up.

Julie suddenly sat up straighter, even though it made absolutely no difference except to propel her slightly higher, so that she had to reach out and fan a little reverse jet with a couple of fingers to offset it. She did it quite without thinking, Tim noticed. In spite of himself, he tensed a couple of muscles to see if it would change his orientation. It did.

"Sir, I'd like to talk about the helmet," she said to Tim.

He almost said, "'Call me Father Tim,'" but hadn't.

"I want to go through the steps for the helmet. It goes on last, after the suit." Her words were rushed, her voice slightly louder. She took a deep breath and glanced at Hank. He was going to let her do it, she could tell; no need to hurry. She spoke slower, calmer. "You'll be standing right by the air lock. In front of a square door, metal; it's gray. There, we'll put the helmet over your head. Then, the door will open, and you'll enter the lock. The lock is a little room."

She paused to give Tim a chance to digest the information. His face registered nothing. His eyes were cast down. Exactly right, Julie thought, he's picturing it, just like they had recommended.

But then Tim raised his eyes to Julie's and said, "I can't. The helmet."

Crunch time! This is where they separate the girls from the goats. Man up, Julie! Or something!

"Yes you can," Julie said firmly. "And I'm going to tell you how. There's a NASA plan."

That made Al smile.

Julie waited for Tim to respond. Would he fight her, or would he go with it?

His eyes, when he finally raised them to her, had the faintest tinge of interest.

She continued. "Think about when we put the helmet on you. Envision it. You're standing outside the lock door. You've got your suit on. We lift the helmet over your head, we lower it, we close two quick-release snap fasteners on the side. Then, you take a breath. There'll be plenty of air. You'll feel it. Just relax and feel the air all around your face."

Julie glanced at Tim. The contemplative look on his face told her was still with her.

"If you start to feel afraid, I want you to do this. I'm going to show you. This might look a little funny—" With that, she closed her eyes and rolled them in a counterclockwise direction, around and around, several times. "Now, I'm changing direction," and she did.

It didn't look funny to Tim. It looked cute. It made him think of a calico kitten he and Tomás had when they were kids. The kitty had thrown such a fit the first time it lapped milk from a saucer, wrinkling up its nose, sneezing in miniature explosions, and making hilarious faces. He smiled at the memory.

Julie looked chagrined. Adios, dignity.

She waited until the grin faded from Tim's face. "Now, you try it."

In a moment, he closed his eyes and slowly rolled them in a circle. Then, he did it again. Then, he did it harder. To his surprise, it did massage something, right over his cheekbones. Cautiously, he reversed the motion. Now, the pressure seemed to be greatest at the corners of his eyes. Interesting. Not sure how it related to his problem.

"That was good," Julie said. "Now, I want you to move your eyes up and down, as far as you can. Try it."

He did.

"Keep your eyes closed," Julie reminded him.

His efforts had provided quick glimpses of either side of his nose each time he'd lowered his eyes. Consequently, it had increased Tim's anxiety rather than produced the desired calming effect.

"Try it again with your eyes closed, and focus on the massaging sensation," Julie said soothingly.

This time, his breathing slowed. Hey! It was working.

"Now, can you switch and move your eyes side to side? Go as far as you can."

Tim noticed he could feel the sensation deep in his temples, on either side.

He finally opened his eyes and looked at Julie. She was watching him intently.

"I want you to do those eye movements as soon as we put the helmet over your head. Right then. Got it? Counterclockwise, clockwise, up and down, side to side. You can touch almost all of the top part of your head with these motions."

Tim nodded.

"After that, I want you to do the same thing with your lips. All the same motions, except with your lips," Julie added. "Let's try that now. Move your lips in a counterclockwise direction until I say 'Stop.'"

He did it. Things creaked and popped in his jaw. Ouch!

"This is the last thing: do all those same motions with your tongue, inside your mouth. Try it now. Don't just go around your lips; go around and around that big muscle in your cheek. Both sides. It's kind of triangular. Feel it?"

He did. He noticed how tense the muscle was. It wasn't very pleasant to touch, but it felt more relaxed when he was finished. At the very end, he sat breathing quietly and waiting for further instruction. His face felt—cheerful.

When Julie said nothing else, he took a sip from his cup and sucked it in. "How does this go down into my stomach, without gravity?" he asked.

Everyone breathed a sigh of relief. Again with the rational! So far, so good.

"It's as if we were designed for outer space. Who knew?" Hank answered, seriously. "It goes down into your stomach by muscle action. And blood circulates the same in weightlessness—better, actually. Even the lymph system works in no gravity, at least as well as it does on Earth with gravity. In fact, there is reason to believe it works better, too. It's like we were made for it. Lucky, very lucky, design." Not that Hank believed in a Designer!

"But they have gravity on the *Halliburton's*," he added. "Almost everywhere on the colony, except where they don't want it. Part of the contract."

Hank's voice had trailed off, and distracted by his thoughts. his eyes had become unfocused. Weightlessness was a big deal to attendants who spent so much time up in the air. Such a glamorous job, yeah, yeah. If your muscles quit functioning, not so much. But he'd been lucky, no health problems. In fact, his blood pressure was down.

Julie frowned, and Al tapped Hank's wrist.

Appropriately rebuked, Hank raised his eyebrows and plunged on. "Let's go over the schematics. Think you can handle that?"

He "hung" a wide-angle visual in the air. "This right here is the gridway. Julie already told you about the air lock. This is how the outer door on the ISS will look after you float through the gridway." He touched a section of the schematic, tracing the outer door.

Next, Hank pointed to a small object on the schematic. "This is where you put your hand on the gridway to pull yourself along. Here, take a closer look." He changed the angle on the view, and suddenly they could see, as if they were out there looking up at it, all the handholds marching upward into the near distance, and everything else went a little out of focus so that the handholds could be clearly seen.

Nice, very nice. Very Tufte. Visuals were kind of Hank's hobby.

"In twenty feet, more or less, depending on how close our pilot can get to the station, you'll see this door."

Hank threw up another schematic of the door, a representation, not a photo. "You're outside the station now, and this is what you'll see. Here's where you'll enter the four-digit code." Hank pointed to a recessed keypad with large buttons.

"What do you think the code is? Could you guess it? If you were a hacker or some kind of bad guy?" Hank had asked this routinely in presentations to engineering students and gotten a laugh and a lot of good guesses.

Tim winced. Bad guy? If Hank only knew who he really was! It sure felt funny to be illegal.

"Zero, zero, zero, zero?" Tim ventured. "Does it, like, make you wait, if you mess up the first time?" Tomás actually had been awesomely accurate at hacking passwords, when they were kids. All Tim could remember now was that if zeros didn't work, try one, two, three, four.

Hank laughed. "Good guess! Or *are* you a hacker? Yeah, four zeros. And no time out. They're not expecting pirates. But, actually, it can be reprogrammed from inside, if there ever *were* barbarians at the gate. It can be bypassed completely. Like, if the keypad was damaged from an asteroid strike or space debris, something like that. There is also a built-in charge to blow the lock from inside if all else fails. And if that doesn't work, they have tools to remove it the slow way; they're stored in this little locker, right here." He touched a small box on the schematic and sighed with professional satisfaction.

Hank was comfortably unaware that Tim had just pictured the scene in which he couldn't remember the code and was locked out, and he'd have to wait for them to blow the lock, and his air was running out and they wouldn't tell him, and he'd take the next breath and the air-would-just-be-gone. Or maybe they'd blow off the lock without warning him. Tim started to pant.

Julie saw the change in his breathing and frowned. She didn't want them to talk about "fail" and "damages" and "asteroid explosions!" Harsh words that could scare the chest muscles.

"Okay, then," she interrupted. "Nothing like that here. 'Cause I'm gonna text the station and tell them to just bypass the code right now, this very second. Honey—I mean, sir—we're *all* going to be watching the whole time. You won't even have to ring the front doorbell."

She shot Hank a quick poisonous glare. "Now, Hank, don't you think you should go on down to the bay lock and get things ready?"

Taking her words as the command it was, Hank quickly gathered up his schematics and floated away.

She turned her attention back to Tim. "Here's another little trick they taught us: put your fingers right here, below the collarbone." She demonstrated on her own person, and Al politely looked away. "Now, I want you to make little circles. No, go outwards, like this." She showed him how again. "That's right, go around, all the way around. There you go. Do it again."

Julie nodded as Tim followed her instructions.

"Okay, now, I want you to change the motion. Keep your fingers here," she again demonstrated on herself, "and make little taps. You don't have to go in a circle."

Tim tapped his chest.

"Good. That's right," Julie said. "Now, make the taps harder, like gentle but firm slaps."

Tim did.

"Do you see? Can you feel it? It's easier to breathe, right? You're waking up the chest muscles, opening up your airways. Isn't that good?"

Tim glanced up and gave her a small grin. It *was* better.

"Okay, let's go back and talk about it again. We're going to go down to the bay. You're going to put on the suit, and then we're going to put the helmet on you. Do you remember the exercises we did with your eyes, and your lips, and your tongue? Do you think you can do them again?"

She was so hopeful and helpful that Tim didn't have the heart to say no. He nodded. Yes, that probably would count as a lie. One of several he had told to get himself into this fix. Although, since he had gotten himself here, to where he was needed, maybe they didn't count with God? He had a way to go in the moral theology department! Maybe if he could get that helmet on and go out that door, maybe this little white lie wouldn't count, either. Maybe all of them would count more like promises than lies. Darn this free will, anyway! Life would be easy if all you had to do was, like the clouds, obey the wind.

"As soon as that helmet is secured on your head, you'll step through the door and into the lock. It's just a small room, a tiny compartment. And then, you'll take, like, two steps—in, like, one minute—and you'll go into another room with another door on the other side.

"The soles of the suit are lightly magnetized, so you can walk to that other door and stand there. We'll open it from inside. When it opens, you'll step into the and you'll go through it like a ladder, but you'll just need your hands."

"All that time, whenever you stop or pause as you enter the lock and go through the grid, you'll do that massage with your eyes and your mouth."

Julie paused to see if Tim had been processing any of what she'd said at all.

"You can talk to us the whole time. We'll be right there," she assured him.

Tim looked up into her eyes, and after a moment, he nodded. It didn't sound so alarming; just go through a couple of doors, and through a wire tunnel to another door and through another door, and then to an injured man to whom he could deliver the sacraments and help into heaven, if he were that injured. He had already done last rites, let's see, at least nine times in his priesthood. Thinking of those times, it crossed his mind that this visit might actually be an improvement over visiting a hospital. They tended to be creepy. And smelled funny.

"We have a few minutes. Is there anything I can get you? Something else to drink?" Julie didn't offer food, not now. The clock was ticking, and she was thinking of nausea, but she didn't say it.

Tim considered. He had his bag; that was all good. "Do you think I might have a few moments to pray?" He had his breviary, but this might not be the best time to pray it, although his heart gave a little longing lurch at the thought of those passionate, stately psalms from thousands of years ago, written by a desert king from—so far, far away. He reached for his rosary in his jacket pocket. Dovie, again. He had packed his worn wooden rosary, but she had added her mother's rosary of fat Florida pearls and a silver crucifix, and it was this one that he found in his pocket now.

They all sat peacefully with their own thoughts or prayers. Al and Julie gazed at the big blue tilted Earth in the window. Tim's eyes were closed, his attention cast inward.

Tim chose the sorrowful mysteries because it was Friday—on Earth, anyway. The beads looked amazingly beautiful, luminous ivory drops floating around his hand. He had time to finish the whole rosary and to ask for all its graces, to ask the Mother for patience and purity, for contrition and persistence, for courage, most of all. At the end, he held onto the crucifix and mentally took up his own cross, trying to be as cheerful about it as Christ. He stood up and waited for them to follow.

The transfer to the bay locks from the conference room was the opposite of stealthy, as they chose the major and wider corridors instead of the maze of small tunnels that honeycombed the big craft and were accessible only when the shuttle was in freefall. Before they'd set out, Al had whispered to Tim, "Keep your head down at the corners," warning him about the inevitable cameras, just in case they worked. Concentrating on that necessity may have actually helped Tim to master the situation. Tim did not, in any case, experience any panic; he tried to keep his heart rate slow and his breathing light and not think about his claustrophobia. It was like looking at stars with your peripheral vision. It was pretty easy to forget about it with the novelty of moving without gravity, with no up or down, and with the novelty of others traveling the same way, coming and going in the corridors. Tim got it right away. Julie said most people *do* get it right away. Even better. Safer in the herd, with the flock. He even towed his own black bag right along.

Al took advantage of his minor role in these preparations to think about what might come next. He figured, if and when Tim returned through the bay lock, he was going to insist that Tim was exhausted and that they both return to their seats without further interview—no questions, no debriefing. Then, somehow, he'd arrange a distraction just before the shuttle docked at *Halliburton's*. And somehow, God willing, they'd slip off the ship unnoticed.

To Al's thinking, it was just an engineering problem. So he had his eyes open, looking for the weak spot. He needed a surgical fix, a precise fix, something that would affect the crew but not the whole population. Because general panic might affect Tim.

Al's seditious thoughts had just turned to the shuttle's plumbing system when Hank drifted over and made him jump by whispering, "We're at the station. The mechs are setting up the grid already." Al wondered whether Hank was using the term *mech* for *mechanic* or ignorantly, for *Mexican*. The words were practically synonymous, because they were an awfully good bunch of guys with a wrench, from his experience.

The bay locks, two of them, were big open spaces, side by side. Across each wall were secured stacks of wire-mesh panels that could be fit together and anchored, used for securing any big mechanicals the shuttle might need to transport to the colony or the mining asteroid. There were only a few contraptions being toted this trip—the most noticeable, a conveyor of some sort, which seemed to be floating in its cage in a corner. The colonists found that few of the mechanicals used to assist production on Earth were adaptable to manufacturing in a weightless environment, because so many of them were designed to help cancel gravity. That wasn't necessary on the colony, where they could cancel gravity at will. Other manufacturing equipment was designed to use gravity to achieve a task—for example, to move objects from one production station to another. In space, workers just gave those objects a little push; of course, then they had to keep the objects from floating away. And most of the heavy-lifting equipment could stay on Earth, which was good because it cost the annual income of a small country to launch, say, a single gantry crane out of the atmosphere.

So the colony was a blank slate for enterprising engineers. They were finding other ways to move things and grow things by just using what humans seemed to always have at hand. Al had followed the blogging from the colony with great interest. It was a hoot! For one thing, they were rediscovering the treasure of manure, especially as a radiation shield. Sort of like pulling yourself up by your own bootstraps, except it wasn't exactly your bootstraps.

It was such a rush, almost better than free fall, not to have to consider energy costs in any project. Al could hardly grasp it. Energy free? All around! Just reach out and grab some! Mankind had found the mother of all light sockets, right in their own solar system, almost home! Unfortunately, start up was sluggish. There just wasn't enough spark; demand for energy on Earth was down ever since the troubles. To conserve, they had taught people not to dream, not to risk. Big mistake, apparently.

Sociologists had traced this curious new passivity as far back as they could. It was like a mental virus, you could trace its spread just like a virus, a virus that affected relations between the sexes. The huge international NGO Planned Population kept popping up in the interminable professional discussion, implicated in every fall of the fertility index, but only South Korea had the sense to kick them out. But whatever! However! The point was mankind had reached the mother-load of energy just as they had essentially ceased to procreate--from worry about energy. Ironic, right?

Demographers thought the birth dearth had started in Japan or Thailand. Maybe, they conjectured, the virus was buried in Buddhism, in all that enlightenment, in all that business about human beings being no different than any other living things, perhaps all that turning inward. Or maybe it was just good old mashed-potato liberalism that had struck the final blow. America would have been the carrier in that case, Al mused, giving a nod to Mary. You were right again, my darling. They *did* kill love.

Now, the fleas were abandoning the corpse, but it was not Earth that had died. There it was: a big, fat, blue globule bursting with juice. Earth! It was mankind who had died. Suicide.

Al and Tim followed Hank and Julie into the bay lock. It was empty; the mechs had already gone out with the gridway. The big overhead arc lamps were off, and the lock was shadowy. The suit was in the meeting area, tethered to the wall in the corner. It was white and glowed against all the plastic and metal.

The suit looked enough like a cross to be creepy, floating there, arms outspread, Tim thought. But he didn't dwell on it, the creepy part. He was trying to psyche himself into being braver than he was, reciting his credo. Putting on the helmet was his own true cross for today, he believed that, and every day had one; this day was no different than any other. That was his faith, and this was his mission. He was going to accept the fact that today's cross involved putting on that suit, putting on that helmet clipped to it, and then going through that door into an airless void. So what? Had not priests always done that? Define your airless voids. He was going to accept it and then he was going to do it. Sure he was.

They gathered around the metal table. They could've gathered anywhere and pretended to sit down, but the table was next to the suit, and anyway, "sitting down" together was familiar.

Julie had suggested it should be only the four of them. She and Hank had discussed taking Tim through the control room and introducing him to some of the other people who would be watching him through their cameras and monitoring his helmet cam. But Julie had argued that the fewer voices and elements, the less likelihood of confusion. Confusion was the enemy. Tim had to fight it and stay in control. So her proposal was that only the three of them would talk to Tim and only they would talk to the control room for him. In the end, she had prevailed. It was the first time Julie had ever won a staff conflict. This could bode well, she thought. Anyway, they still had to work out, among the three of them, who would talk to Tim, who would talk him through it. Not Hank! She had to make sure of that.

Tim and Al contemplated the suit.

Al was enthusiastic. "It has eighteen thousand parts, did you know that?" he said to Hank. "It has everything an astronaut needs to stay alive. Eleven layers. One of them keeps the human body at exactly the best temperature, including extremities, feet, hands. One of them shields radiation. One of them collects waste. It works great! I actually helped design it, on the committee. We're talking state-of-the-art plumbing, buddy! State-of-the-art technology! State-of-the-art everything! It's puncture-resistant, of course. And nothing sticks to it, either."

Al floated closer and peered at the fabric. "See, they don't want anything brought back in the house, no space dust or anything." He touched it. "Wow!" Very close weave. Curious texture. He'd heard of fabric described as *hydrophobic*, but this fabric seemed to flee from his finger. Just *phobic*.

Then, Al noticed the disapproving expression on Julie's face. Apparently, she didn't like the direction of the conversation. Well, maybe it was a guy thing. He was betting the term *puncture-resistant* would be comforting, even to Tim, and Al liked it just fine.

They huddled there, next to the empty table, for a few minutes. It was kind of dark. Julie put one hand on the table, surveyed her fingernails, took her hand off the table, and let it float in her lap. Hank absently smoothed his one unruly tuft of hair and silently rehearsed his report. Al gazed at the suit fabric affectionately, and Tim just gazed at the suit. As the seconds ticked by, they became aware of all the sounds in the ship—the clicks, metallic twangs, hisses, and the deep thrum.

Finally, Tim said, "Well, aren't we on a schedule?"

That put them all in motion. They'd been waiting for Tim, actually. They didn't want him to feel, later, that they'd hustled him into anything.

"You have to get undressed to get into the suit," Al reminded Tim.

There was nowhere private to change clothing, of course. Part of killing love had been to wave all that away and to make modesty old-fashioned. So Al had glanced at Julie before speaking. She'd picked up the cue and suddenly got busy with her handheld, turned away from the table as if to take a call and drifted away a little.

While Hank opened up the suit, Al helped Tim remove his clothes and maneuver himself into the suit. Both Hank and Al examined the closures, and Hank clipped the black bag to the suit.

"Here we go," Al said.

With Al towing the helmet, they all moved over to the bay lock. Suddenly, the green light inexplicably turned red, and a moment later, the heavy door slid open and two men in spacesuits floated in. One of them waved genially and made the best thumbs-up sign his glove permitted as they floated past the foursome and over to the lockers.

The mechs. So the grid is up, Al concluded.

Just then, Hank's handheld beeped. Confirmation from the control room: good to go. Hank nodded at the three of them, but no one moved.

"Okay," Tim said. Again, he'd had to initiate the action. "I'm ready."

Hank looked at Al; Al looked at Julie. She nodded.

Hank double-checked the light. Green. He hit the button. The light turned red and the door slid open. The four of them floated outside the small lock that only one of them would enter. It was time for the helmet.

Julie floated a little closer to Tim. He looked young and small in the suit, but he didn't look scared, exactly. He did look as if he were standing on the edge of a cliff, though. His eyes were all pupil.

"Want to go over what you're going to do when we put the helmet on and all the rest?" she asked Tim.

Looking at Julie, directly and only at Julie, he spoke as calmly as he could. "I'm going to massage the upper part of my face by moving my eyes in those sequences. I know them: around and around, up and down, side to side. I'm going to do the same thing with my lips and mouth, and not forget the big muscle. Uh, and I can do that anytime, if I start to panic."

Actually, he had already started to panic, but he was going ahead with it, anyway. *I can't do it* is a feeling. So you feel it. You just keep putting one foot in front of the other, no matter what you feel. Feelings don't rule Catholics. Right! Until they pass out or explode. And he felt like he might. He was trying not to look at the space on the other side of the door. He could faint right now.

But a badly injured man over there needed him. And Christ had died for that guy. And Tim was Christ's man. So Tim was going to let them put that helmet on him, and if he passed out, he passed out. He'd pass out doing Julie's exercises. He really looked at her then, focused, and smiled shakily. "Do it."

"Wait," Al said. He'd been quiet until then, while Julie did the heavy lifting, with Hank as her backup. Now, Al drifted between them and Tim, leaned forward, and spoke quietly into Tim's ear. "Check this out. I've seen the two switches to open the locks. I see how it works. Few civilians know this, but at NASA, everybody knows the human body can stand space without a suit—for about thirty seconds, that's the most they tried. They don't know the maximum yet. As long as you can hold your breath, I'm guessing. We don't explode, and we don't freeze. Skin is amazing engineering, buddy. Thirty seconds is plenty long enough for me to get out there and get you back, if it comes to that. So I will. Got it?"

Al took off his glasses, struck his Superman pose, and smiled slowly. He waited until Tim registered it all, and then he put his glasses back on and motioned for the helmet. Time to go.

The helmet went on swiftly, actually. Engineers had made sure of that, although they had been more concerned with being able to take it off fast than with being able to put it on fast. Two well-machined hand-screws, and it was done.

Tim began to roll his eyes like mad. After a second, they gave him a little push, and he floated through the lock door and felt it slide shut behind him. He never looked at the inside of the lock itself, because in the next second, the exit door on the other side slid open and his momentum carried him through. All the while, he kept rolling his squinched-shut eyes, so he was all the way out into the grid when he finally quit and opened them. He never got to rolling his mouth at all.

Because his mouth was wide open at the sight.

It was huge. Earth all white and blue bloomed on the other side of the shuttle and filled almost half the sky. Beyond that and all around him, space stretched out—vast, velvety, dark, dense, flickering with lights—like a forest full of fireflies. He was aware of the black bulk of the space station to his right and the other bulk of the shuttle to his left, but overhead (and beneath his feet!) were millions of points of light, clouds of them receding into infinity.

He was aware of his own warmth. He could feel the warmth of his face. He could feel his feet. He could feel the blood rushing through him, warm and alive. Alive! He could feel his life, pulsing in the huge rock-filled emptiness. And hear it! It made noise. His life made noise!

Suddenly, he became aware of something else—another noise. It was low and soft. It sounded almost like a voice. It was so like a voice! A deep, deep voice.

After a second, he sent the small noise of himself out. He kind of offered it, like a question. It was as if he'd pushed it, rather than spoken.

The other noise came again. Like an answer! *I am here.* It echoed: *I am here. I am here. I am here.*

He waited and wondered. A coincidence? He called again, and again that low musical swelling from everywhere. He couldn't swear it was a voice. Or even a noise. He shook his head inside the helmet and concentrated. It might be a noise. Or it might be a feeling. What was it? But it answered! It had *answered*. He had called, and it had waited and then answered. As sure as you could hear a conch calling over an island or the tolling of a bell.

But it *couldn't* be a sound. Didn't sound travel in air? Wasn't sound vibration of matter? What could it be?

It was God. That's all.

Oh yes. Right.

Tim knelt down. He didn't know where down was, but mentally he knelt, he prostrated, he bowed his head, and worshipped.

Oh, what a church!

It was filled with that low murmur. It was coming from everywhere, and everywhere stretched into eternity. God was here. Space wasn't *empty*. You could feel Him, or hear Him, or something. *Better* than on Earth. Maybe something, maybe so much life on Earth, interfered with—what? The signal? The signal, the sound or the feel of God, was much stronger here.

Could it possibly be that gravity interfered with perceiving God? Was this another thing you could do better in space?

Tim stayed like that, worshipping, peacefully appreciating creation and the Creator, until his helmet mic chittered.

Julie's treble voice whispered, "Sir? Uh—how's the view?"

"I like it," Tim answered abstractedly.

Then, he forced himself to turn his attention away from his prayer. He looked up for those handholds. Time to get to work. He was humming the simple tones of Salve Regina like those sailors of old climbing among the masts, hand over hand in the gridway.

Abu Dhabi Blue

A'ida sat at her aluminum table in her ceramic kitchen nook with the two boxes that held her Ramadan treasures. She had brought them, instead of food or clothes, on the journey here. It was uncertain, her family joked, that if ColCor had said A'ida would have to leave behind either those boxes or her last-born child to meet the baggage-weight restrictions, A'ida would have chosen to take her Ramadan cartons.

Despite their teasing, her family always liked the results. A'ida glanced with satisfaction around her home. She lingered over the gauze draped down the metallic walls and canopied across the ceiling, which made of the dining nook a perfect little desert tent. She appreciated, for the thousandth time, her floors gleaming with a bold stenciled foliage motif. Her heart beat with joy at the sight of her favorite, the four oak planks, worth more than gold here on the *Halliburton's*, placed in a central wall like a shrine, and lit from below. Their creamy, lightly pitted earthy texture was almost magnetic, and in fact, her family and guests had a habit of touching the panel as they passed by, with a look of reverence. A new observance.

She loved her kitchen. It could have been cold and sterile with all that metal and ceramic, but she had, simply by using the teachings of her faith, a few touches of gold, and a little blue paint exactly the color of the winter sky in Mussafah (although the paint makers had named it Abu Dhabi Blue!), made it a lovely Muslim home. She was sure that people in the future would say that outer space and Islam went together: big clean empty places so suitable for prayer, a place where life itself was reduced to an artistic Islamic abstraction, so many cubits of oxygen, so many grams of protein, so many nanoseconds of light and dark, so many clouds in the artificial sky. Space and Islam: perfect! She loved her new home in Harmony Village almost as much as she had loved her spacious apartment in Mussafah when they were young, when she and Isadi were just beginning.

Isadi didn't love it as much, because they didn't own it. They had owned even their first home together. This was the first place they lived in that they didn't own. Isadi didn't like that.

In the boxes were the Ramadan lights, the streamers, the sparkling chain you took a link off every day until Eid al-Fitr. When you held the last chain in your hand, the celebrating could begin. Oh, the memories!

A'ida reached into one of the boxes and lightly touched one of the golden stars and the silver moons that her children had clumsily cut from foil when they were young. A sudden sob caught in her throat, remembering her children so small. What would she not do to hold those little hands again! Her children were farther away from her now than Earth was. She meant their complicated grown-up selves.

She shook herself, shook it off. It was unworthy. Children's growing up was just what happened; mothers had to dry their tears. The stars and moons were foil, not the fruits of the festival that would last. The real decorations of Ramadan were the spiritual ones. The focus should be on the prayer and the fasting, the return to Allah, the practice of Kaffarah, atonement, expiation. That is what all the women said as they sat after sunset, sipping apricot drinks and recovering from the day's fast. But A'ida could not lie; she liked her lights. She had chosen them out of many, for their simplicity and color. She would be the first to tell you, with an embarrassed smile, "Not the point, of course I know that."

All of her daughters were more devout, may Allah be praised. Her daughters had the devout bone. A'ida had the decorating bone. She made a rueful little face and returned to the matter at hand.

Because, now—what? Now that the president had said it and their *mujtahid* had affirmed it, Islam was part of the new One Faith. What were they to do about Ramadan, beginning in just three days? What of Ramadan? A'ida had spoken to several of her neighbors, and she was waiting for her husband. Surely, they could not end Ramadan? She'd already ordered the chicken and the sweet Deglet Noor dates! A fortune!

A'ida heard the rain begin outside. Yes, it rained on the colony, Allah be praised! Every day just at this time. Very polite rain, like living in a garden world. It gurgled and sang. Isadi had made rain bells at the forge and hung them in the downspouts, where the musical stream cascaded into a clay pot set on ceramic tile molded into a pattern of honeycomb. A'ida had thought it a perfect combination of earth and water, the clay and honeycomb and glistening metals of the downspout, the crystal glitter of water flowing down. So also there was fire, in the sparkle of cascading water And last she had hung a wind catcher, a cylinder of pale yellow gauze printed with patterned blue flowers, finished with blue and gold metallic streamers, close to the downspout. It whirled in the breeze. She had made it out of scrap cloth. So that made it complete, there was earth, air, fire, and water, like every perfect garden in Islam.

A'ida sighed in satisfaction and glanced at her hands. Smart hands. That is what they called hands like hers, hands that could make things, balance things, arrange things, match colors, match people, and smartest of all, cook. Her home here in this strange place was the envy of her community, just like it had been back home, like it had always been in every home she'd ever lived in. Plus, she had handsome children. And high *good* cholesterol. A'ida settled back comfortably in satisfaction. Allah be praised.

She loved it here on the colony, for a fact. She had never told anyone that. It was bad policy not to complain about everything. She had loved Detroit as well! She had put it into words on several occasions that she loved a country where all were free to worship as they wished. You could wear a veil or not. You could send your children to the mosque or not. There were no impediments in Detroit to the full life of *sharia* law. Just like here. It was on you to be devout or not. Nobody could tell you what to do.

She could stay in Harmony Village forever, where she worked at the day care, where lots of the women wore *hijab*, where Allah was honored, where they could pray, where they were not a freak show. She hardly ever had to go outside the village, where it was rough, her family all told her. Her pretty, delicate face grimaced at the thought of the things her children reported—those poor godless women out there! Ugh!

A'ida was Shia, and so were her immediate neighbors, in an otherwise Sunni community, but there was peace in Harmony Village, and it was strictly kept. A'ida had her mujtahid; her village had its imams. She and her Shia sisters had the advantage of birth control, which Sunnis rejected. They, the Shias, also had the disadvantage of *mut'ah*, the temporary marriages that usually ended in disaster, for the women at least. Sunni's agreed that it was practiced in the Prophet's time but believed they could reject his example and forbid it now, just as they believed they could reject his choice of successor! What of tradition? That is what the Shia asked.

But Harmony Village soldiered on, with Sunnis and Shias side-by-side. At least, it had up until now. Now, there was a new church—a new One Faith.

Perhaps there were no more Sunnis and Shias! A'ida had no idea what to think about it, as she sat waiting for her husband of twenty-three years in the kitchen nook of her home on a street in her village on the colony called *Halliburton*, whirling in near-Earth orbit, where she'd managed to summon the spirit of a cool desert retreat from a blazing sun.

Finally, A'ida heard her husband's footsteps at the door.

Isadi clumped in. Men were so noisy! He slumped at the table across from her and did not look at her. Of course, she would have to ask him.

"The water is hot; I'll get your tea," she said, instead.

She went to search for the blue cup she knew he liked. When she set it before him, steaming with the scent of the pungent green tea he liked, she waited until he had inhaled its grassy scent and taken a sip. Only then did she ask, "What do they say?"

He had been at the emergency meeting of the village men.

At first, when they were all new, they had met surreptitiously, organizing Harmony Village. But then, they had realized the administration could be manipulated through their laws about democracy and religious freedom, not to mention the ordinary human laziness that constant surveillance frustrated. And so, ultimately, their village met openly both in prayer and in political discussion. For really private discussions, they, like everyone else, had their slice of the Combs.

There was the iron fist in the velvet glove, of course. If their discussions had ever yielded anything threatening, action would certainly have been swift. Then, only the infidel heathen laziness of the *Halliburton's* administration could be counted on.

Isadi took another sip of tea, stalling. He wasn't sure how his wife would take what he was about to tell her. He would much rather face their wrath than hers.

"Well, they sent a representative, that same fellow from Central that they sent the last time. Remember, I told you? He and Imam Aboud and the muhtahid sat together. This was their second meeting, not their first. They had already talked about it; they had even already met with Graham Fletcher!"

It distressed Isadi that they had met behind closed doors over such important issues, without telling the rest of them. He felt betrayed. He thought democracy was supposed to be different. It was the old way, wasn't it? When the tribal leaders settled everything in a tent? Hadn't they overcome that? Democracy was different, and they had to live up to it. It was the only way. He believed that.

"What they said was, we're going to have one celebration. We will no longer meet for prayer five times a day, but only twice, in the morning and evening. So will the Christians. So will everyone. That fellow from Central said, 'Look what an improvement that will be!'"

Isadi and A'ida both considered whether it would be an improvement. Not for their village; they always prayed. But did he mean the secular villages, too, where no god was recognized and religious sentiment hardly tolerated? For those villages, any prayer would be an improvement! Were the secular villages to pray twice daily, too?

She asked him that.

"Yes. They mean all the villages. They seem to have gotten very religious. They said they would tax those who refused to come." He gave her a wry look. "Really, we were all astonished! You should have seen Imam Tantowi's face when they said they would tax those who did not come to pray!"

"Are we to have Ramadan?" Protectively, she touched the nearest box.

"No, A'ida."

What? Her look said it all.

"Oh, no, we are still going to have the celebrations," he hurried to explain. "We can put up the lights, and the Christians will put up their lights and their Santa Claus, and the Hindus, too. We're going to have *a* celebration—*one*—a single religious celebration that, Fletcher said, will be 'worthy of Earth.' They have a new name for it."

He considered stopping there. If he said it, the stupid made-up name, his wife would reject it and the whole idea. And then what would they do?

Was it important? He knew when his wife said Ramadan that she did not mean exactly what he meant. He had never given up trying to explain to her that one fasted not to fit in with one's friends, to enjoy the camaraderie of shared suffering, and possibly to lose a pound or two, but to discipline one's rebellious heart so that it was worthy to approach the living God. In the end, though, Isadi had concluded that his wife was over-fond of her rebellious heart. And truly, it was one of the things he loved about her.

"But the lights will not celebrate Allah? They will be for all the gods?" A'ida looked troubled.

"Well, the imam talked about that. He said we were not to worry ourselves at all. *Tawhid* is true because it has to be true, A'ida, not because we say it is true. There is only one God. That is the God we shall be honoring. It does not matter if another fool thinks he is worshipping two gods, or blue gods, or three gods in some kind of trinity. There is only One God. So the imam said this One Faith is certainly correct, is certainly the correct interpretation of the Quran, and therefore is certainly pleasing to Allah."

"Will we still call him Allah?"

"I didn't ask that." The word, *Allah!* Allah be praised! How suddenly distant seemed the world that had given them this light, cool, perfect name, when the throat opened so easily: Allah. Oh world where the sun rose and set and Mecca was always and ever in the east. Where there was an east. Isadi felt sad, and in the end, he hadn't asked all his questions nor shared all his thoughts.

"But we can do it as we like here in Harmony Village?" A'ida still smiled.

"There will be new prayers."

"But there will be prayers?" She would not have missed the prayers as much as the Ramadan lights. Sometimes the prayers seemed so old-fashioned and repetitive; they could do with a rewrite anyway.

Outside, the rain stopped. The sun came out. It was artificial sun. But it felt just like the real sun, and it got its energy from the real sun.

Suddenly, A'ida smiled in amusement. She got it now. "So which God do you think will hear them? There is only one God, and so there is no problem!" Her smile faded to simple contentment, and she opened the box nearest her. That president was a genius!

Isadi breathed a sigh of relief. "Well, wait, hold on a little. The celebration isn't at the old time. They're posting a calendar of worship for everyone in the neighborhood centers; it came from Earth. They said it was written by all the leaders of all the religions on Earth. Think of it! They have combined things in a very clever way, the man from Central said. They are still working on translations for some of the smallest idioms; that's why it's not out yet. He said we are to have a celebration every season."

They still had seasons, of course. For the plants.

The door clicked. A'ida heard that and another sound besides. They turned. It was Adn, pale as a sheet. "They've got Laiq!" she said, and collapsed in the doorway.

Only then—it had been so long since she'd heard it—did A'ida recognize the other sound. It was the sound of Muslim women crying in that high-pitched, ululating wail.

At Last, an Angel

Marley answered the phone, and just like that, everything changed.

She'd been washing the dishes and making a few calls during her off-shift. She'd checked on Stephanie, who'd left her a garbled message (or more garbled than usual). But Steph hadn't answered when Marley rang her back. Then Marley had set up a delivery of some herbals from their guy in the AgPod for her mother's underground pharmacy, and then managed to convey the meeting time to Mrs. Delgado, and then, last, set up an appointment with the midwife for the wife of Tomás's friend.

All this was technically illegal. The midwife herself was seriously illegal, since she had been denied the state's certification for her refusal to cooperate with abortions back on Earth. Next, Marley had arranged to get the pregnant woman off the mining asteroid for the appointment; that, too, was illegal. As soon as she'd hung up, the phone rang again. Then the surprising words of her contact (who was actually a neighbor with whom Marley more typically shared bread yeast than coded information): Live shipment, one angel, middle bay, personnel shuttle, UTC 15:00.

Did she really say "one angel?"

They'd agreed on the code word long ago: *angel*.

But was it actually happening, and now, when things seemed impossible? Then, her phone had rung again, the Bugs Bunny stutter announcing a scrambled transmission. It was Tomás.

He'd spoken slowly and carefully. "Angel, Marley. *Angel*. I just heard from Uncle Max. And that's not all. Wait for me; I'll be there before—" he paused, he might have been looking at his schedule--"before you go to dinner. Wait for me."

Marley had nodded, like Tomás could see her, and hung up without speaking.

"'That's not all?'" What could be more *all* than getting a priest? Getting a bishop. Ha ha. Getting the pope.

She finished wiping the sink, and held out her hand. "Come on, Laney, let's go lie down for a minute."

Laney glanced at his sister's face and understood, and took her hand without commenting. They were playing for the cameras.

Every home had cameras. You could spot them, most of them. People who cared looked for theirs and then took steps. They hacked them and had back-up loops to edit in, or they modified their houses; most people did both. Some people just ignored the obvious, thanked Big Brother, forgot about it, and lived their lives under badly functioning cameras. Those same people also believed everything their doctors told them and never parsed colony statements too hard.

Marley's family was not that kind. They found their cameras and proceeded to fool them, as did their neighbors. They also didn't believe a thing their company doctors told them, or the government, until they could find as many sources as possible to get at the truth.

So Marley and Laney went hand in hand down the hall to a bedroom whose door was conveniently out of the line of sight of the living area lens. In the bedroom they waited until the hidden camera there, whose movements they had studied and now could decipher, was turned to one wall, and then they quickly rearranged the pillows on the bed to look like sleepers and slipped into a big walk-in closet, all by the time the camera's eye swept back. They had disappeared in their own house.

In the closet, Marley slipped two metallic lab coats with hoods over Laney and herself. She slid open a panel that revealed rough and pitted aluminum stairs and began to climb down with Laney, pulling the panel shut over her head. At the bottom she keyed in a code and opened a door into a bigger room. It was their own family storage room, and it had a locked door leading into the deeps of the Combs.

In the Combs, Marley's family had a life outside the eyes of the police. Many other families did, too.

The Combs was never more than twenty feet deep. In some sections it was a single spacious hall; others had two levels with a ladder between them. The space extended all the way around the colony between the outer hull and the inner. It was made, among other things, of the dead—packaged and labeled and racked in special rooms.

The Combs also housed the colony's shit, pardon, the sewage, freeze-dried and bricked. And its garbage, what wasn't recycled or composted, though that wasn't much. And left-over mining debris. These were the components of the interior partitions, the ceiling of the inner hull, the lining of the outer hull. It was a giant receptacle for anything and everything, as long as it performed the one essential thing: shielding the living on the other side of the double hull from space radiation.

This led to health regulations forbidding human entry. The protective shielding also meant the Combs couldn't be electronically surveilled, at least not easily. Not that the government didn't try, with hardwired cameras and audio bugs as well as with robots and humans (suited up). But manpower being what it was, they couldn't keep up. So the upshot was that the colonists had a place of their own most of the time. The builders had packed everything in, leaving lots of room for more dead and more waste. Then, the colonists slipped down and rearranged all of it, under and around their habitats, and had their secret life. And watched to see if they would turn green, or if the protective gear would be enough.

The Combs were creepy. It wasn't just the radiation and the snoops. The Combs were haunted, everyone said. What had made Marley think of that? She paused to listen. Nothing unusual among all the sounds of the Combs—the whooshes, and tinkles, and chimes, and low bellows, and deeper, under all, the space hush. Nothing electronic. And nothing haunted! Right? She glanced at Laney, but he hadn't heard anything to worry him. Laney could hear things in the Combs.

Nothing can hurt us if God is with us, Marley thought, as she unlocked and opened a cupboard while Laney watched.

The cupboard held the most special things Marley's family possessed. She carefully unwrapped one of those treasures from a folding case of leather: a chalice of solid gold. Another Catholic had made it for them when they'd first come to the colony, out of the abundant mining ore that was, early on, almost completely uncontrolled. Then, both gold and platinum were just tumbled in with the less-prized metals on Earth and sold at the same price per weight, less than real meat at the commissary.

But its precious metal wasn't what made the chalice valuable, even when gold was rare. It was valuable because of its use in the liturgy. Marley's family had commissioned this chalice in anticipation of this special day, and now it was happening.

Marley unwrapped a second object and laid it beside the chalice. It, too, was gold, and gleamed like a small, burnished sun in the low light. It was a paten, a special plate on which to place the unleavened bread that would become Christ. The chalice would hold the wine that would become His sacred Blood. The secret words Christ uttered first and then gave his apostles would be pronounced again, and matter would be transformed. It was magic. Yes, Catholics admitted, we believe in this magic.

Shortsighted men protested, but they had been wrong in so many ways. They could not explain the appearance of life itself with its incredibly complex DNA, for example. They tried to say it happened by chance alone, no designer necessary, even though their own statisticians tried to tell them the odds of that happening were greater than the number of atoms in Earth's whole galaxy. One in a trillion trillion. Or, in other words, not likely. Not even conceivable. Better look for another explanation. Yet, the blind materialists persisted. It was important to them that man's measure be the only measure, the range of man's senses be the only measure.

In the ancient ritual known as mass, Christ Himself would be offered to His Almighty Father in reparation for the sins of mankind. It was how mankind had been saved by the cross. It was how mankind continued to be saved. Mass gave ordinary people the strength to be good.

Marley paused and whispered all this to Laney. She did not offer to hand him the objects, or to touch them. They were sacred. Soon and hereafter, they would be in the care of a proper priest, and no one else would touch them.

Next, Marley unwrapped the candlesticks and the beeswax candles. They were very costly, having come from Earth. Beeswax, really? But it had to be. There had been consultation of the old rubrics, and finally the difficult answer was, yes, it has to be beeswax—and also real bread and real wine.

These items were necessary for mass. Long ago, in a desert on Earth, God Himself had communicated His Way, the requirements of worship, to His little pets, the Jews. By means of burning bushes and big winds, God had linked their survival to the survival of bees, in that their liturgical candles should be of beeswax. There was no getting around it.

When Christ fulfilled the Old Law and established Christianity, this relation came forward: men and bees; must have beeswax. And now look, even here on the colony, far from Earth, bees in no gravity. They were thriving in the ag pods. But the beeswax for these particular candles came from Earth, Marley knew, because she'd set up the shipment. It stood to reason that beeswax candles would have been contraband, because Halliburton was dead-set on teaching them that everything is negotiable—your age, your sex, your status, your diet. *Natural* is a construct; *artificial* is fine. Whereas the colonists, or at least the Catholics there, were making a different assertion, a political assertion that was also a religious assertion: we have a nature; don't freak with it. Oops! Marley was sorry about her language. But she was not sorry about the intensity of her feelings. We have a nature; *let it alone*!

Finally, Marley unrolled the linens that would cover the wide shelf which could become an altar. Yes, it was all there, as well as a small supply of the other elements and objects that were necessary to give the faithful the seven sacraments of Catholicism. They had assembled them from their own struggle and labor and had obtained them from others, black-marketed them. It had been plain hard work, and it gave Marley a grim little smile remembering the many phone calls and errands she and others had performed to assemble these precious items.

"Look, Laney," she said, stooping down to him. "Look! Everything for mass. You don't remember mass, you were too little, just a baby. But now, they told me, a priest is coming. A priest, Laney!" She smiled at him, and he smiled back, even if he didn't get it. A *priest*!

"Laney," she added, very slowly. "We cannot speak of this to others. To no one, right?"

Her little brother nodded, his eyes huge.

Marley wrapped everything back up. She and Laney knelt for a moment in prayer. Then, they slipped back the way they had come, hurrying, every step electric with anticipation. Mass! Oh, happy day! But Marley had a new item on her long to-do list: getting an illegal person past security and into hiding. Surely that's why Tomás had called. That was often her task for other shipments coming on the shuttle. In about, let's see—she paused on a ladder rung and glanced at her phone—three hours. She expected Tomás in an hour or so.

It was the first time for her, a "live shipment." But she knew it had been done by others, and she'd talked to some of them. Because the government was incredibly slow in allowing for the immigration of family members (in spite of all the promises they made during the recruitment process), people took matters into their own hands. Marley had made it her business to find out how.

What she found out was there were lots of ways to get it done, and it might have be easier now than in the past. Each new government administration had been more gullible than the last, until illegal people, and illicit money, and black-market goods literally waltzed through soft checkpoints while the dummies in Administration wrung their hands and mouthed, 'How did this happen? How did this happen?'

Marley personally believed that was a no-brainer: it happened because, since liberalism, the world had denied original sin and so never protected "we the people" from bad guys. Every hack and scheme and theft was discovered too late. Corruption just grew; corruption was the only growth industry *in* the economy. No border held against it. Apparently, space was just another porous border. Yes, it could be cracked, people were cracking it. And now it was their turn to receive a live shipment. Marley's straight, dark brows concealed a storm of plans, and her heart raced.

How to catch an angel?

Is Ferdi the Dude or the Sheriff?

Ferdi and Ray gave up the chase under the arch, at the edge of Honesty Village, and watched the two figures they had been pursuing disappear around the outbuildings on the outskirts of town before the bare rolling interior "hills" of the colony began, hightailing it toward the city in the distance.

Ferdi and Ray had taken chase after catching the two scoundrels knocking over the statue of Our Lady outside the school where Ferdi and Ray were doing a little landscaping in their off hours. It had happened before, the vandals slipping in and toppling her.

Now, Ray lobbed a parting stone after them and leaned casually on the arch, panting, his stringy blonde hair hanging over his face. Ferdi stood in the middle of the road with his arms crossed. He looked very stern, even with a backwards baseball cap, and Ray thought, not for the first time, that he'd hate to be on the receiving end of a Ferdi glare. Nice as the dude always was.

At least the vandals didn't have spray paint—yet. Not a priority on the colony, where almost everything was made from aluminum or rock or glass or sand, or any combination, and didn't need any paint. Paint had not come online, not even on the black market.

Before they'd spotted the guys desecrating the statue, Ray and Ferdi had been spreading several shades and textures of gravel in patterns around Honesty school. It was what passed for colony landscaping, very Japanese. As they'd worked, they'd been talking about heroes and Ray's disappointment in the fake heroes in the old movies that were shown on the colony amphitheater on a screen so big you could see it from Earth, it was said. Now, Ray resumed the conversation he and Ferdi had been having while they worked. Or rather, Ray had been talking and Ferdi listening.

"So, you know, Yoda was an idiot, right, dude? Bad advice! 'If you leave now, help them you could, but you would destroy all for which they have fought and suffered.' What a load of crap! Right, dude? 'Cause that's not even what happened! They all got saved because Luke went! Right? And what about this! 'Do. Or not do. There is no try.' What kind of crap is that, right? *Everything* is a 'try' until it works! What was he smoking? Right, dude?"

Ferdi nodded thoughtfully. They strolled down the main path through Honesty Village. It was a yellow brick road, or rather a manganese bronze, harder than bronze, and cheaper than a vacuum in space. They were surrounded by the bronze metal, and with all that free sunshine, there was no energy cost to mine it. The road was edged with red aluminum, cast to look like pitted stones. The houses were set back from the road, and all had yards around them that one day would be actual grass (like in the pictures they were shown before they'd signed up) but presently were just little green chunks of chrysoprase. It was pretty; somehow they'd managed to capture many flower colors without any flowers!

Asteroids giveth—Ray thought as he looked across the center of the colony, with the trains running right up to it on the spokes that led to the neighborhoods, and on up through the observation windows into space —and maybe asteroids taketh away, if one came straight through that window. It was a worry the colonists lived with. They had anti-ballistic bots on patrol, of course.

A few of the houses had live flowers in containers, though. The agricultural pods—the farm pods, as everyone called them—had put those in early, and secretly, since the world government was very firm that the *Halliburton*'s was to have no frills. And they could enforce it. Halliburton owned the houses, and the farm pods, and the villages; the whole thing was a giant company store. They had insisted on that. If the colonists were going to earn higher wages, they could damn well pay higher rents. That was Halliburton's take on the subject. Still, they were pretty nice houses, you had to say that. Ray was not inclined to quibble. Some people did. They wanted to own a piece of the rock. Ray's temptation was to smoke a piece of it, a temptation he resisted almost always, thanks to good influences in his life.

"Good morning, guys," said a trio of young women in chorus, as they passed Ray and Ferdi, giggling, dressed in the colony's most modest attire, tunic-length blouses over trousers. Often in the course of the workday, colonists passed through the semi-weightless areas of the colony, and skirts alone did not quite work now for modest Catholic women.

Ray slyly eyed the girls as they passed, and then turned and watched them walk away. Ferdi walked calmly on. Generally, it was the girls who turned and watched Ferdi, which Ray observed this time, too—the woman in blue, Kiyoshi's sister. Caught you looking, he grinned at her! She frowned back, but just for show. She gave it up and grinned back at him, and hurried to catch up to her friends. Ray turned and followed Ferdi, who had started walking in the opposite direction.

Ray and Ferdi went back to the school. First, they righted the statue of Our Lady, dusted her off, and placed her back in her niche. When Ferdi knelt to say a prayer, Ray took the overturned urn to the fountain, filled it with water, brought it back, carefully put the flowers back in the urn, and placed it in front of the statue. Then, he, too, knelt in prayer. It was very peaceful there, with the great observation wall of windows wheeling about them and the colony stretching off in the distance. They could hear, not the sound of birds, not yet, but at least the sound of the children playing in the yard at recess. Oh, were they squabbling?

Anyway, it was time to get back to work. Ferdi and Ray both crossed themselves and rose. They walked back in the direction of their work, from which they had been interrupted. When they passed the children, two of them ran over to Ferdi and pulled on his shirt.

They were mad as hornets! The little boy held a red ball, and his face was very red. The little girl had been crying and was sputtering a protest to Ferdi.

"I had the b-b-all and Jermy t-took it!" She burst into tears again.

Ferdi looked at them both and then held out his hand for the ball.

Jeremy complied but not without a protest of his own. "She tulled my hair!" he wailed and burst into tears himself.

Ferdi looked at each one of them for a moment and shook his head. Then, he turned each one around and marched them over to a storage bin. He opened it, took out another ball, a blue one, and held out both balls, one on each hand. Each child reached for a ball, but Ferdi raised them above his head for a moment, until he had the children's attention. He waited. They waited.

Finally, Jeremy looked at his little enemy and blurted, "Sawwy!"

Ferdi nodded happily. He turned his gaze to the little girl.

Blushing, she responded in kind. "Sar-ry."

Ferdi handed them each a ball. Then he and Ray continued around to the back of the building, where they were spreading a new sand area for play. They had already marked out the area with string and were getting ready to do the leveling.

Ray picked up the conversation where he'd left off. "So, dude, like I was saying, all those old movie wise guys, it's bogus! Did you see the one they had last night, *The Karate Kid*? That Mr. Miyagi? Dude, so bogus! Okay, listen, he's trying to get this kid to get some heart and to fight back against these bullies, and, see, the kid hasn't got a dad or anything, and he's a loser up to now in everything. So, to encourage him to study karate, this supposed-to-be-wise man says, 'No such thing as bad student, only bad teacher.' Can you beat that?"

Ray grinned intently into Ferdi's face. Ray was not short but he had to look up. Ferdi nodded in understanding.

"Wish I could play that card, myself," Ray went on. "Would explain my grades in high school, right? Crap! So that's what happened with Hitler and Kaddafi and all those creeps! Nothing a good teacher wouldn't have fixed!" Ray looked thoughtful. "I guess that Karate Kid wise-guy doesn't believe in original sin, like we were talking about before. Huh, Ferdi?"

This time Ray had to look down because Ferdi had stooped and was peering at the line level on the strings they'd stretched. He gestured, and Ray hurried over, untied the string on his end, and repositioned it until Ferdi waved *stop*. Then, Ray began to smooth the sand up to the string.

Ferdi got up and went over to dump another bag of sand. It read AST34451, the name of the asteroid name from which the sand that was originally in the bag came from, but they had long since reused every bag several times. So the packaging meant nothing, except that the sand had come from an asteroid. They were just folding up the bag again when a teacher came out of the school and hurried toward them.

"Ferdi! Ferdi!" she called, "Marley called. Something's happening on the bay dock. She said come quick."

Ferdi and Ray both glanced in the direction of the city and the bay docks. Ferdi made eye contact with the teacher and gestured at the tools scattered about: get these? She nodded and waved goodbye to them as they were already sprinting toward the village. They'd be gathering the posse, she guessed, and bowed her head in a little prayer for them. But it would be okay. Ferdi would fix it, whatever it was.

Laiq Meets Adn

If you saw uniformed police on the colony, something had gone wrong. Normally, all the cops were undercover. It worked out better that way. If the public needed a cop and couldn't find one, well, too bad. So when Adn turned the corner on her way to the docks and ran into the group of young men, she barely gave them a look—until she saw that Laiq was in the center of them and they were actually hustling him along like a soccer ball!

Laiq suddenly stopped, and the men around him stopped, too, in some confusion, trying to orient themselves, trying to see what had gone wrong when they had been moving along so well. First one and then another saw the girl in that stupid Muslim head getup standing mutely, her face pale as a sheet, her hands clasped in front of her. Clearly, it was the perp's girlfriend. Look at him!

Laiq's face expressed everything. He was trying to act like he didn't know her but failed utterly. He looked chagrined and embarrassed. She looked horrified. They stood that way for a moment. Then, Laiq stopped looking at her and raised his eyes to the leader of the four men jostling around him and hemming him in. They were not robots. They had girls. They had hearts, maybe, too. Laiq's face was a study of entreaty: my girl; can I say goodbye? Because they all knew where he was going and what would happen there.

Finally, the head guy—in dark-rimmed glasses, his Monday disguise of a techie, corny, but it was a dumb public—nodded and partially turned away. The other guys saw the gesture out of the corner of their eyes and subconsciously imitated it, some moving more, some less. Then, Laiq slipped between them in one moment and had his arms around Adn the next.

"You'll know everything, can't waste this. Listen …" he whispered. But he stopped; he didn't know what to say! This might be the last time he would see her, this first time he'd held her, if you can believe it! Their parents were strict. How sweet she was, how wonderful to hold her close. Praise Allah for love. What must he say to her, what would last? "Listen, whatever happens, don't doubt that God is merciful." Was that good? He slurred it a little, she caught it and looked curiously at his face.

"Come on, man," the techie cop murmured.

"Don't worry," Laiq said to no one in particular. Then, he kissed her. And in that surprising way (they had never kissed, never once), he passed to her the small, plastic-wrapped cylinder of paper with the asteroid coordinates. He'd grabbed the plastic at the last minute from his snack in the lounge, thinking perhaps they would not search his mouth until they got him where they were going. When, in that case, he'd swallow it. That's what he had thought out. And it had been true, opportunity had arisen, as if God were watching out for him.

Adn behaved perfectly. He knew from that moment on what she would do in a crisis. She would trust him, as she did now, betraying nothing, not her surprise at his kiss, nor the imposition of the cylinder. She acted perfectly the part of a simple woman in love, enjoying a kiss. So bold, so bright, my girl! How he loved her at that moment.

Then it was over, and he never did say a real goodbye. The techie cop took his arm, half-smiled and waved like a friendly techie guy would, and they all moved off around the corner, just a few guys from work, nothing to see here, folks, leaving Adn standing there staring after them.

In a moment, Adn turned and walked away in the opposite direction. Several blocks later, she reached down to her shoe as if to adjust a stocking, shielding her face against her skirt, quickly removed the small cylinder from her mouth, and slipped it into her pocket. Then, she began to walk faster toward home. She wanted to cry, but this was not the time for tears.

Blow It Up!

Sahl was walking to the rendezvous from Sector G. It was the designated time for night in that sector, one of the remote housing pods, an inflatable for five hundred people. The lights in the section were turned low, and he walked through shadows. His steps echoed. Leaks dripped and ran from corrugated metal. There was no landscaping here; that was volunteer work, and apparently this neighborhood had no volunteers. It looked dismal, and Sahl cursed himself for the thousandth time for believing the colony hype.

He especially cursed the Gallup Poll. They asked all those questions in the Gallup Poll: "Would you move in the next five years if you thought you had an opportunity to better the chances of your children to receive an education?" And what followed was hope. Then you did ridiculous things, like moving to England, or Sweden, or the space colony. Son of sixteen whores, that Gallup Poll. And he had fallen for it!

Sahl didn't bother to hide his face as he walked along the catwalk. There were too many cameras on the asteroid to avoid them all the time. He would just say he forgot something—his comb, his card—if he were questioned, if it came to that. Better not say comb, he thought, ruefully, and ran his hand over his balding head. But he didn't think they'd ask him, anyway. Too many cameras, not enough human readers. The bots couldn't do it. The bots thought either everybody was guilty or everybody was innocent. If the distinction between guilty and innocent was too grey, they froze up and needed to restart. The techs could not find the line of programming that caused it. They could not write the code that would fix it.

His hand compulsively felt for the glycerin in his pocket. What would he say about the glycerin, if asked? "*Glycerin* is a thick, colorless, sweet-tasting liquid. Extremely common in beauty products, *glycerin* is also used in explosives." That's what Wiki said. He sure wouldn't say that. "Oh, yeah, see, my wife has a little skin problem; we're gonna blow it off her." Sahl didn't have a wife.

He ducked a little, entering the corridor tunnel to the bays. This was the lazy place to surveil, in a housing unit. All you had to do was concentrate on who came and went. Like shooting ducks, it was mostly about who was sleeping with whom.

So, at least for the moment, he didn't worry about it. His face was forgettable, anyway. His whole character was forgettable. People found it hard to remember if he was Sahl or Sal, maybe he was Middle Eastern or maybe not. Maybe he was Italian, or Spanish, or a New Jersey Jew. Or no, surely he was a Palestinian. Or maybe he was Argentinean. It was hard to tell from his broken-down bald head and his punished nose. He could even be Lithuanian or Hungarian, and he could do all those accents--it had been a hobby. He was just a beat-up kind of a blank.

He didn't have a wife. And he could follow a wiring diagram.

It all made Sahl so useful.

He entered the corridor, a moving walkway, even in the low gravity. Because time equals money and money equals profits on the Bernina Harrison, and it sucks the fun right out of everything. Damn them, Sahl thought, still tasting a little enjoyment from the flying feeling of the walkway even though it only got people to work faster. The corridor opened into the first bay. That was his destination. There, the game was different. There, the cameras were definitely live, and there would be watchers. There is where they kept the mining pods.

Suddenly, he wanted to pull out something and consult it, consult anything! But it wasn't written down. He had memorized it. Yes, of course he had. Don't panic. Then you *will* forget it.

He had only that short message from Adn: "They've got Laiq. Blow up the pod box. Sector seven, station 14, has that orange green logo. You know Laiq's pod, Sahl. Blow it up. Make it look like an accident if you can." And then she was gone, the shielded transmission as brief as necessary. So much she hadn't said. Make it look like an accident? Blow it up how?

But he was supposed to know that, and he did. It had been a long time, true. If he'd been trying to forget, tough luck. It'd been a long time, but it was ridiculously easy, once you knew how. Doing it was not the hard part. Even dying for it was not the hard part. Living with it, that could be interesting.

He closed his eyes, stooped for a brief moment, and looking down, checked his watch. Then, after the camera had swept past, he moved quickly. Again, he waited, crouched low enough, below the line of sight, until the next camera swept past. He repeated the process until, soon, he was hunkered beside Sector Seven, Station 14. And there was that tired orange and green logo on Laiq's pod, a secondhand reject. You got the message every time you looked at it: good enough for a Muslim pilot, in case we lose it.

Very quickly, Sahl slipped to the door and keyed in the code. Just as the door slid open, Mohsin was at his side, like a ghost, and they both entered the pod, and the door slid shut behind them. Mohsin had given Sahl's heart a lurch, but his stealth was reassuring. They looked at each other, shook hands, and turned toward the command center, where the objective of their mission waited: the box that kept the data. The rest would probably burn, too, but by then, the fire-suppression mechanisms would activate. Sahl thought he could make it look like an electrical failure, if the investigators were particularly stupid, which they often were. Lazy sons of donkeys. Fat sons of fart. No, he was not cursing, Mother, he was praying that's what they would be like this time. One more time.

He took the glycerin out of his pocket and held it out in front of him. Mohsin reached in his pocket and brought out the package of HTH, which was not part of the lock-up inventory at the low-gravity pool where Mohsin worked, and gave it to Sahl. HTH was a chlorinator and expensive. And it had many uses. But they didn't lock it up. Stupid!

Sahl held both the HTH and glycerin up to the light and eyed both bags carefully. Yes, the HTH was about three times the amount of the glycerin. That was the correct ratio.

Once he poured the HTH into the glycerin, they had between 15 and 30 seconds to exit before the mixture burst into flame. That flame would probably get them another 30 seconds, maybe more, until the sensors caught the heat and set off the alarms.

Would two minutes burn up the box? Would one minute bring them safely into the corridor with the crowd? It depended on the cameras, the timing. They were going back through a different corridor than the one to Sector G. The shift change should be happening, and there would be traffic. They should be able to blend into the workers going back to the housing units.

Sahl glanced at his watch. Okay, the timing was good, 135 seconds to the shift change. He motioned to Mohsin and then to the door. Mohsin quickly moved over to it and hit the switch, and the door slid open and revealed the walkway beyond. Ready.

Mohsin returned to Sahl's side. Sahl opened the HTH vial and was preparing to pour it into the plastic baggie but stopped when Mohsin shook his head vigorously. Mohsin brought out a piece of brown paper with a wax coating and motioned for Sahl to use it instead. At first Sahl didn't understand. What's the difference? Why paper? Why change from the plastic bag? But then it came to him: sure, the waxed paper was like the wrapping around the wires. Maybe it wouldn't be noticed, but the melted plastic bag would for certain! Sahl grinned at Mohsin and took the paper.

Quickly! They could hear sounds outside. Sahl dumped the glycerin onto the waxed paper, milking the plastic bag for the last few drops, and then poured the HTH on top of it as fast as his shaking hands could manage. It would not have made a passable origami, like in a terrorist movie he once saw, that's for sure. Then, he carefully placed the paper on top of the black brain box, and they both slipped out the door, which closed automatically behind them.

The door would delay the first fire bots for a few seconds, at least. By then, Sahl and Mohsin would be long gone. In 15 seconds, right on schedule the paper burst into flame with a soft little *whoosh*. Two minutes later, the black box was melted. By the time the bots burst in, half the command console was gone, too, taking the motherboard with it. Not an explosion, but that was better. A simple fire. Perhaps from mechanical failure. They would investigate first, the routine steps—at least until it became clear whose pod it was.

Sahl was so grateful when he watched the news and there was no mention of the fire. He had watched all those terrorists-are-so-dumb vids, and he knew that if he and Mohsin had messed up, it certainly would have made the news, for the insult. So they had done well. Allah be praised. Well, he'd owed Laiq, poor bastard.

A Goth Girl's Dream

Stephanie jerked in her dream. In the nightmare, she was naked in the back of the van, where she was about to be raped. She was very fat, too, like she had been, once. The guy had that same chilling grin on his face, and he was telling her: "You're just like me. We're the same. I do what I want, and you do what you want. Ha ha. I mean, you eat what you want, and I do who I want. But it's the same, see? Right?"

That had been the worst part of the whole experience, worse than the rape part, which if you put it in perspective was pretty stupid, given what he had to work with, pathetic. Those *words* were the really awful part. She *was* like him.

Then, suddenly, she was out of the van and out of that flesh, back in the room where she'd gone to sleep, or it looked just like that room. And What's His Name was right there beside her. But there was this angel in the corner, too, dressed like a Goth. Yep, an angel.

She also thought she was crying—in the dream, not for real, no tears on her real face, she was almost sure—because the angel was telling her, "Lament, lament like a virgin." And that was pretty weird, because if there was one thing Stephanie knew for real, in any dimension, awake or asleep, it was that she was *not* a virgin.

"What exactly am I lamenting?" she asked the angel, willing to do what she could.

The angel gave her a look like, Way to miss the point. And then, suddenly, he stood all the way up and looked upward with exasperation, if prayerful exasperation, to the heavens. And Stephanie saw that he was ten feet tall, give or take. At least ten feet tall. Then the angel opened his wings.

Stephanie stopped trying to estimate the angel's size then, being that it was impossible to both size him up and run at the same time. The creature was like one of those Earth reptiles that suddenly opened a gland or a gill, and the sun broke out from its flesh in a great orange garland, and you died from fright, and then it ate you! The wings! OMG! Golden, at least twenty feet wide! Transfixed (turned to salt? because otherwise she would have been so out of there), she zoomed in on the wings, like you can do in dreams: exceedingly fine golden leather with a sheen like oyster shell. *Angel* skin. Very nice. *Had* to be black market.

And what about that outfit he was wearing, with the red cross and the—was it the Horsehead Nebula? And armor!—platinum, triple-grade, she noticed, with an expert's eye.

Oh, Stephanie suddenly realized, maybe he means lament like a virgin. *Like* a virgin. She could do that. So in the dream she began to lament and in the real dimension to whimper into the jacket she had rolled up into a pillow. That woke up What's His Name, and he warned her with a rough hand on her shoulder. That was real enough. The dream effervesced away then, leaving Stephanie with a sickening feeling that the day ahead was going to be some kind of bitter day. And, since those were the only kind of days she had, it felt okay. Whatever. So she rolled over and around What's His Name and arched her overworked body with its piercings and stains like a skinny little rat, and went back to sleep.

In the morning, she wouldn't even remember her angel dream. It wasn't drugs, thank you very much; it was flat-out exhaustion. She slipped into deeper darkness, the subterranean slumber beyond dreams, and left the angel standing there.

The angel slowly deflated. What, again? She *never* remembered her dreams! What good was it to make a plan, then? What a thick little skull the girl had!

God! He remembered his last conference uncomfortably. God had plans for this woman. Big plans. He and God had discussed how to proceed. There was the Merici model, but instead of women climbing olive trees, they'd have to use the big nets in the bay docks, but then it got a little unclear. This situation wasn't at all like the Merici situation; it wasn't like the handful of women they'd elevated onto the ladder in Angela Merici's vision, to bring it home to the woman what God wanted from her. To Angela Merici, heaven was "up there," in the big blue sky. She *got* it. To Stephanie Blanchard, that was the dreaming Goth girl's name, there was no up, there was no blue, and her grasp of the whole heaven thing was vague. To

Stephanie, a bunch of women climbing the nets would just be a bunch of women climbing the nets, like they often do on the mining asteroid. She wouldn't even consider that they might be climbing up to heaven. So Angel and God had decided to try the other model, the one they'd used with Peter and Cornelius, the one that had brought the two men together and brought such major changes to both their lives—the one, to convert; the other, to preach to the gentiles. But would Stephanie get it? No. Would Marley McKenna get it? Yes. Maybe.

Angel's objective was to get Stephanie to Marley McKenna in the right frame of mind. He had to get her there so she might repent her sins. Convert. He'd rather tackle all of Jerusalem than undertake that task, although he knew Marley and had the highest respect for her. But still! Wouldn't be in her shoes with this girl.

Because, these people! He's never seen such a people, and he'd known some stiff-necked suckers over the ages. These people were a whole 'nother kettle of wax, or ball of fish—how did they say it? Curse his dyslexia. But, dear God, listen, these people!

Stephanie was bad. She was not the worst, but bad. Empty. He had no context on with to work with her. She'd never even heard the whole God the Father idea, but even if she had, she personally had no father, null set, emotionally speaking. Fathers were what other, lucky people had. Her mother—the same, from alcohol. Angel knew Stephanie's mother's angel personally, and he knew what their efforts to save Stephanie's life had cost them. Poor little Stephanie, her life so frail after the botched abortion.

This girl, and her people, what a mess. They had no idea of a creator. The angel personally could not conceive of the mind of someone with no idea of a creator—I mean, given a well-designed cell phone, they'd give some credit to the designer, yes? Not these people! Stephanie had not a thing, gratitude-wise. She was starving. She had no hope. She had faith in no one. Every time love peeped up in her poor little heart, she smacked it down. No one loved her, and no one had ever loved her. For all she knew, "love" really was only about sex, which, after all, was sometimes pleasant enough and even sometimes resulted in some pats and hugs, until the guy went to sleep.

Angel didn't know how to give her hope, but that was his job. Oh, the formal job description was more specific: be a conduit for God's grace to this girl, this most unfortunate girl named Stephanie, who had started life all wrong. And for whom God had a mission. Go figure!

Well, why not try again? Dawn was a way off. Angel checked Stephanie's REM cycles, and just as she slipped into another round, while he was flipping through Google's image base, he suddenly had an idea and began a new dream in her little shaved head. In this dream, she could see herself, Stephanie, sitting at the fountain in the square of her colony village. She still had the shadow of the tattooed tear drops below her big brown eyes, but now she looked happy. She was wearing special clothes fashioned more or less like his angel gear—a white nun's habit and a white scapular cinched at the waist by creamy leather, real leather. This was fighter gear, with a red crusader's cross on the chest, so of course, she'd have leather. Directly over her heart was a small rendition of—let's see, the Horsehead Nebula. No, no, not the Horsehead Nebula, he saw in a sudden burst of genius, not the Horsehead Nebula: the Heart Nebula! The Heart Nebula and Our Lady inside it, offering her unselfish, immaculate heart to the universe! It might be the most beautiful representation of Our Lady he'd ever seen! And covering Stephanie's scandalous hair, the crowning touch, was a short, glowing white veil that in gravity fell like an ordinary veil, but in low gravity, floated around her head like a halo. Like those old French sisters, with their starched wings. Lovely! Stephanie sat by a fountain, a pile of lovely modest clothes by her side. She was surrounded by girls in immodest Goth fashions. She was washing their faces, one by one, and giving them the new clothes. They knelt at her feet and looked up at her. Such tired little faces.

At first, they were all Goth girls. He thought that was best. They were so easy to conjure, for one thing—lots of shock, very little effort. One had spikes like thorns coming out of her head in a hellish crown and blood (fake) trickling from her eyes. Another had an ax tattooed on her forehead and an *X* in black tape across her mouth. One had stark white hair and a horrible (makeup) scar running from her ear to the corner of her mouth. Stephanie would know it was all makeup, but the chains they wore were real enough, and she would know that better than any of them, too. Angel had tweaked the Google images to look a little like her friends here on the *Halliburton*, or girls she had known on Earth.

But Angel had other girls, too, not only Goths, in the dream. Because that was part of God's plan. There were Asian girls from the Bernina Harrison, agricultural workers, and techs. Stephanie was washing all their faces in the fountain and giving them the clothes, and after that, their chains and piercings and fake blood and real scars were all gone. They had joined the Faith when they slipped on the clothes.

Those visual details were easy to arrange. The hard part was guessing how it would be reassembled in that human skull, which God had made a no-fly zone for angels, having given the creatures free will. How Stephanie put it all together was strictly up to her. Some people got it. Some people never did. God always kept offering, grace after grace—in dream after dream, in chance encounters, in messages hidden on billboard ads, or in the wind. But not everybody cared to hear, to see.

Not that Angel wasn't happy with the details just because they'd come to him without any great effort! Stephanie's habit had taken thought! It had to be modest in low gravity, and thus, had required a new direction in religious fashion. This habit had loose-fitting pants, not a long skirt, as among nuns of old. The pants were covered by the traditional scapular, though, the rectangle of cloth draping gracefully over the shoulders and covering front and back to below the knees. It was cinched with a leather belt at the waist and then loosely tethered lower, above her knees, so it wouldn't float over her head at zero-G. That short veil was inspired! Angel could not help thinking it stood up well to other habits suggested by his angelic peers over the eons to various saints forming religious orders.

The pants would, of course, raise a small sensation in some parts of heaven, he thought ruefully. Fortunately, God had his back. Angel was only the project manager; the whole thing was God's idea. It was God Who wanted Stephanie to found a religious order to save women on Earth's first space colony, and

He'd been personally interested in the clothing aspect. God, Himself, had suggested the red cross, the old crusader cross, just to show the scope of the job, and then, as an afterthought, the pants--soldier's dress, perhaps that had been the connection, but then it certainly worked for zero g. The Heart Nebula was totally Angel's idea. It was his personal favorite design idea of all time, although his first idea, the Horsehead Nebula, had also been great, he had to admit it. What could tempt Goth girls to virtue so well as a dark, blood-colored stallion in Orion? Right? And yet, the Heart Nebula was even better.

And not nets, ala Merici, but close to it and so classical, a fountain and face washing. God would be pleased. Angel emitted an angelic purr.

The moment of self-congratulation was short-lived because, *oops*, he remembered that Stephanie Blanchard was technically unable to form a women's religious order for the mission of saving women. Because she was not a Catholic—yet! *That* was where Marley McKenna came in. Angel whirled around, and it was a sight to behold, more beautiful than the Heart and the Horsehead Nebulas together. He bowed low and began whispering again in Stephanie's oft-pierced little ear. Quick! It was close to what counted for dawn on the colony. Close to the uptick of lights and the blast of rock and roll that woke the secular villages. They liked to wake to something loud that would drown out the truth.

What Do You *Mean*, They're Gone?!

"What's he doing? What is that?" Julie turned off her mic and asked Al.

"Um . . . he's singing." That was as much as Al knew about it.

The song had just risen up in Tim as he'd begun to move: *Salve Regina*, the hymn to Our Lady the ancient sailors had sung at the end of every day while they were setting up the ship for the night watch. The one that tells her how sweet she is. He kind of hummed it, kind of sang it. It was not the end of *his* work day, but it had a nice rhythm for climbing the handholds, as it had for those sailors singing it at dusk while they climbed the masts so long ago.

Later, after Tim had heard the man's confession in the disarray of the station, anointed him, come back through the grid, after he'd unsuited, after Al had run his story about exhaustion and insisted they both rest in an otherwise empty sick bay without further discussion, after Al had plugged into the system through the terminal in the sick bay and upped the vacuum in the crew's bathrooms just enough to cause an unpleasant toileting surprise—after all that, Tim had a few moments to savor the experience.

He could no longer hear or feel the frequency, the Presence, he'd experienced out there in the grid. But it was inside him now. Like, some people can store the harmony to a song inside them and find the first note after years and years. Anyway, that deep, sweet bass was inside him now. Also, he was fixed. No claustrophobia. He never thought of air now, and he supposed he'd never think of it again.

Then they'd docked, and in the crew's disturbance and distraction over their aggressive vacuum-toilets, Al and Tim slipped out with the rest of the passengers. No one had gotten their names or even a usable camera shot. Hank would take the heat for that. Julie would get promoted.

Al and Tim missed Marley's plan, which never executed because some kind of trouble on the docks had distracted security. So the tall black guy and the smaller white guy just sprinted across the checkpoint with the rest. It was easy. The vids on that scene, when security scanned them later, were useless, too! People had learned to run with their heads down!

Trouble on the Docks

The bay locks were the heart of the work on the colony, and it was work time now.

A hundred or so men stood about the long cargo area outside the security center, waiting for the passengers to disembark from the shuttle so they could off-load the cargo (and incidentally, to pass to crew members whatever precious metals were going back illicitly, always in exchange for the illicit good stuff from Earth). What's His Name stood lounging with the other cargo handlers, considering the economy to pass the time as they waited for the security lines to start up. He didn't have any particular expertise in that area, but it took his mind off that bi— that Stephanie—who'd walked out on him before he could ditch her! No loss. He liked the vids better, anyway. More room in the bed and way less work.

Basically, the man figured, on the subject of economics, the colony officially took in three things: people, sunshine, and a whole lot of rocks. The sunshine was beamed on to Earth from *Halliburton's*, sold to Earth, after siphoning off juice for the colony. Sold it to the colonists, too—oh, at employee discount, right? The *Halliburton's* administration prided itself on that. Transfer of solar energy to Earth was accomplished by a string of mirrors beaming microwaves to receivers on Earth. From a distance, they looked like a necklace of square black sequins hanging in the sky, like on a dress What's His Name's mother had. (Don't get him started on his mother.)

The rocks—the asteroids—were captured in their orbits. The colony's workers surrounded them with gas to slow them down, netted them (that part was frigging dangerous and made What's His Name glad of his dock assignment), broke them up, and then maneuvered the slurry of gas and rock into the *Halliburton's* manufacturing bays. There, in the bays, the materials were processed and turned into water, air, and dirt. Oh, and a thousand other less-common things, metals of this, molecules of that—*most* of which the colony administration knew about.

The people, those willing idiots, were processed into colonists. Of all that mess of work, What's His Name thought, the people were the most trouble. Everybody hated the days when the shuttle landed. Crowds, noise, confusion, accidents. The immigrants made mistakes and screwed up business! You had to watch them every minute, because they hadn't been properly trained—just one training vid is all!—for the dangers of a varying-gravity environment. In his life, he'd been called a lot of things—stevedore, longshoreman, wharf rat. He didn't mind those, but he didn't much like—everybody laughed when he said this, the word contrasting so well with his one wall-eye—no sir, he didn't appreciate being called a *nanny*. And that is exactly what every new crop of colonists needed.

What's His Name's father and grandfather both had been longshoremen when longshoremen earned some real money, back in the day. They'd had a house and garden and all that good stuff, around San Francisco Bay. In Oakland. That was before the shipyards all closed. He'd been lucky, sitting stinking in Alameda prison on a ten-year breaking and entering, when they'd offered him this gig. A job? On the space colony, in the family tradition? Absolutely! Yes, he'd sign where it said if he couldn't hack it or messed up, he'd be back in prison on Earth. Where were *they* going to sign to guarantee Earth would still be there, huh? Tell me that! He grinned at his own joke. Tell me that, huh! His yellow teeth were too big for his jaw.

What's His Name jerked to attention from the day dream and looked at the other men to see whether anyone had seen his dumb smile. Nope. Just standing around, waiting for the shuttle to tie down. Then, they'd have to get all the immigrants' stuff off the ship first. Waiting got old, even to a lazy man. He flipped open his cell and opened his e-mail. He read the latest, from a buddy who'd gotten out of the big house on a regular release about the same time What's His Name had. He laughed at the guy's email ending: "I hope you're still getting chicken every week." Ha! The con's benediction. He laughed again. Just as long as you're getting chicken once a week, things can't be too bad. That's what the old cons said.

Funny thing, that was becoming an issue. There'd been rumors flying all week that the colony was going vegetarian. He didn't much appreciate it. He didn't appreciate being hustled. They offered a man a contract, and he signed it. Done deal. Maybe the contract hadn't said "meat," specifically, but it damn sure hadn't said "amino acids," because he'd have remembered that. It damn well better be chicken amino acids. A man had his limits. At least in prison you had chicken once a week. Don't push a con too far; you don't know *what* will happen. That's another thing the old cons said.

Finally, the bay doors slid open, and the new colonists started walking through toward security. Just then, What's His Name's work mate gestured at the dock vid: the news.

What? Suddenly, everyone was talking, but he could read the scroll at the bottom. Well, I'll be damned! It was an announcement: "The wise allocation of—*buffering*—resources indicates that healthy—*buffering*—vegetarianism is an affordable—*buffering*—option for colony diet." *Buffering*. "The Health and Safety Committee will make the presentation on the evening news." (Couldn't they ever stop that damn buffering?)

What's His Name stood dumbfounded for a moment. All around him men were turning to each other with disgusted faces. So now even cheap chicken was too good for them? These were men who'd known some cheap food. They knew you could grow fat and tired from cheap food, even plenty of it. Too tired for sex. But not too tired for low-grav work. Nope.

Damn it! What's His Name thought angrily, I can do without women. But I cannot do without meat! That's when he reached down and picked up a rock. There were a lot of rocks on the colony, but you can't eat rocks. He hurled the rock with all his strength at the vid. Around him, other men began to do the same. Then they turned on the administrative buildings flanking the checkpoint.

Suddenly, security was streaming in. The bots and security men at the gates, after hesitating for a moment waiting for orders, joined in the fracas. For a few minutes, the new immigrants stood uncertainly on the other side of the barriers, but as rocks started flying from all directions, they began to sprint through wisps of tear gas.

Welcome to the *Halliburton's*. Whoo-ee! Run for it!

Among the fleeing new arrivals were a priest without his cassock and a sanitary engineer without his superman suit. They sprinted with the rest of them, raising their faces only long enough to assess their options, and then they wisely chose a narrow side street rather than the closer broad avenue directly across from the shuttle terminus. The priest and engineer slowed to a walk, made a turn and then another turn, reversed direction to follow a crowd exiting a light rail, and blended into the colony.

But not before Marley, standing at the edge of the dockworkers, saw them. They were coming straight toward her. She immediately spotted the man who looked just like Tomás! And then saw that another guy seemed to be with him. The shock ran all the way down to her toes, partly the resemblance and partly the sudden disengagement of her brain from the plan she'd been so intent on following—to save the guy who, apparently, was already saved and hurrying away from her, walking fast but not too fast.

She'd never know now if the plan—to distract security while Marley grabbed the angel—would have worked, but she didn't care at all. Whenever God wanted to take the controls, Marley was all for it. She made a fast call to inform her provocateur as she whirled around and went after the priest and his companion while pretending to dodge flying stones, with Ferdi and company following her at a discrete distance. They soon left the dock area behind, and she caught up to the pair.

"Hello," she said in a low voice, containing her excitement. "I'm your future sister-in-law. You don't know me yet. I'm Marley." Without waiting for the words to sink in, she grasped his hand and kissed it, old school. A priest was in the house. A *priest* was in the house! (Thank God, the cameras didn't catch it!)

Soon, thanks to Ferdi having deftly managed the whole necessary choreography of the security cameras, they were all at Honesty Village and then deep in the Combs.

It was all Marley could do to arrange for confessions so there were would be no awkward crowds. A priest was in the house! Only Catholics knew the joy.

Sacrifice in the Combs

It was really quite amazing what Tomás and the others had accomplished in only a few hours. A space had been prepared in the Combs, under Honesty Village, of course. They had opened some individual family spaces and joined them into one big space, and made their church. The original entrances remained. That those were also exits and that there were several of them had occurred to most of the several hundred people kneeling in the hushed, dark space. The security risks of the gathering pressed on them all, and they listened closely for any sound that might announce the arrival of the bots with their stunners. Or worse, live troops and perhaps even live rounds.

It was quiet enough to hear everything. Marley, Stephanie, and Laney knelt in the first section, as close as they could get to the altar, with Laney between the women. Neither Steph nor Laney understood what was about to happen, Laney having been just a baby when he'd attended his last mass on Earth, and Stephanie being only lately among the faithful and not even baptized yet.

Stephanie had come to Marley's house after the riots on the bay docks, during the daily rain shower, and stood knocking outside Marley's door with her Goth makeup running down her face. She had never left. Stephanie was glad her old life was over, glad to be here, and glad to have visits from angels in dreams. But the last words from What's His Name had been cutting.

Cutting. Take it from a girl who knew about cutting.

He had hurt her. He had hurt her and called her names, accurate ones, unfortunately. In that moment, she had realized it was all about him and always had been. So much for all that talk of liberation. She had finally seen him for what he really was: a man who sold out on everything. Sex with him was like making it with a hologram.

Actually, *she* was the hologram.

But the angel in the dream had said, "Go to Marley." So she had. It was a decision she'd made, to obey the angel instead of the other option, hitting the kill switch on the dumb girl she'd turned out to be, which would have been easier. She knew how it was done, all right. God, it was worse to be dumb than to be fat. How come she was always getting played?

But she had not hit the kill switch. She'd gone to Marley instead.

Marley's mom had called Marley to come home and then settled Stephanie in the rock garden behind their home, where she sat under a shade umbrella, for camera shielding, not for shade (it was the new feng shui), sipping precious green tea, waiting and thinking.

Stephanie felt so alone. And she hated it; she had always hated it, her entire life. She had traded her body to not be alone, but she had felt even more alone then. And as she'd sat there, in the home of her friend in the middle of a whole village of people who could not be more unlike her, so safe and secure in their families, she felt just how truly alone she was.

But how did you escape your fate? Her family was trash—no other way to put it. They came from trash; trash beget trash, generation after generation. Kicked out of wherever they'd come from, likely (at least she'd left Earth voluntarily). Drunks. Thieves. And lots of whores. Pretty whores, it's true, especially her mother.

But how did you escape, if you wanted out of all that? Because it runs in the blood, it runs deep. Stephanie had sat there under that silly little awning, thinking those dark thoughts, watching the blue blood run in her thin, white, scar-crossed arms—and remembering that angel.

Then Marley had come home and joined her under the umbrella, and they'd talked and talked and talked.

Stephanie had told her about the dream, how she had been washing girls' faces and giving them new clothes. Marley didn't know what it meant, only that it was clear she, Stephanie, should get the heck out of the room with What's His Name. She invited Stephanie to stay with her, and a promise to arrange a room in the single women's house when one was available, where she would be safe.

And that's what Stephanie had done. She had waited until What's His Name had gone to his shift. Then, she'd collected her stuff, wrote "A-hole" on the mirror with black lipstick, tossed the tube in the trash, and got herself gone.

Stephanie had learned a lot since she'd moved to Honesty Village. For one thing, these people apparently believed in angels, for real! In fact, they believed each of them had their own personal angel, a *guardian* angel, they called them, who was always with them. And they spoke to their angels! It was *prayer*, they said. This made Stephanie feel better, although none of *their* angels talked back, apparently, like hers did.

Thinking it over, Stephanie realized she had always known an angel was with her, all the time, not just in the dream. But it was like they had agreed to not see each other.

It explained so many things—like, how she knew certain things that she couldn't have known. The exact time. Directions. What temperature it was! She had a knack for those things. Maybe it was her angel's knack! If so, her angel was apparently good at directions but not so good at cooking. All Stephanie had to do was ask, although she rarely did, except in some freaking emergency, like the time she'd gotten off the train at the wrong station when she was little, a terrifying event that had never left her. Her mother had been drunk when she'd put her on, and forgotten to tell the attendant to put her off in her grandmother's little town. She'd asked the universe for help then, for sure, and even though she was so little, her angel guided her to the right people at the station, and they helped her. But she'd never thought of it as prayer, before. She just kind of squinched her eyes together and said silently, "Please help." Sometimes not silently. Once, she screamed it.

Stephanie had learned from the other girls in her dormitory in Harmony Village that, besides speaking to their angels, they also spoke to God. Their God was not made of anything. He lived in an unphysical dimension. Sort of like anti-matter, maybe. Catholics actually believed in a second reality completely different from the physical one! Well, so do Goth girls! But that seemed to be all they had in common. Compared to her old friends on Earth, her dorm mates on the colony were happy. Nobody expected these Catholic girls to trade sex for anything. These girls were free of all that. These girls were free, period. And that was so funny because it was the opposite of what she'd always thought. Where had she gotten the idea that it was the other way around?

Now, Stephanie was at her first mass, deep in the Combs, where she had never been before. She was clueless. What was going on? All these people were as happy as if they were gonna get ice cream. Laney was all eyes. Marley was radiant. But they were all very quiet.

That's because it was dangerous to be gathered there. It had always been illegal to go into the Combs. But for a religious activity outside the new law? It would not be a matter of a slap on the wrist and a fine. The authorities would come down hard on them, if they were found out. Might even use deadly force!

All ears strained, but so far, all they could hear was the sound of the Combs stretching out beyond them, pings and moans bouncing off a thousand surfaces, and always underneath, the deep bass hum of the great fans that moved the air through the Combs. There were a half dozen exits from the space. Even now, the police could be gathering behind any one, or more, of them. But so far, although everyone was listening for it, no one heard the electric whine of drones coming for them. No one heard any unusual noise at all.

The big room was dark. A light shown on a long, low table placed against the support wall, and elevated a step up by some alum skids they'd covered with real carpet. The table was draped with two pieces of real cloth (you could tell it was real; it was that *luxe* even from a distance), which draped to the floor on each side. The under-cloth was so snowy white it almost pulsed in the gloom.

Marley whispered to Stephanie that it was an altar. Stephanie didn't know what, exactly, an altar was. She looked at Marley: huh?

"For a sacrifice," Marley whispered.

Holy crap! Stephanie thought. Talk about Goth!

"For our sins," Marley added. "We offer Christ to God at mass, for the sins of mankind. Payback. We used to offer goats— I mean, the Jews did—until Christ offered Himself."

Stephanie understood that. Any Goth would. But you had to wonder at the way Marley had said "Christ," as if he were there, part of the conversation.

"Is He here now?" Stephanie asked.

"Not yet."

Holy crap! Stephanie thought again. Oops! Sorry! Ought to clean up my mouth.

But really? *Really*, Marley?

Yet, if anyone had asked Stephanie who was the smartest, bravest, most honest person she knew on the colony or anywhere else, she'd answer, without hesitation, "Marley McKenna." Ask *anybody* on the dock, and they'd give the same answer. If Marley McKenna said that Jesus Christ was coming, well, you better shut up and watch.

Just then, the silence was broken by another treat: the clear sound of a well-metaled bell. (That was one thing Stephanie ought to know, right? Good metal?) All the people turned themselves slightly toward the farthest circle of light, where she could see some figures coming down the aisle. They had on funny clothes, but everyone recognized Tomás and Ferdi, walking side by side, and two other guys from Honesty Village, who walked together, too. But behind them, at the end, walking alone without a partner, was a guy who looked just like Tomás! Stephanie knew the man was Tomás's twin brother, who was a priest and had actually sneaked onto the colony yesterday during the food riot. You had to notice: all guys. Did Steph care? Nah.

As she watched, they began to walk down the aisle toward the altar. It was like a parade; everyone had their place. They were dressed in very interesting clothes. Like robes. Lots of lustrous white cloth—What was it? She struggled to remember. Oh, yeah, brocade. Very Goth. And real cotton! Under all the white layers, they wore black robes that came to the floor. The last guy, Father Tim, was carefully carrying something in front of him, kind of square, not too big, also covered in white brocade. Something to do with the 'sacrifice'?

Marley had told her about mass that morning, in their house. First thing, Marley had said, everyone would say a prayer called the Confiteor, their sorrow for their sins. They said it in Latin, a special language they kept just for God. While they said it, they'd bend over low and hide their faces. After that, the priest would give them absolution. Meant forgiveness. He had the power to speak for God in this matter, Marley said. Father Tim could give them God's forgiveness, even Stephanie, not Catholic yet, provided she was truly sorry for her sins and meant never to commit them again. So cool! Stephanie had thought. It was like washing up your spirit. She couldn't believe she had never heard of it.

Next, they would do a couple more things with water and incense; Marley had explained that this was about making the altar and the space and all of them holy and clean. Then, the priest would read the gospel. The gospel came from information God had deliberately revealed to mankind in the beginning, long ago. We didn't make it up ourselves, Marley had said. God, Himself, had written it down in stone for some Israelites, thousands of years ago on Earth. He had led them out into a desert to get away from the Egyptians who had enslaved them, and then when he had them out there safe, he taught them what He wanted them to do. How to worship Him. It was not for His big ego or anything like that; all of it was to keep them safe. He spoke to them in burning bushes and stuff like that. Not with His real voice or by showing His real face. Too strong for them. Oh, He gave some stone tablets to their holy man, Moses. Marley said it was something to *believe* and *not* something to analyze. Remembering her angel, Stephanie didn't have any problem with that, either.

After the gospel reading, Marley had told her, Stephanie, as a catechumen—A cat what? Stephanie had asked, and Marley had explained, it was somebody still studying the faith, not baptized yet—Stephanie could step outside during the rest of mass. But, Marley said, she could stay if she wanted to, just not go to communion. It was her call, to leave or to stay. What would happen after the gospel, Marley said, is they would get into the heart of the sacrifice. The priest would take some plain bread and wine, bless them, and say a really ancient formula, some powerful words that Jesus had taught them. (Like a spell, Stephanie thought.) With those exact words, the priest would turn the bread and wine into the flesh and blood of their Savior. The priest had that power. Christ had given him that power.

Then, they ate the bread and drank the wine, Marley said. It was a miracle God performed every mass. It was one of His best presents to humans.

But Stephanie had stopped listening. *He's a genius!* She was lost in that thought. Because she knew all about the magic of food. How you took it in, how it became part if you. How you were what you ate. He was a genius! She sat stunned at the reality of it. He gave us himself as food! OMG! And this time she meant it.

After explaining about mass and communion, Marley had stopped and looked at Stephanie. She had expected skepticism, or confusion. Instead, Stephanie looked thoughtful.

"So," she finally said. "There's more, but you can't learn it all at once. So what do you think? I guess you think it's totally crazy, right?"

Stephanie shook her head. People sure were funny! "You're kidding, right?" she answered Marley. "Look around, Marley! If God could create all *this*—" she waved vaguely at the observation window, which they could see from Marley's garden, outside of which galaxies receded in an infinite distance and pulsed like Christmas lights "—then I guess He could do *that*! Right?" She gestured at the picture of bread and wine in the book and shrugged. So, after He made everything, He gave Himself to His friends as magical food? What a concept! Awesome! Stephanie wanted some of that good food. Who wouldn't?

Now they were at the actual mass, and it was happening just like Marley had explained it. Tomás's brother and all the other guys were kneeling at the bottom of the altar, bowed down humbly, and Stephanie guessed they were saying that Confiteor thing.

Bowing her own spiky little head with everyone else, Stephanie whispered, "I'm sorry. I was dumb. I was dumb. I was dumb."

The men at the altar said, "*Mea culpa. Mea culpa. Mea culpa.*"

Stephanie sighed. She felt light and clean, like cool water had spilled over her. Where had this been all her life?

Then, the priest, Father Tim, the bishop of the colony (although Stephanie didn't know what that meant, probably like a supervisor, she guessed) went up to the altar. There, he did some more praying, and he kissed the altar once. Then, it was time for the sermon part. They sat down on the floor; others around the edges of the space could grab a handy box or just stand. Stephanie sat down to listen, too, as Father Tim turned away from the altar to face them.

First, he read something in English, the epistle and the gospel (They all stood up again! Then they all sat down again!), which he said were from the feast of Christ the King. He had a nice voice, young, but confident. Stephanie listened to the gospel and understood some of it, although the language, even in translation, well, talk about your medieval! The upshot: Jesus is a king, not of just the Jews, what they had been going for. No, of the whole universe. Then Father Tim crossed himself and changed to the sermon part. Everyone else crossed themselves, too. Stephanie noticed the people seemed unsure of themselves; it had been a long time since they'd had mass, Marley had said, and many of them had never been to this kind of mass, a traditional one. Stephanie crossed herself, too. Would they mind?

Then, the priest said what a surprise it was to read the words of Christ that established His kingdom over all nations, here, of all places, on a space colony! Speaking of places! He grinned. And when Father Tim grinned, he *really* looked like Tomás! Twins are freaky! Stephanie thought. The people relaxed a little and smiled, too. Yeah! Christ in space! Who would have thought?

Father Tim went on to say that this feast day was particularly applicable to what was going on right now, when mankind was being tempted to mix Christ with false gods and to form a new church. A monster, not the Church founded by Christ, not the one purchased by His Blood, but a new church that denied sin, that made liberty to sin the measure of freedom. And most of all, denied that Christ was king.

Zombies, thought Stephanie. She feared them most. Make us zombies!

"It's just like what Pope Pius XI said in 1925," Father continued.

As if people would remember that far back! Stephanie almost laughed at the thought. But when she glanced at Marley, she didn't seem amused or perplexed by such an ancient reference. Imagine caring what someone said in 1925!

"They promised us peace if we would merge our religions, shoving Jesus and His Church out of our lives. But we can't get peace that way. Mankind must look for peace in the Kingdom of Christ, because only Christ, no other god, is the one source of Salvation."

Father Tim paused and looked out over the people in the shadowy room, lit only by the four little candles burning on the altar. Stephanie wondered if they seemed strange to him, so small, just coming from Earth, where they could probably have all the candles they wanted—huge ones! She scratched the itchy shaved part of her head, and felt a stab of worry about security, for some reason. "This is not the first time we've been asked to honor false gods," he said. "It is not the first time we've been threatened with harm should we refuse to give in. We won't give in. So we must be ready to die."

Well, *now* Stephanie knew why her hair--the part she hadn't shaved--was standing up on end. Dangerous words. Didn't her old teacher call that *sedition*? "But that's how it's always been for Catholics, and we've always been willing to share the cross with Christ," the priest ended. On a happy note, apparently. Seriously, he actually sounded upbeat about it.

Weird, Stephanie concluded. So not Goth, this part. Goths do not die for God, or for Jesus, or ideals like brotherly love.

Wait. She sat for a second. Would I?

Well, would she? Is there a God? Is there *really* a God? Stephanie knew that, back in the day, the scientists had changed their minds about God and decided that gravity and natural forces like that explained the physical world, the way that guy Darwin had said about the evolution of life, just natural selection stemming from the laws of physics. But then, when it got down to the beginning of life, that idea fell apart. They couldn't explain one-celled life, and they totally couldn't explain intelligent life. As old as the universe was, if you did the probabilities, the same math they used for every single other phenom, there just weren't enough years after the Big Bang for the stages of evolution to have happened. Her old science teacher had said that. Stephanie had paid a little attention in school when they'd talked about this because she liked him and it was sort of like a mystery story.

Another thing to note, the teacher had said, is that they could perhaps say that matter itself was eternal, and that had seemed reasonable to Stephanie, anyway. *Something* had to be eternal. But life, he'd said, couldn't be eternal. Why not? Well, because of heat. The Earth had been too hot for life, originally, until it cooled off. So they had to explain how life just "accidently" happened from that point, not even from the very beginning. See? They couldn't use *all* the time from the beginning of the universe to work the probabilities on, only the time from the cooled period on Earth.

And then, from that point in time, they had to have had some kind of swamp soup, or whatever it was, on which the laws of physics, like gravity, could just "'accidently" work. The way the evolutionists theory went, they had to have had gravity plus warmth, but *not* heat—*plus* the right chemicals, like methane and many others—*plus* some kind of jolt (maybe lightening?) that made them join.

But they never found that soup. They found something very different. That's what Mr. Hauser said.

Because, see, digitized microscopes opened up microspace, and they sure didn't find any generic slop there. They found a whole organized world—a whole complicated other universe, nothing primitive about it.

Take the most basic creatures: a one-celled spot of gel separated from the outer world by nothing more than an electrical charge and a prayer is how Mr. Hauser put it. That single-cell creature took the form of a double helix that was more complicated than a cell phone. Codes written in chemicals that gave the creature its whole structure. Codes written in chemicals that programmed the sequence of an orchestration of interplay of physics and chemistry, atoms and electrical charges, resulting in the reproduction of the creature. The whole code, millions of lines of programming, written in various chemicals in certain combination. How did it get there? By *accident*? Pretty funny! It still made Stephanie smile. Like saying the colony had suddenly appeared in near-Earth orbit by accident! But the colony was not nearly as complicated as that single-cell creature!

So it was back to considering design, and for that, her teacher said, you had to select a restore point in the nineteenth century, pre-Darwin, and restart, right? Because life clearly was designed. The science fascists did not find the necessary chaos, Darwin's slop, and they could not account for the too-short time, anyway. The rate of mutation was known. The amount of time was known. Do the math. There was no way life could have evolved out of chaos. Stephanie had thought it hilarious, the way Mr. Hauser had said it. Come to her house! She'd show you some chaos!

Stephanie guessed that was why they had given up trying to kill religion, like now, with what the president was doing. The people couldn't buy it, atheism, any more after the fake science part of it fell apart. Stephanie didn't buy it—and that was even before she'd seen an angel. So, if there was a God, well, he was singular. There could be only one. Room in town for one sheriff only. So, if there was only one God, to act like there was more than one was just a big, fat lie. Deal with it. Even the Prez of the World saw it. After that, Christ was possible and plausible. Besides, Stephanie really liked Jesus, the little she knew about Him. And His love for her was true, if the cross was real. Not like the other guys.

Well, you can either smile or slit your wrists. Oops! Too late! Stephanie smiled her crooked smile. *Okay*, she'd die for it—for Him. Sure.

Then, the sermon was over, and Father went back to the altar.

Marley glanced at Stephanie. Stephanie guessed, then, that the part of the mass for beginners was over and she could leave, if she chose. After thinking about it a moment, she decided to do it old school. She was already a little blown away and shaky, anyway. So she gave Marley a little wave and made her way toward the back of the room, to the exit she knew led to Marley's folks' house, and there she opened the door.

And on the other side were bots and troops!

Silence. The human security force looked at her in surprise behind their shields. Stephanie looked back at them. A second, maybe two, of dead silence.

Quickly, Stephanie closed the metal door, looked for a lock, found none, turned, and with all her breath screamed: "Run! *Run!*"

A sea of faces turned and looked at the new girl with the Goth doo near the exit, yelling. Then, in an instant, they scattered, racing for the exits.

Stephanie ran, too, with the bots buzzing behind her, right on her heels. But when she skidded sideways, the bots went right past her. Their objective was the priest at the front, not some Goth skank.

Run?

Many of those who'd escaped the police found their way to Tomas's big mining pod, where they huddled in the huge hold, stunned by the horror of their new priest being arrested. and wondering what would become of them now. Had they been ID'd, were they next? It was natural they'd ended up at the pod, called POD386 on Halliburton's roster, called by them *Regina Coeli*, Queen of Heaven. Many worked on the pod or serviced it from the docks. In the crisis, it seemed safer there than going home.

The aluminum ceilings of the hold receded into darkness above them, and the walls were shadowy in the distance. The pod was half as big as a football field. It had cost a cool billion and had yet to turn a profit. Demand was down, no matter how much space platinum they could squeeze in. The men and women congregated in one corner, where the crew kept some comfort items on a big table—coffee, tea, snacks. Tomás and Ferdi were in the middle, and scattered around them were most of Tomás's mining crew and Ferdi's posse. There, too, were Marley and her friends, and that Goth girl. They leaned against the wall, or perched on crates, or sat on the floor along the wall. All their faces were sober. They had lost their Church and their priest in the same day. And they'd just gotten the priest!

They were scared. Their ears strained for sounds at the door. They had no idea how many of their identities had been captured when the bots broke in. They didn't even know what law they had broken, what the charge would be. Maybe their only crime was being in the Combs without authorization, or maybe the authorities now called that treason. On top of that, they had a priest in prison. For those reasons, they knew, or at least some of the group on the *Regina Coeli* knew, that their days on the colony were numbered. They also knew they could not return to Earth, except in hiding. They were outcasts—because they believed in something *exclusively*. They believed in an exclusive club. You had to be good to be in it, and they had the nerve to define *good*. And that was no longer acceptable.

Just then, a door opened and a ray of light shot across the group. They winced with dread, but thank God it was only that nice Muslim girl, Adn—Marley's friend. What was *she* doing here? They'd all heard the rumors about her boyfriend, that Muslim pilot, Laiq, how he'd been picked up on some beef. But any friend of Marley's was okay. Marley was better than an optical scanner at reading people. Besides, Muslims were on the wrong side of the law, too. So the group of outcasts turned their attention back to the meeting.

Adn, too, was keenly aware, passing among them, that she was the only Muslim there. She felt them looking at her. No one likes to intrude where they're not wanted. But where else could she come with the coordinates Laiq had passed to her in their one kiss? Only to Tomás and Marley. They were the only two people she knew who might have a chance of a plan.

She regretted bitterly that she could not say the same about her own community, who were gathered in the commons of their village at that very second, arguing fiercely about how to shield themselves from this new attack. And they would argue all night. And all tomorrow. And never arrive at a plan for them to keep their religion and their lives. That meant they would give in and give up their faith. Adn had felt capitulation and compliance radiating from her mother like heat. No, like cold. Because that kind of life was like being dead. Dead among the dead.

Neither would Adn's people even consider trying to spring Laiq. It wasn't that they couldn't hide him; there were plenty of illegals on the colony, just like on Earth. But they were so afraid of the "terrorist" label. They'd thought they had escaped that concern in escaping Earth.

Oh, to resist! But how? But how? Of course, Adn did not want to be a terrorist, either. Nor did she wish to be even *called* a terrorist! Ugly, ugly word. But what alternative did they have?

The asteroid. They had the asteroid!

The tiny scroll lay nestled in the little bag that held Adn's *tasbih*. On that paper were the coordinates of the secret place where they might hide, if they could make it there—to the asteroid in the Oort Cloud. She had not even thought to bring it to her parents or to their own leaders. It would have been purposeless. Laiq was their only Muslim pilot.

So Adn was here. Among Unbelievers. The desire to survive intact, to survive as a true Muslim girl, burned inside her! If it meant to suffer this, so be it. But, oh, the pain!

She glanced around. What a big space! What a fine ship! Laiq's was nothing like. She'd heard that Tomás and his crew had done a little retrofitting off the record, out in the asteroids, treading space between shifts. She was well-stocked, this ship they called—what did they call her? The *Regina Coeli*. But upgrading a pod wasn't unusual. Every crew who could do it retrofitted. Nobody counted on colony administration to save them in the event something happened. They would save the ship, sure, but they might take their time. You didn't have to be Muslim to be thrown under the bus. This ship was well stocked, you could bet on that. Best to have enough of the essentials when you worked on the *Halliburton's*.

All this Adn had heard whispered and then confirmed with Marley. What Adn didn't know, because Marley hadn't shared it, was that the *Regina Coeli* was also armed.

Many eyes lingered on Adn as she passed by them, but they were people she had known to be good and kind. Of course, they were curious and would gawk. When she got to Marley, though, she saw they had turned their attention back to the discussion. She touched Marley's shoulder, smiled, and gave her own attention to the subdued conversation.

"But it could be done," Tomás insisted.

He had just proposed getting arrested on purpose so he would be sent to the same holding center as his brother. Then, he and Tim could break out. Somehow.

Tomás looked around the group. His gaze stopped on Ferdi. Ferdi was always the last vote of every decision they made. Ferdi looked thoughtful.

"Let me just say something, Tomás," a young guy spoke up. It was Augie. His red hair stuck up in all directions. "You know I built that section, right? I know all the circulation ducts and the layout. I know it like the back of my hand." He rotated his square, freckled hand for proof.

"That's right, he did, remember?" Ray offered.

Ferdi smiled at him. Tomás nodded.

"So *I* should go," Augie said.

Tomás nodded again. He supposed they could do something together to get thrown in jail, fake a fight or something. "I guess we could both get arrested," he said out loud.

Ferdi shook his head.

Tomás addressed him directly. "I have to go, Ferdi. He's my brother."

Again, Ferdi shook his head.

Tomás understood: They had two other pilots, but he was the best and he knew the ship. (But why was Ferdi thinking of pilots?)

Then, the new guy, Al, the black guy who had been with Tim on the shuttle, spoke up.

"There's the sewage ductwork, too. I can get the specs off the server, I think." Al had already considered a plan—well, sanitation was his go-to solution, after all. Of course, he might be locked out of the server. Nobody could guess what admin knew, things had been so confusing at the shuttle docking, but for sure they would check the data as soon as they freed up the manpower. They'd sort it all out. Eventually, they'd know that shuttle passenger Albert Taylor, assigned to sanitary engineering, had not registered with department security. Al knew with certainty that they *would* sort it out and lock him out of the system.

Lord, what had he gotten himself into! Mary had always cautioned him about being impulsive! But she'd also always told him to trust his gut. No, she hadn't; she'd said "Follow your heart," or something more refined like that, which seemed to contradict her warning to be more careful, less impulsive. But Al thought he got it. And he'd done it.

"But even if I can't, uh, get into the sysop," Al continued. "I, uh, designed those ducts. So I know them. I ought to go."

Al didn't know exactly why he hadn't checked in when he'd had the chance, after he and Tim had scrambled through the lines. He'd just thrown in his lot with Tim, that's all. Boom! Done. He hoped Mary understood. As far as he was concerned, it was a permanent arrangement. Like family. Just like family. He'd never thought he'd end up with a son who was a priest—and a white kid to boot! One *brave* white kid, you could not deny it. Al could imagine what it had been like to put that helmet on and go into that lock. He, personally, had never faced anything so bad in his life.

Christine raised her hand. Christine worked in the AG pods, Tech Specialist One. Tomás gave her a nod.

"Even if we get him out—and that would involve a lot of ifs, right?—what are we going to do then?" she said. "We'd have to hide him. They'll be looking. Do you honestly think we can hide him? How? Where? You know what they'll do when they catch us. They'll make an 'example' of us." She looked around at them. "Do you want to go evac? Really?" She paused. "Because wolves are back in Germany, my grandma said."

They shuddered. Some countries had already collapsed and had given up trying to keep order or to protect their citizenry. Compared to that, they had it good up here in space. Work, wages, climate-controlled, and younger here than there. Food—well, at least they *had* food.

"Sure, we can hide him. In the Combs," Tomás said.

Christine nodded, reluctantly. "We can shield it from heat seeks and radiation, too, I know that," she added. The drones had heat sensors, of course. "We can make more than one place, a couple. I'm thinking of a couple of spots, which we can talk about. But think what we're risking!"

They all knew the Combs was risky to your health and to your wealth, if you got ID'd by a drone and got snatched. They'd heard stories of people who'd pulled it off, who resided in the Combs. Maybe they were only rumors; nobody actually knew anybody in permanent hiding. But you could see how it *could* be done. Everybody kept any scraps that could be used for shielding, anyway, for their own personal subspaces. People were already doing it and not talking about it.

Ah God, what a cross for Tim, Tomás thought. "Father Tim's a little, uh, claustrophobic, is all," Tomás said out loud.

"I think he got over that," Al put in.

Roy raised his hand. He looked upset. "But hey! Hey! The World Government is really serious about all this, this religion thing, you know they are, because they got nothing. That's the most dangerous time with these people. They're serious, all right. And I-do-not-want-to-get-on-their-shit-list! Hide a *priest*?"

He paused for effect, expanding his muscles as he inhaled. It was some effect. Roy worked out; he could keep swelling for entire seconds.

"Why," he sneered the word, "don't we just try cooperating? For once? The Holy Father was there with the President and everything. How could it be a bad thing?"

Ferdi looked troubled. In fact, the whole group had a constrained look. They always got that same look whenever they encountered Rome's strange cooperation with these forces, these powers that clearly were against them, against the little guy, the flock, the sheep, the low folk on the totem pole. Rome was taking the wrong side every time! Rome shook the wrong hands again and again in the last few decades! Yeah, the pope was at the side of the president when he'd announced the One Religion. At least this time he hadn't been beaming and joking, like the last time he'd appeared with the World President. The people couldn't understand it. It was so un-Catholic. So they got this pained look.

Others, especially Muslims, came forward in opposition to the resulting liberal policies, though. Sometimes in violent protest, sometimes just resistance, like Hungary's quiet revolution, in which an enormous majority of the electorate had changed their constitution to reflect authentically conservative pro-life values, infuriating the whole EU. Rome sided with the EU and denounced Hungary. Go figure! But they couldn't go figure. How could you be pro-life in your teaching and practice over centuries and centuries, and suddenly reject pro-life law? It just didn't make any sense.

But really, maybe Roy was right. Why mess with the status quo on the *Halliburton's*, where you could at least still enjoy a couple perks? As long as you had those dumb dweebs over on the asteroid slaving it out, well, why not? Wasn't it just like Earth?

Judging from the silence in the room, other people at the meeting were entertaining similar conflicting thoughts.

Finally, Ferdi shook his head.

Then, Tomás spoke slowly. "I say we go underground. And keep our own priest, and our own God, our Trinity, and the old faith. *Try* to." He looked around.

The AgTech bunch, Roy and Christine and Randie, looked doubtful, maybe a bit resentful. So did others. But most of the group, although sober at the prospect, seemed to draw together their mental resolve along with their facial muscles. And when Ferdi nodded, they all nodded, too. They would go underground. Like rabbits. So, okay. It was not the first time for their embattled Church.

"So job one is to get Father Tim out." Al brought them back to the task at hand. "I say we rely on stealth, not confrontation." He gestured at Augie. "Me and this fella, and that's it. Me and him can work on the specifics first, and you tell us where we should go after we make it out. Or just me, if it fits the plan better. You'll have to prepare to hide Tim and move him often, right? And you've got communication issues to work out."

They stirred, some looking toward Marley's group, where the communication plan likely would come from. Others looked at Ferdi and his guys; there would be preparations in the Combs for them to arrange.

Then, a voice spoke up from the darkness—a woman's voice, trembling a little.

"There's another way." Adn stood with her hands at her sides, a small figure among them. She looked shyly at Tomás and addressed him personally, almost a whisper. "Do you know about it? About the asteroid?" She watched his face intently.

Tomás nodded. He hadn't told anyone else but Ferdi about what he had learned from Laiq the night he was taken. They'd all know sooner or later, though. Might as well be now. Might give them hope of an eventual way out. If there's one good asteroid, there's probably more.

"What if you went *there* to hide?" Adn asked.

Tomás looked at her in stunned surprise. It was not what he had been thinking at all. The asteroid was Laiq's, for one thing. And Laiq was in jail.

"So you think Laiq would give us the coordinates?" he asked.

"I, well, I—" Her voice waivered. All eyes were on her.

Tomás looked away from Adn and addressed the group. "This is Adn. You know her; she works with Marley. Her fiancé, well, you know he got arrested. He and I talked just before he was taken. He found an asteroid, see, an asteroid with the perfect configuration for terraforming—water, all the elements for atmosphere, and besides—it's in the Oort Cloud."

He waited for their reaction. The Oort Cloud. Far away, but perfect. Far *and* perfect. The Oort Cloud, where a man could get well and truly lost, just disappear in that com-slashing jungle, find a chasm as big as Jupiter and disappear in it. The perfect spot for people who *needed* to disappear.

Tomás turned back to Adn. "When Laiq and I talked, they hadn't synched his box yet. Is that still true? They still don't know the coordinates?"

Adn looked down and nodded. That black box was ashes. Sahl! "They don't know."

"Who *does* know?" Tomás asked her.

"Laiq, that's all." Before she could add, "and me," Tomás had again turned to the crowd.

They were all sitting alertly. They were definitely on the same page. To escape! To take their families, and the supplies they'd been putting away, and some herd animals, and some plants, and their priest, and escape! Oh yeah!

"Then we have to get Laiq out, too. You realize that, right?" Tomás said to them all.

He looked intensely at each of the key players, beginning with Ferdi. Because rescuing Laiq complicated things considerably. Laiq, as a pilot, would be in a different holding facility, the one for dangerous or especially trained or skilled criminals, not the one for the general population, where Tim was. It added a whole new element. It might mean physical confrontation, even mounting some kind of attack.

"We'll have to bust out Laiq," Tomás repeated, his eyes on Ferdi. "And that won't be easy."

Ferdi sat calmly, considering it.

Adn realized she had definitely complicated things. She and Laiq weren't even one of them, one of these people.

"No," Adn said. "You don't have to bust out Laiq."

She swallowed. It was sad, leaving her love in jail. While they, these strangers, some of them even hostile toward Laiq, escaped to his secret refuge, his asteroid. And it *was* Laiq's. God, after all, had led him there. But it was the right thing to do. Her own people could not use what she had in her little *tasbih* bag.

Adn took a deep breath. She raised her head and spoke clearly.

"I have the coordinates."

With that, Adn reached into her pocket and pulled out the tapestry pouch. She unzipped the bag and withdrew a small slip of real paper, a little scroll. They all watched her do it, the glow of her white hands in the shadows. She held it a little aloft so they all could see it.

Then she sighed and handed it to Tomás.

"These are the coordinates of the asteroid," she said. "I did not look at them. No one else knows them, I'm quite sure; Laiq would have found a way to tell me that."

She did not further explain their last few moments together, or how she'd gotten the scroll. She was focused, rather, on the fact that she'd just given away the coin that might have saved her future husband. Why? In Allah's name, why? Because it was the right thing to do. Their lives, these men and women around her, should not be forfeited without necessity. It was just the right damn thing to do, may Allah be praised, please excuse my language. She was addressing her father in her heart. Suddenly, she felt tired, overwhelmingly tired. She was acutely aware, in that moment, of how much her whole body yearned for rest—and for Laiq. Laiq, whom she'd just given away, probably to torture.

Tomás took the scroll and unrolled it carefully. He examined the coordinates, nodded, and then walked over and handed the scroll to Ferdi.

One of Tomás's mates, Hugh, a young guy with a fight-bent pug nose, expressed the sudden relief of all when he said, "Well, that's one problem gone, right?"

They all glanced at Adn to see how she would take it. Adn looked at Tomás. Tomás looked at Ferdi. Ferdi looked thoughtful.

Then, the group resumed the earlier discussion: how to flee?

"So, tell me, are we ready to run?" Tomás said as he glanced around the room at the entire group. "Could we possibly get ready to run? Do you *want* to run?" Then, he addressed only Ferdi, "Is it the *right* thing to do, to run?"

Ferdi only looked thoughtful.

The crowd broke up into intense conversation, leaning over each other to talk with family, friends, work comrades, and neighbors. They'd been preparing for something to happen, they didn't know what, for some time now—stockpiling necessities and trade goods, studying deep-space survival skills, a hobby that engaged most geeks on the colony.

Walt Ferguson was the survivalist expert, as everyone knew, and he didn't hesitate to answer Tomás. A tall, thin guy, he stood up to do it, still talking animatedly to the younger man on his left even as he turned to Tomás.

"We've got the gear. We've got the skills. We don't have the ship." Then, he sat down.

Because the *Regina Coeli* was not theirs, of course! It was Halliburton's!

The group looked in consternation to Tomás and then to Ferdi. They'd had the Regina's use for so long that it seemed like a part of them!

"Well, we could just take it. It's not like they don't take from us." Ray drawled what many were thinking.

Ferdi shot Ray a quizzical look, and Ray looked sheepish.

Several people sprang to their feet.

"That's not how it's done!" Jacob, the dockworker, protested.

"How is it done, then?" challenged Roy, instantly belligerent.

Walt raised his hand. Tomás nodded. Besides being the colony's go-to survivalist, Walt also was the resident expert in theology. He had been a seminarian way back.

"It has to be done God's way," he said. "This is what Saint Thomas taught about it; I'm remembering it. He said this in the *Summa theologiae*, that all choice of bad means—a bad means is doing a bad thing—for any end whatsoever, good or bad end, is bad. Period. Always. *All* choice of bad means. It doesn't matter if you mean to do good with it. It doesn't mean if you plan to do *major* good with it. Let's see, I think he cited Romans III—

that 'damnation lay in saying that good may come from doing evil.' Something like that. I'm paraphrasing."

Walt paused to look around and then added, "So you can't rob a bank to give to a worthy charity. That's a bad means to a good end."

"And you can't take a ship that's not yours, even to escape," Tomás summed up the situation.

Still, Ferdi looked thoughtful but said nothing.

Bill, the engineer, objected. Bill was a reliable guy, too. "But didn't Saint Thomas also say that in case of necessity, I'm talking about survival, I think that by *necessity* he must have meant survival, a man could steal to feed his family?"

As Bill sat down, many were nodding in agreement with the sentiment Bill had expressed as well as of their approval of Saint Thomas. Their acquaintance with Saint Thomas and the *Summa*, however, was slimmer than their acquaintance with Bill. Most eyes drifted to Tomás and Ferdi. Ferdi gave no sign of decision.

Finally, Tomás said, "Well, it's something we have to pray about, right? We have the coordinates. We could run. Maybe we pray that God gives us a ship to run with."

Now, Ferdi nodded.

"Back to matters at hand: how to bust out our priest. And Laiq, of course," Tomás added, turning momentarily to Adn.

She looked surprised, and then grateful, and then joyous! Had he just said they were to bust out Laiq? Oh, Allah be praised!

"We have to, because he knows the coordinates," Tomás said.

Adn looked confused.

So he explained, glancing, as he did, with raised brows at Hugh, who hadn't thought of it. "Laiq knows the coordinates—and they'll know that."

Then, Adn realized what Tomás was saying: of course! Laiq knew the coordinates. Adn hadn't thought of it because she was sure, completely sure, that he'd never fold under pressure, not even under torture. In fact, she was so sure it that it had not even crossed her mind.

Whatever! They were going to bust him out! So Adn looked happy, really happy, whereas everybody else just looked tired, and thoughtful, and ready to do what had to be done. Even the ag techs were on board now. They all had plans to make and a long night ahead. If they didn't have a direct role to play in the rescue, they had some knee time to put in, begging the good God for a ship, a ship like the *Regina Coeli*, or for any other solution, or for an argument that would permit them to steal. One thing about Catholics, they believe God has big ears. Many had already pulled out their rosaries. You could say *everyone* got down to work.

Adn, personally, thought they would run. Personally, she knew God would send them a ship.

And she and Laiq would be on it.

Elma is Short for *What*?

Why was everything always so much more difficult in the real world than in school? Elma almost swore when she hung up the phone and stared at the view before her.

As one who shared the office suite of Graham Fletcher the Great, she enjoyed an expansive view: the private observation window behind her desk looked out over her own little slice of heaven. Ahead of her desk she had a central shot of the huge colony observation window, with Earth on the left half, the mining asteroid on the right, and at dead center—wow!—the Milky Way glittering like a bling watch. Beyond, stretching away in the margins, was deep space, with wheels of galaxies like old-fashioned rhinestone broaches set on velvet. Besides all that eye candy, Elma had the inside view of the whole interior of the colony, breathtaking, because Graham's office suite floated high above the villages of *Halliburton's*.

She hated it.

She *hated* it. She should have known she'd hate it. Why hadn't those mandatory college field trips to the outbacks of Earth been enough to teach her! She'd hated that, too, the dust, the putrid latrines, the sun beating down, the rattlesnakes. And she'd hated being the only girl—only woman. Anyway, that's what she'd *thought* she hated.

But she'd loved the way the words rolled off her tongue, the magical terminology of geology: obsidian and agate, magma foam, placer, poo gold. And it had not occurred to Elma, even though she'd hated most of the places on Earth where the liquid or adamantine riches lay buried, that she'd also hate space, which seemed at the time to be the opposite of those dusty and over-bright badlands. But now she knew. It was not the rattlesnakes she had loathed about her major. It was the emptiness.

Sure, the classroom work had been fun. Wonderful. Nothing like sitting comfortably, laptop on well-breakfasted lap, dimmed lighting, gorgeous slides, and that attractive TA who offered private office hours. She'd had straight A's, and she'd collected two degrees, a bunch of football mementoes, and a boatload of student debt.

Who knew it would end in actual *work*?

True, she'd chosen the colony job. It was better than her only other offer, with that mud-logging outfit in Midland, Texas, once again the only female, training with a 300-pound fundamentalist Christian ex-con in a trailer. So, instead, she'd ended up being Chief Geologist on Earth's first space colony, sharing a space not much bigger than the trailer in Midland with a guy who was a whole lot skinnier, a whole lot richer, and just as fundamentalist, in his own sick way.

He *did* smell better. Graham. Gra-haaamm. Make it British. He did, but he was from Detroit, which was made much of in the many biographical vids.

Very big deal for her, right? Not! The only thing that stood between Elma and those poor Asian bitches on the asteroid was her degree. Her two degrees and her 4.0 GPA. Because, otherwise, the geology profession, colony-style, was all about maximizing profits by increasing the work rate. Every worker on the mining asteroid wore a wrist monitor that told all—every breath, every rest, every fart—while ice chunks as big as New Jersey were coming dead at you. It made rattlesnakes seem positively pleasant. Elma did everything she could to stay off the asteroid. She shuddered just thinking about it.

Fortunately, she had a second assignment. Elma was also the colony treasurer, and it kept her indoors. Indoors with Graham Fletcher, but what could you do?

Most of the time she could bear it.

She poured another cup of coffee (real, none of that ersatz stuff in this office) and sat thinking about the phone call. That was really funny. Stephanie, all saved! And wanting a pod! A *pod*! As *if*! But you had to hand it to the girl for nerve!

Elma had known Stephanie on Earth. They'd both had the problem. That's how they'd met, in Weight Watchers. Then Stephanie had gotten raped, and OMG, that had changed her! Besides the physical violence, the guy had said stuff to her that made Stephanie completely freak. So Stephanie had lost the weight, like overnight. *Boom!* That's when she'd started to hang with the Goths. She and Elma had lost touch then. Meanwhile,

Elma went paleo and lost the weight, too, got the second degree, and took this job in outer space because, hey, it was preferable to Midland, Texas. Can I get a witness?

Then, unbelievably, Stephanie was here! A mining tech, but not on the asteroid; on the colony docks, safer, decent pay. They didn't hang, but they touched bases pretty often. Elma really liked Stephanie. You just couldn't help it. You could stand there and watch the world break her heart. You just wanted to put your arms around her.

Elma had to thank her own dark stars (for once) that Stephanie had proved faithful to their friendship, which, in this environment, meant being close-mouthed about their shared adventures. Elma was sure Stephanie still had some old vids they'd taken together, party scenes at a favorite dive bar. One in particular. Stephanie could have done some damage alright, but she never had. Maybe this phone call would break the pattern. This time, for a change, it was Stephanie who needed something, and maybe some pressure could be implied.

Elma was usually—okay, *always*—the needy person in their relationship, which was funny, given their actual positions on the colony. It had always been like that. Was it their names? Elma had thought a lot about names. *Stephanie Blanchard*, for example—just so white bread, so American, so safe. Like *Graham Fletcher*. No baggage, no bad luck. Her name?—not so much. She'd been told her last name had a story, as if pronouncing it wasn't drama enough. It came from way, way back, some ancestor who'd become famous for something, which then became her last name, the way names happened back then. Her last name meant "little kiss" in Croatian. Elma could guess what it *really* meant, what that long-lost ancestor was *really* famous for. But perhaps she was just projecting.

Talk about baggage. Your name, like fate, you could not escape. It was a weight. Even if you immigrated somewhere farther than the farthest outpost on Earth—somewhere, in fact, weightless. You would still be Elma Ljubić. You *bitch. You-*bitch. Ljubić. People jumped when she introduced herself. And not in a good way. No one had ever *once* asked her if they, uh, heard that right?

Elma would have changed her name if she thought it would help. But she knew it wouldn't. The damage had already been done; the heart stake lay deeper, in the blood, in the cell, passed on from many, many centuries. She owned the name. It owned her.

Well, back to the phone call: true to that girl's lucky name, old Stephanie was on a roll, at least emotion-wise. She sounded what Elma could only admire: happy and calm, sweet and sure. She'd quit sleeping around, she said right off, and moved in with some kind of born-again Catholics. She was loving it. She was learning Latin. She'd quit cutting!

She just needed one little thing: the title to a pod. That is, pod386, and was there any way Elma could help her, as the treasurer?

Title to a *pod,* dear lucky Stephanie? You mean, one of those billion-dollar mining pods?

But Stephanie had an idea. Didn't they have that buyout program, where a qualified pilot could get title on a government-backed lease-option deal? Wasn't there a cooperative ownership arrangement? Could she check on it?

Steph was right on the first thing; Pods had titles, alright, just like cars and airplanes. And yes, there was that buyout program. Earth had insisted on it. They'd needed that cover, because Halliburton owning *everything* in outer space was such a tacky giveaway to the rip-off.

Nobody had ever actually *gotten* one of those billion-dollar ships. You should see the application procedure! All the pods still belonged to Halliburton, that's how Halliburton liked it, and were self-insured by Halliburton, of course. It was Elma's job as Treasurer to keep track of the insurance. The titles kept track of themselves. There was no maintenance on a title because there was no renewal and no tax collected, not on the pods or any other darn thing Halliburton owned in near-Earth orbit. Outer space was quite a write-off, as it turned out.

Steph hadn't shared why she wanted title to a pod, to this particular pod, and Elma hadn't asked. So, she assumed, it was shady. So? Stephanie Blanchard had always hung with one wild crowd or another. This, of course, beat all for magnitude. Had to hand it to her for guts.

"Elmo! Skull session!" Graham Fletcher's rich voice summoned from his sanctum.

Ah, the day begins. She gathered a couple of folders in one hand and grabbed her coffee cup in the other. She nervously brushed a strand of dark hair back from her face with the wrist of the hand not holding the coffee, bonking her ear with the folders and managing to spill the coffee too. Oh great! She took a deep breath. Meeting with Graham Fletcher was like falling into something dark that made her dizzy. She felt sick.

Staying off the asteroid was her goal, though, and that depended, logically, at least, on her doing the treasurer's job well. But Graham made it hard. He'd given her a list of responsibilities and then made it practically impossible for her to fulfill them, putting up one stumbling block after another. Not the least of those obstacles was her complete lack of training in accounting, not that that was an unusual condition on the labor-starved colony. But it was almost as if he wanted her to fail. She could never tell if her success in staying away from the asteroid would be measured by how little her treasurer's projects succeeded or by how much.

A game was in progress, but she didn't know its name or its rules. She only knew she hardly ever understood anything Graham said. He was supposed to be a genius. Maybe that was why. Or not. Maybe he was hiding something. She got the feeling it was the latter, and it made her stomach hurt. Because, of course, she'd find out. And then what? Then she'd be dead. Assigned to the asteroid. Death was waiting for her there, she knew it. Yes, it was superstitious. Yes, it was ignorant. But her great-greats went back into deep, dark places, and they had been able to feel the future. And so could Elma. Unfortunately.

Graham was facing the observation window when she came in and swiveled around to flash her a smile that celebrated his implants, not Elma.

"How was your weekend?" he asked.

But Elma had learned, by then, that his inquiry into her well-being was entirely rhetorical. So she gave the expected featureless answer, to which he did not respond. Then, she sat down gingerly on the armless aluminum cube by his desk and waited.

If she came right out with her agenda, he would take offense, and that offense would come in the form of refusing to listen to or to read any item she put before him, all of which were "actionable" (his favorite word this week) and all *her* responsibility. She had to pay for his ear. The payment was to listen to whatever self-promoting story he'd seized upon that day. He began today's tale, about his first tech job (which had been showcased in the documentary; everybody in the world had heard it for Pete's sake!), while Elma watched an imaginary tennis match that kept her face alive and neutral. Finally, he finished his narration, stretched languorously, and turned a bored gaze on her.

"So what do you have for me this morning? Let's hope it's at least entertaining," he drawled.

Elma handed him the first folder. It held the draft of the shareholder's quarterly report. Her heart raced a little faster as he scanned it, but it was only a autonomic reaction to the little game she played. Every report she gave him had a deliberate error. It gave him something to correct, but it was something she controlled. She really hated doing it. It went against her upbringing, which was probably faulty, emphasizing honesty as it had. Maybe her upbringing should have emphasized survival instead. Maybe she was just being a stupid Good Girl. Anyway, that's why her heart beat faster every time. Deception, however harmless, even in self-defense, just felt wrong. But she had to play the game. To keep her lousy desk job. To stay off the asteroid. On the asteroid she'd have to wear a monitor like everyone else. Then there'd be no more hiding the heart-beat.

"Uh," he said, pointing to page three. Right on schedule. "Uh, you forgot Sector Thirteen."

"Thirteen?" she dutifully responded and, damn it, blushed.

"Time analysis," he said. "Page three. It's not populated in Sector Thirteen. Didn't you count the sectors, at least?" He rolled his eyes.

"O-M-G!" she squealed dramatically. "I can't believe it! I'll fix that right away. I've got the numbers right here, see? I've got the numbers!"

She took the folder and fumbled around in it for the loose sheet she'd included. Of course, he was way too egotistical to notice the coincidence. She thrust the data sheet at him, which he took as if it were offal, found the numbers with his colorless dead eyes, handed the loose sheet back to her, and continued to look at the report pages. Seconds ticked by. He was on a roll this morning. It was the longest she'd seen him concentrate in weeks. Guess meth had come online at the colony.

"Okay, this insurance item," he finally said.

"Yeah?" she said. Her heart was racing!

"Uh. Look, why label it like that? Look what you put: 'Insurance Revenue from Asteroid Fire.' I mean, Elma, need we *fuel* negativity, with so much of it all around us?" He permitted his eyes to flick over her. "Negativity, Elma," he lectured. "Negativity."

"But that's where the revenue *came* from," she said.

She could have a heart attack right here. She was sure he could see her heart beating through her dress.

"It means we got a profit of, let's see," he squinted at the print, "three point four-seven percentage points—from a fire. And then you think of people hurt, and let's see, didn't we lose, uh, three girls in that fire? It makes the profits seem dirty! And a fire means somebody screwed up, and did that somebody pay? Inquiring minds! Now, why remind stockholders of all that?"

"But that's where the revenue came from," she said, more weakly. Of course she didn't want to remind them! But since that's where it came from, that's what she had called it.

"Let's see if I can help you." Graham put his fingers together in a pyramid and pursed his everted, ugly lips. "Let's see ... Oh, I have it!" He smiled in beatific self-congratulation. "Call it, 'Revenue Enhancement from an Involuntary Conversion of Fixed Assets.' Got that?"

He paused, again smiled gently at himself, what a genius he was, and waited for her to write down the words. She controlled the impulse to roll out each word as she wrote it with as much sarcasm as Monday morning and a hangover could manage, but she repeated it just once and sans interpretation: "Revenue Enhancement from an Involuntary Conversion of Fixed Assets." Then, glancing at him quickly, she added, "On the Bernina Harrison Asteroid." And then, "On Galactic Time 13.24.00."

"Lose the date," he remarked. "They might Google that." He handed the folder back to her. "What else you got for me?"

Elma handed him the second folder and again her heart raced. But not because she had left a poison tidbit for him to find in this folder. No, this was a different risk, her own project, her own attempt to do the treasurer's job for realies.

"I have to make the Treasurer's Annual Report, in two months, you remember. You asked me to comply with company standards and to prepare an analysis of our procedures on the colony. I think I've uncovered a problem."

His eyes flicked briefly at her. "Yes?" He waited.

Did he, or did he not, want her to fulfill her responsibilities as Treasurer? Her clue would come next! Although she might be struck dead for it!

"It's an item under Operational Risk."

He raised his eyebrows at her: explain.

"It's on the Financial Risk tree," she continued.

He frowned.

She hurried. "It's supposed to work like those loans that administrators can get for development. There's supposed to be a second signature as well as an automatic update within six months. You know, a follow-the-money trail."

He was squinting at her now.

"We don't have that." Here it goes: this was like taking a breath at the bottom of the pool. "You've made six of them in the last two years. We should have had six reports in. I mean, if we're following Halliburton regs. And it's the world regs, too." She waited, resisting the urge to count up out loud: One, two, three, four, five, six ...

"So?" he mocked. Then, he shook his head and said in a patronizing tone, "You've really geeked this one out, Elmo. Don't you have enough to do?"

"Well—" It fell on her neck like a weight. She knew what she *should* say next, what a real treasurer would say: let's prepare those reports and update our procedures book. Like we're supposed to. Instead, she said, "Well, what should I say if they ask?"

"Let me think about that," he said. "Because they haven't asked."

Several beats passed. He looked in the vicinity of her face; she looked in the vicinity of his.

"By the way," he finally continued, "Thinking about the productivity digits . . . the asteroid, that's your geography, Elm. I'm wondering if you wouldn't better serve the colony in that capacity for a while. Over there. That would make shareholders happy. Don't you think, Chief Geologist?" He turned his colorless eyes full on her. It took all her courage to sit upright and keep from screaming. Here: the face of evil.

"Yes, sir," she said. She could hardly breathe.

"So don't worry about it. I'll tell you what to say, in due time." Mercifully, he looked away. "Now, I've got *zero* cycles left this morning, Elmo, and you've used up yours. Same time next week?" He smiled at her.

She threw a shaky grimace in the direction of his desk and hurried out.

Elma slumped at her desk staring into space for several minutes. Suddenly, she sat bolt upright. She slowly blinked her eyes and set her jaw, as the look of despair on her face morphed into one of resolve.

Squaring her shoulders, she keyed some entries into her machine and printed out a page, on precious real paper. She signed it and stamped it with her official Treasurer's seal. Then, she picked up her phone and texted.

"Steph, come by. I've got something for you. Meet you in the courtyard in a half hour, okay?"

Elma resumed staring out at the emptiness of space. A snatch of a song ran through her mind: "I do what I can / 'cause I am what I am." She tapped her fingers to the beat and thought of her agenda. Before Fletch the Great Liar knew what'd hit him, she'd be outta here. On the next shuttle back. She'd probably face charges. Technically, though, they would find she had not violated her authority. Handling that fake buyout program was in her job description. She hadn't abused any parameters for the program because Halliburton hadn't set any, having no intention of ever implementing it. So she wouldn't go to jail. But she didn't think she'd be working in her field anymore. She'd be waiting tables again. Thank God, she still remembered how.

Rome Finally Gets It

In the end, miraculously, everyone had escaped the raid on the mass in the Combs except for the priest, Father Tim. The drones had not functioned well in the shielded Combs, and they had neither killed nor stunned nor arrested any of the parishioners. The men and women who had gathered for mass knew the Combs very well, and after the first moment of panic when that Goth girl screamed, everyone took advantage of the many small byways and exits. Eventually, they all had emerged from the Combs, and realizing the colony was in a state of distress and distraction, had simply slipped on home or reported for work. Some of the workstations were closed. So at first those people went home, too, shaking their heads. Eventually they'd headed for the *Regina Coeli*, hungry for news and uneasy at home. Although many bots roamed the neighborhoods, they were apparently scanning faces for something else, because no one was questioned or arrested.

The people were not as distressed as they might have been in earlier times, when they were new to the colony. In those times, any little thing that went wrong was cause for great anxiety. After all, they were in a great emptiness in which they would die if certain critical actions regarding air and heat—which were difficult for flawed human beings to deliver even under the best of circumstances—were not performed by certain people at the exact right time, in the exact right place, and in the exact right way. Always a little miracle! But little by little, they had come to realize that space was no more and no less frightening than many places on Earth, and it was possible to survive with just a spacesuit and some oxygen. There were places to escape to, if you had any form of propulsion. You didn't have to be helpless. If there was major disruption on the colony, whole sections of it could be sealed off. It was designed that way. Engineers were not inclined to be liberal, and they had *forced* Halliburton to protect its workers.

Marley was one of those who ended up going home to Honesty Village—and to Tomás. The docks were closed because of the riot. Maybe there hadn't been enough drones for the job in the Combs because most of the bots were too busy managing the Chicken Riot. That was how some people were referring to that mêlée. So many arrests had been made at the riot that the holding centers were completely full.

 Tomás and Ferdi had placed an urgent call on the shielded network to the Vatican. Until then, no one on the colony had ever called the Vatican. But Tomás figured it was the right place to report that their new bishop had been arrested on the *Halliburton's* in the act, the very act, of celebrating the Holy Sacrifice of the Mass. No one knew whether Tim had been charged with illegally holding mass, or with violating the prohibition to go into the Combs, or both, or what. The end of 'religious liberty' was so recent that they didn't know which charge might be worse. In any case, the Holy Father should know about the arrest. Perhaps he could find out the charge more safely than Tomás or Ferdi could.

 First, though, Tomás had asked a few other people to meet him and Ferdi at Marley's apartment: Ray, and a friend of Ray's, and Joseph Edcore, who worked in Administration and was a lawyer and a Catholic. Joe knew colony law. Maybe they could get Tim out legally. They had no such hope for Laiq. Prosecutors would call him a terrorist. Terrorists had no rights, and the term had no definition. They could hold Laiq without charging him with anything.

 So, then, they had placed the call to the Vatican by simply looking up the number on the interwebs, and were now waiting for it to go through Google. It was almost dinnertime in Rome. The vidphone connected. A man in a clerical collar peered at the screen.

 Tomás stepped forward. "Uh, is this the Vatican? Is this where I can reach the Holy Father?"

 The man, the priest, continued to squint at the video screen. "Who is this?" he finally responded. Then he glanced around the shadowy room where he was seated. He was nervous. He turned back to the screen, and his face, an Italian face, looked very drawn and tired and frightened. Yes, he was frightened! Their stomachs clenched. Perhaps things were about to get worse, when they had so hoped they would get better.

"This is Tomás Monaghan. I'm calling from the *Halliburton's* space colony, and I have an urgent message for the Holy Father."

The priest's eyes widened. "My God, man! We were just talking about you—I mean, about the situation."

"About the situation? Do you already know about it?"

"Uh, which situation are we talking about?" the priest replied. Before Tomás could respond, he waved his hand and said, "Never mind." He sighed deeply. "I am sure the Holy Father will take your call. I'll get him now, if you'll excuse me." He looked away, and his face changed. He looked ten years older, and afraid. "It might be a moment. We're—expecting company." He left. The screen blinked on an empty room.

They waited. They thought about what the priest might have meant by "which situation," and that they "expected company."

Suddenly, the Holy Father seated himself, leaned forward, and peered into the camera, filling the screen. They could see more than they wanted of his pores and nose hairs. When the pope saw the colony group on his screen, he drew back and smoothed down his hair. The colonists seated in front of the screen in Marley's living room glanced at each other in concern.

"Holy Father," Tomás began. He didn't know what to say, and so the first urgent and immediate thing came out of his mouth. "We're calling you because, well, Father Tim, who you sent to us, has been arrested. And we don't know what to do."

The pope did not look as surprised as they had expected. Several expressions passed over his round, cheerful features, but none of them were surprise. He put his hand over his eyes for a moment. Then, he asked them, "Where is he being held? And what will you do? What *can* be done? Do you have a lawyer?"

Practical questions. Tomás felt comforted. Just what was needed!

The Holy Father continued, "Tell me about the situation there. What is happening? What are they doing to you?"

Tomás looked at Ferdi and Marley and the rest of them. They could chime in anytime! But they were leaving it to him. So he went on. " Yes, we have a lawyer." He gestured at Joe Edcore, who leaned forward into the camera. "They told us this morning, in the Civic, I mean, the transmission from Earth, that everything had changed. You know about that; you were there. They said there was going to be one religion, which was the culmination of all existing religions, something like that. So we're not supposed to celebrate our religion any more, but Father Tim had come, and we'd waited so long, and so we had mass. And we're not going to obey them, anyway!"

That last part was hard to say. Catholics were well aware that it was a sin to defy legitimate authority. And hadn't the Holy Father been on the platform that morning, right with the President of the World? Wasn't that like saying it's not a sin?

No one else chimed in, but they'd all nodded when Tomás had finished.

"What should we do, Holy Father?" Tomás added. "We'll try to get him out of jail, of course. But what must we do about the world religion?"

The Holy Father was first concerned about his priest. "What does the lawyer say about the arrest?"

Joseph leaned forward again. "Your Excellency, Joseph Edcore here. I need to find out the charges. Then I can go from there." That would have been his answer to the same question in any circumstance—no matter who asked it, where, or why. The law was the law, on Earth or on the colony (at least he hoped it still was!).

He was shocked when the Holy Father shook his head.

"I know what the charges will be, Joseph." The pope suddenly looked sick. "It will be—treason. That is what they said when they called me."

Treason. A hanging offense, as they said. No more of that, of course. All by injection.

"They *called* you? You already knew?" Tomás asked. But he was thinking in horror of that word, *treason*, and what it meant for Tim.

"No," the Holy Father said dreamily.

Was he drugged? It crossed Tomás's mind briefly.

"No, they did not call me about Father Monaghan. They called me—because they are going to charge me, as well. And the charge will be treason, as well. They mentioned him, though. To say it was the same charge." The pope looked down then. "I, too, have defied them, in the name of the Church. Since the announcement. They did not tell us what we had gathered there for."

But they had, Tomás thought. They surely *had* told him at other ecumenical meetings, of the many the Holy Father and his recent predecessors had enthusiastically attended. Not paying attention to *those* meetings is what had brought them to *this*.

But, *treason*? The colonists were stunned. It would apply to them all!

"But what happened, Holy Father?" Tomás referred to the sell-out, the Vatican's long capitulation to secularism. Tomás knew the Holy Father's answer would implicate their decades long strategy.

Because, the whole One World Religion thing was the logical consequence of the Vatican's cooperation with evil since the last century. Many theologians had predicted this very thing, but not a word of response from the Vatican, and suppression of good men. The dread of the inevitable future had fallen on the faithful, and resentment had built over the decades as the false demand for religious liberty turned into its opposite. Traditionalists had tried and tried to tell Rome. They had blogged and petitioned and prayed. Now, Tomás was settling a score by asking the question, just as Tim had with the bishops gathered in his Florida living room.

Everyone in that room with him knew very well what Tomás meant: because you were there, Holy Father, you were on their side, what happened to that? Not just on the platform today, but for three generations, at least, the Catholic Church had taken "their side"—the side dictating that all religions had to be equal and equally invisible, that no religion could use the "coercion" of truth, could "pretend" to have the truth, could elevate itself, could demand compliance to a code. Yes, the Church and the pope had been there the whole while, agreeing, complying, and asserting only that no matter the belief or system, the important thing was to realize that each man had a "dignity," a transcendent dignity that is his, by nature. That is, all men had that dignity whatever their "beliefs" and subsequent behavior, and all states had to recognize it, and that would be sufficient for peace and happiness. Whether they were socialist, or fascist, or monarchist, or Islamist, or witch doctor; whether free market or regulated, free love or married, deliciously gay or laboriously faithful, a kind employer or a slave master. It would be enough to recognize the personhood of the individual, and everything would be fine. Just fine. No church had to insist on its teaching, its saviors. People were naturally good when left alone. That Original Sin belief stuff was old-fashioned. Oh how it had hurt them to hear it denied. Because anyone could foresee the consequences!

Rome occasionally argued back. True, Christ had said, "I am the Way," but those were *His* times. That's how they had argued. *Times change*, you rigid dummies! On a smaller Earth, one must adjust. The Holy Father had been there all along. Five popes had been there all along. Those were their arguments to change the Church. That is what they had been thinking. And see where it has ended up! What a load of garbage it had all been.

"What happened?" Tomás repeated, speaking for them all. It was a reprimand, and he spoke for tradition.

Perhaps the Holy Father knew what they were thinking. He swallowed hard. It took him a moment to answer. "They lied. I told them so. They lied to me!" His face was the face of a chastened man.

"Holy Father, there is something else." Marley diplomatically, mercifully, changed the subject. "A new development. There is an asteroid; it's in a special place. We think we could get there and be safe, Holy Father. They don't know its location, we're pretty sure of that."

The Holy Father seemed lost in thought. Perhaps he had not heard her. Perhaps he didn't know what an asteroid was.

They were suddenly aware of a commotion in the room at the Vatican. They heard a crashing sound, and the Holy Father turned as a hand reached out, perhaps the Italian priest, taking his arm urgently. Then, they heard another crashing sound, just as Tomás managed to say one last thing.

"Holy Father, what should we do?"

The pope turned to the camera and leaned forward. Just before the screen darkened, he said clearly and firmly: *"Run!"* And then he was gone. Google hung up.

Hello, God? Are You Sure I've Got the Right Guy?

As cells go, this one was not so bad, Tim thought. His frame of reference, of course, was *monastic* cell, not *jail* cell. As an ordinary priest and as neither a monk nor a felon, he had never actually been in either kind of cell, up to now. This jail cell was new and clean. But it was small. And it was locked. And there were no windows; the air was perfectly still. Tim could remember a time when that would have freaked him out.

So would have the plastic handcuffs he had worn until about 30 seconds ago, when they had just fallen off—*poof!*—after an angel had waved at them. A minute before, that same angel had smacked Tim on the shoulder and wakened him, and then waved at the cell door, and it had opened. Now, the angel stood in the corner looking back and forth between Tim and the open door—at Tim and back to the door, at Tim and back to the door—like a big, good dog.

Before this, Tim had seen angels only in dreams, rare dreams. Of course, he had dutifully, his entire life, said the ancient prayer to his guardian angel, and celebrated with the Church the feast days of the great angels mentioned in the Bible—Saint Raphael, Saint Michael, all the archangels. He knew the story of Lucifer's fall during the battle that took place in heaven. He had learned about devils, about their continuation of the war, especially at the hour of a person's death, about their hunger and thirst for human souls. But Tim couldn't say he'd actually *felt* angels. Nor *heard* them, exactly. Nor *seen* them with his own two eyes. Or even in his *mind's* eye. They were creatures of another realm, like anti-matter!

There was a woman in his congregation in Florida, though, who'd often reminded him about the benefits of devotion to angels. She sent her own guardian angel to people, she'd told him once, with the instruction to hug and kiss them, if she thought they were sad, or when someone was hospitalized, or facing a challenging day at work. More than once, not even when he was at prayer (when you might have expected it), Tim had felt an unexplained flood of well-being, and it made him think, had Mary McInerny sent her angel?

Then there was this thing with Tim and machines. When he and Tomás had gone through their go-cart crazy days, Tim had a knack for mechanics. It was sort of like his hands knew what to do. Hard to explain—but not a bit hard to recognize. He ruled at the sand-lot racing track that Tim and his brother and the other kids had laid out in their back field. He could just fix things. And privately, it had crossed his mind—since he knew the scant extent of his formal knowledge of engines and brakes and bolts—that maybe his guardian angel was just into cars! Tim's hands just knew where to put the English on a wrench.

Tim thought of his guardian angel often. His mom had seen to that. He and Tomás had one of those old pictures from the catechism on their wall; their mom had clipped it out and hung it above their beds. It was just a cheap print of a popular old illustration, the one with the angel in a white dress floating above a little girl and boy crossing a bridge over a raging river, and his hands are stretched out and lightly touching both their heads. The Guardian Angel prayer was written in curly script right below the picture. Tim had said it every day. He still did, although the picture was long gone. "Angel of God, my Guardian dear/ to whom His love commits me here/Ever this day be at my side/ To light and guard, to rule and guide. Amen."

In fact, the night before, Tim had tried to use his good hands to help him find a way to escape from this cell. He had felt and probed every corner, since his hands, providentially, were handcuffed in front of him. But he had discovered no breach. Then, after he lay down on the cot, he had a dream about Saint Peter, the time Peter had been captured and imprisoned in a cell, and his chains had just fallen off, just like that, and he'd walked out of the joint. There'd been an angel. Just before dozing off, Tim had remembered the epistle from the mass commemorating that event, August 1, it was, *S. Petri ad vincula*, Saint Peter in Chains, from the Acts of the Apostles. He remembered it very well.

Herod the King, the epistle said, "stretched forth his hands, to afflict some of the Church." Herod had killed James, the brother of John, with a sword. Then, he went after Peter.

"Now it was in the days of the Azymes," the epistle noted the period precisely, when Herod had "apprehended" Peter and put him in a prison guarded by "four files" of soldiers, intending to "bring him forth to the people" in the morning, to parade him in triumph, of course. "Here's your great leader, you stupid people." Subtle, Herod was not.

The epistle continued. "Prayer was made without ceasing" by the people for their Peter. That night Peter was "sleeping between two soldiers, bound with two chains," with more "keepers" outside the door, when "behold an angel of the Lord stood by him and a light shined in the room, and he, striking Peter on the side, raised him up, saying: 'Arise quickly.' And the chains fell off from his hands."

Tim could remember it exactly, word for word, it was so dramatic.

"And the angel said to him: 'Gird thyself, and put on thy sandals.'" And Peter had done that. And the angel had instructed him to put on his cloak, too. And Peter thought it was a dream; he was sure it was a dream. The epistle records how he thought he "saw a vision." In the dream (because at that moment Peter was still thinking it was a dream), they passed right out of the prison, and they came to the iron city gate and passed right through that, too. As soon as they passed through the gate to the street, "the angel departed from him." And Peter "came to himself" and went off in search of his people. It hadn't been a dream at all!

It was comforting to remember that epistle, under the circumstances. Tim had hoped his own flock were praying for him. He, personally, had not prayed for an angel. His prayers before sleeping were only to bravely face whatever came. Police had ways to get information or to get you to deny what you believed, and he could only pray for the strength to resist, as the martyrs had. His prayers had focused on that.

After he slept, Tim had dreamed of Peter and this prison, where Tim was being held. He dreamed of two soldiers sleeping right outside his cell, dressed in their navy blue colony-police jumpsuits, which they wore only on official duty inside, never in the street. Tomás had told him that. Actually, no guards had been stationed outside his cell, only cameras.

In the dream, Tim had clearly heard the prayer from the mass: "O God who didst loose the blessed apostle Peter from his chains and didst make him go forth unharmed, loose, we pray, the chains of our sins, and in thy mercy ward off from us every evil."

He had been repeating that prayer when he suddenly woke up, and he woke up because an angel had socked him. Smacked Tim right on the shoulder and not too gently! Nothing dreamlike about it.

Or was it? Sometimes dreams seem very real. But *this* real? Everything around him seemed to be quite normal and logical: his feet (in the black socks he'd put on that morning—yesterday morning, now) were on the floor, all two of them. And he had one head, he felt it gingerly, and two hands. And nothing was spinning or misty. Everything normal. Except that angel standing in the corner.

He could suddenly appreciate Peter's dilemma. Yeah! Not so easy to tell the dream from the real. But this seemed so real! He was pretty sure this was real! It *had* to be real! There's no way his imagination could come up with the details of that angel standing over there in the corner! Could it?

It would help if the angel would say something. But the angel was silent. Tim imagined the angel did not speak to him because there were cameras. Maybe the cameras could not see an angel but could hear one? Or maybe the angel knew where the cameras were and was standing out of range. Anyway, Tim knew what the angel wanted. He didn't *have* to say it. The angel wanted him to go through that door.

Oh, forget the "out of range" theory, because now, cameras or not, the angel was walking over to Tim and leaning very far over him, with his powerful pale arms straight down at his sides, his fists clenched, and staring with great intensity into Tim's face. The angel seemed to be experiencing a moment of doubt about whether he had the right man! Apparently, what Tim had learned in seminary about the instantaneous nature of angelic cognition had a couple of gaps. Not all *that* instant! Because Tim saw genuine perplexity in the angel's face. Angels were scary, especially close up! They stared into each other's eyes for a long moment.

Slowly, the angel stood upright, still staring hard at Tim's face. Now, Tim got a really good view. The angel almost touched the top of the ceiling, plus it was barefoot and wearing a dress, just like in the old pictures. It had gunmetal-gray wings folded neatly against its back and skin so pale not even the Goths could have achieved it. This was your textbook angel! It was human in form, at least its holographic rendition (because angels normally occupied a non-material dimension), and it clearly came from the mind of the same Designer who'd designed humans and birds and things—you know, the symmetry template: the two eyes, two legs, two wings model. But way taller!

But that was only the design. Tim felt strongly that he and the angel--were different. As different as--he searched for it, as water from air, or matter from anti-matter. And the funny thing, the angel was taller, maybe more beautiful, but not *better*. He had felt it, locking eyes. And it matched the theology: men were created in the image of God, but not angels, it didn't say that about angels. What that meant he hadn't a clue, but he felt it. Another difference: some men sinned, some angels sinned. But only men were forgiven. Bad angels were damned eternally to hell--but at least they ran the joint. Tim had to think, he almost laughed, we don't have to look for aliens in space--we already found them! Angels!

Suddenly, the angel turned toward the door and gestured for Tim to come. After a moment, Tim shook his head as if to clear it, looked around, stuffed his breviary into his bag, checked his pockets for his rosary, and followed the angel. They stepped out into a shadowy corridor. Tim was sure there were cameras, but they clearly didn't worry the angel. They moved through two dim hallways, quickly and quietly. Actually, the angel glided, but then, there on the colony, where, as Tim had already experienced twice, gravity could be adjusted, that wasn't as startling as it would have been at home on Earth. *Anybody* on the colony could glide, given the right gravity.

They came to a security door, and by then, Tim figured it would open with a wave, and it did. On the other side of the door was a room with a desk, over which two men in navy blue jumpsuits were slumped, sound asleep. One of them snored gently.

Tim's fingers tingled with tension as he tried to control his breathing and make no sound, painfully aware of the thunder of his pounding heart. The angel approached each man and gazed into his face intently. The older man suddenly snorted and jumped, and Tim's heart leapt in his chest, but the guard only adjusted his arm under his head and slept on.

The angel glanced around the desk, and then moved to the lockers against the wall. He gestured, and one opened. He reached inside and took out a T-shirt and a jacket. He removed a coin that flashed like gold from his pocket and placed it on the locker shelf. Then, he handed the clothes to Tim. Apparently, a little adjustment of the script. Tim was wearing his cassock, possibly not the best apparel to escape in! Tim unbuttoned the top of the cassock, pulled it over his head, put on the T-shirt (advertising a heavy metal band, he noticed), tucked it into the black trousers he wore beneath his cassock, and folded the cassock into his bag.

The angel moved toward the other door in the room, and Tim followed. The lock on that door was more complicated, with a keyboard to enter a code. After the angel examined it, he made a triangle with both hands over it, and the door opened outward. The angel gestured for Tim to go out.

Suddenly, they were out in the street, and the lights indicated the time was dawn. Tim glanced around and saw a couple of early-morning pedestrians. He turned right as casually as he could manage, pulled up the hood of his jacket, and followed them. He glanced back at the angel. It was gone!

Tim remembered the last prayer of Saint Peter's mass: "Now I know in very deed, that the Lord hath sent his angel, and hath delivered me out of the hand of Herod." Yep. Yeah. Delivered. *Deo gracias*. And thank that angel, too, Lord.

Then, like Peter, Father Tim set out to find his friends.

He passed another rather larger group of people, all hooded, anonymous colonists. He pressed closer to a closed shop so they could pass by, and one of them glanced up into his hooded face and suddenly turned around. She tugged on his arm and exclaimed, "Father Tim!" and her hood flew back. And he saw it was Marley. Marley!

The group surrounded him and swept him up. Then, they turned right around and went back in the opposite direction, walking quickly as the dawn fully bloomed on the *Halliburton's*. They had gotten their priest back, without even a fight. *Deo gracias!*

License and Title, Please

The colonists were praying the rosary in the dark. The rosary was the Catholics' most desperate of prayers. *Mary! Mama! Do not desert us! Help us, dear Mother of God*. Over and over, the prayer asks for victory, or if not victory, then courage.

They were kneeling in the dark in the pod. It felt safer there than in the Combs. There were guns on the pod, and if they were attacked, they would use them. They had discussed it briefly but, hopefully, thoroughly enough. Saint Thomas had come up: what did theology teach about self-defense? When was it legit, when not? If you were defending yourself, your family, your neighbors, it was legitimate. Besides hand guns, they had the ship's laser cannons, which were normally used for rock mining but could knock a drone out of the sky. The tools for profits were also tools for defense; it could not be helped, or Halliburton would have helped it. The Catholics hiding in the pod had only one big entrance to defend—the main airlock—and they knelt close to it in the bay, so they would hear any commotion outside and have the guns only a step away. Meanwhile, their best weapon was already in their hands: fifty-three beads and a cross. That's how they saw it.

The group included both men and women as well as kids scattered amidst the adults. The colony's head librarian knelt in the first row with her old wooden beads—worth a lot, now, there on the colony. Among the colony's Catholics, she was legendary for her hard work on their behalf, fighting for education funding when Halliburton wanted to treat them exactly as it treated the machines, like profitable tools rather than people with living brains, spirits, and souls.

Also kneeling up front was at least half the colony's medical staff, some still in uniform, and they were the best half of the bunch, the ones who could be counted on shift after shift. Never absent, not complaining. The best ag workers were all there, too, those who had a way with plants. And the good techs. There, too, were the really good maintenance men, and the mechanics with good hands, and the best teachers, and the most skilled toolmakers—the colony's only toolmakers, for that matter, all two of them.

Apparently, Catholics filled key positions, and if *Halliburton's* management knew who all was there praying on their knees to be delivered from the political mess that raged outside that air lock, they would have been right there on their knees, too, praying to keep them. But, of course, Administration would never pray, would never kneel down to God, and in their litany of equalities would never acknowledge their dependence on key workers. Oh, they would have been there, alright—with clubs—had they known where to find them. Clubs or jail cells or fines, their tools. Somebody should rename the ruling liberal party Neanderthal.

True, some Catholics were missing. Some, like Roy, the ag tech, had made it pretty clear they wouldn't go along with resistance. The people there could only add them to their prayers—that they wouldn't talk! And they probably wouldn't. It never paid to get too close to management, unless you were willing to join them. Others were missing for different reasons, at work or still at home in the village, which had suffered some attacks by the hooligans continuing to riot throughout the colony.

Word was slowly getting out that some colonists were defying the plan the president had announced. The Catholics were going to fight it, that was one rumor. So attention began to focus on Honesty Village, even as news of struggle woke up others all around the colony. In most villages, in fact, people were making aggressive plans—to take over communications, to shut down key colony functions, to commandeer the oxygen, to hide in the Combs. People had had enough! And the colony was far enough away from Earth to do something about it. What would Earth do then? Blow them out of the sky? Maybe they would.

The Catholics in the *Regina Coeli* hold, though, were only praying for help, any kind God cared to send. They had no plan. There were so many variables. Their new priest was in jail. There was that asteroid everyone was whispering about, the secret asteroid with an incredible profile. But they had no ship of their own.

They would like to argue that they could steal this fine one, given the state of emergency. They weren't being killed, though; they couldn't argue that point. No one had a gun to their head. Yet. Oh, the temptation, though! Tomás had all the operation codes. He had the code to change the code, and no one in Administration had that code; their own coders from Honesty had taken care of that, first thing, along with the codes for the air locks and everything else on the ship.

But perhaps Tomás could work out a way to buy it? The men and women kneeling there were not entirely without financial resources.

And there was still, always, the possibility of a miracle.

So they knelt and prayed.

They had worked their way through six decades, all the Joyful mysteries and up to the second of the Sorrowful. The man leading the prayer, Augie, that red-head, had just begun it in his Aussie drawl—"The Second Sorrowful Mystery, the Scourging at the Pillar. We ask for the Fruit of Purity. Our Father Who art in heaven"—when the buzzer sounded at the air lock.

They froze. Everyone looked at the monitor: a group, not clear who—.

Before they could quite make it out, the air lock suddenly opened by itself! Oh, it was Tomás, Marley, Ferdi, Hugh, a couple other guys from Tomás's crew--and the priest? No! The *priest*? Had to be; he wasn't wearing a cassock but he looked like Tomás. Yes! The priest! Quickly, the group passed through the lock, and the door slid shut behind them. Then, they turned jubilant faces to their fellow Catholics. Thanks be to God! Thanks be to God!

The group didn't interrupt the rosary to explain. They just took their places among the kneeling people. After a moment, Augie took his rosary and gestured toward Father Tim, who had knelt beside him, pointing to the second decade, and whispered, "Sorrowfuls." The priest took up the task.

The rosary had changed, become one of thanksgiving, instead of petition for Tim's release. One problem down, perhaps the heaviest one. Mother Mary, help us with the rest! They felt more confident, as would anyone whose prayers had just been answered and as would Catholics whose prayers are led by a priest, a man chosen and ordained by God to offer the sacrifice that saved the world every day. Their "other Christ," as priests were called. To baptize them, and forgive them their sins, and lead them in prayer, and bury them. Their priest was back where he belonged. They sunk into the prayer. It was almost like a current running through them, like something had connected and turned on.

Suddenly, the buzzer sounded again, shocking them. Again, they looked with apprehension at the monitor.

It was the Goth girl, Stephanie. She wore that same bored expression all those girls had—mouth open, chewing gum, eyes glazed. And she stood with one hand on her hip, flipping her bright-colored hair, glancing up now and then at where everyone knew the camera would be mounted. She was such a cute girl, with such sad eyes. You just wanted to make her smile.

Hugh glanced at Tomás, who nodded, and he got up and went to the control panel and opened the lock. Stephanie came in and squinted to make her eyes adjust to the dark, and then she spotted Tomás. Stephanie unzipped her jacket and took out a paper. Her dark eyes got very wide. She kept her head down but walked slowly over to Tomás and handed him the paper. He had to get up and go over to the control panel's glow to read it. Stephanie ambled behind him.

Tomás's eyes scanned the paper and scanned it again. He looked up at Stephanie in disbelief.

"Is this for real?" he asked quietly.

She nodded with the same open-mouthed, bored expression. But suddenly her eyes brightened and her slack jaw broke into a big grin, a real smile, and she was a thousand times cuter, if that were possible. And the whole assembly smiled with her, without even knowing the reason, just happy to see her smile. She had a dimple!

Tomás looked at the paper again, and then at the girl, and then at them all.

"It's the title," he announced. "All signed and stamped. It's official. It's the real title. To the *Regina Coeli*." He shook his head in disbelief. "We have a ship!"

Tomás paused and glanced at Ferdi, who nodded, and then again at the rest of the faithful gathered there. Hardly a word need be said. It was done. A small band, but a great one, and it would be larger soon as word spread.

"Let's get Laiq, and let's get gone." Tomás paused again. "After we finish the rosary."

He put the title in the console of the control panel, where the manifests were usually kept. Stunning. How—? But he didn't have time to think about that. However it had happened, the ship was theirs now. Now, quickly, they had to stock it. And run!

Goodbye, Goodbye

Adn threw clothing into a sack while her mother stood in the doorway watching her. She had never looked more beautiful. It hurt Adn's heart. Oh, my mother! How will I live without you?

"Come with us," she begged, still packing.

"But it's crazy, Adn, dearest. Listen to me, darling. It's nonsense! I forbid you! I forbid you, do you hear me, Adn? Wait 'til your papa gets here!"

"No, Mama. It's not crazy. What's crazy is to stay here! And you and I know that Papa lets me make my own decisions, anyway. Come with me! We'll be safe!"

"Come *with* you? Come to an *asteroid*? Start all over? Leave our *home*? Leave our village? Leave our *own* people? Go with *Catholics*?"

"Mama, the administration is going to take the village! It's over, can't you see? I wish it weren't, but it is. The new religion is not our religion, can't you see that? On the asteroid, we'll be able to continue practicing *our* religion."

"That's what they say," her mother said. "That's what they say. But they just mean their religion will rule! Catholics will rule. And Islam will be in the shadows on that asteroid of theirs."

"But it's *real* Islam, not a made-up one. All of them going are real religions—Catholicism, Islam, Buddhism. To each his own, our own traditional faiths. No made-up religions," Adn said.

"What difference does it make?" her mother protested.

"I don't know. I don't know," Adn said. She shook out a headscarf, folded it again and put it in the bag. "It's just different from a made-up religion. They can't change the rules on you just because they want to. A made-up religion can't be right. No true God! What kind of religion is that?"

"How do you know, Adn? How can you be so sure?"

"I just know. Besides, I know Marley. There's nobody better! She says we can live our Muslim life privately and safely, with no harm."

"And you trust her? More than you trust me? You'd leave your family for people you barely know?" her mother wailed.

"I'm not leaving *you*; I'm leaving this God-forsaken place, Mama. They're going to get Laiq out of jail, and then Laiq and I are going to make our life together. We're going to have children and love them. How could we do that, the way it is here? This place is crazy! And I do know Marley! I know I can trust Marley—with my life. You just don't find that often. Maybe it was easier for you, in your time."

What could her mother say? It *had* been easier, when she and Adn's father were young. This world was bad, really, really bad. Actually, A'ida didn't even know how bad it was here. She did not go outside the village if she could help it. That's how bad it was. She loved her home, but it was also her jail. She hardly spoke their language, and she didn't want to. She could not even *look* at them—the women. Deformed! Deranged! What religion could possibly allow them to go on, day after day, embarrassing themselves like that? Dressed like that! Living like slaves! She vaguely understood that whatever religion they made up, it would include those women just as they were. The new religion would not make them into good Muslims. It would teach good Muslims to have to accept them, women like *that*.

But did it matter? Couldn't she still be a good Muslim woman, inside?

"You could still be a good Muslim wife inside," A'ida said to her daughter.

Adn stopped packing and looked at her. "No, Mama. The force is too strong. People who don't believe in God—people like that, who proudly denounce belief in God—they make the air poison, you know? I can't breathe among those people. With people who believe in God, even if they don't believe in Allah, may He always be praised, I can still trust them to be, like we say, 'people of the book.' People of law. But those zombies who believe in nothing—they suck the *life* out of me! And they're *dangerous*!" She looked stricken.

Her mother didn't disagree. Adn knew that. But she didn't understand that the situation was different than it had ever been. She didn't understand that the so-called 'one religion' would be a non-religion. A God-less religion. Not religion at all. Adn didn't know how to explain it. She also realized, sadly and not for the first time, that her mother didn't care about it as much as she did. It was slavery, with prayers to make you a better slave. That's how Adn saw the new religion. And Adn just wasn't willing to do it. Would not. Could not. Nor, apparently, could she explain that to her mother. It was as if her mother lacked something. It hurt, to think about it.

Adn sighed. She put down the pajamas she was stuffing into the rucksack, went over to her mother, and put her arms around her.

"We will be able to communicate, Mama. Don't worry. They can bounce a signal, make it untraceable; they say they can, anyway." She sure hoped so. "And don't worry, we'll make sure it's safe on both ends before we try. Your security comes first. We're not gone so very far, really Mama, don't cry," she said as her mother's tears fell on her bosom.

She knew her mother really loved her, even if she loved Allah less than Adn, herself, did.

"We'll send pictures and everything, did they say we can?" A'ida said through her tears. "The first thing, to decorate for Ramadan." But then she took a shuddering breath, and Adn knew her mother was thinking of all the things Adn wouldn't have, couldn't take.

And *that* spoke to the difference between them. Because Adn knew the meaning of Ramadan wasn't in the knick knacks her mother adored. Adn had everything she really needed right there in her heart.

"Mama, hug Papa for me. I'll try to come back to say goodbye, if I can. Now, pray hard that they can bust out Laiq! Mama—goodbye."

She turned then, picked up her bag, and forced her feet to walk toward the door. It wasn't until she'd stepped through it and was halfway down their front sidewalk that she turned back around. Her mother was standing in the doorway of her home, as regal as a queen. A hostage queen. What did the Prophet say? "This world is a prison for the Faithful but a Paradise for unbelievers." She'd not thought of it quite like that before.

Adn stood for a long moment, gazing at her mother's beauty.

Then, she smiled and waved, turned, and hurried on.

She would help in the evacuation. Sirens shrilled in the distance—just like on Earth. Adn flexed her shoulders, loosened her neck with a quick side-to-side motion, grabbed her bag with a fresh grip, and strode toward Honesty Village. Work to be done.

Exodus

The bay docks were crowded and chaotic, as usual. It was like being part of a cheap reality show! The drama! People shouting and cursing all over the place! One woman dropped a few f-bombs when somebody stepped on her foot. First, she yelled it in pain; the second and third times were just for emphasis. A big bald-headed guy exploded with various epithets involving female body parts because some other guy dropped his sheep right in front of him—that's right, a sheep. And it wasn't the only sheep in the bay docks that morning! The blessed bay docks looked like—pardon—an effing zoo.

A wedge of soldiers, real soldiers wearing uniforms, swept past, looking tense. People scurried in all directions. Many of them were carrying parcels. Of course, the AgTech folks carted plants and animals and what-have-you, as they always did, for transport to the ag pods or to the *Regina Coeli*, as was also normal operating procedure. The ship had carried pigs and goats on several occasions, and the crew still joked about a phantom stench.

To add to the chaos on the dock, every so often the intercom would buzz on and add to the roar: "Citizens are directed that Sector 17 is closed. Do not report. Repeat: Sector 17 is closed. Do not report." Of course, everyone knew that meant people were rioting there. Now, thanks to the announcement, those who wished to take part in the rioting knew exactly where to go. Those who wished to start their own riot elsewhere knew where security's attention was focused. Administration could not do one single thing right. They couldn't *not* announce it, either; letting people show up for shift in an active sector just added—witnesses. They had tried texting only those affected, but most people ignored Admin texts on principle. So they announced everything on the intercom. Never with the intended result.

It was perhaps not the best place for Marley and the rest to meet, but at least the throngs provided a little cover. Marley's group had drifted into an alcove, where some tables had been set up for repacking shipments, as needed. It was slightly off-range of the nearest camera, but you could still keep an eye on passersby. That's how Marley saw Stephanie and reached out and touched her arm.

Stephanie whirled around and joined Marley and the rest in the alcove: Ferdi, Tomás, Ray, two of Tomás's crew, Roy, and his friend from AgTech. Roy had been against the plan at first, but the developments on the colony had convinced him otherwise. Chaos will do that.

"Were you looking for us? Marley asked Stephanie. Do you want to help evacuate?" Marley knew a couple of teams could use a few more hands on deck.

"Yes. But no." Stephanie gripped Marley's hands and looked into her face. "I'm not going. Do you remember my dream?"

Marley nodded. Impossible to forget. But, given Steph's background, not entirely reliable. Given *anyone's* background; the devil can bring dreams, too. Stephanie's behavior since joining the Catholics had been encouraging, though. She'd been baptized after a marathon crash-course in the Church's teachings. Now, she prayed the rosary daily with all those who met for that purpose and read everything she could get her hands on.

"I'm gonna stay here and do it, like the dream. Save the Goth girls. Save all the girls. Save as many as I can. I know I don't know enough to do it. But I think God will help me, even so."

Marley gazed into Steph's face. She was the same old Stephanie. The big brown eyes, the tattooed tears, the half-smile. But new on that little face: peace. Good to see, so good.

Marley thought fast. There was no time to consult. Even Tomás, right there beside her, was deep in conversation with Roy over getting every bit of AgTech resources they had on board right away.

So Marley had herself, alone, to ask: what would they have done in the old days? Should she help Stephanie do this? Maybe Stephanie should come along with them; God knows, there was plenty of saving work to do anywhere you went! But she had to think of the saints in the old days. Women were always making these wild schemes to save orphans, or teach kids, or tend the dying, doing it all for God, especially if they could wear romantic getups to do it in.

Still holding Stephanie's hands in hers, Marley asked, "Does this involve special clothes?" She had to smile, thinking of Steph's fashion history. Steph believed in dressing the part.

"Yes! You should see! All white, red cross, Heart Nebula insignia, Our Lady in the foreground! Just like Angel had on."

"You won't be able to wear it—outside," Marley said. "You'll have to be secret."

Stephanie nodded, sobered. Of course it would be dangerous now to identify as Catholic, to wear the habit. Still, the thought of dressing for God made her so happy. She and her sisters would wear them when they met to pray, and they would make a point of dressing modestly outside. "Okay. Listen. Go to my house," Marley instructed. "My mother is there. Ask her to give you my books."

Marley had three real books from Earth. Three! One was the old traditional 1962 *Angelus missal*. It had everything, it was like the ultimate Catholic encyclopedia, even the complete music for several votive masses. It had the burial mass and the burial rite, the marriage rite, last rites, everything. Marley knew other evacuees who had it, too, so the *Regina Coeli* people would have the resource. She also had the *Against the Heresies*, the complete set. And she had Liguori's *Preparation for Death*, the abridged version. Well, with those three books, Stephanie would have a fighting chance to learn the faith. Even if the colony never had a priest again. It would not be the first time in history.

"And here," Marley took Stephanie's handheld and texted in a number. "That's the number of a woman who is staying. Her sister is too sick to evacuate, and she won't leave her. Her name is Joyce Howard. I believe she will be interested in your dream, and she might join you. She's really nice. You'll love her. Take care of each other!"

Marley and Stephanie held hands and looked at each other for another moment. "May God keep you," Marley whispered. "Perhaps we will meet again. I'll contact you when it's safe."

With that, Stephanie whirled away and into the crowd, and Marley returned to the matter at hand. She had never had a happier parting from Stephanie, she thought fleetingly. Wasn't that funny?

The group that Marley turned back to was still discussing evacuation plans. They already had been secretly stocking the *Regina Coeli* for hours, a mammoth activity made possible only by the cover of the crowds and the distraction of the riots. Everyone was doing the work of two and not stopping to rest. They had tapped all of their resources. Of course, they had been preparing for *something*, they had not known what exactly, as long as they had been on the colony. The Combs had held a little of everything.

Now, Tomás and his crew were getting reports from all the sectors: AgTech had material from every plant that had come online on the colony plus the undeveloped stock that had just come from Earth. They had animals, certainly not *all* Earth's animals, but a great many species. They had—incredibly luckily—animal bedding made from plastics and not from too-dear organic material. It was an absorbent, biodegradable plastic. Really freed up one problem in AgTech. And other necessities were being addressed one by one. Dormitory spaces were already set up on the ship, and hardware for mining was being strapped down in the biggest hold. Safety equipment had been secured and stowed. Safe rooms were stocked.

The priest was safe on board, along with the evacuee's children, except those big enough to help. It was down to the last steps. Load the rest of the livestock and supplies. Get Laiq. Then, blast off! They were on their way!

When Marley rejoined the group, they were discussing how to get Laiq out of jail and onto the ship. Al Taylor, the black guy who'd come with Father Tim, was explaining something about the sewer system, and the others were nodding. Tomás turned to Marley and summarized the plan. Al was going to get into the jail on the pretext of a sewage problem, find Laiq, and run for it. They had two groups of helpers, one at each end of the street, ready to escort Laiq and Al to the ship, with firepower if needed. They were going armed.

Now they needed the dummy number, the one that duplicated a disconnect with the system-error message: "We apologize for the inconvenience. System failure due to overload.

Try your call again later. Thank you. Goodbye." Marley had that covered.

Al handed her his handheld. She consulted her own device, then typed a number into Al's, checked it again against her own screen, and handed it back to him.

"When?" she asked Tomás.

"We're waiting for the flight crew to make the pre-flight, and then when we're ready. All the other sectors have boarded." Marley parted her lips to speak, but he added, "Your mom just checked in," before she could.

"Everyone is on board but Laiq—" Tomás looked around at the small group. "—and us.

"So as soon as possible," Marley concluded. Tomás nodded.

Their good luck could run out at any second, as soon as some bot noticed the unusual amount of hot—that is, living, human—traffic around Pod386.

When Augie started to open the tool bag, Jacob and Hugh were first to step up and choose their weapons. Then Augie pulled out a small pistol—plastic, but enough for their defense. Bots were fragile if you hit them in just the right spots, and Halliburton didn't buy vests for its human soldiers; against the colony image, of course. Augie handed the pistol to Joong Yu and pulled out another. Tomás took it.

Marley held out her hand for the pistol Tomás had been passed. Tomás hesitated. Marley kept her hand out and gestured for the pistol. Still, Tomás did not give it to her. He glanced at Ferdi.

They all paused: Augie, Ray, Patrick Wade from the crew (a loner ever since his kid, Mick, had died a year ago on Earth from cancer before he could join his dad on the colony), Al, Joong, Jamie Syzmanski from MetalTech (a friend of Jay's), and James Scott. They had been practice shooting together for a while. Now, they all stood there silently, looking back and forth from Marley to Tomás to Ferdi.

A can of worms had been opened, something they hardly ever discussed. The woman thing. Darn it! They didn't want to discuss it now!

But they wanted Marley to go.

Feelings ran deep. It was a long-standing argument. Some traditional Catholics believed that women should be wives and mothers, period. Women did not need an education, especially if it meant borrowing money to get one, because their primary job, their most important job and maybe the most important, critical job in the world, and furthermore the one currently most neglected, was bearing children. Second only to that, perhaps, was demonstrating obedience (women sharing a disproportionate burden of guilt, thanks to old Eve!). Obedience was hardly despised among Catholics, believing, as they did, in obeying God, first and foremost. It's a virtue, okay? The husband and father was the boss of the family, just like God was the boss of mankind. Jesus had taught them the benign Christian meaning of 'boss.'

This attitude, or a general version of it, could be found among many traditional Catholics, including in Marley's family and in Tomás's family, and most of the time they thought of it as the traditional Catholic position. These same folks also believed in free markets (mostly free labor markets!) and unrestricted profits, although few of them owned anything, aside from their training, with which to make a profit. They thought their beliefs about women and about an economy came from traditional Catholicism. They were wrong, though, on both counts.

Those known as "liberal Catholics," the group celebrating the protestantized new mass and opposed to traditionalists, typically bought the whole feminist rant. They didn't bother to call it traditional because they had given up all things traditional in the last century. That Church was over! That's what they said. You've got to fall into line with the modern world if you're gonna convert the modern world. Yada, yada, yada. So this faction argued. Vintage Vatican II.

The third group, a small and generally reticent traditional group, disagreed with both of the other two camps on many counts. For one thing, they thought the "hard-line, free-market attitude" toward economics was protestant to the core. It wasn't Catholic at all! Back in the day of the great European Catholic states, there was no free market, profits were restricted, rightly restricted, and the guiding policy was, first off, that prices and production levels had to be good for *everybody*. Not just a few who might or might not trickle it down to the rest. You were even supposed to pass up work if you had enough for your family. Your daily bread, that you were supposed to have, but you were not to be trying to amass extra. It was Catholic economics. And it had worked for many centuries, building a just society of owners responsible for their living, until greedy protestantism had finally overturned it and subsequently made a government responsible to help those who fell by the wayside. That government could be socialist or communist or fascist, they were all just ways to keep the people from rebelling against the unrestrained greed. That's how the third group saw the economic question. Not that it came up often--because nobody had any chance to do anything about the current system. Change to that system was not on the ballot! Ever!

    The woman thing seemed the same as the economics. An exaggerated protestant reaction to the protestant feminism which had been there from the very start of the rebellion, a disguise for forcing women into the labor market. It wasn't Catholic, either, it seemed to the third group of traditionalists. Back in the day, the day of the real Catholic state, women could get an education, free all the way through university, the same as anybody else, and the old records showed that some did. Most didn't, but only because they didn't want to, nor did some men. They didn't *have* to, and book learning was dry, and they were very satisfied to be the queen in their own domestic kingdoms, thank you very much. Nor were their husbands the ultimate boss the way it was in protestantism. Their parish priest was the boss, of everybody, and he could tone down a harsh hubby, and the records and the statements of women—saints!—showed he often did. That is, when the priests weren't toning down kings--in their spare time! Priests had power. That's why protestantism got rid of them. They wanted the only power to be money.

    What about women in the Bible? Supposed to be the guide, straight from God, right? Real traditionalists could cite it. Biblical women were shrewd and resourceful, and they were good business people, working from home, buying and selling land, selling wool and corn and whatnot, turning a just profit, as the Good Book related, feeding and clothing their big households well with the proceeds. Women were listened to, in the Bible.

They were consulted. It was another kind of feminism, real feminism, you could say if you wanted to use the dishonored term, one that was kind to women. Our Lady Herself, the Queen of Heaven, was always there, after Christ, in the foreground of society, demanding respect for humanity and especially for women, respect for their bodies, their babies, their obedience. Mary Queen of Angels stood awfully tall among nations for a little pregnant girl from Nazareth. Undervalued? Not. A powerful and protective model for womankind.

Those biblical women fought for their people, too. Literally. When needed. Killed a few bad guys, as needed. Were not above a beheading, and strong enough to do it. Hebrew women. Christian women, too—Joan of Arc, the most famous, but many more over the millennia.

It was true, tradition said that women could not be priests. There was a reason for that, and it wasn't at all a putdown for women; more a protective thing for the valuable child-bearer. Because the priesthood was the hardest job in the world. Because his job was to die every day in place of Christ. But what *else* did that mean, for women? What *else* could they not be? The three groups argued about it continually. The guys here didn't want to talk about it! Not here, not now! No time, and it broke your head!

But here was Marley with her hand out for a weapon. Well? Come on, what else could women not be? The question could not be avoided.

Joong broke the silence and his custom of keeping his eyes down. He looked right at Tomás. "Uh, okay, this is not a personal thing, Tomás." He paused to give Tomás a second to prepare. "We all love Marley. Okay?" Joong kept looking at him. His look was kind of sorrowful. Men don't go out to die without some feelings. He continued. "But the thing is—"

"We gotta get Laiq!" Augie finished it for him.

"He's a liability in their hands, with the coordinates," Al reminded them.

"Marley is our best shot." Jay said the key thing, what they'd all been thinking.

She was, literally, their *best* shot. She had a way of breathing—not breathing—when she pulled the trigger. And a way of standing, with her knees "loose as a goose," is how she'd put it when she was trying to teach it to them. She'd giggle—and then hit that mark dead center! Every time! She'd tried to teach it to them, and they'd all gotten better. But Marley was the best.

"She's also the mother of our kids—future kids," Tomás said. "But yes. She is. Best shot." He gestured with the gun hand. What can you do?

Tomás looked at Ferdi, and Ferdi nodded thoughtfully.

So Tomás handed Marley the gun. With that, a matter of some five-hundred-years argument settled, they passed out the rest of the guns and ammunition. Then they pulled up their hoods and dispersed, drifted apart as if they weren't together but all heading toward the same destination: the holding center their contacts had identified as the most likely place the authorities had stashed Laiq.

They had a plan and they had a purpose. Get Laiq and get gone.

Showtime!

Al stood outside the unmarked door and took a deep breath. He was dressed in the civilian version of camouflage, which he had been wearing since he'd left home to catch the shuttle on Earth. Well, not the same clothing, of course, and not the typical version of camouflage. He was wearing one of the three outfits he'd brought with him to the colony, all the same, a black man's camouflage: black jacket, black slacks, black shoes, button-down plaid shirt (green; he also had a blue plaid one and a maroon plaid one, now stashed on the *Regina Coeli*). He straightened up the collar and brushed off the pocket protector with the pencil in it. He had to say, he looked the part of a nice, humble sort of sewer expert. He had his tool kit. It had to look authentic, it was his real workbag, although he'd taken the heavy wrenches out.

Throughout his life, Al had tried mightily to stay out of exactly this spot. But, after all the work—the degree in engineering, the careful choices of friends, the judicious selection of colleagues—and, most of all, after Mary's influence, here he was, where he'd never wanted to be: a black guy about to enter a jail. It was like a bad joke! His instincts were screaming, bad move! He sighed and closed his eyes for a minute. He wasn't kidding. He was scared.

He rang the buzzer by the side of the door anyway. And waited. He took off his glasses and put them in the breast pocket of his jacket. He took them out and put them back on again.

Finally, a voice answered on an intercom. "Yeah?"
Showtime!
"Sanitary engineering."
"Huh? We didn't get any notification. Please provide your supervisor's contact info and then stand aside."
"Sure," Al said a little wearily, fumbling in his breast pocket for his handheld. "Sure, but you got to hurry up. There's a blockage somewhere in the system. I got orders. It could get messy, and—" He deepened his voice and slowed his speech for

emphasis. *"And I do not feel like cleaning up your shit today. You got that?"*

Al raised his head a little, so the guy could get a good look at just how much Al did not feel like cleaning up any shit today. And how tall he was. And beefy. He scratched his nose so the guy could see the size of those paws.

"Well, come on in while we check it, then," the guy said hurriedly and buzzed him in. Al had thought he would.

They weren't all that particular about security on the colony. It was part of the image they wanted to project, to counteract all the security abuses they were racking up on Earth. The number Al was going to give the guard would ring and then disconnect after the standard error message; Marley's little app. Happened all the time on the station. Perfectly plausible.

The door opened silently and Al went in.

Security was just a guy behind a simple aluminum counter. No need for all that glass, not yet, even though this was a high-security unit for prisoners who were "pending transfer" to the prison pod that circled the colony. That was where the real work went on. In practice, nobody brought to the "transfer station" ever got transferred out again—or charged, either. They left through the morgue. That was the rumor, anyway. The inmates were all "terrorists," allegedly. Nobody to check on them. No law to help them.

After this day, though, they'd probably put up enough rig at every security station to keep out the Terminator. Al himself didn't have anything that would hurt the guy—except his fists, of course. Those he was prepared to use, if need be.

The guard scribbled down the fake number that Al rattled off. The guy blew dialing it, so they had to start over. Al gave it to him again, as he drummed his fingers on the counter and looked annoyed.

The evac group had talked the whole thing through, not just the plan but the morals, too. Those Catholics, Al considered, they sure had their rules against the use of violence. But they figured this was war now, for real, so that meant you were allowed to do what you had to do to defend yourself and your community. But there was one little kicker in the use of force. Your force had to match the situation. *If* you could step it down, wound instead of kill, warn instead of wound—you had to. Match the use of force to the enemy and the threat. It was not hard to argue that this enemy was dumb and could be tricked as easily as killed. You work with people every day, you see how they think or how they don't. You can fool this bunch as easily as fight them, so try that first. That's how they'd come up with this plan.

It was a plan that depended mostly on bravado. *Chutzpah. Cojones.*

According to plan, they had a group of armed fighters, actually two groups of them, ready on either end of the street, in case they needed to use stronger force in the end. Al had the lead man's number up on his cell.

Nobody in the group had bothered with the usual tricks to outfox facial recognition. They figured this was it: they got Laiq, they headed to the *Regina Coeli,* and they were gone. Or they were dead. The bots would get everybody in range, something big like this, an attack on a holding unit.

Meanwhile, the rest of their folks were busy evacuating everything they had collected through their own work or could beg or borrow. They were almost finished. Al and the rest of the fighters had paused and watched the parade on their way to their mission. The *Regina Coeli* looked a little like Noah's Ark! Turkeys and bunnies, oh boy!

The guard finally shook his head in frustration and looked sheepishly up at Al. "Disconnecting," he said, as if it were his fault.

Al sucked his teeth and tapped the counter with the ID that the guy who worked in HR processing had supplied.

"Forget it, let's get on with it," the guard said, and took the card.

The ID said Al's name was Jim Jones. It had surprised Al when Augie handed it to him, newly minted. Damn, man. Then he got it. Liberals were the worst racists deep down under the smarm. Al understood the choice of names. They'd be too embarrassed to doubt it. They'd be too embarrassed to confront him about it: this can't be your name. Really?

Nah. They'd believe Jim Jones because they wanted to. And they'd believe he was a sanitary engineer because they wanted to. And they'd never question either thing because it would make them look racist. Maybe, probably, they also believed it because they *were* racist. Oh, well, maybe also because he actually *was* a sanitary engineer--that didn't hurt. And of course they were also horrified of sewage. So to avoid a shitty mess, and because they'd never question a black guy, especially a big black guy, they'd let him do whatever he wanted. Things that are never discussed. You're not allowed to put those things into words. It was a perfect cover. That's how they'd come up with the plan in the first place.

Mary would not have liked it. She did not believe in treating people as dumb as they actually were, as greedy and lazy and proud as they actually were. She believed in treating them as Jesus had, that is, respectfully, and she'd pay the difference, as Jesus had. She'd make up for it in her flesh. Patience takes that.

Sure enough, true to form, you would have thought the plan was devised by magicians. The guy glanced at the ID, remembered how impolite it was to profile, refused to look Al in the face, refused to check his face against the ID. He just muttered something like, "You got everything you need? You don't need to bring anything in?"

Al first nodded and then shook his head (impatiently) to all the questions.

The guy shuffled toward the second entry door.

So far, piece of cake. *Thank the good God for me, Mary, dear. And ask Him to take care of me now and forgive me my sins. I am truly sorry for my sins.* He enunciated it carefully.

That was how you prepared to die. Mary had taught him. Push your ego out of the way, grab being sorry, and hang on for dear life.

Al followed the guard into a darkened room with bars on one side, a row of cells lining a corridor. Men sat on cots against the walls in the cells Al could see. The inmates did not look up when the two men entered. Drugged. Al knew the sewage lines ran from the toilets to a central line in the corridor. The toilets were up against the bars, not against the back, for this very reason, to shorten the run to the main line and to minimize the need to enter cells to fix blockages. You could reach almost everything from the corridor; you didn't have to go in. But the guard wouldn't know that, Al was willing to bet on it. Bet his life on it, maybe. Maybe he could end up right there in one of these holding cells. Man, he would not like that.

Al clutched a GPS unit in his hand. It came from Marley's father, who had it because he passed back and forth to the free-orbiting ag pods several times a day. He was part of a beta unit that was beginning the work of establishing near-Earth orbit waypoints. As if space was just an extension of the Grand Canyon or something—which, of course, it was, and someday they'd be trekking it.

"Okay, got to enter these," Al said. "Gotta check the lines."

The guy blinked. Oops. Did he know the layout? But then he said, "Uh, okay," and placed his hand against the sensor.

The door slid back.

Al moved toward the back of the cell. Then, he turned to the guard and said, "Are you gonna move this guy?"

"How long will this take?"

"Don't know. Depends," Al answered.

"Look, he's not dangerous. Can't hardly move. Look at him. Just do what you gotta do. I'm going off shift in a minute."

Moving a prisoner meant all kinds of protocols and wrestling the guy into restraints. The guard wasn't going to argue with Al about it, He leaned up against the bars, folded his arms, and closed his eyes against further discussion.

And that was fine with Al. Fine and dandy. Exactly what he'd hoped for.

Al moved toward the wall and squinted again at the inmate's face in the shadow. White guy. Bruised, raw with scrapes, eyes stupefied. He glanced back at Al with fear. Not much change in the penal department, same ole same ole. But it was not the guy whose picture Adn had shown him. That guy was an open-faced young man in his twenties, younger than this guy, wearing a white skullcap. And he was handsomer; no offense, buddy.

Al squatted down. Keeping his body between the wall and the guard, he moved the GPS gently over the floor, as though the device were some kind of handheld plumbing scanner. In fact, no such plumbing scanner existed, yet, even though the technology existed and functioned to scan vehicles at every border crossing.

Al had often thought he ought to develop one for sanitary engineering, but never had. He worked his way around the perimeter as if he were actually reading the device, and then came out.

"Not here. Next one," he said firmly.

The guard wearily closed the cell, glanced at his watch again, and opened the next one.

Again, Al moved toward the back of the cell, and the inmate raised a bruised face to him.

Bingo. Al's hand involuntarily gestured: *Quiet!* The man saw it and instantly lowered his eyes.

Now, Al had to stall until he could find a way to get Laiq out of the cell and out the front door. He paused at a section of flooring in a corner, went over it again and went over it a third time, like he'd found something. He took a deep breath to get his nerve up, pocketed the GPS, and turned to the guard. He had no clear plan at all. What could he do now? Pretend to call his boss? Pretend to need tools? He didn't have a thought in his head. He had to make something happen. So he just grabbed the guard and pulled him into the cell. He clamped a big hand over the guy's mouth.

"Listen," he said. "Shut up. I mean it. I don't want to hurt you, but I could break your neck in a second, right? So shut up. We're getting out of here, me and him." Al gestured with his head at Laiq, who had risen unsteadily and was looking back and forth between Al and the guard as if they both might grab him, as he steadily, if shakily, edged toward the door.

Al glanced at him. "Laiq."

Laiq blinked.

Yes, I know your name.

"*She* sent me. It's okay." Al didn't specify *which* she. But it worked.

Laiq immediately moved to Al's side to assist, as if he could in the shape he was in.

Al considered hitting the guard and knocking him out, but shook his head and repeated, "So shut up."

The guy understood and appreciated Al's decision. And he stayed shut up when Al let go of his mouth and pushed Laiq out the door. As he closed the cell door firmly behind him, Al considered if the guard could reach around and somehow activate the sensor, but decided not. The two men moved down the corridor, with Al's arm around Laiq's back and under his arm to steady him.

But Al's luck ended as they neared the door leading out. The new shift was coming in. Two guys were behind the counter stashing their gear in the lockers. They looked over at Al and Laiq in disbelief. They'd been expecting the guard who was going off shift.

Al's mind raced, trying to think of something. "Medical officer," he flashed the ID as authoritatively as he could.

But nobody was loving him now, and they drew their service weapons from holsters they hadn't even put on yet.

Al shoved Laiq through the outer door just as the shot caught him in the back. His big body fell to the right and blocked the door, as Laiq found his legs and sprinted out and around the corner, where the rest of the rescue team was waiting for him, a group on either side of the street, as planned. Both groups jetted toward the *Regina Coeli*.

As for Al, the heart they caught with the shot had been full of love. Lucky Al. His last thought was, Why is it always the black guy who gets killed, huh, Mary? But he was smiling, so she'd know he was joking. He saw, rather than heard, her reliable answer; Mary was mute: she held up the crucifix. Then he was in eternity and he saw everything right away. Oh yeah, so *this* is real life; that other life had been mostly a dream, like time in a womb, already fading

.

The Fight on the Bernina Harrison

It looked like a big, bumpy, baked potato with a bar code. The Bernina Harrison, Earth's first space-mining project. The last of Italy's old money. The gantry rails on the surface of the working sector were orderly gashes in the otherwise irregular asteroid terrain, with solar panels stretched out on either side of the crane like lines of code. Butt ugly.

Never mind that the one little sector they were presently working held more PGMs than had ever been discovered on Earth, ever. PGMs: platinum metal groups. Just that one sector alone held more than they'd ever found on Earth in the whole long (and dangerous) history of mining. Too bad the market was down.

They were pulling up slowly. Tomás, working without a copilot, since they were still holding Laiq in sick bay, had not yet hailed the command center. The *Regina Coeli* was going to enter the portal as usual. And then plead they weren't on the schedule due to colony error, and get permission to land or just land without permission, if necessary.

Next, they would . . . that part was a little hazy. Should they just run through the place shouting, "Escape"? The asteroid didn't have a regular security force, but management had arms and the bots could kill you just by running you over. Whatever they were going to accomplish on the Bernina Harrison, it would take a while. How much time would they have? (None! They could expect pursuit any minute!) How much time would they *need*? That was the question. And that they didn't know. The miners would have to hear them, understand them, and act. And when did human beings ever do all those three things together like that? And a lot of miners were not native English speakers and that could slow things down.

They didn't have time to go into details. They had to get moving! So? What *could* they say? "We know about an asteroid! In a secret location! We can hide there! Come with us if you want!" The rest of the details would have to be supplied by their good reputation.

So, ultimately, the mission was not perfectly worked out. It wasn't until they were pulling out of the colony docks that they had considered giving workers on the Bernina a chance to escape, too, before they made their run for the Oort. It was Tomás who raised the idea.

At first Tomás hadn't known if he should even bring up the idea. But conditions seemed favorable and sweetened the risk. Authorities had made no public announcement of their flight, at least none they had intercepted, and no one was pursuing them. Eerie. It was like everywhere they passed through as they rushed to the ship was empty! Where was Administration? So, once they were in flight, Tomás had taken a deep breath, decelerated and put the ship on autopilot, stepped into the bay where the colonists were gathered, and told them his crazy idea.

He had told them about the Krishnamurthy family and their threatened baby, as well as the Catholics and other non-Catholics on the asteroid who might wish to escape with them. They could not leave them if there was a chance to save them, right? Christian charity means always doing the right thing for your neighbor, if you could reasonably do so. Right? Okay, it's a hard standard, especially in this instance! But think, Tomás had asked them, think if it was you or your wife or your daughter or your friend who was caught on the asteroid and the colony was in chaos and could not resupply. Think if it was someone you loved, run down like an animal and forcibly aborted.

They shuddered.

Tomás had gone on to argue from another perspective. What did Christ say about it? That what you did for your brother you did for Him. Right? So how can we leave them there? You know what the asteroid is like, and they won't even have their faith to sustain them. They'd have to go through the motions of practicing some made-up religion, if they wanted to live.

Besides that—Tomás had looked pained—we *owe* them. We ought to admit that. These workers and the others just like them on Earth are making a horrible lie possible. This is the lie: that our wicked, awful, godless, secular, profit-driven system can exist peacefully, unrestrained owners on one side, unprotected workers on the other, with no conflict and everybody leading a good life. That's not true and the Bernina Harrison proves it every day. In capitalism, some workers get a better life than others who don't. Some workers make peace with the owners and somebody else pays for that peace, and that's these workers, just like on Earth, on the Bernina Harrison. They get less so we can get more, and we shut up. An exchange, an unfair one. We owe them, then. Maybe some people can ignore the injustice, but Catholics cannot. St. Paul taught us that, there is an equality among us. It's in the mass, St. Paulinus's feast day--I never forgot it. 'There should be equality, as it is written, "He who had much had nothing over, and he who had little had not less."' Or something close to that--Corinthians, I think it is. So, the point is, we owe them better than this. And there's baptized Catholics among them."

And that's not all, Tomás had argued. There was another thing. Think of the training and skills these particular workers had. The *Regina Coeli* was headed for an asteroid, and they'd have to mine it to survive. That required a special skill set. People on the Bernina Harrison had those skills. We could use them.

The unspoken question was, how exactly could they be "used" without repeating the same abuses? Used profitably—that is, in a good way, producing more resources than they consumed, in terms of air, water, food, warmth, light, and so on. If those things were equally distributed somehow, were they sure adding people on was sustainable? Was that possible using the economic model they were fleeing, and did they know any other? How could they avoid capitalism and its bounce, its evil twin socialism? No one actually said that or anything close to it, though. Hard to put into words on the spur of the moment like this. On the run!

They hadn't discussed any of those economic questions, in fact. Not on the colony when they were hiding in the *Regina Coeli's* hold before they escaped. That was a very big discussion—and they hadn't had time for it. Tomás hadn't meant to bring it up at this critical moment, either! He could just ask them to have faith that they could solve the economics, being Catholics and being sworn to justice. They would eat. They would have enough air. They could work out the details later!

But they had discussed something almost as tough, not the economics part but the religious part. What if they *did* save the

Bernina workers, then what about mixing non-Catholics and Catholics on their new asteroid? They'd glanced sideways, there in the hold, at the several Muslim couples among them, but they were few and so, maybe not enough to tip anything over. Maybe. But still, hadn't that very same mixing gone wrong on Earth? How would they avoid that if they brought along non-Catholics, and especially if they brought along people who were as fervent in their false faiths as the Catholics were in Catholicism? They wanted to escape the life they'd had on the colony, not reproduce it on the new asteroid! They didn't want porn in their faces and sex selling everything. They wanted Sunday, to worship and to rest. Frankly, they didn't want homosexuality in their faces, either. Sin, if you must, in private, in secret, but don't expect it to be legalized or not to backfire. Catholics wanted to live where God was respected—just one God. That was about as far as they had gotten in the discussion. They were not for 'religious liberty.' It didn't work. What they might put in its place had been deferred for another day. Any kind of change hadn't been an option right up to this second, anyway.

But now it was. So, rescue the miners? Really? Better to avoid the mistakes of Earth. Right? Or not? Well, how then!?

Tomás had had no ready answer. None of them did.

But in the end, after they'd tossed the idea around a little more and after they'd discussed, just hypothetically, how it *might* be done *if* they decided to do it, they just settled in to the conviction that they were perfectly willing to go rescue a baby Hindu. They couldn't help it. Catholics had struggled so hard for babies' lives on Earth, to save them from abortion; saving this life was just a reflex. It was, like, the heart of their Faith. It was what Jesus with that Sacred Heart *meant*. They would try to save that baby. That was the plan--just about the sum total of the plan. No one had grumbled.

They might die for it. They would also risk getting other people killed. Innocent people. (Well, fairly innocent. There weren't, upon investigation, very many totally innocent people in the world.) They would be endangering the lives of people who hadn't *chosen* to risk their lives. Maybe it could be put like that. They would be making that decision for them, if everything went sideways and it came to that, which they hoped it wouldn't. And that was a big responsibility.

They were thinking all that, jumbled up as human thoughts tend to be, when they slowly pulled alongside the Bernina Harrison and tentatively opened radio contact. Tomás waited for the reply, ready with his carefully worded confusion about their absence on the flight schedule. It skirted being a lie. It was more like an evasion. "We're not? What are you talking about! Are you sure? Can you look again?" He was ready with it. He had silently rehearsed sounding a little annoyed.

But he was delivered from the temptation. All was silent on the asteroid. And it was unusually dark, too. What the heck? Lights out! Nobody home! What was going on here?

Finally, Tomás just pulled into the outer portal and waited for the second air lock to open and the *Regina* to slide into a sling. It was a smart lock on the second door, and it would open on scan if he was unblocked, and he was pretty sure he was unblocked because he'd already checked his account, and he logged in, no problem. He had to hope there were so many scheduling errors that it wouldn't be programmed to automatically lock down in the absence of a tower clearance. He held his breath and said a prayer.

The door opened. He docked, checked his instruments, and put the ship on Sleep. He keyed something into the log, and then he slid out of the captain's chair and headed for the bay.

Ferdi and the rest of the fighters were waiting at the smaller personnel bay door. Vijay Patel, a friend of back on Earth, had joined them along with two more of Tomás's crew who regularly target-practiced with him. Marley stood among them. In addition to the fighter, many other people waited in the bay, too. They had friends on the mining asteroid and were going to try to find them and invite them to escape.

Tomás addressed them all. He figured, he told them, they'd try to locate Krishnamurthy, find out what was going on with his wife, and get them both. Then, they'd contact as many on the mining asteroid as they could, as quickly as they could. He could not say (he looked at Ferdi questioningly as he said this, but Ferdi just raised his eyebrows and shrugged) how much time it should take. They *could* not take much time. Even though the asteroid had little security, management would certainly contact the *Halliburton's* forces as soon as they were notified of a breach, and the trip from the colony to the mining asteroid was not a long one. They should all keep their handhelds close, listen for text notifications. Be ready to get back to the ship!

Marley suggested they partner up for a check-in system when they returned, so no one would get left behind inadvertently. The group quickly picked their partners.

Then, they all went out into the asteroid's interior through the personnel door. At the last moment, Tomás directed Richey Epps—who was hanging around the bay even though at twelve he was too young to go with them—to open the big cargo door and stay by it until they returned. Then they went out into the asteroid.

Tomás swung along with the posse: Ferdi, Marley, Augie, Jay, Mick, James Scott, Joong Yu, that ChemTech kid, Syzmanski, and Hugh. All armed and good shots. They passed through both bays and headed toward a corridor leading to the living quarters. There was not a living soul or bot or anything in the bays. It looked as though people had been called away in the middle of work, the way equipment and tools were scattered around, clearly in use. But nobody was there! It was very, very strange. What on Earth could be wrong?

With the asteroid deserted, the stark conditions of the Bernina Harrison lay exposed. The enormous interior cavern was full of shadowy darkness and the hellish clatter of lightweight belts that criss-crossed the interior and rose ceiling-high to exit the room through a wide corridor into the complete darkness of the deeper region of the asteroid. The belts clicked and screeched, and the noise mixed with the patter of liquid dripping from slime-crusted overhead pipes. The floor was grey with thick dust that, stirred by their walking, rose almost knee-high.

Tomás remembered a conversation he'd had with Ramdoss a couple of weeks back. The mining asteroid's base, its processing bays and living quarters, had been constructed in the interior of the asteroid rather than on the surface, and sealed with air locks. Ore was often brought back into the interior from outside, shifted down by the gantries from the slit on the surface. Experts generally considered surface habitats to be safer than interior ones, because a small body like an asteroid was vulnerable to the repeated hard blows of mining, and volatile gases shifted as easily as ghosts into interior spaces, including the human habitations therein. All you needed was a small leak and a spark, and *boom*! Investment all gone. But maybe in this market, with the right insurance, that wouldn't be all bad, right? Naturally, *that* was never said. Naturally, but it was an underlying principle of modern business. Oh a few souls blown to hell? Peripheral damage. The experts arguing for a surface habitat had testified before Congress and the media had covered it, on a sidebar, for a day or two. Bernina and Harrison had elected to construct an interior habitat, anyway.

The arrangement *did* have its benefits, and they'd glossed them up. For one thing, it shielded from solar radiation; that was their best shot, when Bernina and Harrison had argued the case. They pushed it hard, complete with dramatic vids of solar flares snaking out into space. But those nasty dangers originating in the interior? Administration had admitted there were volatiles in the asteroid. They'd scanned them before they'd ever selected this particular asteroid to work. But, they'd argued, what asteroid didn't?

Because it had those sweet PGMs, people! They painted that profitable fact large at the hearings. Certainly, yes, they'd sealed the interior habitat well Certainly, yes, they'd used those high-tech new material that could flex. They brought some of it and demonstrated it to the panel. Rather, a buxom blonde demonstrated it to the panel, flexing for all she was worth. It had never been tested, of course, to determine how well, or even whether, those materials could flex with the blows of mining explosions on the work face, or with the inevitable earthquakes, or with the rotational shifts of an asteroid around its axis, which Administration sometimes engineered, delaying the rotation, or accelerating it as needed to optimize extraction. They could hardly be expected to have field-tested in *space*.

Bernina Harrison, Inc. simply touted their attention to safety, touted it early and often, and after the hearings every media outlet recycled the same story and the same vids over and over, with the same absence of details. With lots of shots of the blond. (Don't be rude and ask boring follow-ups, or you won't be invited again.).

But no one familiar with the history of mining on Earth, *no one*, believed them. Except for the members of the Congressional Hearing Committee on Joint Public/Private Space Development.

Krishnamurthy, as Tomás remembered it, had been very concerned about safety issues on the asteroid—small stuff, maybe. But who was going to complain? "Consider it from management's point of view," Krishnamurthy had said sarcastically. So what if, in case of mishap, so you lost some bots and some human debris on the vast outgoing tide of Earth labor markets? The bots cost the most, those highly specialized mining bots. The humans? Meh! But have no fear, Bernina Harrison Inc. had "taken every precaution." Of course they had!

That's why you could smell methane.

Krishnamurthy had told Tomás of one incident when he'd complained that he thought he smelled the deadly gas near a certain ventilation grid. He'd gone to the safety officer's desk and tried to file a report. The officer had laughed at him.

"Methane has no smell," the guy had announced with a smirk that supplied an unspoken *dumb ass*.

Krishnamurthy had had to back-pedal, trying to remember the name of the gas that often came along with methane that *did* have a smell. That was probably what he had smelled, and it was what he had meant to say. But he couldn't remember it. So his complaint had fizzled out right there, although the safety officer magnanimously promised that he'd check it out, anyway (supplying the name Krishnamurthy couldn't remember: *hydrogen sulfide, dumb ass!*).

Still, although embarrassed, Krishnamurthy had followed up on the complaint a week later, stopping by the safety desk to ask about it. True to form, the safety officer denied there was a problem, said they'd gone in with the full battery of detectors and the odor was cooking smells from the living quarters. But the next day Krishnamurthy saw somebody had smeared glue— looked like the same kind they used to laminate surface panels in the living quarters—on a substantial fracture snaking out from the grid cover. Glue? Really?

But, then, Krishnamurthy was not a materials specialist. Maybe glue was just the right fix, and anyway, who would he complain to? The safety officer made a sour face every time he saw Krishnamurthy, a punishment and a warning to stay away, and Krishnamurthy was not in a position to draw further attention to himself. He'd said that apologetically, and Tomás had understood his point. Dhwani was newly pregnant. Krishnamurthy needed all the friends he could get in management.

The corridor Tomás and the others had been following after they left the big antechamber at the locks ended in the other large space of living quarters, where Tomás had first thought to check the clinic, to make sure Dhwani wasn't there. He'd initially thought (back on the ship when he was trying to make a plan) that he'd just ask someone to direct him to Ramdoss or the Krishnamurthy quarters. But that wasn't happening—there was no one to ask. Where had all the people gone? What had happened to the people?

Tomás and his team entered the large vestibule that opened into the living area beyond—and stopped. Instead of the opening, they were looking at a ceiling-high pile of rubble so fresh the dust was still finding its way down. The way was blocked. There had been an explosion; that was clear. And here at least were people and bots.

Their side of the blockage was still well pressurized, judging from the unsuited humans standing there. They had been talking with excitement when Tomás and the others entered. The animated group consisted of David Booth, the Bernina's administrator; his second in command, Alex Arthur; the safety officer, whose name Tomás didn't know; a couple of guys in hazmat suits; some of the dock personnel; and a whole battery of bots. Now, they all swung around to face the newcomers. The bots had more facial expression than the trio from Administration.

An engineer by trade, Booth was a techie wunderkind who had made so much money with his breakthrough in the use of low-frequency vibrations to power miniature electronic devices that he'd bankrolled most of the Bernina Harrison operation. But he had not the mother wit to realize he was professionally unsuited for the position of Chief Operations Officer of a working metal mine. Krishnamurthy was full of stories about Booth's disastrous decisions as COO.

"What happened here?" Tomás asked.

Booth had been about to ask Tomás, "How did you get in here?" But he let that go, preoccupied with other issues. Like his glasses. He took them off, wiped them, put them on, took them back off, wiped his face, and put them on again. His phone rang in his hand, but he did not answer it. He was absorbed in his own thoughts, which flitted across his well-tanned face, but he could not track them. He had no thoughts! All he knew was that his career had ended about half an hour ago. Whatever he did next, it was *his* head on the chopping block. *He* was the sacrificial lamb who would be offered up, with an apology and a payoff to the families and all that.

So Booth could give a crap about talking to this guy—a pod pilot, a nobody. There was absolutely nothing a pod pilot could do to make this situation better for David Booth. Ef it! He looked away.

Disgusted, reading the man, Tomás repeated the question to the others. "What happened here?"

There was a long pause, and then it was the safety officer who responded. "There was an explosion in the quarters. As you see, it has sealed off the corridor. We are presently trying to make phone contact, or radio contact, with the other side."

When no one else followed up with additional information, the security guy added, "Methane, probably. As you know, methane is a highly volatile gas, and ordinary mining practices can disturb methane under the best conditions. The company has taken every precaution to avoid this, uh, this—Act of God."

"Why aren't you blasting through the blockage to get to them?" Joong Yu asked with some urgency, thinking of his friend on the other side.

Alex Arthur and the safety officer exchanged glances, which the dock personnel noticed. They wanted to know that, too! They all leaned in to the conversation.

The safety man sighed. He wished Booth would step up and take charge. "We have to know if there's unexploded methane inside, and we haven't been able, yet, to activate any sensors or to activate any drones to check the sensors."

One of the dock workers raised his eyes tentatively and asked what he had been afraid to ask until these outsiders showed up: "Aren't the ventilators supposed to automatically change the air every two minutes? Isn't that powerful enough to prevent another buildup?" Because that's sure what they had been told when they signed on!

Alex shot the man a poisonous glance and cracked his neck aggressively. He was a muscular young man. Then he went back to staring at Tomás.

"There's a problem with the ventilators," the safety said.

"Yeah?" Tomás said. "What problem?"

"We don't know if the ventilators are working. We were having some issues a couple of weeks back, and we thought we'd fixed them. But the explosion may mean we didn't get it right."

"You don't know? Does that mean oxygen may not be getting to the survivors?" Tomás continued.

"We don't know," the safety repeated.

"What are you doing to find out?" Joong Yu asked in frustration, gesturing at the men standing around.

"Well, everything is on the other side," the safety said defensively. "Our stationary scanners. Just on the other side. They're in the clear, we think, but there's really not much we can do from here."

That brought Tomás back to the task. "You know how far this blockage goes, then?"

Booth turned his worried eyes to them and rejoined the conversation. "This corridor makes a bend about six feet forward, and then it forks. We're thinking it's possible the collapse was controlled at that point."

"We sent in a probe," the safety said.

The eavesdropping dock workers looked alert, because they were actually the ones who had "sent in" a probe, a real one, not an electronic probe, but a piece of well-used rebar. They'd used muscle to extend the probe, so they'd be less likely to provoke a spark, turning and pushing it gently, pressuring it a little right, a little left, a little up, a little down, going slowly and carefully around and through the blockage. It was delicate, tedious, nerve-wracking work. About four feet in, they could feel the resistance evaporate. The tip was in free space. They'd gingerly pushed it in farther, at least six feet, and then it would go no farther. They'd figured it had hit that wall where the corridor divided, with one branch going to the dormitories, the other to the common area—the mess area, the clinic, the vid lounge, the workout center.

After that, on the safety's order, they had pulled the probe back out and sealed up the hole made by the probe with foam. Less chance of introducing free methane on this side, the safety had said. Now, suddenly, he was all concerned about methane. Right.

"So let's just blow a hole through this blockage," VJ said.

"Ah, no," the safety said. "We can't do that." His tone was final. "I told you—methane."

Then what exactly was the plan? They all looked at the safety for more explanation.

Meanwhile, on the other side of the blockage, darkness reigned. Dust hung thick in the still atmosphere. You could see little, but you could hear. Voices were calling, and there a harsh metallic staccato—drumming on pipes. People were signaling to rescuers. The vents made noise, too, cycling on and off repeatedly, but nothing came out of them. The sounds clashed in the darkness.

The atmosphere on the Bernina Harrison was generated deep in the asteroid, where hydrogen and oxygen were taken out of the asteroid's abundant free water. The oxygen was combined with other gases and circulated throughout the interior in both the working and the living areas. The circulation motor was running, but something had gone wrong upstream. There was no air. Perhaps the vents had been blocked by the explosion.

In a residence room in E sector off Corridor 12, three figures lay on the metal floor with their heads inward. They lay face down, in their Bernina Harrison "leisure uniforms" of loose pants and even looser over-tunics, like pajamas. In the darkness, it was hard to see whether they were male or female, until the characteristic clues of identity—the slope of the shoulders, the shape of the skull, a birthmark—made it clear. Then, like a camera autofocus coming in, the individuals were suddenly visible: Gen Bao, distinguishable by her boyish haircut, her roommate, Yi Meifen; and oh yes, those were the bitten fingernails of Jai Birdi, a young man on their work team, an Indian. Both his hands were visible up near his head. He had been visiting Meifen and Bao in their room, carrying on his endless argument with Meifen about which was worse for its people, China or India.

They had been arguing about castes. Jai maintained it was so much worse in India, in spite of sixty years of legislation. Meifen had countered that it was worse where it wasn't recognized, like in China. She'd then told him about a girlfriend of hers who had loved this guy, but see, he was from Shanghai and she was from this village way up north and west, Jiangsu; you've never heard of it. And she could not get papers to live in Shanghai, so she would have to give him up. She would have to marry in Jiangsu because her family was from Jiangsu and China followed that system, *huji*—where your family was from, that's where you were from. Forever. Just like castes! And she had just blown a big concluding bubble with the bubble gum she always kept boiling in her mouth, and when it had popped, that very second, there was the explosion. Like Meifen had caused it.

It had gone dark right away. Jai had crawled to the bed and snatched the blanket, and crawled over to the door and asked for tape. "Gas," he'd said. Bao had groped in the side table drawer and crawled over and handed the tape to Jai, and he'd taped the blanket up to the door, all around it. Bao had helped. It was hard to do in the dark.

Then, with no atmosphere blowing out from the vents, they'd felt along the wall for the panel that held the re-breathers. There were two, for two occupants. And one didn't work. So there was one. They'd thought it was good for an hour but had been uncertain whether there were two kinds, two brands, with different time capacities. They'd remembered some kind of boring technical presentation before the subject was dropped. So they'd figured, among the three, they maybe had twenty minutes, but they wouldn't have to start using it right away. There had been some air in the room. But when that had gotten very low— they held on as long as they could—they had finally turned on the re-breather.

Now, they were all lying the same way, with their arms and hands stretched toward each other into the center, and passing around the re-breather. And doing it with as little movement as possible, staying as close to the mouthpiece as possible. The other re-breather, the dead and useless one, lay on the floor across the room, where Meifen had flung it.

They couldn't talk—no air to waste. They were left alone with their thoughts while they concentrated on keeping a slow and steady breathing rhythm, on keeping calm, on keeping still. It took everything Bao had. But she continued to manage it. A mystery. Take the mouthpiece, breath in, breath out, hand it off. The machine was recirculating all the atmospheric gases in the breath, except for the exhaled carbon dioxide, which it sucked off and replenished with oxygen. Hold your breath, lightly, lightly, don't panic, don't move, until it came round again. Breath in, breath out, hand off.

She brushed Meifen's hand, a tiny touch—Hang on, Meifen—when she passed the re-breather. Then resumed the hard work of staying calm.

In spite of herself, Bao was thinking of home. It made her breathe faster. She tried not to. But, of course, it was fate that, if she were to die here, her last thoughts would be of home.

It was hard to think of home and stay calm. Your brain settled on the one thought that was guaranteed to hurt.

So she kept remembering the day her dad had hit her. He had hit her twice, and the second blow had knocked her down.

Gen Bao had been fourteen and living in the village with her Lao Lao, her granny. Her mother and father were home for the New Year. It was a big deal. Everyone was home, and everyone was on their best behavior, showing off. The whole village had new clothes. It was not a time for honesty, with so much saved-up living riding on the visit, but Bao had been trapped. Her grandmother had held out Bao's school report, which her father must sign. She was failing, for the second year in a row. Her father had drawn a ragged breath and cursed. Bao had said something rude back and that she was dropping out of school, anyway, and she had gotten a job—she was going to tell them later!—in a mine north of them, outside of Huainan, the river Huai ran by it. She'd said all that in one breath! And then her father had struck her. As she'd recoiled back from the blow, he'd stepped forward like a fighter and hit her again, and she fell to the floor. Then, he'd gone over to the table, sat down, put his head in his hands, and sobbed as if his heart were broken.

She had known the truth, even then, deep down. But she had not put it into words. She had never been a girl to put things into words. But she had known. He was not crying because he had hit her. He'd meant to hit her. He would hit her again if it would do any good. He was crying because it would *not* do any good. He was crying for himself, because he had worked so hard, so very hard, every day, so that he could say he had done everything a human being and a good parent could do, for only one goal: so she could escape it. So she would not do as he had done, exactly as he had done—dropped out of school and gone to work. Just to have a few coins in his pocket. Just like her.

His only child was doing exactly as he had done. Bao could almost read his mind, although the details of her parents' painful life in the city far away was usually a subject she studiously avoided. He was seeing, she was sure, the long, sad days that had already passed far away from them while he'd worked. So he had never known her, really, for whom he sacrificed. And he must have been seeing the long, sad days still to come, stretching far ahead, with the same low pay, and bad food, and sewage smell, and sleeping by his machine, and washing up in a basin on the floor—for nothing. His hard life had all been for nothing. And her mother's!

Oh, no, no no do not think of Mother!

But the report had lain there on the table by her sobbing father, a fact. She did not understand school, and there was nothing she could do about it. It was her *mìngyùn*, her fate.

So they all had acted as if he were crying over his loss of face, for hitting her like that, his only daughter, knocking her to the floor, on the one visit they had in a year. That was bearable. You could regain face. He'd stopped crying then, and they'd gone on as before for the rest of the visit. False. Feigning peace and prosperity for the sake of the neighbors. So polite to her. "Bao, have some more of this pork bun. Here." He'd put it on her plate. Lao Lao had given her the good plate with the peony on it.

Of course, she had not seen the whole picture then. She had thought it would end differently for her, surely. Coal mining was not textiles. Miners got extra pay. They got excellent benefits. She would never be like her parents.

That's how she'd ended up on the colony, from that job in Anhui province. When they'd come to the mine to interview and promised so much. Things were going to be different in space.

Bao tried to think of something else. She tried not to know just how right her father had been. She tried not to think of him. His mustache. His hair all spiky in the morning. Her father's face. If only she could undo everything! If only she'd given school one more chance! If only she could show him how much she loved him! She had barely spoken to him after that scene in their house in the village. "Hello." "Goodbye." Hardly more. She had gone home for the next two holidays, but then no more. Oh, my father! I am so sorry! Because they still lived, her father and mother. They still bathed in a basin on the floor.

But that was not their worst suffering. She was their worst suffering. Their only daughter, Gen Bao. Not good in school.

Breathe in, breathe out, pass it on. Hang on, Meifen. Try not to panic.

Jai resumed kicking the metal wall behind his feet for a moment. He could not continue; it used too much air. "Rescuers," he muttered in a small voice.

But Bao was not comforted. If rescuers were coming, they would have come long ago—to China. But still her heart could not help but cry out: rescuers, please come!

Breathe in, breathe out, pass it on. Meifen's hand felt cold. There could not be much oxygen left in the re-breather. But don't think of it; above all, don't panic. It only used air.

"The rescuers are coming," she whispered to Meifen.

But on the other side of the blockage, the rescuers weren't coming. They were still arguing.

"So let's just blow a hole through this blockage," VJ had said.

"Ah, no," the safety had answered. "We can't do that."

Tomás sighed. "So set up vacuum hoses to suck the methane out, and tear down the blockage by hand. Carefully. No sparks. It's not a big job, six feet of rocks, we could have an opening in, like, ten minutes."

This set off a round of buzzing among the dockworkers standing about. Apparently, they had been saying the same thing before Tomás and the others had come in. Now, they resumed their discussion, gesturing at areas of the blockage and moving forward as if they were about to commence in spite of the safety.

"No!" the safety shouted.

Instantly, the bots moved forward toward the miners. The workers froze and looked at Tomás.

"No!" the safety repeated. "We have our directives from the center. There is a forty-six percent probability that there's free methane on the other side. That is above industry standards for rescue without specialized equipment. They are sending it; the ship will be here this afternoon."

"By then it could be a recovery operation," Tomás said.

"Probably. And the infrastructure and Earth's investment will be saved."

"It's a recovery operation now, already," Alex put in. "Those ventilators aren't working." He sneered. Effing tech nerds could never do anything right.

"But the survival equipment?" Hugh asked. He'd worked with Walt long enough to know it should be there.

The safety guy shook his head. "If they could get to it. It was their break shift; they were not necessarily in their rooms. And we've been having some quality problems, too, with, uh, the re-breathers. We were working on that." He gestured to Booth.

Booth nodded vaguely.

"But there is some survival equipment?" Tomás pressed.

"Yes," the safety said. "Central says the odds are small that survivors could utilize that equipment, under these particular circumstances. Central says to wait for the specialists,"

Tomás glanced around his crew. The safety saw it, and the bots, responding to his silent command, moved closer. Their asymmetric right arms, like long tentacles, began to pulse.

Jay, hanging close to Ferdi's right hand, as always, smiled at Tomás and drawled, "Tomás? Did you hear those odds?"

Tomás nodded.

"They're wrong." Everybody paid attention, with Jay, statements like that usually ended with a good laugh. Math was not Jay's strong point.

"Yes?" Tomás waited for the punch line, although Jay never meant his observations as a joke.

"'Cause everybody knows the odds are fifty-fifty."

Hugh laughed. "Fifty-fifty odds on what, Jay?"

"We live, or we die. That's fifty-fifty, right?" He grinned.

Tomás could not help but chuckle. Jay! Always a grain of truth in his nonsense. Then, he looked at all of them.

"Do you like those odds?" he asked. He broadened his glance to include the other men in the room—the men in hazmat suits and the unsuited men who looked like they had just come off break themselves. "Fifty-fifty sound right to you?"

One of the suited men responded. "We like them better than Central's."

"Hugh," Tomás said. "I want you to go back to the *Regina Coeli*, tell Laiq to back the ship off and stand by. Wait until the ship's moved out, then come back."

Hugh nodded and bolted from the room.

Tomás looked around the room. "Any of the rest of you want to get on the ship, go now, with Hugh. If you stay, prepare to help. We're going to open that blockage."

He paused to give each man a moment to make his decision.

"Safety, where are the re-breathers for this room? Everybody needs one." Tomás waited, as if he expected to be obeyed.

The safety just stood there, silent, and lowered his head.

One of the guys pointed at a locker, and Augie went for it. But the bots moved in front of him and began to move their arms in their curious dance. Those arms could crush a man. Alex, Booth, and the safety moved to stand beside the bots, and their intention was clear. Alex was flexing his shoulder muscles and warming up. He never took his eyes off Tomás and he smiled a cold, wicked smile.

One of the hazmat guys on the side went behind the bots to a locker, opened it to a rack of re-breathers, took several, and started to pass them out. A bot moved toward him.

And then it was on!

Alex sprang at Tomás, but Marley fired the shot from behind and neatly disabled him. He fell to the floor holding his leg and cursing. Meanwhile, Tomás took down the bot that was advancing on the hazmat worker. It clattered to a halt, its one robotic arm crazily broken. The other bots began moving in unison toward the humans. Mick shot and missed a bot. Joong Yu got hit in the shoulder by a bot. Syzmanski went crazy and took out two bots, one-two, just like that. One crashed down with a boom, the other froze in place. Then, Marley got the one that was going for Syzmanski. The fight continued for several minutes, with no major injuries to the Catholic fighters, but they managed to do some serious damage to the bots.

Hugh, returning from the ship, drew his pistol at the door and took out a bot that was going for Marley. It was the last one. All eight bots were disabled.

Alex sat on the floor, pressing his hand to bleeding thigh. Booth and the safety tentatively put their arms in the air. But no one paid them the least attention.

The Catholic fighters and the asteroid workers had already turned to the blockage and were carefully removing rubble and setting up ventilator hoses into the cleared areas. Marley quickly organized a line to hand off the debris, and after a couple minutes, Booth quietly joined that line and went to work.

The safety just stood and stared. Finally, he walked over and picked out a re-breather, tested it, and put it around his neck. When the ventilators had run for several moments, enough to clear the areas immediately adjacent on the other side of gas, he reluctantly cooperated to the extent of judging it sufficient to enter that area only.

They broke through a larger opening then, not clear enough to enter, but open. Was there methane? All they could smell was dust—no scent of fire, no scent of gas, no smell of anything except maybe cooking. They could hear sounds from beyond the blockage—bangs and cries. Still, they waited until a hazmat guy fetched the handheld infrared ESP-TGA gas detector and scanned the opening. No gas. They went to work harder, less worried about sparks now. The hazmat-suited guy wiggled through first, with a light and the detector. They kept clearing until the opening was passable. Then, they set up big portable ventilators at the opening to move atmosphere inside. Finally, a crew crawled through and began to fan out in the corridors to find the survivors. The tech got to the main ventilator controls, found the problem (a reset, that's all it needed! What had the programmers--not--been thinking?), and their dry hum took on a productive whoosh.

The rescuers *were* coming!

Bao was still conscious and felt the air on her cheek as, freed of obstruction, the ventilators resumed their work, just before she heard the noise of the rescuers. Meifen stirred, but was too groggy and weak to sit up right away. Jai Birdi lay on his back, his eyes open. He was dead.

Bao took another cautious breath, then reached over and closed his eyes. She had to make two tries on one. "Okay, India was worse," she said. "You were so right."

She held his hand until the men opened the door and the blanket fell down. Then, helping Meifen stand and walk, she went with them to the *Regina Coeli*. So did most of the other miners.

Tomás and Augie soon found Ramdoss and Dhwani and rushed them onto the ship. The couple had been hiding from Administration in a friend's room when the explosion, or collapse, or whatever it had been, happened.

Within an hour, the *Regina Coeli* was headed away from the colony and the mining asteroid into deep space. Those who had chosen to stay on the Bernina Harrison were securely tucked in a safe room with David Booth in dubious command, waiting for Central's disaster team to arrive. There might be after-shocks, but they'd be okay in the safe room. If you didn't mind some of the company.

Pharaoh's Army

"We're painted!" Laiq exclaimed, observing the beta scan and the new blip.

It was a drone, that was clear from the size of it, coming up fast, and its sudden course adjustment revealed the *Regina Coeli* had been spotted.

Tomás jinked right, as fast as a mining pod *could* jink, glanced at the screen, gripped the blaster, and fired a rear shot.

"Boola boola," Laiq murmured off-handedly, staring at the screen as Tomás's blast hit home.

The drone sparked briefly on the scanner and disappeared. But there would be others. They'd been painted, and the coordinates had been instantly broadcast. It was on!

"Turn on the music," Tomás said.

Laiq adjusted his dials to broadcast static in their wake, jamming their pursuers' radar—he hoped.

"Can we up the G's?" Laiq asked.

The more space they put between them and their last known coordinates, the better, as far as the Galactic Positioning System went.

Tomás saw the point and pushed the *Regina Coeli's* ramjets to the max. Tomás sat in the pilot's seat. He'd commanded the *Regina Coeli* for as long as she'd been commissioned, so deciding who was in command had been an easy decision. Besides, he now *owned* it, astonishingly enough. Stephanie had told Elma to put Tomás's name on the title.

Laiq sat in the copilot's chair, rubbing his sore shoulder. He'd hurt it in the skirmish on the Bernina Harrison. Otherwise, taking stock, he felt fine. Never felt better, physically or mentally. He was comfortable with Tomás. You knew where you stood with Tomás; Laiq liked that. The two men had joked with one another when they'd taken a breather in those first moments after the *Regina Coeli* had escaped the Bernina Harrison with their load. Not a load of ore, as usual, for a mining pod, but another kind of gold, human beings—Catholics and others, like him and Adn. She was in the big hold now, with the rest—the colonists and those they'd rescued from the mining asteroid.

They were on the run to the legendary Oort Cloud. Even with ramjets, it would be a hike, many months, but nobody minded. The farther away, the better. The deeper into the Oort, the better. It held fewer terrors for pilots like him and Tomás, men with actual experience, who'd flown there and knew the wild debris-dodging stories were exaggerations. In fact, the Oort Cloud had a relatively low density—if you knew how to finesse your instruments, it could be traversed.

The Oort Cloud was famous for all the wrong reasons. Crews demanded hazard pay to go into it. Halliburton demanded higher government subsidies for exploring it, though they weren't getting them, demand being down even for riches easier to reap than those to be had in the Oort. So they left it alone, like an Earth badland beyond steep mountains and deep rivers and waterless desert—in the Oort, all three at once! No profits in that madness.

The Oort was a hot mess of asteroids and comets and debris and gases. No, not hot mess—*frozen* mess, all methane, ethane, carbon monoxide, hydrogen cyanide. All gently rising and falling in a galactic tidal reaction to the pull of the Milky Way. Made it impossible for the Galactic Positioning System to get a fix. They thought the Oort had first formed—or, more precisely, had begun to form but hadn't been able to finish— closer to Earth's sun, and it had been spun out of orbit by Jupiter, the giant, losing its net of anti-matter in the upset and for that reason never taking its true form as a supergiant. Most of the rest of what they knew about the Oort was colorful conjecture, legend. They thought the Oort had taken its own sun with it into exile, a little sister to Earth's sun, a red dwarf or a brown one. They thought it had many planets, but that you could not see them, could not get a fix on them. Something was wrong, off, crazy with the orbits of *everything* in the Oort, the numbers suggesting the presence of ghosts, invisible gas giants pulsing and pulling. You could never be sure of anything in the Oort Cloud. Now you see it, now you don't. Some way to run a universe!

But a brilliant place to hide.

When Laiq had been on the longest scouting run he'd ever had at *Halliburton*'s, and then thrown off his orbit by electromagnetic activity (the daily storm reports had missed calling it, as usual! No warning at all!), he had dialed up the coordinates on his GPS. He stared at them in disbelief, rubbing his eyes like a cartoon character. It just wasn't possible, he had thought, for his ramjets to have carried the ship *here*. What had gone wrong with the programming fail-safes? The flight program was impossible to override. But some glitch had permitted it!

And it had taken him right to the front door of the perfect asteroid!

Now, here he was, headed back to the Oort Cloud with a full ship. And the *Regina Coeli's* mining blasters, well, they were going to come in handy long before they got to their asteroid. Because the Halliburton powers-that-be were not about to let them go. Laiq would bet on it. To hell with who actually owned the ship. Star Command would arrest them and sort it out later, with apologies and payoffs to the families of the dead.

Of course, Laiq was sure Tomás knew all that. But the legal title meant something to him, just like it would a Muslim. Not to Administration. Dogs!

Laiq checked the radar, which was thankfully empty, and glanced around. For such a big ship, it was a snug cockpit, a two-seater behind the wide windscreen with a nook of a bridge behind them for the minimal crew Halliburton allowed on its miners, and crammed with digital tools for the profitable recovery of asteroids in space. Much better than Laiq's clunker, though! In the center of the console (with a pasted-up crucifix beside it, which bothered Laiq way less than the porn in most cockpits) was the telescopic spectroscope. The scope could remote-scan an asteroid surface for nickel, iron, magnesium, gold, and platinum—all of which were mined for profit—as well as for the hydrogen and oxygen that the ship used for propulsion, and of course, for water and air.

Laiq's old pod's scanner had been first generation, low contrast and liable to power failures at every passing solar burp. Still, he had been the best among all the pilots at reading an asteroid, even with a bum scanner. He'd gotten a bonus for his accuracy and consequent cost-to-profit ratio. "Sixth sense, gift from Allah, you know," the other pilots said snarkily, behind his back, but he knew they said it as surely as if he could lip-read. He hated the way they sneered the sacred word: *Al-lah*. Made it sound, dirty, the devils!

Yes, a nice cockpit. One they might die in, Laiq thought as he eyed the radar. Nothing yet, praise Allah. He went back to checking out the *Regina's* setup.

The cockpit was arranged as usual. The pilot seat had the default controls and a handle for the blasters. The copilot had the second controls, and the handles for scraping and tunneling, and a second handle for the blasters, the tool they used the most, since they had found that just about every asteroid had its treasures conveniently well-distributed, not like Earth. The quickest harvest, it had turned out, was just to blast off a chunk of the surface and pull or push it back to the Bernina Harrison for processing, instead of setting up a whole operation right there, on-asteroid, as the Bernina Harrison investment group had first planned but never executed after experience showed them the easier way.

The goodies were more likely to be equally distributed on an asteroid than on Earth, which had been hot-formed and spun so that the heavier elements had gravitated to the center long before the crust had formed. Not so the asteroids—at least not the million or so of them in our solar system; it might be different elsewhere. Every last chunk yielded a taste of what the whole rock offered, as it turned out. No need to set up the big tower that guided the three-story, 1.5-ton drill to get into the core. You just read your spectroscope, checked the ultraviolet, and called your readings into Central Administration. Then they checked the markets and gave the nod, or said move on. If you did harvest, after the girls on the Bernina Harrison processed the chunk, you might come back for another big slice.

And nobody bothered to put the extracted rock into the hold anymore. They just nudged it back home with little blasts. That was after they'd experimented with towing it, which had worked out about as well as towing on old car on a chain--not for the faint-hearted. Pushing was better.

Yep, mining in space had become routine.

Selling the products, that was the rub. No markets. Markets were down. Down, down, down. Always the same story. Space was easier to finesse than markets!

Well, perhaps Laiq was done with the weariness of that dynamic. How *were* they going to arrange things, though, when they had their own asteroid? Technically, Tomás owned they ship. They might all be working for him! Where would the profits go? How would they resupply? Although, as Laiq had learned, there was a black market for everything!

If they made it there at all. If! The thought caused him to glance again at the radar.

Sure enough, blips. Tomás saw them, too, and reacted, jinking as randomly as he could manage so that their algorithms would be less predictable, their destination coordinates masked. Not that Tomás had put in the exact coordinates in the first place.

Laiq clicked on the ship's intercom. "We have incoming. Prepare the hold."

He did not see them kneel at once, down in the hold. That was their preparation!

Then, their radio woke up.

"Attention, Pod386! This is Star Command with a message from Mother. Stop your jets, oxygenize the locks, and prepare for boarding. I repeat, this is Star Command. Your flight is not authorized. Stop your jets and prepare for boarding. Failure to comply will result in immediate firing of the locks. I repeat, we are prepared to fire. Don't be stupid, *Regina Coeli*! Respond! Respond!"

Laiq knew the voice. It was Brad Ford. The creep kept a scorecard in the pilots' locker room of the young girls he'd "laid." It made Laiq's cheeks burn with shame to hear him brag about the strategies he used. Laiq hated the man, and Ford hated him.

"No way. It's *our* ship, and *we* authorize it," Tomás muttered.

He put the *Regina Coeli* into a steep dive, sheering left, and then pushed the ramjets handle to the floor, straight ahead. On the radar screen, Laiq saw the fighters follow them. Tomás varied first the horizontal and then the vertical orientation, rocking the ship. Laiq figured it was to keep the fighters from getting that zero-angle right up the *Regina's* tailpipe.

A shot blazed past them on the right, then another on the left. Tomás prepared and launched a blast of his own, which didn't hit anything, and gripped his blaster handle as another fighter drone managed to get in front of them from underneath, turn, and come straight at them. Laiq hesitated one second, praised Allah for success, and fired. The fighter exploded in a fireworks display, and Tomás sank the *Regina* rapidly, dodging the debris.

Tomás nodded at his copilot, and Laiq felt the praise like cool water, but he had no time to enjoy it. Another fighter careened in on their left. Tomás had him in his sights, when suddenly the radio barked on again.

But it was not Brad from Star Command. It was the stuttering delivery of NASA's weather service. Tomás hesitated and did not fire, but the fighter did, and they felt the shudder as the shot hit home. The *Regina Coeli* trembled for one long instant but did not explode. What was it? What was hit? The screen refreshed, reporting a fin, only a fin. Praise God! Then Star Command stopped firing, too, because they were all—the *Regina Coeli*, Tomás, Laiq, Brad—caught up in the alert.

"Attention, all personnel. Attention, all personnel. This is your NASA weather service with a public service broadcast. This is a warning of severe solar weather. Repeat, this is a warning of severe solar weather. An unpredicted Coronal Mass Ejection of previously unexperienced magnitude is currently traveling through Galactic Sector 414359, and it may extend in full strength through adjacent sectors. All sectors, including Earth, will experience satellite disruptions with consequences in all communication vectors. Switch to manual controls, as auto controls may fail. Repeat, switch to manual controls *at once*; auto controls may fail. This is a warning of an unpredicted solar flare of a previously unknown magnitude. All personnel must take shelter. Repeat: take shelter." There was a pause. And then the disembodied voice continued, more colloquially, with a distinct edge of hysteria. "This is the big one. This is the kill shot." And then the message began to loop.

Tomás and Laiq looked at each other. They were dead in the middle of Sector 414359, according to the GPS. Take shelter? Where?

On the colony, they had safe rooms. The ship came equipped with a shield adequate for the garden-variety solar flare, but this didn't sound like that. This sounded like NASA meant an apocalypse! To be exposed in a strong solar flare was to burn from the center out, from the center of each cell out, to melt from the inside out. In extreme flares, all that was left was bones.

"Shields up!" Tomás cried.

Laiq hit the toggle, and the ship was instantly sheathed in a protective net of electrically charged spheres made of pure gold. It had never been tested by extremely high radiation, but Halliburton had exploited the idea that it was made of gold to convince pilots to forgo hazard pay for deep space, where you could get dosed not only by Earth's sun but also by distant supernovas, even though the metal gold was cheap enough, now, to use for tea pots and trinkets, because of the asteroid mining.

Tomás switched on the intercom and addressed the ship. "Attention," he said, "we have received a warning from NASA. A powerful flare is expected immanently. Bring out the blankets. Take the children to the locks."

The locks were more heavily shielded than the hold itself. The blankets were hydrogen-filled foils. They offered some protection, and every ship had a set. Tomás had made sure they had extras, as many as he could gather before they'd left.

"And pray," he added and switched off.

Apparently, their pursuers were engaged in similar preparations, except for the prayers part, because new shots had been fired. But they hung close by the *Regina Coeli's* flanks.

Tomás and Laiq thought furiously of how to implement NASA's command, which was still repeating, "Take shelter! Take shelter!"

They could see the flare on-screen now, moving across their GPS, coming straight at them. It looked like fire. It was bigger than a thousand Earths and moving as fast as light. It looked like hell was coming.

In the hold, Father Tim knelt with the people. They clutched their protective blankets and bowed their heads. Father

Tim prayed Psalm 59. "You have rocked the country, O Lord, and split it open. Repair the cracks in it, for it is tottering. That they may flee out of bowshot, that Your loved ones may escape." He knew it by heart because it was a tract in the mass. So old a prayer, from the dawn of their faith in the desert, the syntax strange now, seismic shifts in it. But they understood. "That Your loved ones may escape." Amen to that! Please! Then, he blessed them, and they covered themselves with the blankets and God's protective love.

In the cockpit, Laiq and Tomás searched frantically for a solution. As they passed a large asteroid, Tomás sat upright.

"Laiq," he said, "how fast can you scan that rock?"

Laiq had the scanner working before Tomás stopped speaking.

"It's a water mine," he answered almost at once. "Hydrogen, oxygen, traces of other volatiles. Carbonaceous. The usual."

It was, in other words, ice, typical of asteroids in near-Earth orbit. The kind they pushed back to the Bernina Harrison on a regular basis, where it was turned into propellant and base supplies of oxygen and potable water. The kind that had just killed a girl when a chunk of it had crushed her against the hold of the mining asteroid.

"It's a big one," Laiq added. "A huge one."

"Ice?" Tomás said. "Are you sure?"

Laiq nodded. He was sure.

Tomás typed something into his handheld. He waited for the results.

"Okay," he said. "The CME's got a north/south axis; that's the fat way. It's on edge east/west."

Laiq still did not catch the drift as Tomás reached for the controls. "Let's get ourselves east/west. And when I say ready, I want you to blast it."

"Blast the asteroid," Laiq repeated, and felt stupid.

Tomás was already changing the ship's orientation. "Yep. Pulverize it."

"Because water in any form—ice, steam, whatever—shields from radiation," Laiq said, nodding. He got it. It was brilliant.

"Worth a try," Tomás said. He took a deep breath and reached out and touched the feet of the crucifix.

Both men had their eyes on the screen now. The storm was almost upon them. They glanced at the pursuers in their wake. Star Command had not understood Tomás's reorientation maneuvers (Laiq could almost hear them chattering about it, relying heavily on the f-word, per usual), and the pursuers stayed north/south but close on their stern.

The CME was here.

"Okay. Now," Tomás said calmly.

Then Tomás bottomed out the ramjets as Laiq hit the forward blasters with every bit of energy they had. An instant later, the *Regina Coeli* plunged into brilliant blue steam—all that remained of the asteroid.

Time stood still.

The ship trembled, and held.

The storm passed over them without touching them.

But in the *Regina Coeli's* wake, all the humans of Star Command were suddenly a bunch of bleached bones. The lights, the motherboard, the bots, had all shorted out, and fires were beginning to bloom. The ships began to drift apart, even as the *Regina Coeli* shook like a wet dog (Tomás testing the controls) and turned slowly around toward their pursuers. Tomás called for survivors. Waited; called again. Scanned for bio-signatures. At last, finding no sign of life, they resumed their course to the Oort.

Laiq would never look at Tomás again without thinking of Moses. But he never told him so. They rarely discussed religion. They just lived it.

The Meeting in the Hold

The hold was still dark when they began to gather there. They had enough room for all of them but not enough chairs. They sat on the floor, or perched on shipping containers, or leaned against the walls. Tomás and Ferdi stood up near the front, in what they called the "patio"—the area outside the kitchen where they kept the chairs and ate in shifts.

Marley was there (she was Marley Monaghan now), and Walt Ferguson, the ex-seminarian, and Father Tim. Laiq and Adn were there (now Adn Amanpour—she and Laiq had been married at the last minute, as they fled the colony). Adn sat in one of the chairs. She thought she might already be pregnant. She was not the first pregnant lady among them. Ramdoss Krishnamurthy's wife, Dhwani, leaned against him, her baby-bump quite prominent and a look of grateful relief (permanently etched, it seemed) on her pretty face. Her trauma and nightmares about the horrible experience on the Bernina Harrison were fading.

When Armand Hebert came in among the latecomers, he joined the group in the front. Armand did not walk—he strode, with his arms pumping and his hands balled into fists, his geek glasses firmly planted, and his dark hair sticking out every which way.

"Armie!" Tomás smiled genially in greeting.

Armie Hebert smiled back.

The two men had known each other from the Bernina Harrison, through Krishnamurthy. Tomás liked him. Once Tomás had seen him win a toe-to-toe shouting match with one of the administrators over scheduling abuses. It had been a thing to behold! Armie had stood his ground as if he didn't even need the job. Tomás had admired him ever since, more so when he'd found out they shared the faith. Armie had been a boss for the Man, but he had earned the respect of both Administration and workers on the mining asteroid.

After the storm, day-to-day life had resumed and developed on the ship, and men and women like Armand Hebert had stepped up and offered their skills. Marley, for one, who was always a go-to problem-solver on the colony, and Father Tim, Ferdi, of course. And many others—including a woman named Marlene McLane from AgTech, an Asian girl from the Bernina Harrison named Meifen, who chewed bubblegum and really knew the inside of a hydraulic shovel. They had all been official or unofficial leaders on the colony or on the mining asteroid. Marlene had AgTech up and humming.

And they were the ones people turned to now. Some, like Marlene, had been colony officials with several degrees and high-level positions, and they had given up more than others to come with the fleeing Catholics. They had earned high pay from Halliburton and had been looking at a real retirement, the real company-funded kind that hardly anybody had any more.

All of that was gone. Yes, some had paid a higher price. Others like the Krishnamurthy's hadn't had so much to lose because they'd had so little on the asteroid and colony. But of course maybe they had more to lose than anyone knew.

In any case, flight had seemed like a good idea at the time, even for the relatively well-off, what with the One World Religion bearing down their necks. Maybe now reality was setting in. What the hell were they doing?

That was one of the things they had come to the hold to discuss, now that they had taken care of the basics of survival. Now that they were out there in deep space, in the middle of nowhere, actually *living* there. What were they going to do now? How were they going to manage it? What about pay, and retirement? How would they live? That practical stuff!

Humans live short lives, and media and money had controlled the history they were able to learn in those short lives. So they had few social alternatives in mind. Actually, they had no alternatives in mind. All they knew was things were royally screwed up.

Most of them were well-trained technicians in their fields, but they were far more confident of the technology they commanded than of themselves (even if they would have to improvise the technology using duct tape!).They had always been someone's employee. A week ago, they had been Halliburton employees. They got paid; they weren't slaves. They got paid through a plastic card. They used that same card to buy their necessities. All the "stores" and "restaurants" were owned by Halliburton, that is true. But they got to choose which ones to use! They weren't slaves! Well, except for those unfortunate ones on the Bernina Harrison. They hated slavery—but never enough to make waves about conditions on the Bernina Harrison. Many felt a little guilty about that now, side-by-side with the victims they'd rescued on the way out.

Behind them was the colony, the devil they knew. Ahead of them was deep space, something no human being knew—yet. They feared both.

So, yeah, some of them wanted to go back. They were talking about it at the meeting there on the patio. It could be, they were saying, that, after a while, things would change so much on the colony that maybe they could negotiate a deal. That is what they told themselves. It was plausible. Things had been in such an uproar when they left, who knows what could happen? Privately, they were counting on the chronic labor shortage to broker their forgiveness. Sure, they could go back. They missed the colony. They missed television! They missed video games! The *Halliburton's* was a great employer. Everybody on Earth envied them their jobs! What had they been thinking? So they'd have to pretend to follow a new religion. So what? Big deal! Like it was a first time in history that had ever happened?

Of course, not many of them thought apostatizing—which is what going along with the new religion meant, denying Christ; apostatizing was just the word for the mortal sin it was—was "no big deal." Only a few were that far gone. Most knew the truth.

They had, for one thing, recited the Catholic Credo at every mass. "I believe in one God and His only Son, Jesus Christ," the gist of it. Not in Kali, or the Prophet, or Buddha, and so on. "I believe in the holy Catholic Church." Not in the Mormon Church, or the Church of Scientology, or the Unification Church. And so on. Thus, they recited the core and the heart of what Catholics believe, have *always* believed, and *have* to believe to be Catholic. And they did; they *did* believe. But they had not necessarily *applied* those formulas to the issue right before them, not head on. Definitely not on the colony or the mining asteroid, being as how being logical could get you expropriated, imprisoned, even killed. They had simply hoped to survive the new religion intact, alive, as Catholics always had, as people usually did, for that matter—so far.

A chain of events, though, had brought them to this unlikely place. Now, in retrospect, the notion had surfaced, perhaps they had been hasty. Perhaps, in retrospect, they had been unwise. Maybe they could go back to the colony, maybe that's what they should do, and hope for a miracle. Like, maybe Halliburton's stock had taken a downturn, or the labor shortage had made them more precious on the *Halliburton's* than they'd been before. Maybe that's the best thing: go back. Right? Some were thinking and feeling that.

The crowd had stirred when Armand came in, as though they had been waiting for him, and seeing him arrive, they settled down on their various perches.

Now, Tomás addressed them. "Good evening," he said, for it was evening in the ship's day/night schedule. "It's good to see all of you. You know why we are here. We have to talk about our plans for when we get to the asteroid.

"It seems to me that we can divide things into two parts: social plans and technological plans. The technology, well, maybe that's the easy part. We have workgroups to prepare project plans for us, and they're the best people for that. They were already doing that, even before we left, before we even knew what was really happening on Earth, so, we already have the basic materials we need to turn the asteroid into a safe and productive place—into a world, actually. Even though it might take a while. But the ship, as you know, can support us for a long time. There's no pressure there. If we can manage the maintenance, which we think we can. We have the infrastructure basics under control, thanks to your hard work. So technology isn't our biggest challenge. It's the social plans that we have to figure out."

Tomás paused. "And also, by space law, we get to name it—name the asteroid." He grinned. That was the fun part. Possibly the only fun part. "So I open the floor." Oh boy, here it comes.

All those present cast their eyes down and thought about what Tomás had said. That moment was to be the only silent one for a stretch.

Meifen's hand shot up, and Tomás nodded at her.

"Maybe we don't have to name the asteroid. Or make any big plans." She glared at the crowd. She was furious, and snapped her bubblegum like a machine gun. "Because some people want to go back. Even some of *us*!" She meant the workers from the Bernina Harrison. They had forgotten Jai Birdi already; they had forgotten those who'd died on the mining asteroid! Meifen had to swallow hard not to cry, she was so indignant.

Tomás nodded. Meifen was right: might as well go there right from the start.

Everybody glanced down, looked uncomfortable. Tomás waited.

Finally, Keith Costner waved his hand and spoke up. "Yeah, I been thinking about that. It's hard not to. I mean, do I have a job? Where is this job? How much does it pay? Where are we gonna spend the money? Are we gonna live on a ship the rest of our lives?"

He glanced around, having said his piece, and nervously scratched the little goatee he'd been growing since they ran. He was kind of embarrassed that he hadn't thought of all this before he joined the rush of his workmates toward the ship. He'd had a great job as a programmer. Work a couple of hours, muck around the rest of the time. There were certain—uh, amenities—on the colony he'd miss and was pretty sure would not be available with this straight-arrow crowd.

Rasheed Rogers raised his hand and began before Tomás gestured for him to speak. He seemed a little peeved. "I'd like to know that, too! I mean, I liked life on the colony okay." Rasheed grinned as he smoothed his pearl gray jacket. "Don't laugh, now, but you know how I am. I like my threads." He chuckled. "Unless somebody here can promise me they can knock off an Armani, is there any chance—" he looked up, serious now, knowing that what he was about to say was harsh, "Is there any chance we could, you know, apologize or something? Like, go back?" He sat down.

His words hung in the air, in the big echo-y hold. *Go back. Go back. Go back.* They missed what they knew. Seemed like life now was just always missing something, from blue sky to pizza. Bitterness flooded them. They could hardly remember that, when they'd had those very things, they were not happy then, either. That was the real tragedy: they missed *something*, but they did not know what it was. That's the worst.

They were frozen with longing. Ferdi looked at Tomás. Marley looked at Tim. Little Anka looked at Layne, under the table where they had been playing while the grownups talked. Everybody looked at somebody, as we humans do when a major point is scored. *Go back*. Even the children knew what that meant. Their school, the big observation window, the train that moved fast, all the strange people. Their house. It had not been so bad. It had been great! The low-gravity fields at the center of *Halliburton's*, where they had the recreation areas, had been *awesome*! (Of course, they already had one on the ship, but it wasn't as good. Just climbing nets and baby stuff.) And they had television on the colony. And movies. All they had here were those old book archives and vids. If they wanted new music, they had to make it themselves.

Walt Ferguson raised his hand, politely waiting for Tomás's nod to begin. "I think we need to talk about how we could do things on the asteroid, how we can survive. I have been thinking about how we could do things, and I have some ideas. I've talked about it to Tomás and Ferdi. I'd like to talk about it now."

Walt walked up to the front. You could still see in his demeanor the seminarian he had been—the quiet face, the thoughtful eyes. On the colony he had been a mid-level operations manager, but everyone was more familiar with his lifelong avocation of survivalism, which in space boiled down to figuring out how the human body could survive a colony catastrophe.

On the colony, Walt had drawn upon much of NASA's unpublished and mostly anecdotal reports regarding the body's ability to withstand the conditions of space. Because of Walt, the colony had a number of safe rooms that could withstand high-level radiation and an atmosphere blowout. They were even stocked with self-propulsion units—like, as if they could send somebody to go get help in a suit! As if! But Walt had insisted it was possible, since more and more small, independent habitations were springing up in space, sponsored by the various nations and some sponsored simply by wealthy individuals. Alternative shelter was available, even there, so they should prepare to get to it. It was merely sensible, if saving life was your objective (over profits), but Halliburton had fought the cost of it, you'd better believe.

Walt tended to talk about macabre subjects, but he was otherwise a cheerful man. He believed Catholicism's unequivocal tenet of personal immortality. It gave his survivalism a calm, unhurried quality. Survival was not Walt's chief contribution to the community, though. He knew about *spiritual* survival, too. He knew all Saint Thomas's writings and was well read in Catholic tradition. The community had the sense to appreciate Walt.

Standing in front of them now, he nodded at his audience, and they nodded back. Somebody turned up the lights.

"Well, you know me, the guy who's always talking about survival. So I want to say right up front that if I had to pick our survival chances here on the *Regina Coeli* compared to the colony, I'd say ours are better here." The crowd stirred in surprise. "No, no, hear me out," Walt went on. "They have superior technology, sure, but we have *enough* technology, and we have something else. Maybe something better." He looked around. "What we have, the *people* we have--well, let me put it like this—we have a better social platform. Theirs is very shaky. They don't agree on key issues, and it shows. As you know, when we left, there was a lot of trouble. I wouldn't be surprised if—" Walt paused, knowing that most listening to him had family and friends on the colony. "It wouldn't have surprised me, if more people hadn't gotten together and run after we did, stolen pods or rovers when they had the chance, in all the confusion there at the end. It might have gotten very bad. We don't know what's left."

They could imagine. There would have been police action. There might have been injuries, even fatalities. Sides had been taken, and there were dangerous actors on both of them. Privately, Walt wouldn't even put it past Halliburton to blow up the colony, flat out, if they thought it would be cheaper than an evacuation made necessary by rioting, or by some cataclysmic event, or by seizure of the colony by terrorists (naturally, that's what they'd call them). He'd been aware of the possibility from the beginning. That's what colonies *do*, for heaven's sake, they separate, and owners of colonies fight back, but he hadn't added that particular scenario to the list of potential catastrophes for discussion with management. Fine with him if they hadn't thought of it yet.

"Also, they needed us, and our escape is going to hurt them," Walt went on. "Things will have gotten worse, deteriorated, that's my point. So considering going *back*—I'm not sure what we could go back *to*." He cast his eyes downward then. "We *could*, though, I guess. Go back." He could not look at them when he said that. He scratched his eyebrow and covered his eyes. It was such a bad idea! "Or we could go forward. I'm more for that."

He stepped forward a foot to make his case. "Yeah, I say go forward to the asteroid Laiq found, which qualifies as well as anybody could hope for as a great hiding place. When we get there, I'd like to propose a whole new way of living—that is really an *old* way."

Walt cleared his throat and plunged on. "We have this ship. Well, Tomás has this ship; that's the way this all developed. But Tomás is willing to give over the ship to a cooperative, owned by all of us, for the purpose of terraforming the asteroid—providing the asteroid lives up to its billing, of course." He glanced at Laiq. "Which we have every reason to believe it will."

They had more than Laiq's word. They had their own experience. All the asteroids they had found mining had similar composition. They were dirt, exactly the same old dirt on Earth, lacking only carbons, and there was no reason to think Laiq's asteroid in the Oort would be any different. It was just the statistical probability.

"We would develop the land along with an atmosphere," Walt continued.

They knew about that; they had all seen the vids. You primed the asteroid with atmospheric gases, just about as common as sunlight in space in various forms—gas, liquid, solid, but not combined, of course. You mixed them and released them, gravity would hold the mixture close, and then, with the pod's lasers, you spun the asteroid (pretty much like you'd spin a billiard ball) so the new atmosphere would heat and cool more evenly but not too fast to fling off the atmosphere. It could take several trials to get the balance right. It had already been done on a small test asteroid, in three tries. Walt had been part of the team; so had Keith Costner and Bill, the engineer. They had learned an astonishing thing from it: they could not seem to make atmosphere stick to a *dead* asteroid beyond several weeks. Gravity alone didn't seem to be enough. There had to be life on it. It seemed to take, believe it or not, the effluvia of living organisms to keep an atmosphere in place. They had taken to calling the condition "sticky." They had been working on the right addition of carbonaceous material to the dirt right up to their exodus.

They didn't have to have an atmosphere on their asteroid, actually. Not at first, definitely. They could live and farm under domes, just as people did even on Earth in certain environments, like under the ocean. That's what they would do on the asteroid, at first, and after they had added sufficient carbon to the dirt, they would just move the tents. But oh, when and if they had an atmosphere, that sure would make it—home. Hey, just add life! It could be done.

Walt continued. "But that's how it would be different. It wouldn't belong to Halliburton, see. It would belong to us. The land would be distributed to us, individually, to hold in our families, for *perpetuity*." He pronounced the word carefully. "That means it could not be sold for speculation.

"There could be some jobs off the land, too, in companies owned by the employees or individually owned. I'm thinking schools and hospitals, at least. But most people could live on their own land and farm it or develop it however they liked, and work from home.

"Economic relations would not be competitive, though— they would be cooperative. Hear what I'm saying. That basically means there would be regulation from management teams made up of all the workers in any particular industry or area. Like the guilds were in the building of Europe. The way the guilds worked was different than the management we are used to. Their job was to make sure the work and the gain were roughly evenly distributed. Their objective was to make sure everybody stayed in business, not to put someone else out of business. Not for anyone to get a monopoly. Guilds is what these self-regulating organizations were called in the old days, and that's what they did. That is how the economy was run in the old Catholic states. The point was to make sure that the ownership—of land, of businesses, of everything—was spread out. Like, the exact opposite of *Halliburton's*. I say let's try to re-establish that kind of economy. It's called distributism now."

Roy, the ag tech, raised his hand. "You speak as if we were going to sell things! Okay, but to who? Uh, whom?" He snorted and looked around at his buddies. Grammar!

Walt laughed along with him. "But we're talking at least a couple of generations down the road, right, for everything to work out, line up? Maybe more. Up to that time, we'd trade with each other, we'd own the habitats cooperatively and that should be enough to give us a living, and down the road, we might get strong enough to sell back to Earth, to the colony—if they fixed their demand problem. Keep in mind, too, that we would be in a growth economy on the asteroid. We expect to have kids, as many as God sends us. That would take care of the demand, and of income for the elderly, as well. The old-fashioned way."

Walt wasn't sure they would know why he included that detail in a discussion about economics. Weren't kids a moral issue, a marriage issue? Family stuff? But Walt knew it was economic, too. And of course moral truths would be reflected in natural laws. "Go forth and multiply" was also an economic axiom!

But most people didn't get it. Earth had been debating their economic crisis for several generations while the fertility rate plummeted. They kept applying old economic theories from an older world where in almost any economic system you could count on an automatic annual 3 percent rise in demand without any productivity increases at all. Why? It came from population growth. It was the baby benefit, but did anyone count it? It was like the air you breathed. In the old days you just took it for granted. It had been that way ever since Christianity stopped the practice of infanticide, family by family, tribe by tribe, nation by nation. So, historically, the point was, which economic theory had worked, or didn't, it really didn't matter too much in their situation of predictable natural growth. They were going to grow, no matter which weird theory experts might have applied. Theories didn't help and they didn't hurt; they just gave the suits something to do. The birth-rate effect was the real engine. It had been the invisible boost over all the eons of mankind's history. But that old world of steady growth was gone now. When they'd killed it, with contraception and abortion and gender engineering, they hadn't realized what that meant.

They still didn't. By now, they didn't want to. They'd grown used to a childless society. Oh, no wait, not exactly childless; the grownups were the children. So they'd kept on killing their economies with stupid policies—encouraging delayed marriage or no marriage at all, pushing contraception, promoting a negative vision of motherhood and fatherhood, promoting homosexuality. All exercises in low fertility. And then the economic growth rate fell below one percent, then it fell below a half percent, and it began to go negative and contract, and they just could not figure it out.

Catholics might not understand the economics any better than anyone else, but because of their religion they were committed to the principle that sex and marriage and babies went together. And Walt was completely sure that marriage and children and families would be encouraged on their asteroid. In fact, birth control would probably not be provided at their clinics. The pills were lethal to any environment, excreted and washed with sewage into the water supply, and mechanical birth control devices hurt women's bodies. And contraception was lethal to society, too, in a hundred ways. So Walt included that in his thirty-second economics plan. "Economic growth would work out just like it always has, over all the centuries, until people started messing with the birth rate and screwing it up. We won't limit the birth rate on the asteroid. In fact, we'll do everything we can to encourage it. The growth baseline is about three percent, without any productivity increases necessary—in a healthy community. Earth is now less than a half percent.

"And we won't waste any resources putting each other out of business, either. Capitalism is a wasteful way to run a world. Thank God, we know a different way. So that's why I say we have a better chance of making it than the colony, if we use what we have."

Another hand went up. It was Max—Maxim Andrushkiv, the Ukrainian whose father was Jewish, mother Catholic. He always had a worried look, and he always told jokes. Usually the combination was hilarious. Everyone leaned forward a little in expectation, but this time Max was serious.

"Well, won't prices go up? And won't quality go down?"

He was only saying what everyone else was thinking, what everyone had always said, the same thing, it was the capitalist catechism, even though they knew very well that they themselves, personally, worked harder for love than for money and that competition seemed to bring out the worst in people, not the best. It certainly brought out the worst in the economy, as people, millions, were thrown adrift ,with no way to live but off the government. Which was broke due to the lack of growth. But still they believed and repeated the capitalist creed.

Before Walt could formulate an answer, Hugh, Tomás's crewmate, raised his hand and spoke.

"It's not like prices were going *down* and quality was going *up* you know, on Earth or on the *Halliburton's*. Right? Come on, Max, competition's not all it's cracked up to be. In fact, think about it, we all know how it goes, competition leads to only a few companies being left. They put each other out of business, which costs a lot, like, billions. Then, they fix the prices. *We* always end up losing! You know it's true--remember how the airline industry was doing?" Yes, they remembered! Always lower quality and always higher prices. People had started to freak out on flights, they were so awful. Worse than the shuttle!

And just about everybody knew the history of Halliburton and its great rise over all the nations of Earth. Now, Halliburton was invincible, and wages were lower than ever. It had not worked. Capitalism had not delivered on its early promise. That's all you could say.

Jacob sprang to his feet, his face already blazing red. He was a dockworker. He was a volatile guy, like a bulldog once he got his teeth in an issue. He had been very much against their stealing the *Regina Coeli*, when that possibility had first been floated, and he had not hesitated to say so. But then Providence had come to their aid, and it became a moot point.

"That's what the communists have always said!" he spat out and sat down with a thump.

"That's true, they did," Walt responded. "But so have others. Real Catholics. The thing is, communism does try to minimize competition. But it does it the wrong way. It gives everything to the government and hopes for the best. But a noncompetitive economy doesn't have to be that way. It can be the opposite of that. We could give everything to the *people*. I mean the people themselves, not the government. Real ownership, of land and wealth, the shares, the money, the titles. And then they use it to make their living in a regulated economy where the common good counts, not just profits. It was a comfortable living even with the technology of the middle ages."

The great conflict between communism and Catholicism! It had dominated the Church's struggle for more than a century—almost two centuries. Determined Her allies. Captured Her votes. Catholics had ended up, for lack of an alternative, voting against communism and voting for parties across the globe that were associated with unrestricted competition, with a "free market" (a fantasy right from the first days of capitalism), and with deregulation—just because those various parties sometimes took vaguely pro-life positions, if only because they wanted more native workers to exploit. These parties always strongly took anti-communist positions, which pleased the Catholics. These free-market forces (which originally came from the protestant rebellion) were always emphatically secular, all for 'religious liberty,' which boiled down to, let the fools believe anything they want as long as we get the cash.

Because of this unholy alliance, Catholics had failed to protect the concept of the Catholic state, the Catholic economy. They had failed to fight for the social Kingship of Christ. They had grown to believe the story that all faiths, no matter how contradictory, could live peacefully together under the umbrella of a benevolent, non-religious, secular apparatus. They had continued to believe that right up to the present, when the secular state had reared up and bared its fangs. And its face was indistinguishable from either communism or fascism, because they were all the same in the end, mere strategies of that bad angel Satan, the king of contradiction. He wanted souls; he was getting them. He didn't care at all that his means or his terms were contradictory. Because error can be wrong every which way. Only Truth has to be right.

The cost for this unholy alliance was huge. The Catholic state would've saved some—many. It would have given shelter in the great storms of the twentieth and twenty-first centuries. But sheepfold there was none. The Church had opted out. The hirelings had fled before the wolves.

Walt continued. "Distributism is the opposite of communism. The *opposite*. With communism, all of the means of production—the land, the factories, the stores—it all belongs to the state, and the people have jobs working for the state. With distributism, all of that—the land, the factories, the stores— belongs to the citizens, individually or for certain industries collectively by the workers, but not to the government. The people own real shares or real land, and the government only helps to enforce laws that keep the distribution of these things as close to one hundred percent as it can be. That is exactly the way it was during Medieval times, but certain greedy people, starting in England, overthrew it using religion as an excuse. They called it Protestantism. It was really economic, as well as religious, because the Catholic Church had rules that kept competition in check. Had to overthrow the one to get to the other. So it was social, religious, economic, everything."

He paused to take a sip of water. Then, drove on.

"That rebellion ruined everything. All across Europe, up until the sixteenth century, from Roman times to modern times, there had been progress. People went from being slaves the way most people were in the Empire, passed through centuries of being serfs, and ended up being fully enfranchised citizens of Europe, all owning the means to support themselves in the form of land and tools. The Church guided this transformation—which was a really incredible human achievement!"

Walt sighed and looked at his fellow evacuees sadly. "That's what we *had*. At the end of the sixteenth century, nobody worked for anybody; that was the norm. They worked on their land from home. If something needed for production was too expensive for a single family to own, it was owned by a cooperative, and the people had shares in the cooperative. Well, the ownership of the *Regina Coeli* could be like that, if we accept Tomas's offer. And also the asteroid. And everything on the asteroid. We have a chance here to go back to the old, peaceful way!"

Walt stopped and let them think about it. What he had said was the complete opposite of what they'd learned from their history vids and books, and the Catholic Church itself had given up trying to tell the truth about it, and just gave in when it joined forces with the victors back in the twentieth century. In the protestant version of the history of the world, Medieval ways were "backward," and liberalism had set the people "free" of all that. (Free to starve! And go to hell in the bargain!) Only traditional Catholics had held on to the archives. Only a few among so many, but there were a surprising number of them gathered right here, and Walt knew there was a chance they could convince the others.

There were plenty of worried looks, and not all of them on those who might be expected to want to go back to the colony, like the well-off workers. Some of the traditional Catholics, as well, looked worried and mad, because over time, they had lost their sense of the old Catholic states and the way they were run. They knew only that communism had been ruinous and godless. What could Walt mean, there would be cooperatives? Like communism, right? Wasn't that it, really, no matter what he said? If you shared things, it made you--one of *them*.

Jacob's hand shot up again. "Isn't that at least socialism, then?" he demanded.

"No, it's the *opposite* of socialism, too, Jake," Walt said. "Because what does socialism mean? It means the government takes care of its workers and tries to protect them from the effects of capitalism, if it's a decent government, but the workers still don't own any of it or at least not much of it. Maybe they get to own their house—and the mortgage. But last I looked, leaving Earth, even that was gone. All the real ownership and real power is in the hands of only a few, just like in communism.

"I'm proposing something else. It's not a new idea. Like I said, we already had it. It was the ordinary condition in Europe for many centuries: ownership of land by one hundred percent of enfranchised voters. Not just land, either, but what they call the means to work it with—the tools, the gear, the transportation. They owned all that. They could make their own living. They were not anybody's employees. That went for all the businesses and professions, too, except for the parts of business that were too expensive for any one person to own, and those they owned those together, as in cooperatives, where you own shares, like I said. You know, like a mill. Does that sound like socialism? It's called distributism, but they only started calling it that after they lost it."

"I heard about cooperatives," came a woman's voice from the back. "Didn't they try that in Detroit? The companies fail! Bad management!" The comment had come from Linda Ramos, a waitress who had switched to agtech as soon as she was offered the chance on the *Regina Coeli*. With her bruised-looking, sad brown eyes, she looked like she knew a thing or two on the ground about bad management.

Armie Hebert stood up. "But management doesn't *have* to be bad. I heard about how they did management in those days. It was different, the way they did it. It was smarter! It wasn't done by suits making all the decisions, and then the people who do the work having to live with it and only getting to vote in big elections, never on the job. The way they did it was management on the shop floor, managed by people who worked there. Everybody got to help make the plan. And anyway, cooperatives have to have at least the same support as the competition, and that didn't happen in Detroit."

Armie looked around for the faces he knew in the hold, mostly thin, young Asian ones, worked nearly to death. He had managed them and done his best to protect them. They too knew a thing or two about bad management. And how. But hadn't he shown them some good management? He pushed his geek glasses back up on his nose and continued.

"I heard about the guilds in a role-playing game. But they were the real deal, not a game, once upon a time. They were like super corporations run by their members. They organized everything, from getting the raw materials to transporting the finished product. They identified skills needed and made sure training was available. They ran hospitals. They ran schools. They set production goals for a region based on demand. And they set aside money for investment in the infrastructure. It wasn't unions against management; everybody was represented. And their goal wasn't higher profits; their goal was that everyone had *work*."

Just thinking about it made Armie happy. It was his dream, happening right there and now. He had been living in a nightmare on the asteroid. Seeing Armie happy made those young Asian faces happy. If Armie liked guilds, then guilds sounded pretty good to them! They might not know a whole lot about economics—or didn't know all the words in English, and there were a lot of complicated words—but they knew Armie Hebert had fought for them.

Walt nodded. "Yes, that's pretty much what I had in mind. We have some examples archived," he said. "There were examples on Earth, even in the twentieth century, even right up to the twenty-first. The guilds held the expensive tools in common. First it was the mill grinders, and then the big combines for reaping and thrashing, and later, the machine shops. People shared their use, paid a reasonable fee, got to keep or re-invest whatever profits were generated. Members could get time on the machines without having to own them outright. It was the same deal with banks—community banks, not for profit but for growth, owned by the account holders.

"It will probably work out to be the same with us, with heavy equipment and energy. We can own things cooperatively until we're able to distribute ownership by family and even after that for the really big-ticket machines. So, specifically, what I am recommending is that we ask volunteers to study the archives and present a plan for us to vote on."

Walt looked out at the crowd seriously but not sadly. It was a happy moment, a very happy moment, really. Yes, they were a long way from Kansas. What Kansas wouldn't give for their chance to start over!

For a few moments, everyone sat quietly in thought.

Then, Rasheed Rogers stood up again. "Look," he said, "I don't want to be the bad guy here, but, hey, are we out of our *minds*?" He made a funny face and put his hands on his hips. Rasheed was an extremely good-looking guy, and the effect was impressive. Like a movie. More than a couple of the people watching wished they were only seeing a movie with a good-looking black guy performing his role instead of all of them living the reality way out there in middle of, literally, nowhere.

Rasheed continued. "You're talking as if we're going to be able to follow some kind of plan that, up to now, has been, well, just a school discussion for a whole bunch of university professors! This is real life, people! You're talking like we are going to take an asteroid and do what has never been done. I'm just talking about the technology, and, like, that's not enough, we think we are going to solve us a whole bunch of social issues. That's what Dr. King wanted to do, and *he* couldn't do it!

"Listen, I had a *job*. I had a *good* job. I was the first person in my family to go to space." Rasheed made another funny, rueful face. "You are talking like people can plan sh— uh, stuff. Plan stuff. You know we can't. Not that well. We have to, like they say, let the market do the planning." He sighed. "There were a few things on the colony that could've been better, true, but I think they might have wised up to that by now. Like the vegetarian thing. I'm sure they have rethought *that*."

Rasheed didn't, however, repeat "go back." He sat down.

James Scott passed a hand over his eyes. James was a black guy and an electrician. He got his Catholic roots from his Louisiana mother and his light grey eyes from his dad, a German stationed on an offshore oil rig. He looked pained, sorrowful. James had the kind of face that was handsome when he was happy and ugly when he was sad. But when he took his hand away, he had calmed down and his face was its handsome version. He was resigned to his fate—to argue the damn race issue, right there in front of all these people. He knew he was starting with a handicap: he was obviously mixed race, and that translated to his having a lot to prove. But sometimes you had to do what you least wanted to do and say what you least wanted to say.

"Uh, Rasheed," James said, glancing toward Tomás for the go-ahead to speak. "I hate to hear you say that you don't think we would be capable of owning our own land and of having a say-so over how our community acts. That you would rather go back to a good job then go forward to—to freedom. I have to put it that way. You would rather go back to somebody else making the decisions and telling you what to do. Just so you can be stylish. Well, I think you should think about that. I really do."

James sat down, and Rasheed sprang to his feet. He was indignant.

"What is wrong with wanting to keep my job, man?" His handsome face was brimming with the sorrow of generations in search of a living, in search of only one thing—a job, a job, a job. They counted themselves lucky to get one. He'd *had* a job! A *decent* one!

James stood back up. "There's nothing wrong with wanting a job, Rasheed. When that's all you can get. But don't you know what is happening here?" He looked fiercely at Rasheed. "We are being given the chance to be *free*. We can do our own thing, work as hard as we like, or take a couple hours off and read a book, if that's what we feel like doing, if we can do it. We could have our own land, work for our own family. And it grieves me to hear my brother say—" He paused, and you could see his grief, true enough. "It really grieves me to hear you say that you prefer *slavery*."

The word shivered in the air.

Rasheed looked at him, stunned. He'd felt everything James had said, and it had gone straight to his heart. James was talking about the game. Rasheed knew the game just about as well as basketball. Of course he did. It was a game without any name. It was just the game, about not growing up, about shucking and jiving. It was the grey-haired, grizzled old man still wearing his baseball cap turned around on the L train. Okay, if they were going to treat you like a child, anyway, why not enjoy it? The game. It was not obeying any rules nor accepting any responsibility. It was working slow, keeping your fingers crossed and your options open. And he knew that those who laid it on race were simply wrong. It was *human*. He had seen it in white guys, and in Chinese guys, and in Hispanic guys, any kind of mixture you could think of.

No denying it, he loved the game. Oh yes. He loved his chains. He *did* want to go back to them. They set him free, the way old cons said about doing time. What good was freedom without a comfortable bed and an easy shift? What was the big deal about owning your own land, anyway? Just heartache and grief.

And yet he felt shame.

One thing you could say about Rasheed: he knew when he was wrong. And he didn't answer James back or put on any show. He just sat down.

After that, everyone sat quietly, thinking of their own friendly chains.

Marlene McLane leaned closer to her right-hand woman, Zillah, the Israeli Catholic who was driving egg production, and muttered, "I hope he knows, I hope he realizes, we were all slaves." It was a surprising observation from a person who had been among the best-paid employees on the *Halliburton's*. She sounded bitter.

But was Walt's plan for the asteroid in the Oort any better? When they'd fled the colony, most people hadn't realized what they were getting themselves in for. A whole new society? A whole new economy? And it sounded like they were basing an awful lot on *family!* What if you didn't have any? What if you didn't *want* any? There were a whole lot of single people in the hold. They'd always thought it was by their own sweet choice. That's what they'd thought most of the time, anyway, except sometimes when they cried in the dark. That marriage thing, that family thing—all that was *work*.

Vijay Patel raised his hand and stood. He had been mid-management on the Bernina Harrison, working with Ramdoss. "If we go back, I think we could work out a deal for the mining pod. You must realize that something was wrong with that title transfer, even if it was legal, I don't care who signed it, and they must realize it by now, too. I am sure they'd like to get their billion-dollar pod back. Why don't we take advantage of the situation?"

Several people nodded. That was good business thinking! Maybe they could get something out of this!

James Scott raised his hand again. "Nope, Vijay. I'm pretty sure they'd rather have us dead than get the pod back. Or else they wouldn't have been shooting at us." He paused. A thought came to him. "We represent something they don't want anybody else to hear: I think it's that mankind getting to outer space changes the rules—gives us a chance to make it on our own. It's like in the old days—like a frontier! We've made a break for it. They are not going to let that go unpunished. The idea could spread. They can't afford to let that happen. We go back, we get erased, Vijay. *Especially* us!"

Vijay shook his head. "No, no! They'd rather have the whole package back—the ship and us! They're reasonable men. We're valuable. They won't be able to ignore the numbers."

But Vijay was able to ignore all the instances in his own experience and in the experiences of trusted associates and friends of times when the owners had been perfectly willing to disregard profits and to violate the rules of the market, when pride was at stake. He called his vacillating views on the subject *prudence*. Every evening, Vijay congratulated himself on being a wise man, a scientist. He didn't see the pattern, that his decisions were capitulations and his virtues the virtues of a slave. It wasn't prudence. It was cowardice.

Another man stood, Will O. Yee, name American style. Will was barely more than a kid, with a downy little beard on his cheeks. He'd been a dock worker on the Bernina Harrison. Dangerous job. You'd not have known it from Will. Everyone knew Will; he was quite a character! Will laughed theatrically at danger, to the delight of the girls, and he worked hard. He was determined to star in his own success . He would change his name, to Li Ka Ching. Heh!

Nobody got that joke. It was actually the name of a very famous rich guy, a real guy, a billionaire, Li Ka-Shing. He'd had to drop out of school and work, just like Will. Li Ka-Shing was Will's dream and his philosophy. It was other people's destiny to be poor; it was Will's destiny to be rich. So he laughed at danger (whenever the girls were listening), and off-duty he wore an elegant, old mariachi jacket. Naturally, on him it looked like the court dress of some obscure Chinese sect, maybe a mountain tribe; easy to imagine, China was a big place. Will looked terrific in it!

Will hadn't exactly understood what he was doing when he'd followed Meifen out to the *Regina*. He just always stayed close to Meifen, without thinking about it. He had not thought ahead about what he had gotten himself in for. Now he realized: these crazy people wanted to eliminate billionaires!

So now he spoke up. "Did Armie say that the guilds were not trying to get profits? So how is that not socialist? It sounds just like Maoism."

He sat down again, peeked up slyly, and smoothed the lapels of his jacket. He believed he'd gotten to the heart of it.

Armie stood up again. Guessed the ball was in his court, since he'd chimed in. "Well, the thing is, like Walt has tried to explain to you, it's not socialist because it's not owned by the government. The people own shares. They can buy and sell shares as long as no one owns enough to dominate a market and create a monopoly. That's regulated by the guilds, based on the guidelines established by us. *We* decide the guidelines. Who *owns* the profits and the means to make it is what matters. That is what makes something socialist or capitalist—not that people cooperate to make a better living or to own some things together. That's not capitalist, but that doesn't mean it has to be socialist."

He had to pause for a breath before going on. "The old archives show us a third way. There's this old Catholic principle called subsidiarity, where you're supposed to solve problems as far down the line as possible. Close to the work. That's more democracy—real democracy. On the shop floor. In the field. On the ground. Decentralized authority. Like I said before." Armie sought out the faces in the crowd he knew best. He knew that had hurt them on the colony, that management never asked them to help plan anything, when they were the ones with experience and the ones who could get killed. Hurt them, hurt the work. Dumb.

"Did you say the asteroid is going to be Catholic?" That came from Max, the joker.

Again, the audience waited expectantly for a one-liner follow-up, but again, he didn't deliver it. They fell back to considering, not for the first time, why he had come with them in the mad dash to the pod, but figured, as they usually did, that it was because of his friendship with Cardei Dita, who was a whole other question mark. They sure had collected a lot of rare types in this ark!

Armie replied to the question. "No, I didn't say that. I just said that cooperatives—as well as minimizing rather than maximizing competition and the other things, like subsidiarity—were Catholic. Came from the old Medieval Catholic states. Lots of people have imitated them, or tried to, without being Catholic or even religious at all. But now that you bring it up, Max, I would be in favor of the asteroid being officially Catholic."

He looked around the room. "I know that some of you aren't Catholic. But most of us are. I can argue the point that our best chance of survival is to use that—to name, define, a morality we all recognize and practice to the best of our ability. Naturally, that doesn't rule out tolerance of other people and their beliefs. It never did, in the faith. They talk about some infamous instances, but every time you look, you see it was really a matter of things some individual people were doing, not things the Church taught, not coming from their faith. They were using their faith as a cover to exploit or defraud. Same as now—you know what and who I mean."

Armie paused, and they all glanced at Zillah, the Israeli Catholic. She had seen it in action. She nodded sadly.

"Nothing in the Catholic faith says you can make anybody believe a certain way," Armie went on. "But nothing in the faith—at least before Vatican II—says you can't make laws that follow Catholic morality. So just because someone may believe something doesn't mean they get to *do* it. People can think whatever they want, but not act however they want. And that's fair. I, personally, feel that would give us the best chance of survival, like Walt said. If we bring that stupid religious equality crap with us from the colony, we'll end up like the colony."

He started to sit down but added, "Our best chance would be to establish a standard for public morality. Then, you get a greater likelihood for more honesty in business and more stability of social relations. It pleases God, and it's good business. Most of us are Catholic, we would choose Catholic morality."

Ever the good manager, that Armie, clarifying the benchmarks. Better businesses, better neighborhoods. Not *perfect* ones, notice. *Better*. Managing expectations.

Tomás stood up. "I get it, Armie! It makes sense," he said. "If you want a society where people cooperate with each other instead of trying to get over on each other, trying to make a buck off somebody, twisting things to fool somebody, then 'Thou shalt not steal' cannot be open for some kind of popular vote. And that's what 'religious liberty' means. It's false! It means you can do whatever you want and call it your religion! If you have enough money, you can buy the politicians, make your particular scam legal by day after tomorrow. 'Religious freedom' means everything is built on sand! In the end, it's just a cover to rip-off people. That's the crap you're saying we shouldn't bring from the colony.

"I mean, yes, you have to have a firm standard. You are absolutely right. The standards have to be universal, part of what everybody in the community respects or at least knows well. So it has to be taught in school and at home, and used in the courts, and followed in the hospitals—all that. Because everybody knows, if you want somebody to learn something, you have to repeat it more than once.

"Now, naturally, just declaring that something is a value shared by of all of us does not make it guaranteed, in any way, to work with all people all the time. So I see why Armie said things wouldn't be perfect. We're imperfect. But it makes fairness more *likely* to happen, and maybe that's enough. The consistency makes it easier for us to grasp, and maybe we only need a few more of us to practice what we preach to make a decent society.

"I guess I don't have to go into what 'indecent society' means. Remember? We lived in hell. Their freedom is *hell*. Let's just go ahead and admit up-front that our freedom is limited by the Ten Commandments and we like it that way. We choose that. Mankind lived like that for a long time, and prospered."

"But what about those of us who aren't Catholic? Where do you get off, saying the asteroid should be *Catholic*?" It was Cardei Dita himself, wearing his blue bandanna and an ear ring. Cardei was their professional rebel. Actually, he *was* Catholic, by his family upbringing anyway. He had a curious way of practicing his faith, only through his politics, because he never went to church.

Cardei's politics were simple. He had been for the underdog all his life, in every sense of the word, you name it— school, work, even his style. He always rooted for the underdog. He considered himself to be one.

His bishop on Earth (because, like every Catholic, practicing or not, Cardei had a bishop whose job was, supposedly, to guard Christ's sheep) had exploited this identity and encouraged Cardei to continue to identify with the underdog part rather than with the Catholic part. Or at least to mix them up well. It sure made things easier! Vote for the poor, vote for the oppressed, vote for the victim, vote for the underdog. Easy position, low risk, always covered by the argument of mercy, and you weren't responsible for fixing it! Why, that job belonged to the government, not the Church!

And there was a steady supply of victims, since the system went rolling on, churning them out, grinding them up.

And it was so liberating, from a bishop's point of view, in the homily department! You could take the heroes from any tradition, any tradition whatsoever, and use them. Rather than Christ. Instead of Christ. That meant you could preach a Christmas sermon on the virtues of, oh, pick any one of a hundred good-looking movie stars. Instead of preaching about Christ. Preaching about Christ was embarrassing and difficult, but anybody could get a crowd warmed up talking about how great Flint Westwood was. The many virtues of the fictional characters he played! When the bishop preached about Christ, when he got around to it, it was pretty much the same way. Christ as character, not as real live Savior. (So maybe, thank God, they didn't preach about Him all that often, matter of fact.)

But now, here in the hold of the *Regina Coeli*, it was the reverse, Cardei was being asked, for once, to consider being the *overdog*. Because, this time, the overdog was the right dog. So, Cardei was confused. Up to then, the underdog had *always* been the right dog. The protesters were *always* better than the administration they were protesting. The dominant race was *always* worse—and uglier!—than the dominated one. It had been like that his whole life. It simplified things!

Everyone in the room understood Cardei's new predicament, and it troubled them less than it might because they knew him. Cardei was more worried about his sweet bandana than he was about an abstract principle like truth versus error or justice versus injustice. That wasn't a put-down, just an honest assessment of a guy they had worked a lot of shifts with. Wow,

Cardei might have to cut his ponytail! *Poseur!* They smiled and shook their heads. Grow up, Cardei. They thought it affectionately because you couldn't help but like the guy.

That *was* the hard question, though. Picking a social operating system (which is one of the things religion is) was not about bandanas, or ponytails, or smoking the green herb that had made it to the colony along with the other plants, or having a beer after work. Yes, it was all that, but more. It really *was* about truth versus error, even if not to Cardei. At the heart of it, it was about *truth*. Whether there even was truth or not. Whether words could be used to find it.

And that was a can of worms. They didn't even know how to consider it. Liberalism had this habit of shrugging off little details like true versus false and right versus wrong with a shrug, and it had left them all lazy and disinclined to fight. Hey, whatever! That was their go-to response. Easy to say, with a cute little roll of the eyes, and it worked every time. They sighed; you could hear the exhalation in the quiet hold. This part of the argument was the opposite of whatever. What made them think they should have a Catholic state instead of any other kind? What made them so bold as to think their religion was special?

But the thing about it was, as a human being—as one who wants to get anywhere, anyway—you just can't escape adding things up, judging things, not if you want to see results. Then, in the end, you have to make a decision about what it means for what you do next. You have to. You do that in any scientific field, on any job. You use evidence, all kinds, wherever you can get it, to operate that unmoving brain muscle, and then, in the end, you choose the true over the false. The better over the worse. The valuable over the valueless. You had to pick an operating system in the end. You had to choose and buy a car, a house, a phone. You had to decide where to invest your 401K. Likewise, in the end, you had to pick a philosophic position. If the decision matters at all, there will be a preferred position. Nothing was ever equal.

Well, there *was* evidence to help—compelling evidence. Studies support the narrative that the Catholic faith was truly revealed by God Himself and began thousands of years before Christ. It was possible to examine ancient written records from widely separated sources and to legitimately conclude that the best explanation for the convergences between cultures is that a good God--the God of the Jews was good and loving--was working on Earth. That was at least as good an explanation as "aliens came and then left again" or other stories. And, of course, once you deciphered it from the archives, once you saw that the Catholic Church was the reliable religion composed by God Himself, logically, then, from there on, you also grasp the morality that was revealed. This morality was intended to be expressed throughout the culture—in its laws, in decisions about where money is spent, in schools, in hospitals, in government, most of all in government. It wasn't something to "do" only at home or in church on Sundays.

       The philosophical position of religious liberty flattened all religions, just when the world desperately needed one to emerge in leadership. The President's advisors had seen a piece of that algorithm. But the President's religion was made-up, a jumble of boy scout slogans from around the world: do a good deed every day, save for the future, believe in yourself, smiley face. No. Not enough. Not real. Not supernatural, only natural. People needed the supernatural. They needed a heaven, and they needed a hell. They needed angels. They needed supernatural help from the sky, to be good. A man-made religion could not deliver that. They needed a real religion. A real religion that decent people can be persuaded by evidence that it comes from God. That means doing the hard things: gathering the evidence, arguing it out just like you would for any other decision, once "religious liberty" was off the table. Not only arguing it out, but taking it to the people, teaching it, letting them make that decision with their choice of church. No ecumenism. No "whatever." A hard fight fought with words. But no revolution, either. It wasn't class against class. Or race against race, or men against women. It was sin against virtue. Some people hate those words—until the sinners seize your house, as they are wont to do. Rape your daughter. Or just sleep on the job. (Funny how "whatever" fails to satisfy then.)

       Catholic morality was easy to sum up, it was simple, you could tick it off on one hand, and it was not nitpicky. Catholic morality protects all life against any kind of violence, from conception to natural death. Catholicism discourages theft and lying, even small change and white lies, and calls gossiping about another person (even when it's true!) what it is—not "harmless" at all, but a sin. Catholic morals channel sex drive into life-long heterosexual marriage by restricting all other sexual expression—even sexual thoughts. Simple. Nobody said easy. And what happens when people do not live up to the standards? Stoning? Mutilation? Shunning? No. Confession, penance, and a chance at a new start.

Less known, Catholicism favors a particular economy and a particular politics. It is an economic system against the grain of self-centeredness, and it takes work to maintain.

Such a society is not achievable or not sustainable for any civic entity. Divine help, supernatural help, was required and promised to the Catholic society in the form of grace from the sacraments—mass, confession, consecrated marriage, baptism, all seven of them. To get and keep enough people doing the right thing *needed* help from Almighty God, and the Church kept the grace flowing through the sacraments. Nothing is tougher than simply telling the truth, and yet the best societies were based on that simple platform. It takes the help of God. That's what they were discussing here on the *Regina Coeli*. Calling on that help.

With that simple recognition of God and Church by the state, the culture itself acquires a spirit. The spirit part was harder to define but easy to spot. That Catholic spirit. It was generous, yet in some areas rigorous. It had a lot of feast days, no work then, and women were privileged, not abused. It liked to found universities and hospitals. There were no restrictions on mild inebriation, yet there were, for a balance, fast days along with the feast days, a somber Lenten season, and little "Lents" in each of the seasons of the year, called Ember Days. It set up this rhythm, it went with nature.

In their short human lives, few in the shadowy hold knew their history in great detail. But they had held on to much of this feeling, this confidence in their faith to make them better and happier in the bargain.

Augie raised his hand. "Yeah, but nobody likes dictatorships. Nobody likes being told how to think. At least on the colony we were free, right? Well, isn't that what people always say?"

And yet they *had* been told how to both think and how to act. And if they messed up, it wasn't a matter of being sorry and trying again; it was jail, hard time and a lot of it. And the "rules" kept changing. And the secular world had made a business of prisons, just like everything else. The United States, which touted its wonderful "freedom," had the most people in jail in the whole world. Every working-class family had somebody in the slammer.

"And I forgot, what about democracy? Not the shop kind like Armie was saying, I mean the voting kind," Augie said. He clenched his fists in frustration. He'd rather work a double shift than talk for two seconds in front of a crowd.

Walt answered him. "Well—we would have it. Because democracy works. Most of the time. To a point. We'd write a constitution spelling out that we believed in God and the Catholic Church, make it very hard to amend, so it was stable, and then have elected representatives just like always. I think, like we said, we'd have *more* democracy, because the guilds will develop production goals and everything else, like pay and any fee for using the cooperatives, right on the shop floors, or on the farms. The way I see it, most people will be able to work from home. But where decisions need to be made, people would have a say. Because they'd own it, either outright, like their land, or a share in any cooperative. Not a couple of rich people. That's more of a say than we have now."

Work from home? Wait a second, were they actually hearing it right—*everybody* work from home? Now, the women glanced at each other. For so long, for all of their lives, their mothers' lives, their grandmothers' lives, they had lived with a painful contradiction. They wanted to have careers, and given the economic conditions, they *had* to have careers, but either during their pregnancy or later, almost all of them had wished (cried, screamed, sobbed) to stay home with their babies, a feeling that did not vanish when the infants turned into kids and then teenagers. Women wanted to stay home, but on the colony they *had* to have careers, too, for the security in a divorce-ravaged world. Besides, in some countries, not working was even *illegal*! Nobody (except the elites) could have it all. Women always had to go back to work, on Earth. To have it all, they had to do it all—work, mothering, loving a husband. Nobody had to spell out what suffered. Or rather, *who* suffered. They had accepted it, but the stress was almost unbearable. They had, of course, stopped having kids. Too hard.

So, now, Walt and Armie and everybody were saying—what? Not only could women stay home but men could stay home too? *Wow*. Just wow. Marley looked at Adn, and Adn looked at Christine, who'd just joined their work group. All around the room women looked thoughtful.

Actually, what they were proposing sounded good, it sounded really good, even to the non-Catholics among them, but only if they meant that part about tolerance. But how could tolerance work, anyway, where people were all mixed together? Granted, most of the "settlers" of the Oort asteroid were Catholics, but some were people of other faiths, serious people, not slackers and half-steppers, but sincere people who sincerely loved their religion. It was a very tall order, tolerance. It had not worked so well on Earth. But had, perhaps, intolerance been inflamed by competition rather than religious antagonism?

As if on cue, a hand went up. It was Elaine. She had red hair and a very toothy smile, and she was well placed in food service because, it was widely known, the woman could cook. She put it into words, what many were thinking. "So you're saying everybody has to go to Catholic Church on Sunday morning? That's what you mean?" She had heard that would be the law on the colony with the *new* religion.

Tomás looked at Ferdi. Ferdi looked at Marley, and she stood up, but before she began to speak, a small hand went up in the back.

It was Farah, from Malaysia. She and Marley had that awkward moment: who should go first? Farah smiled and went ahead.

"I can tell you how they do things in Kelantan, a part of my country that has a real Muslim religious state. I am from there. I think we have acceptable tolerance but not complete religious freedom as some kind of right, and I think I can say it works okay for the non-Muslims. It seemed to. That's my opinion and my neighbors,' too; they are, they were, Chinese immigrants. There were rules. Non-Muslims could not promote their faiths publically, naturally. But they *were* allowed to have these special days, I think it was something like, five open house days a year at their places of worship, where they could invite people and promote their faith if they wished. They always cooked their special foods, played their music, the children put on plays about their faith—there were no restrictions. Believe me, it was enough evangelization, it seemed like. Like they could hardly keep up! Five days every year. A lot of preparation went into it. My Chinese neighbor was so busy during those open house days! In our little town we had a Buddhist temple, a Catholic church, a Jewish synagogue, and, I think, a Lutheran church on the other side of town. The Catholics did *not* use the open-house opportunity, as I recall. The only ones." Her eyebrows went up when she said it. It had scandalized her.

"Because Catholics were pushing for 'religious freedom.' That ecumenical idea. They would not evangelize even when they could, like that's against religious freedom. They thought it rude, maybe. I don't know, I could never understand it! But here's my point. They didn't have to do *any* Muslim things at all! Non-Muslims had plenty of options. Like, non-Muslims could buy liquor but Muslims couldn't—by law; it's still the law, as far as I know. If you are in a hotel, you can drink alcohol there at the bar. When we stop to pray, only Muslims pray, but the rest *do* have to wait to keep shopping or whatever until we're finished, that's true. Ten minutes, fifteen. They go sit and drink coffee or stand about and chat. It works fine. Nobody minds. I can see how that would work on the asteroid, too. If we had those open house days."

Farah pursed her lips and went on. "Now, probably some things, some conflicts, you cannot avoid. That would be true in a Catholic state more than in a Muslim state." She said it proudly and glanced quickly at the three women sitting with her, Muslims, too.

There were twenty-one Muslims on the *Regina Coeli*. Farah had counted. That one couple—What were their names? Adn and Laiq?—was even from the colony, not the asteroid. They had *meant* to come with these Catholics. They had chosen. As for Farah, the conditions on the mining asteroid had been intolerable, and she had chosen, too.

Farah gathered her thoughts for a moment and then continued. "For example, Catholics do not believe in divorce, right? And Muslims do." She glanced around. "So, I have to think, your religious government would not allow for divorce, only for separation, right? You *do* allow separation, in the case of abuse, or infidelity, or something serious, right? But no remarriage, in that case?"

She looked at all of them and saw some nods. They were not too sure and not too assertive. They had lived in a protestant, divorce-plagued society for so long. It wasn't exactly clear what the new-improved Catholic Church was teaching.

"That might be a problem for some non-Catholics," Farah went on. "But I, personally, would not mind living with that law. And also the part about monogamy. I would not mind that law. I could live with it. It is not Muslim teaching but I could live with it."

She sat down among her companions. They too looked thoughtful. *Very* thoughtful. Intensely thoughtful! They would not mind that law, either. Could something good actually come of this? They had never had the chance to reject divorce, and Muslim women had suffered so much from it.

Marley added her two cents' worth. "That's what I was going to say! I was thinking of Malaysia the whole time we were talking about it. Like Farah said, another guy I worked with on the docks told me the same thing. We could do it like that. On our asteroid, nobody would *have* to go to church, Catholic or any other. On the other hand, there won't be any Little League games scheduled on Sunday morning." Little League? Seeing their confused faces, she added, "When we get teams, I mean—which, of course, we will." Because Layne and all the kids loved baseball.

A man sitting near them raised his hand and stood. It was Davood, a friend of Laiq and Adn's, an Iranian, too. No one knew him very well, yet. He was a nice-looking guy. His wife was with him; she was a medical worker. Their names were Dorrie and Davood, everybody called him David. He said he preferred it.

Tomás nodded at him. "David."

"I just want to say something about this. As you know, we Muslims are not big fans of secularism." Twenty-one Muslims nodded. "We Muslims prefer a religious state. We are very serious about it because we know you can lose your children to bad lifestyles, bad living."

Dorrie and Davood did not yet have any children, so he was speaking theoretically, but it did show the direction of his thinking. A little pink blush rose in Dorrie's cheeks.

"You will think that I am going to speak against the idea of having a Catholic religious state," David continued. "But I am not. I do not speak *against* it. I speak for it."

He nodded emphatically. "I have studied the Koran. What Islam says is that the state should reflect the religion of the majority of the people living there. I know that it might seem like Islam teaches something else." He glanced around the big room filled with people he knew to be saturated with misinformation, at best, about Islam, and some with hatred for Muslims. "Because there are places where Muslims agitate for a religious state when they are *not* in the majority. But that's because the secular state is so horrible and nobody else seems to be fighting it. We really cannot stand it! Surely, you must see how unbearable it is, what you must witness on the street in your countries. If the people who live in those secular states will not wake up and honor God, then someone must make them! If that's Muslims, so be it!

"But I personally could live in a Catholic state, if it's like you are describing, and I personally would prefer it to a secular state like the one we just ran from."

David paused and chuckled. "That's why I came along, of course. I didn't know any particulars, but I know Tomás. He is not a corrupt man. Not corrupt. That is important! It is enormous! I am, well, I won't say confident, that's probably too strong, what I can say is that I am hopeful that we can actually accomplish what we say you want to accomplish. We have all the technical skills necessary. Economically, the plan you have sketched it out seems very similar to *sharia* law—but, of course, I would have to look at the actual proposals. Which I will do, very carefully. When you say *tolerance,* I need to know you mean my ability to practice Islam in a mosque, on our day of observance. I need to know that I will not be forced to violate any of the principles of my religion. I need to know that we will be able to practice our culture, our diet, our dress, our understanding of marriage—with the possible exceptions of polygamy and divorce, as Farah mentioned, if that is necessary. By the way, divorce and polygamy are under much discussion within Islam, too, and we are waking up to what contraception does to a nation, after what happened in Iran. Homosexuality is not discussed, but we are in agreement on that. Praise Allah."

"What if the constitution is *not* acceptable to you, David, and to the other Muslims here?" Tomás asked. "What if there *were* limitations on your religion, say, with regard to the concept or practice of jihad or to worship outside a mosque? Could you accept that? Because we haven't worked out the details with you. There may be things we haven't thought of."

These "founders" of the would-be settlement in the Oort Cloud had never discussed this, nor had they consulted the archives. There hadn't been time. So Tomás was unsure how they would handle the differences, although he personally would do his best to ensure peace and tranquility to his Muslim friends as well as to his Hindu and atheist ones. There was not a soul there he had not worked with and liked. They were *neighbors*. They had rights under Christ, who died for them too, whether they knew it or not. But still, there might be obstacles no one had thought of.

Everyone waited for an answer. Not a few thought wistfully of the lives that could have been saved on Earth if the question had been discussed sooner there, especially in Europe, before the vigilante wars and the rise of the right wing and the new anti-Semitism.

David pursed his lips and frowned. A moment passed, and then he answered. "Aren't there REVs on this pod?"

"Yes, two," Tomás said. "We keep them maintained. Hid the expense." Halliburton! Ever stingy on remote escape vehicles.

"If the legal structures for the formation of your religious state are not acceptable to us Muslims, could we use those vehicles to return to the colony?"

Many listeners nodded, and some privately added, "'Those Muslims' … and me!" One of them was Keith Costner. Keith had his own reasons for preferring the colony. He knew his absence would hurt the people around him, but—well, he had his own demons.

Tomás thought about it. He glanced at Ferdi and Marley. But it was Laiq who answered, looking directly at Tomás.

"I do not see why that could not be allowed," Laiq said. "But with conditions. The proposals would have to be available before we got to the asteroid, so that everyone could make the decision to go or stay early enough to protect the location."

Laiq glanced at Ferdi. Ferdi nodded. Good catch.

Richard Epps raised his hand. He had been happy that things at this grownups meeting worked just like they did in school discussions. You raised your hand and spoke up, that was it. Richey was twelve, and his voice broke in the echo-ey hold.

"Don't forget you have to wipe the black boxes. The memory. The on-board computer. And don't forget there might be a hidden black box. You know, an extra one."

Richey had seen that in a vid about a missing airplane, back on Earth. They had to find all the black boxes, and he remembered that the news said some were hidden, even from the pilots. Because even if people left on the REVs before the *Regina* got to the asteroid, Richey knew the software could predict future location better the closer they got to it. He had helped write an app at school as part of a game to surprise your friends at an unknown destination, like an ice cream store, just based on three previous locations. It was so easy once you knew how!

Tomás nodded. "We've already got the hidden ones. These are the *Regina Coeli* REVs I'm talking about, and we covered that well, Richey. And we got the black box. No spares, and we really looked. Thanks for reminding us."

That had been troubling, a nagging worry even still, in spite of his reassurance to Richey. Had they missed one? Was it transmitting their location, right now? He was thinking of the security team that had disabled the black boxes on the REVs as well as the official one on the mining pod itself, and several cameras on the colony, too, like the one in the pilots' lounge. They were the best.

"But you're right about the saved files on the motherboard. And the updating mechanism," Tomás said to Richey.

That was because those could be set to automatically update the REVs on board, into the computer itself, rather than a black box, and they probably were programmed for the feature. Halliburton had made very few moves to save their human staff in case of emergency, and they'd fought the REVs. But when the escape vehicles had become a deal breaker, thanks to hardheads like Walt, Halliburton had been canny enough to make sure they'd know where that staff had *been* in those expensive machines.

Smart kid! Tomás shot him an appreciative smile, and Richey grinned.

"I'll get right on finding and erasing the update files—and the trigger line," Tomás added.

He didn't explain that last thing, but he figured Richey knew what a trigger line was, the bit of code that initiated the update, which would have instructions to notify Mother if the update were cancelled. Tomás glanced at Keith, their best programmer, waiting for him to chime in. He'd been awfully quiet during the discussion. What was eating him?

Marley raised her hand. Tomás hesitated a moment before nodding, because their eyes had met, and the love and happiness flowing between them had paused time for them. Everyone saw it. Ah, love.

Marley stood up. "I'm from the United States," she said. "A lot of us here are. Our people came to the United States a long time ago, mostly from cities in Europe, where they were poor and worked for others. They took the risk and made the great journey, and they got land in the United States. *But* they had to learn to work it. They were clueless! They were French and Czech and Swedish, and British, and oh yes, lot of Irish. All kinds of people. They'd lived in cities."

She looked around at the faces gathered in the hold: all those blood lines still there, seen in the colors of their hair and skin and eyes, their expressions, their stature. Then, she went on. "They learned to love the land again. And so could we." She kept looking at them for some stir of feeling for it, but they were so quiet. "I think it's inside us." She sat down.

They had followed Marley's words like a fairy tale, their eyes unfocused. They had never had land, any kind of land, let alone their own land, to make their own living. They were not sure whether they, um, *loved* it. Like all *that*. Most of them, except for the AgTech people, had never even had an African violet or a fern.

Ray's hand shot up. "Marley?" he said. "I know a good name for the asteroid."

He looked ridiculously pleased with himself, and Ferdi had to smile. Marley raised her eyebrows in inquiry.

"*Stella Maris*," he said.

It was the only Latin phrase he knew outside the ordinary language of mass. "*Stella Maris*—you know, Star of the Sea."

And everyone realized it at the same time: perfect. A star. One of the many pet names of the humble girl who'd said yes, who had agreed, Yes, I will be the mother of God. Maris Stella. Awesome choice! Leave it to Ray.

"Let's vote on it," Tomás said.

It was an easy vote and quickly done. And unanimous. The Muslims liked the mother of Christ, too. Who wouldn't love that beautiful name, if you had a religious bone in your body?

Then, they went ahead and arranged the committees to write the formal proposals for Maris Stella. It had to be done as soon as they could, to allow time for any dissenters to take the REVs and go. They closed with a prayer and a blessing from Father Tim.

But more than a few had a feeling that—even though they had talked so much!—they were forgetting something. They kept looking at Ferdi. They felt something was missing and it had something to do with Ferdi. Sometimes they hated that he never talked. But mostly, after such a marathon discussion, they liked it. Who wouldn't

Outside of Time and Space

A group of guys—Ray, Cardei, Syzmansky, Hugh, Laiq, Tomás, Ramdoss, and Armie—waited outside the dorm area for Ferdi, chatting about Syzmansky's sourdough-bread-making project. Seems he'd finally captured the elusive yeast. Apparently yeast liked space life, too. They were a little shy. It felt weird to be standing around together when they weren't working.

They were wearing their best clothes, which were not very good, but what could they do? They had been busy with food supply, and then a hard bout of flu had caught them short on medical items. Fabric production had been pretty far down on the list. For this solemn occasion, they had improvised where they could. Hugh had on a bow tie that might have been part of a Halloween costume at one point. Cardei had taken his trademark paisley headband and fashioned into a tie, or like a cravat, and as a statement of intention, it worked, except it revealed his receding hairline, which actually gave his face an attractive trace of humility. Anyway, they were as dressed up as they could manage. Of course they looked good! They were the *guys*.

Their friendly chat was cut short when Ferdi emerged from the dorm. He, too, was wearing his best shirt, which happened to be an old, but good, red flannel. He had on a purple and red tie. His beard and mustache were trimmed, and his hair was neatly combed but not trimmed. They had talked about that when they were making all the preparations. In times past, those who were giving *up* power got haircuts, it appeared. So he kept his chestnut curls, and that was fortunate because they were his best feature, although no one had ever thought to say it, nor would anyone say it in future, including his biographer, but that's ahead of the story.

Anyway, Ferdi looked handsome. He'd lost a couple pounds. They all had, for that matter.

They formed a procession, with Ferdi at the end. The procession was part of the rite, as they'd planned it. They were walking from Ferdi's home, his bed in the single men's dorm, to the church. It was formal, a real procession. Nobody talked, but they felt comfortable walking together. They'd walked a lot of places, back on the colony, together—except Ramdoss and Laiq, but those guys had fit in from the very first, no problem. They were part of the team now, not as Catholics, no, but as good citizens of Maris Stella. The men walked through the long corridor that ran down the middle of the dorms. They didn't pass anyone, being as everybody else was probably already in the main hold of the *Regina*.

They passed the single men's, the single women's, and the family dorms, all make-shift areas in the larger secondary hold, of which the *Regina Coeli* had two. They were headed toward the main hold. The lights were dimmed. It was quiet. It was a little musky; humans indoors for a long time. Well, that was over now.

The dorms and kitchen had been emptied out of almost everything. They'd been hard at that work on that project for a couple weeks. Every bed, table, box, pot, or pan had been carted to the new living areas on the asteroid. The previous night was the last time anyone would sleep in the dorms, which they would turn back into cargo space. They expected the day would come when they would re-establish trade with Earth as well as with the colony, and they'd need those cargo holds then. It was unlikely they'd be able to trade directly; they'd probably need to use middlemen. After all, they were wanted men, no doubt. But there would be a market, just as there always had been among men. It was only a matter of time before they got a piece of it—if Earth didn't completely collapse from demographic instability. Meanwhile, they had the means, *Deo gracias*, to take care of themselves.

Their first habitat on the asteroid was finished—only meaning, it was operational. Finished completely it was not. It had taken four months to fabricate and fill the membrane, test it, lay out the plots and the commons, move out their heavy duty equipment and get started on an infrastructure. But they weren't complaining. Add it all together—the forty-month journey and the four months on the asteroid—and it hadn't taken anything close to forty years, like some Promised Lands!

They were now getting atmosphere and water from the asteroid itself, extracting it from minerals, and they had mirrors in orbit to focus and intensify the distant sun. More solar reflectors were a priority. Pretty soon it would be Florida in December around there. And they'd have seasons, because the asteroid was tipped on its axis.

Today was the for-real move-in day, and they were making it a very formal affair. They were making history! They hadn't time to think about it, but they knew it. Mankind steps off Earth onto free real estate.

The procession came to the entrance of the main hold. As they entered, every face on both sides of the center aisle, rank upon rank, turned toward Ferdi and his band of friends. Father Tim and six solemn young servers, grouped two by two, stood on the side at the front of the hold. Everyone had been waiting for them.

They walked down the aisle and stopped just before they reached the sanctuary. They genuflected in pairs, like they'd practiced, and then all the men except Ferdi peeled off and took their places toward the front, because they'd be needed again later. Ferdi took the last few steps alone, and then turned and stood at the entrance to the sanctuary, facing the assembly. Tomás stepped forward and stood beside him. They both faced the people. The altar stood elevated three steps behind them in the sanctuary, furnished for mass to begin, the real wax candles lit and the precious linens spread. An empty chair stood in front of the steps.

Tomás addressed them all. "I present to you the future king of Maris Stella: Ferdinand, the first king of the Oort—if you acclaim him. Signify your wish." Tomás stood straight in his captain's uniform, waiting.

Put to them like that, head-on, direct, they paused and thought it over one more time. They thought about Ferdi.

He had *always* had a place among the men and women who'd led them. He had, really, the top place among them. And that was strange. Because he was young, and humble. Because he wasn't a super specialist in anything—in fact, he had been more or less the handyman of the village, a jack-of-all-trades kind of guy. And then there was the fact that he didn't talk. He only listened, with his kind face showing interest and respect and compassion and intelligence, until the discussion was whittled down to a yes or a no. At that point, everybody would look at Ferdi, and he'd either nod thoughtfully or look doubtful, and usually that was it, the inevitable answer. They had never known him to be unkind or to be wrong on anything important. Not that they knew what Ferdi believed on many things, what with the not talking.

What *did* they think, then?

They trusted Ferdi. They were drawn to him. They loved his sparkling brown eyes and his half-smile, and when he'd raise his eyebrows and look dubious, as if to say, *Really?* But more, they appreciated his simple, quiet goodness. Okay, they loved him. And didn't everybody say he had royal blood? Well, then. King Ferdi. King Ferdinand! Alright!

The crowd began to cheer.

Tomás didn't wait for them to finish, just raised his voice. "I present to you, Ferdinand the First, of Maris Stella."

They cheered even louder. It felt good.

As Tomás and Ferdi—*King* Ferdi! They'd get used to it, surely—stood before the sanctuary, Father Tim and the boys entered the sanctuary from the other side.

Father Tim had on a cope—the long cape of a priest. On Earth, it might have been made of silk. Here, the ladies of the altar society had pieced it together from a nice drape someone had carried aboard and embroidered it with threads they'd unraveled from other scraps. Father Tim had on the tall, triangular bishop's hat, called a *miter*. That had been easier to fashion. They had lots and lots of super-thin aluminum, which cut easily and bent perfectly, and they'd covered it with more embellished cloth.

Then, Tomás led Ferdi into the sanctuary and to the chair. Ferdi sat down. He looked very solemn.

Father Tim stepped forward, the servers behind him. One supported a sword on his two outstretched arms, unsheathed. Another held the sword's sheath. Another held a shield. A fourth held a circlet of minerals and gold that sparkled on the cushion on which it rested. All were made of platinum and gold in various combinations and finishes, the sword and shield cast for strength, the circlet for a smooth finish. Rare materials on Earth, just about as common as dirt in space.

The specialized labor that fashioned it, on the other hand, was rare anywhere. Sword-smithing! But Walt Ferguson, the survivalist, had a little experience in metalwork (and everything else), and so had a guy named Jorge. They'd found models on a re-enactment website the evacuation team had downloaded, along with hundreds of others. They had the plans and plenty of metal. Walt devised a forge, and Jorge knew how to heat and hammer the metal into rough shape, and then how to anneal it, the slow heating and cooling for refinement of the shape, and finally, how to grind for the finish. Sitting among the crowd now, the two craftsmen were happy to see the work of their hands put to this use.

It was interesting to see the twins, Tomás and Tim, in their different roles. The one was a regular guy, a leader, a married man, the ship's captain, and their unofficial civic leader, although they'd not had formal elections. That would happen, eventually, along with about a million other things. The other was a priest—the bishop of the official Church in space. Tim was intense, Tomás was laid back. Twins! Go figure! Now, they stood in the main hold of a spaceship parked on an asteroid in the Oort Cloud with an altar at their back and Christ in the tabernacle witnessing a very unusual event, this crowning by the Church and State, represented in the persons of these brothers, of a king. A king! *Their* king! Boy, the recruiters had not been wrong: a job in outer space could be full of surprises!

But they'd talked about it for a long time on their journey. Their faith had never stopped celebrating the feast days and the memories of their king-saints: Louis IX, that shining knight; Stephen the Great of Moldavia, known as "the athlete of Christianity;" Saint Olaf, who civilized savage Norway and ended the oppression of the Viking raids on Europe; and who could forget Saint Ferdinand! Ferdi was a descendent of King Saint Ferdinand III. It was a bit of a joke, because half of Europe, including every single remaining European monarch, was a descendent of Saint Ferdinand. Well, he'd married off his numerous children all across the world, and they'd carried on the family tradition of successful reproduction very nicely. Ferdi was from a little side branch of the family, but it was kind of eerie, you could see it from the archives of old paintings, how Ferdi actually favored Ferdinand the III—the way their beards grew, and their eyebrows!

Yes, the Catholics of Maris Stella, like traditional Catholics on Earth, moving through the great liturgical cycle of the year, did always pay tribute to their king-saints. They were not so inebriated with democracy that they regretted leaders like the saint kings, Aethelberht of Kent, Canus IV, Boris of Bulgaria, Ashot, and Archil, and Amadeus, and Edwin the Martyr. Good kings were they, and never forgotten for it. When a king was good, he was very, *very* good. He was great! It was something democracy needed, Joe Edcore had convinced them on their long voyage. May he rest in peace.

It hadn't been hard to convince them. To say they were disenchanted with democracy was an understatement, and when Joe listed the ways a monarchy could balance and blend the forces that necessarily emerge in the conflicts of life, they could see it. A monarchy could protect them from their own excesses, that was another and no small thing, protect them from their quick tempers and their pride. Not only that, maybe more important to them: a king could protect them from attacks of the majority on *them*. And another: the monarchy in the right hands could motivate them when they were low. Like a winning NFL coach! They needed someone to honor. They needed someone above the fray of elections. They needed someone to *love*.

Kings, Joe said, were qualified. They were raised to govern, taught the arts from birth. (Perhaps not Ferdi; he was raised in New Jersey, wasn't it?) And governing *is* an art, Joe insisted. Within his province of action, a king could act quickly, unilaterally, decisively, and that was—Walt got the point right away and backed up Joe and brought *that* home—so very useful in an emergency. Kings were generally well enough off, or deliberately poor, and too much in the public eye to be corrupt. They were sworn to represent the whole people, not parties or interests. And they were sworn to preserve democracy, although they themselves ruled for life, unelected after that first time, unless they proved unfit, in which case they could—under high standards, under tough burdens of proof, under certain conditions only—be deposed. There were so many benefits, Joe had argued, from a legal point of view. Stability in government is a precious thing.

So they considered the question. A constitutional monarchy. The monarch had veto power over everything, the final say. Under conditions. Under law.

There is a problem with democracy, Joe had said often enough. It becomes excessive over time. The judiciary cannot control it because the judiciary itself is either elected or appointed by those who are elected. Manners will not control it—manners are made in church, and the state attacked the Church. Morals in democracy are eventually relegated to sentiment, to fashion, and are only maintained in some kind of deformed state by the stubbornness of a few human beings who cling to habit. Democracy: can't live without it, can't live with it.

People in utterly degenerated democracies sometimes didn't even know it! Joe had often quoted an early American lawmaker, Fisher Ames, speaking of Rome and freedom. It amused Ames no end that the Romans bragged of their freedom minutes after having elected a dictator. "It is remarkable that Cicero," Joe read to them from a download of Ames, "Cicero, yes, Cicero, with all his dignity and good sense, found it a popular seasoning of his harangue, six years after Julius Cæsar had established a monarchy, and only six months before Octavius totally subverted the commonwealth, to say, 'It is not possible for the people of Rome to be slaves, whom the gods have destined to the command of all nations. Other nations may endure slavery, but the proper end and business of the Roman people is liberty.'" It was delusion, pure denial, and it was common—even today, right on the colony! If you asked people, they would say they were free! And get mad at you for asking!

So that's how they got to this day. A king! And a new planet! Going to be some serious partying! They wished Joe could be here to see it. Maybe it was too late for Earth to reverse the centuries of denial, but not here. They could reverse them. They meant to crown a guy who could and would be the boss of them, as necessary. Good!

They stopped daydreaming when Father Tim spoke again. He was speaking to Ferdi. He handed him the sword the boys had been carrying, and Ferdi took it in his left hand. Father Tim handed him the shield, and Ferdi took it in his right hand, and the shine of it from the overhead lights lit up his face for a moment with a warm glow.

"With this sword you will punish crimes, and with this shield you will protect the weak," Father Tim said. He was reading the words of a medieval coronation ceremony they'd found archived. They had located several, from merry old England, from fierce Norway, from the far western tribes. "With this sword you will fight for liberty against tyrants, and with this shield you will defend virtue, which cannot be fully attained without liberty. With this sword you will fight the vices that lead to slavery, and with this shield you will defend with patience our liberty in all things, especially the liberty to speak freely on all subjects whatsoever, for whatever reason as long as virtue is not cast away. With this sword you will attack force and fraud, though they be as furious as lions and as wily as serpents. You will fight for the law, for liberty, and to defend the faith, for these are gifts of God."

Then, looking earnestly into Ferdi's glowing face, he added, "Do you so swear and promise?"

They all leaned forward. They had never heard Ferdi speak!

"I solemnly promise to do so," said Ferdi.

Well! He had a nice mellow voice. They liked it. He was going to talk just like any regular guy, they concluded. He sounded just like himself!

Father continued. "Do you swear and promise to govern the people of the Maris Stella, this asteroid legally claimed by us as provided in the interstellar space treaty of 2050, according to the statutes her government agrees upon, and the laws and customs of the same?"

One thing they'd found out from their coronation sources: people talked funny when crowning kings and queens—formal, as it should be. "Of the same." Awesome.

"I solemnly promise to do so," said Ferdi. *Solemnly.* Yup!

"Will you use your power to cause law and justice in mercy to be executed in all your judgments?" asked Father Tim.

"I will," answered Ferdi.

And they believed him. That's how Ferdi was.

"Will you use your power to maintain the laws of God, and the proclamation of the gospel, and all the traditional teachings of the Roman Catholic Church?"

"I will," answered Ferdi.

"Will you use your power to promote tolerance and to protect those among us who practice a non-Catholic religion so long as they promote the common good?"

"I will," Ferdi promised.

The server brought the gospel book and stood next to Ferdi. Ferdi laid his hand on it lightly. He had fine, freckled hands.

Father Tim asked the last question. "Will you use this sword and this shield to protect and defend us all?"

"I will. So help me God."

The server then brought the gospel book around to in front of Ferdi and lifted it with both hands. Bowing his head regally (okay, maybe they were imagining it), Ferdi kissed the gospel book. A number of young ladies in the assembly sighed.

But Father Tim did not then take the circlet to crown their new king. Instead, the servers and Father stood at the foot of the altar while Tomás moved Ferdi's chair to the side and Ferdi reseated himself. Then, Coronation Mass began. They had learned that from the documents, too; kings were crowned in mass, during mass, as part of the sacrifice. The familiar liturgy began. Father, the servers, Ferdi, and all present first acknowledged their sins in the Confiteor prayer—"I confess to Almighty God that I have sinned, through my fault, through my fault, through my most grievous fault"—and received absolution at the foot of the altar. Everybody had to be clean in order to ascend. Only then could Father go up to the altar.

Catholic mass is a sacrifice. Altars and knives. It came right out of the ages, right out of the desert. The drama was very old. Humanity sinned. Their sins had legs that could run for centuries, in their families, within their communities, inside themselves. With catastrophic consequences.

Every crime left a mark. The feeling of being dirty, itchy, scabby, oozing, dirty, a bad smell in a clean creation. Everywhere the sinner looked was a rebuke. Nature rebuked him. There was the beautiful sun rising, obedient. There were the clouds running before the wind, obedient. There was the wheat growing toward the sun and the animals following their nature, all obedient. And there was mankind, there was the man and the woman *in flagrante delicto*, there was the disobedient little sinner, the jam still on the rosy cheek that was to have been for all for breakfast. The liar and the lie told and retold. The betrayal, the theft, the murder, the forbidden kiss.

Then, despair. It could come to so many, the heart sickness that follows sin. Mankind was given free will, special among the animals, astonishing language skills, an attractive physical package with an spectacular soul, and then we used that free will to sin. Something changed in the universe then, something got a negative charge, something real. The light dimmed, the milk soured, the sinner's stomach turned as he grasped the truth: five more seconds and he might have—*would* have—withstood the temptation. He knew it. But he was a coward. He hadn't had to commit that sin. He just did. And then despair clouded his mind. When despair dominates enough people in a society, it's over. Deconstruction. Devolution. The lights go out. It happened to many societies. Rare, actually, when it didn't.

Eons ago, the Jews received from God (speaking in burning bushes and quiet breezes) a remedy for the pain. A restart button. An app. It was because they were special that God told them the secret: sacrifice. Destroy something you treasure, and offer it with true sorrow for your sins. Then I can love you again, you will please me the way you used to do.

It was magical. They could offer to God some special animal, a perfect lamb, a plump pigeon, they could offer that fine animal, meaning, take it out of use, not breed its fine blood or brood its eggs, and they could transfer their sins onto its back. The priests actually laid hands on the sinner, and then on the sin offering, and then killed it, and sprinkled the blood onto the altar. Or you could let it loose to wander out into the cruel desert. It worked like medicine on their troubled hearts. A lynch pin discovered in that complicated human brain. So primitive, yet not really: like poetry, the opposite of primitive. Sin was real; you had to take that as a given. Sin was serious. It did not have weight, but like anti-matter, you knew where it had been. Sin had consequences. Sin was so much bigger than you ever thought it could be, after the fact. Before the fact, it was nothing, minor, a little transgression, God wouldn't mind.

But after, ah.

So the merciful God had revealed this way. Take something you love very much, and give it to me. That will prove you're sorry. Words, not so much. I will be able to love you again in spite of the other reality, the sin.

Thousands of years later, the mass did the same thing, without the blood. Christ had been the last blood sacrifice. He had been the one perfect Lamb. Christ was a God offered to God. It was the only possible balanced equation to expiate the sins of a whole world—of a whole universe. The mass called up Christ's presence with the power Christ had given only consecrated priests, and then offered Him to God again, every day. Offered for all mankind, it stayed the hand of justice and opened the fist, to give blessings.

And it made them feel better. God was so generous! Like the Jews in the desert, if the sacrifice was the one called a peace offering, they got to eat the meat afterwards. It was theirs after the priest's portion, the good charred meat left over from the liturgy consumed for supper. It was like big-hearted God gave it back.

Now, there, in the hold of the *Regina Coeli*, their tribe was about to enter a new desert, on an asteroid in the region known as the Oort, the farthest mankind had wandered yet, the real outskirts of town. But already it was just like home, cluttered with sins, small ones, big ones, and then the thick film of sorrow, paralyzing or anesthetizing. Either way, you were done for, caught in a cognitive trap no less lethal than one with steel jaws.

But they had a way out of the sin trap! They were going to play their God card. Fire up their hyper drive. Burnish the brass on their magic door. They would begin their adventure with mass, the ancient desert ritual. Admit your sins first at the foot of the altar. That was essential. The priest will channel forgiveness from God. He will then ascend the altar and take the people with him in his heart.

It all unfolded in its solemn way to the epistle. Father read the epistle from the ancient Coronation Mass at the altar, and then descended to Ferdi. Servers followed with the crown on a metal tray and with a round glass bottle etched with the initials SC in a beautiful old font on a second try. The initials stood for *sanctum chrisma*, a mixture of olive oil and the sweet-smelling oil of balsam, which was blessed by a bishop once a year on Holy Thursday for use at the sacraments and to anoint the sick. It had not been used to anoint a king in hundreds and hundreds of years!

It was the beginning of the crowning. First, the priest and servers and all turned, faced the altar, and knelt, and then Father led them in the litany of the saints. It was, like, the Hail Mary play, calling on all the saints. What they were beginning on this day would take Divine help. Get those saints in the game! It was eerie the way their prayer, a call and response, filled the hold. They prayed it in Latin, except for the Greek part that had found its way in over the ages. It had a beat. *"Sante Ráphael / Ora pro nobis."* Like a heartbeat, faintly marching. Sometimes the call, the first part, was plural: *"Omnes sancti Innocéntes."* And then the response was syncopated: *"Ora-te pro nobis."* It rocked—discretely.

How powerful it was, calling out the names, one by one, of those holy men and women now with God! Simon, Matthew, Andrea, John the Baptist, and Catherine. She was a virgin martyr. Francis, and Saint Nick, and John, and Gervase. He was a twin, martyred as a child. The martyred mixed with the merely holy, bishops with the defiant virgins, and the humble nurses of the poor with kings, born in the faith or converted from many lands, coming from all classes, ranked by one rule: virtue. Ah, how rich in heroes this faith is, thought the Muslims who'd gathered with them there to formally process out into the Maris Stella, to take possession of their new land. The Muslims were also there to witness this ritual, though not to worship through it—although they, too, had heard often enough that "it was the same God," when anyone knew it was not. But their hearts were moved by the simple cry for help: "All ye holy saints, pray for us!" Because if there were any of the ancients who could hear us, the Muslims thought, fine, pray on.

Because we're a long way from Mecca.

They remembered *tawakkul* then and tried to have faith in the providence of God, which anyone needed plenty of to terraform an asteroid in the middle of the Oort.

The Hindus present prayed, too. Among the Asians, of scattered and various faiths, all heads were bowed as well. How much better it is to be gathered like this among believers, many realized, than to be among the godless trying so hard to manufacture a public life without God. Not here. It felt fine. They'd been so hungry for an end to the chaos they'd done some bad and stupid things. That was over now. They could live in peace now.

Father Tim concluded the litany with the final prayers. "Almighty and everlasting God, who hast dominion both of the quick and the dead," he read it in Latin and they followed the vernacular in their missals, "who likewise hast mercy upon all men, we commend unto Thee all those for whom we now do offer our prayers, whether in this world they still be held in the bonds of the flesh, or being delivered there from have passed into that which is to come. / Beseeching Thee that at the intercession of all Thy Saints they may of Thy bountiful goodness obtain the remission of all their sins. / Through our Lord Jesus Christ, Thy Son, Who liveth and reigneth with Thee in the unity of the Holy Ghost, God, world without end."

"Amen," said the people.

They wanted to begin their new lives with that *amen*.

Father made the earthy nature of the plea clear in the concluding prayer. "Prevent us, O Lord, in all our doings with Thy most gracious favor, and further us with Thy continual help, that in all our works begun, continued, and ended in Thee, we may glorify Thy Holy Name, and finally by Thy mercy obtain everlasting life."

Because the "works" they were about to begin, specifically, the transformation of a hunk of dirt into a home, weren't separated from everlasting life; it was the way to get there. You didn't have to be on Earth to work for heaven. You could win that by being a great engineer on an asteroid, as long as you did it for God. Saint Engineer. It was a sentiment almost everyone shared, from all their faiths. And they loved the passion it gave to work, even beyond family, greater than nature.

"Amen," the people said.

And they meant it. Their cross, their work, was their way to heaven. They got that, Christ's unique message. And what a ride!

Still, though, mass did not resume yet.

Father Tim rose and turned, and the servers followed and stood beside Ferdi, who had unbuttoned his shirt so that his chest was exposed. Father took the crystal bottle and opened it, and sprinkled the holy oil on a small square of fabric, and moved to stand in front of Ferdi.

As Father dabbed the oil in the shape of a small cross on Ferdi's chest, he said, "I anoint you with the holy oil, in the name of the Father and of the Son and of the Holy Ghost. May your heart be pure and brave except for fear of the Lord."

He put more oil on the fabric and, leaning close, made little crosses on each of Ferdi's hands, elbows, and shoulders. Leaning even closer, he reached inside Ferdi's open shirt and anointed the space between his shoulder blades, again saying the anointing words.

Then, Father said, "May you be strong against the enemy, mount up on wings like eagles, run and not be weary, walk and not faint."

Ferdi buttoned his shirt and sat up straighter.

Father made a cross on the top of Ferdi's head. "I anoint you with the holy oil, in the name of the Father and the Son and the Holy Ghost."

Then, he turned to God. "God Almighty, may this Thy most holy unction fall upon his head, descend within, and penetrate even unto his very heart, and may he by Thy grace be made worthy of the promises which the most famous kings have obtained, so that in all happiness he may reign in this present life and may be one with them in Thy heavenly kingdom, for the sake of our Savior Jesus Christ, Thy Son."

Finally, Father took the slim crown from the tray and held it above Ferdi's head. "Receive this crown," he said, and placed it slightly crooked, fixed it, and continued, "which we, with one accord, give you and choose you for King, and we pray God encompass you evermore and in all places with the right hand of His power, so that strengthened by the fidelity of Abraham, possessed of the patience of Joshua, inspired with the humility of David, adorned with the wisdom of Solomon, may you be to Him ever pleasing, and walk evermore without offence in the way of justice, and henceforth in such wise succor may you direct, guard, and uplift the church of the whole kingdom of Maris Stella and the people belonging to it, and may you administer right royally the rule of God's power against all enemies visible and invisible."

Father stepped back. The servers, too.

Then, Father turned to the people and said in a clear, strong voice that echoed out into the tall arches of the hold ancient words that floated there as well as any medieval chamber, "Long live the king!"

Tomás grinned and said it loud, "Long live the king!"

After a moment, the people took up the happy shout as if they'd never put it down. "Long live the king! Long live Ferdinand!"

As mass began, Ferdi knelt inside the sanctuary, wearing his crown and his red flannel shirt. Neither crown nor clothes made him a king. It was the part you couldn't touch that did that. The part where grace glowed like an inner fire. That was the Catholic part; that wasn't even the king part. Ah, God, how blessed are Catholics! And about the king part, he had vowed to be the best king in the universe, and he meant with all his heart to keep it, with God's help and Our Lady's.

The mass proceeded, led by Father Tim. With solemn intensity, the sacrifice rolled forward through the several prayer offerings of the victim to God in the bread and wine. With the sacred species they included in their prayers all their own personal offerings—their work, an offering; their aches and pains, an offering; their sadness, their loneliness, their art, all offerings to be transformed on the altar into merit, the coin of heaven. They prayed for their loved ones, their neighbors, their enemies, that God might transform all into better beings than they were.

Then, using the words, the formula, given by Christ the night before He died, Father Tim bent low and whispered the words of consecration of the bread and wine. And viola! Christ was newly present. They adored. It was quiet in the hold.

Next came the prayers for the dead. They already had their own dead, they didn't have to refer only to their dead on Earth. Included in the prayer were Joe Edcore and Al Taylor, whose bodies lay in the refrigerated room, awaiting burial. Al had been shot getting Laiq out of that holding cell. Only a week out into deep space, Joe had been the first to come down with the flu so many of them. He'd gone into respiratory distress right away, and before they could get him stabilized, his heart went, just like that. CPR hadn't worked, and they hadn't set up yet for anything else. For the next sick person, they had gotten their protocols down and their equipment ready. Al and Joe would be first in the graveyard next to the church in the commons on Maris Stella.

They came to the last part of mass. The moment had arrived. They were taking possession of Maris Stella. They would take the Blessed Sacrament out of the tabernacle in the ship into the new stone church they had built in the settlement.

Father Tim placed a consecrated Host in the monstrance, also newly fashioned by Walt and Jorge. Father and the servers formed the beginning of the procession in the center aisle. First came the server with the cross. Then came two servers with lighted beeswax candles. The candles themselves were more precious than the solid platinum candle holders in which they rested. Next, on Earth, would have come the organizations of ordinary Catholics, the lay associations, like the Knights of Columbus, but they didn't have those yet on Maris Stella. After that would have come any religious Brothers and Sisters, but their only one—that Goth girl, Stephanie—had stayed behind on the colony to save the girls there. So next came two boys with incense in the thuribles, and a server behind them with the precious stuff in his little gold boat, the navicula. He was the smallest server, and his skirts were a little long. Last came Father Tim, holding the monstrance high. They lacked the canopy to cover the monstrance. They would have it someday. As they made their way down the center aisle, the people filled in behind them. The Muslims, Hindus, and other small groups came last; they understood the protocol, knowing it meant only that a good God was being honored and godless secularism was not, and thank Allah and thank Shiva for it! They all slowly made their way to the big main doors to the hold.

The doors opened before them.

The habitat lay beyond. Their new land. Maris Stella, Star of the Sea.

Before they'd arrived, none but Laiq had ever seen it. At the end of that long journey, they had slowly circled the asteroid, running an analysis and looking for a good place to set down. It was smaller than Earth's moon and well-shaped; they would have to do little in the way of water injections to round it out. Bands of craggy peaks circled broad valleys. It was easy to imagine them green. Laiq had been right about the composition, too. It was mixed, the most desirable kind for human habitation. It was partly metallic in composition and partly carbonaceous, rare in Earth's sector but prevalent out in the Oort. It had a 23 percent water content, not to mention the presence of the gases they could use to make their own water from scratch, or they could always tow in a little water asteroid. It was so full of minerals it made the richest old mines of Earth seem poor. Yes, it was rocky and bare, but that was momentary; they had known at first sight what could be done. It was definitely prime real estate.

Now, it was bright mid-morning in the habitat they had made first, where they would live and expand as they prepared for an atmosphere. They could see across the whole mile of it. Another linked segment was already under construction, to the west. That one was five miles across. It would contain the first family-owned farms. Everyone else would continue living in the first habitat, for the time being, anyway, per the arrangements they'd worked out for their beginning.

They'd worked out the plan based on a lottery. They'd have a mixed economy until they could make the transition to fully distributed ownership, except for basic essential utilities, which they finally decided would be cooperative. They were comfortable with that plan, and they were prepared to put up with the difficulties that mixed economies and compromises on responsibility would bring. Socialism was bad for people. But some of the elements of socialism would have to operate for the nonce. If their goal was clear, they thought, they could resist the pull toward unnecessary government and slavery.

The first thing that struck the eye from their vantage point up inside the entrance of the ship was a tubular vane mounted high from the topmost membrane struts. It rotated slowly and silently to circulate the air enclosed in the membrane, sweeping the warm air down and the cooler air up. Single-sheet louvers embedded in the membrane shielded them from direct exposure to the sun, which even at this distance could deliver a punch. The membrane itself was self-healing, one of the new metal-plastics. Nevertheless, from the first day they had made use of the bots that equipped every mining pod to sweep their air space for debris. The membrane was filled with atmosphere mixed from minerals on the spot. They were still reminded of the incredible energy benefit of space economy: put out your hat, pull in some sun, plug in. Their challenge was labor, and it was no small one.

Slowly, they began the procession down the ramp and into the habitat. Father Tim held the monstrance high. He did not have to watch his footing. They had made sure the processional way to the church was well swept. They passed the infirmary first. Everything had been laid out in stone blocks. It looked vaguely Roman. It would be beautiful when it was planted. When would that be? They had so much to do! But it was lovely even now, perhaps it was the order imposed on the chaos of rocks, especially with Maris Stella sky, so much more various and busy than the sky of Earth.

There'd been no planting in the civic areas yet, only in the crop areas surrounding them. The planted sections were green with kale, cucumber, barley, oats for the animals, corn, and coffee—quite a variety, since the temperature was always moderate and they could modify the light intensity and duration to benefit the maximum species. It worked well for humans, too. They had adopted a Guadalajara climate, only a little more humid. The soil was already okay, richer than many of the soils of Earth, but virtually identical, really. As it turned out, dirt was dirt. The dirt on the asteroid just lacked the organic elements, and they were busily putting all their own fertilizers and the animals' into it. They had wheat, and rice. They even had grape vines. So far, so good.

They were not farmers. They were like the people thrown from Europe in the great cataclysms that followed the Protestant rebellion. Those people had already been wage slaves by the time of their journeys, already disappropriated of their land from the old Catholic times. Not farmers for a long time. They had stood dumbfounded, staring at the flat, ugly Great Plains of America. Nebraska had been a vast, dry prairie with enormous storms marching toward them over the edge of an enormous horizon. They had been frightened, shocked by the huge emptiness of it. Earth like that they had never seen. But they had plunged in, and some of them began to love the land again with a great passion, and the plants growing in it, and the winds that blew over it.

Now, these refugees of planet Earth could feel something similar stirring in them. Perhaps it had always been there? They would have land to work here, and they found they liked the idea. No, it would not be like Europe in the fifteenth century. It would be like the solar system at the end of the twenty-first century, with hovercraft and email and free energy. Nobody would be remote, even in the Oort. They would be high-tech rednecks. Yeah, they liked the idea.

They passed the school in procession, and then the smaller buildings where those among them of other faiths would worship. There were plantings around the school; Ferdi and Ray had done that during their rest periods. They passed the family quarters, and the female and male singles' quarters. In the new habitats, in progress, they would have their own homes on their own land, but for the present, they had to compromise. It was okay; they knew where they were headed.

The procession came to the Catholic church. Like everything else, it was made of blocks of stone that the *Regina Coeli's* lasers had cut out. It rose heavenward, exactly as if it were on Earth, not more nor less crude (or magnificent) than churches rising in raw communities on every frontier. Their next church would be grand. This simple one still led the eye toward the Creator, and it would serve.

Out here in the Oort, they were not actually farther from Holy Mother Church than had been those early bishops of America, whose dioceses stretched far south into another country, stretched across vast deserts and ranges of mountains. Those bishops must have felt light years from Rome. Far, far from the Church, but not cut off. Meanwhile, way out here in the outskirts of Earth's solar system, they had their own bishop. Rome in space. He would consecrate other bishops. That was first on the list after the ordination of priests, for which they already had two young men in training with Father—with Bishop Tim. They would live at the rectory beside the church. More would enter. It would all take time. Human beings—short lives and big dreams, which could never be achieved without Christ, without living the way He had taught, to live in a City of God based on virtue, not a city of Man based on pride.

    They went up to the door their newly named church: St. George. George the dragon slayer and the patron saint of boy scouts, and that seemed about right; they might someday expect dragons from the sky, and they already had them some boy scouts. Henceforth the Christ they carried in the monstrance would live here, where they could visit Him. Following the monstrance, they entered the church, and suddenly, like they had turned on the lights, there was in that most remote section of the universe a whole new glow. Now it was home.